Juh held up his gla⸺ ⸺oyalty and friendship," he said. "The loyalty and friendship that can exist only among those who consider themselves a family."

Somewhat startled by the man's naïveté, the Sicilians raised their glasses in salute, brought them to their lips, and, with Juh, tipped the glasses skyward. Before they had replaced the glasses on the table, two dozen Apaches stood as still as stone at the edge of the clearing. Each had a rifle pointed at the men around the table.

The Sicilians didn't speak, didn't utter a sound of surprise. One of them reached under his jacket, and three shots sounded as one. The man's head exploded, and he crashed onto the table, dishes scattering.

Across from him, blood, brains, and pasta sauces sprayed onto the shirt and into the face of Al Capone, who sat without moving, his face gone ashen . . .

By Jake Page:

Mo Bowdre mysteries
THE STOLEN GODS
THE DEADLY CANYON
THE KNOTTED STRINGS
THE LETHAL PARTNER
A CERTAIN MALICE

Science fiction
OPERATION SHATTERHAND
APACHERIA

Nonfiction
WILD JUSTICE: The People of Geronimo vs. the United
   States (with Michael Lieder)

APACHERIA

Jake Page

A Del Rey® Book
THE BALLANTINE PUBLISHING GROUP • NEW YORK

A Del Rey® Book
Published by The Ballantine Publishing Group
Copyright © 1998 by Jake Page

http://www.randomhouse.com

Library of Congress Catalog Card Number: 97-94509

ISBN 0-345-41411-X

Manufactured in the United States of America

First Edition: April 1998

10 9 8 7 6 5 4 3 2 1

HISTORICAL and Fictional characters in the order in which they appear:

JUH
GOYAKLA (known also as GERONIMO)
TOM JEFFORDS (also called RED BEARD)
NAICHE
GENERAL GEORGE CROOK
JOE BIGNON
BIG MINNIE BIGNON
Margarita
Billy Milgreen
LITTLE GERTIE (also called GOLD DOLLAR)
Deputy Sheriff Danny Kincaid
LOZEN, THE WARRIOR WOMAN
ISHTON
Little Spring
CAPTAIN EMMET CRAWFORD
CHATO
Kozineh
Charlie "Jawbone" Phelps
Oliver Fredd
MANGAS
PRESIDENT CHESTER A. ARTHUR
LOCO
VICTORIO
Sergeant Jeremiah Danforth
Lieutenant Kraus
GENERAL NELSON A. MILES
PEACHES

Lieutenant Bixler
GROVER CLEVELAND
GENERAL PHILIP SHERIDAN
LIEUTENANT CHARLES GATEWOOD
Tom Jeffords Cleveland Bignon (also called Big Ears)
Homer Nye
TEDDY ROOSEVELT
Nakahyen
CARRIE NATION
CHARLIE ALZAMORRA
WOODROW WILSON
Muriel Freeman
Puffy Vanderbilt
Abner Boniface Freeman
CLIFTON WOOLDRIDGE
George Hearst, Jr.
PANCHO VILLA
GENERAL JOHN J. PERSHING
Rasheen (Jessica Wilbur)
Charles T. Holly
JOHNNY TORRIO
AL CAPONE
BIG JIM COLOSIMO
DION (DEANIE) O'BANION
FRANKIE YALE
HARRY DAUGHERTY, U.S. ATTORNEY GENERAL
J. EDGAR HOOVER

∽ ∾

Prologue

1839

The boy named Juh ran well behind his companion over the flat red rock, but knew he could overtake him before they returned to camp. The others were out of sight, far behind them, boys and girls all learning the endurance of the warrior, carrying clamped in their mouths a gulp of water, holding it for the duration of the race.

Juh breathed deep and easy through his nostrils and watched the brown legs of his friend Goyakla, One-who-yawns, churning over the rock ahead. Beyond the flat rock lay a walled canyon that rose steeply up into the mountain, and a stream raced down through boulders, its waters high, fast and icy with snowmelt. Trees along the watercourse would make dense shade, a relief from the sun that scorched overhead, and it was in the canyon that Juh would make his move and overtake Goyakla.

Some of Juh's people had made their annual journey north to visit. Juh's people were known as the Nedh'ni band, the Enemy People, and they spent most of the year in the fastness of the Sierra Madre Mountains, occasionally bursting forth into the countryside overrun now by the Mexicans. But each spring, with the melting of the snows, Juh's people trekked north to visit the other bands of the Chiricahua, and Juh could not recall a spring when he had not run and wrestled and fought and competed and laughed with his short, stocky age mate, Goyakla.

Both boys were now nine, Juh slightly older and taller by several inches. Goyakla was short-waisted, broad of shoulder, and usually kept his mouth clamped shut in a thin line. Perhaps, Juh suspected, he wanted to live down the name his father had given him, One-who-yawns.

Up ahead, Goyakla veered off under a large willow tree and disappeared into the shadows of the canyon. *Now,* Juh thought, and his stride lengthened. Moments later he was directly behind Goyakla, and when the trail widened slightly between the slabs and boulders that had tumbled down into the canyon and its streambed, Juh took the lead with a burst of added speed. He saw Goyakla, grim-faced, his mouth a tight line, glance at him as he passed, and then, over the sound of the air rushing in and out through their noses, they heard the gunfire.

And, distantly, the screams.

Moments later, breathless, they crouched behind boulders at the upper mouth of the canyon, staring horrified at the chaos loose in the camp they had left only a few hours ago. Bluecoats wheeled and slashed on horseback, twenty, thirty of them, and women ran, stumbling, falling. The glen was alive with shrieks and the roar of gunfire. Bodies lay sprawled like worms in the dust, blood seeping out, pumping from slashed throats. Juh watched a horseman bolt out from behind one of the wickiups and pull up beside an old man squatting in the dirt. The old man was cradling in his arms the bleeding head of a woman, Juh's aunt, and Juh saw the flash of flame and the old man's head torn sideways, and the old man crumple.

From the corner of his eye Juh saw Goyakla bunched up, as if to pounce, and Juh grabbed his hair and pulled him down.

"No, no!" he hissed. "We can't."

Goyakla struggled and went still. The gunfire was now sporadic, the White Eyes firing uselessly into the woods above, after the women who had managed to escape. Juh's eyes flashed back and forth, counting seven Apache women and the old man—all dead. His mother was not among them. She must have escaped. The soldiers were gathering at the far end of the clearing, laughing. From behind a wickiup built by Juh's mother from willow branches he had fetched from the canyon three days ago, he saw movement. One of the dead women was not dead, was crawling, inching along the ground, trying to get out of sight.

It was his older sister, she who had just come of age and had her new name. There was blood on her arm, on her hand.

Stay still! Juh shrieked in his head. *Don't move!*

But her bloody hand clawed at the dirt and she moved, evidently trying to reach a nearby boulder and get out of sight of the cavalry troop. And suddenly a White Eyes shouted, wheeled his horse, and loped the thirty yards to where she lay. Two others followed, staying on their horses while the first— an enormous man with a protruding stomach and a dark, greasy beard—dismounted and stood over her. There were three gold stripes on his blue sleeve, and he wore gray gloves. He reached down and snatched Juh's sister by the hair, wrenching her onto her back. He turned to the other two and said something, and they laughed and climbed down from their horses.

Juh and Goyakla watched, frozen with horror and shame, as the bluecoat tore off the girl's deerskin skirt and threw it over her face. The three men, one after the other, then exposed themselves, their horrid, hairy swollen selves, and manhandled her, thrashing and heaving like beasts between her bare, slender inert legs, cheering one another on. And finally, the fat man with three gold stripes stood over her, and the sound of the last gunshot of the day echoed in the glen.

BOOK ONE

∽ ∾

The Last Indian War

It is the primary right of men to die and kill for
the land they live in.

—Winston Churchill

∾ ∽

One

AUTUMN 1884

Three men watched from above as an eddy of dust far out on the tawny floor of the valley of San Simon resolved itself into a column of cavalry, a hundred and maybe more blue-coated horsemen inching westward like a line of ants across the sun-parched land. Behind the soldiers, to the east, the Peloncillo Mountains lay across the earth, blue in the shadows of mid-morning. Less than a day's trek to the south, where the Peloncillos faded into other mountains, lay old Mexico.

The troops inching across the desert, three thousand feet below the three men, were headed for Fort Bowie, where the White Eyes exerted control over Apache Pass and offered protection for the trains of wagons that toiled west toward Tucson and east to New Mexico, many bearing silver from the mines in Arizona. The troops below were the fifth such arrival in two days, a growing stream of men and horses pouring confidently toward the fort in the belief that the final pacification of these lands was near at hand.

Two of the three observers high in their eyrie were of the second generation of Apaches to watch such intrusions by blue-coated United States soldiers. They had never known the world without the White Eyes. They had fought, they had run, they had hidden, and then they had fought again and again. In war parties bent on vengeance for the deaths of their own, they had sent countless numbers of these intruders to their deaths. But the endlessly replenishing stream of miners, settlers, and soldiers had worn them down. The People were fewer now. Looking to the exhaustion of their women and the fearfulness of their children, no longer able to lead the old life but forced instead to run, to be on the alert, always on the move, some courageous men among them had sadly, bitterly, said: enough.

Many now lived on the reservations set aside for them, most at San Carlos, to the west and north of the Gila River—a terrible place of heat, flies, and boredom, where warriors were instructed to scratch in the dry earth for a living, which was bad enough, but where the earth came forth with little as a result. The People survived only by lining up each month in hopes that the White Eyes' promised rations would be sufficient.

The Apaches knew that *all* the other tribes were gone— defeated. The Navajos just north were on a reservation, the Comanches run out of Texas, the tribes of the great plains—all sequestered, their spirit gone along with the last of the buffalo herds. Only the Apaches—and only some of the Apaches— still roamed free, if running ahead of the cavalry could be called roaming free.

This destiny, the end of the old ways and maybe the end of life, had often engaged the three men now watching from high in the Chiricahua Mountains as the detachment of horsemen crawled across their land. The white man they called Red Beard—known otherwise as Thomas Jeffords, the friend of Cochise—peered through binoculars at the advancing column. They were Buffalo Soldiers, the ones with the black curly hair of the buffalo, thick lips, and darkest of skin, the most relentless of the soldiers that crisscrossed the land in ever-increasing numbers these days, an infestation.

"Company B, Ninth Cavalry," Red Beard said. "They've come from Fort Stanton. Your Mescalero cousins over there must be calm." He grinned at his two companions through reddish brown whiskers tinted with streaks of white. "Old Hotfoot Hatch wouldn't've let any of his troops go if he thought he had a problem over there on the reservation. He'd just as soon keep his boys out of Crook's hands. Him and Gen'l Crook don't see eye-to-eye on the best way to rid this here country of you pitiless savages."

The two Apaches grinned. Red Beard was talking about Colonel Edward Hatch, the white officer whose Negro soldiers had helped chase the Comanches from Texas, and then raced two thousand miles around the landscape in one year in pursuit of Victorio and his small band of Apaches before Victorio disappeared into Mexico, there to be reported dead at the hands of the Mexicans.

General Crook had been in this country long before, and reappeared just recently, sent to bring a final end to the Apache depredations in the Southwest. It was he who had earlier persuaded so many Apaches to go to San Carlos—even Geronimo had been persuaded—and it was Crook who now was in charge of the relentless pursuit of the last free-ranging Apaches—the "renegades."

George Crook, the Tan Fox, with his voluminous side whiskers and his erect frame, was hardly ever seen in the blue uniform of the army, but in the tan canvas clothes of the civilian. General George Crook, the White Eyes whom Apaches respected above all others of his kind, was a man of his word and a worthy enemy. Crook told Geronimo, and all the Apache leaders with whom he met, that they could live in peace on the reservations set aside for them, or they could be hunted down by him and killed, even if it took him fifty years to do it.

In this endeavor Crook preferred the black troops, the Buffalo Soldiers, over all the others, for they were almost as tireless and "pitiless" as the Apaches themselves. They could ride throughout the day and into the night, day after day, month after month. They could go hard under the fierce sun, and go long without rations.

But more dangerous were the Apaches whom General Crook paid to be scouts. They wore blue jackets over their breechclouts and rode with Crook's officers. They were former warriors who knew the land, knew the location of all the hidden springs and most of the mountain strongholds, knew the

Apache ways of war. It was Crook's use of Apache scouts that Colonel Hatch—and his superiors—disapproved of.

Thanks in part to the counsel of Thomas Jeffords, the two Apaches watching the little stream of cavalrymen on the valley floor knew all of this about their enemy. One of the two Apaches was Naiche, a son of Cochise. But for a deerskin bag hung around his neck, he was naked from the waist up and wore only the traditional white breechclout tucked into his belt and a pair of high-legged deerskin moccasins that were now folded down onto his calves. A red cloth tied around his head kept from his face the long black hair that hung down his back and was whipped by the high mountain breeze.

Naiche's face was smooth and unscarred except for deep lines of pain that surrounded his wide-set black eyes—eyes that looked intensely outward under low eyebrows and over flat cheekbones. Below a long straight nose, his mouth tilted upward on the left-hand side, giving him an expression of permanent skepticism, or what had been taken by some to mean uncertainty.

The great Cochise had hoped that his son Naiche would inherit the mantle of leadership among the Apache groups called the Chiricahuas, but that had not happened. Some, thinking Naiche indecisive, had gone with Taza, Cochise's other son, and yet others had retreated into their traditional bands, hoping to live in the old way, a way that Cochise, as he lay dying in his stronghold more than ten years earlier, had warned was no longer the path of survival.

Naiche now looked over at the third man, a Nedh'ni Apache from the south in old Mexico, the man they called Juh. He had been visiting among the Chiricahuas now for more than a month, living in the high meadows in the mountains among Naiche's people, talking. Juh spoke haltingly at times, unable to get his mouth and his tongue to make certain sounds without a great effort. His voice was deep and always quiet, barely above the whisper of a wind, and people listened with special attention whenever he chose to speak.

Nearly six feet in height and thus tall for an Apache, Juh

was now somewhere in his fifties, and recognized by most of the people as one of the fiercest of men. All his life, Apaches had been at war with the rest of the world, and he had killed many White Eyes, many in hand-to-hand battle—fighting that he relished, especially when he used the old-fashioned Apache lance, which he wielded with stunning quickness and the strength of an athlete.

Juh's chest was notably thick and he was longer-waisted than most of his kinsmen, with long powerful arms and hands with broad palms and long flat fingers. He sat now on a red slab of rock, bare-chested and dressed in the same manner as Naiche, leaning on one hand while with the other he held the barrel of his Sharps rifle. In repose, he had a deceptively lazy look, like a mountain lion at rest.

There was no Nedh'ni warrior who would not follow him, and most of the Chiricahuas who had taken Cochise as their leader in the 1860s and early 1870s now perceived Juh as the rightful heir to Cochise's mantle. Just as important as all the enemies he had killed, when a war party led by Juh surged out of the fastnesses of the Sierra Madres and descended on the Mexicans, wreaking vengeance and death on them, few Apache warriors failed to return, few women had to wail and keen in mourning while the others rejoiced at the return of their men.

The most startling aspect of Juh's appearance was the obsidian eyes that seemed almost to burn in narrow triangular slits under heavy dark brows. From the slitted eyes, his cheekbones fell straight down like cliff faces past a prominent, wide nose that was bent from a blow he had received as a young warrior in a raid on the Mexican town of Janos. Dark fissures ran down past the corners of his mouth, which was typically set in a full-lipped frown. His rare smiles were like the sun emerging from behind a cloud.

He smiled now, enjoying Jeffords's phrase—"pitiless savages"—and then pointed with his lips to the column of horsemen down below. The column had turned slightly north, avoiding the site of an old massacre, the only sign of which now was a shallow dry wash in the earth where a flash flood one spring had carved a sharp-edged new arroyo in the flat desert. Years ago a group of Cochise's warriors had hidden in the new arroyo and ambushed a wagon of military supplies, sending half its fifteen guards to their death, the rest fleeing ignobly across the desert.

"You see," Juh said. "They have long memories. They remember everything we have ... done, so they think they know what we will ... do." He grinned again, even teeth suddenly gleaming white in his coppery face. It was a predator's grin. He stood up and stretched languorously, arching his back.

"Let us go back to camp, my friends," he said with the elaborate courtesy of the Nedh'nis, and stepping lightly between two pillars of red sandstone, he vanished. Naiche and the white man stood, Red Beard grunting as he rose.

"I'm getting too old to run around with you young warriors," he said, and walked stiffly to the place between the two pillars where Naiche had by now vanished as well. Slipping between the rocks, he caught up with Naiche and they followed a familiar though almost imperceptible trail through the craggy rock, leading upward to where the dark spruces shared space with the white-trunked aspens whose round fluttering leaves would soon begin to turn yellow. Juh was already a hundred feet ahead of them on the trail, moving rapidly but without evident exertion, the way Apaches were always taught to move.

Naiche listened to the white man, Jeffords, huffing and puffing behind him, and smiled to himself. He was not easily explained, this man Jeffords with his red beard and thick red hair sticking out in unruly clumps from under his wide-brimmed hat. He had come early to this country, when Naiche was little more than a boy. It was he who had brought the stagecoaches into Cochise's realm—always stopping at Apache Pass, where there was a permanent spring. He was in charge of the Butterfield stagecoach line then, often driving the teams of four horses himself in the early years. On several occasions Apache warriors had ambushed the stage, running off with the horses, and twice in such raids during the first two years that the coaches came and went, the drivers had been killed.

Sometime later Jeffords had appeared in the Dragoon Mountains west of Apache Pass, riding alone, seeking a meeting with Cochise. No white man had ever ridden into the Dragoon Mountains, where Cochise's stronghold lay, and returned to speak of it. But this tall lanky White Eyes appeared among the huge round boulders sprinkled about the foothills like marbles strewn by some vast god and, confronted by Apache lookouts, called out in the Apache tongue. Not Spanish, which most Apaches also spoke, but their own tongue. Impressed, the Apaches let him pass, and finally he came into the presence of Cochise, who was equally impressed by the man's calm and unshakable courage.

So impressed was Cochise that he agreed to give Jeffords's stagecoaches free passage through his territory. The word went out to all the Chiricahuas that Jeffords was a friend of Cochise, and indeed they met often thereafter, always clasping each other in an embrace and always sitting alone, talking of many things, often all through the night. At such times, Naiche would sneak up as near as he dared, trying to overhear the two men, and often he heard them laughing.

When the United States Army offered to make the traditional lands of the Cochise Apaches a reservation strictly for their use, Cochise agreed, stipulating that Jeffords be appointed the agent for the reservation. For several years Jeffords acted as the sole white authority on the reservation, and as the government failed to make good on its promises of rations and other supplies, Jeffords always toiled in the Apaches' best interests.

After Cochise's death in 1874, Jeffords did his best to keep the faith with both Naiche and his brother Taza and with the other bands, always trying to balance their often competing interests and demands. But when the United States government abolished the reservation and demanded that the Chiricahuas all go to San Carlos, Jeffords quit and bought a ranch east of the Dragoons, where he eked out a living running cattle. But he had never lost his regard for the Chiricahuas, and they all knew him as a friend whose word, once given, was as unshakable as a mountain.

And here he is all these years later, Naiche thought as they reached the edge of the spruce forest, with us in these final months.

The White Eyes often did unexplainable things, contradictory things, things that made no sense, but Naiche had little trouble explaining them. They were driven by the yellow metal that was forbidden to the Apaches by their creator. They groveled in the ground for the yellow metal, gold, and otherwise directed their lives to accumulating money. Money was first in their hearts. They killed each other for money. The soldiers came to protect them as they groveled for money.

That was all plain to see, if hard to understand. But Jeffords, Red Beard—he was not so easily explained.

Up ahead Juh stood silhouetted in the shadows of the spruce forest's edge. Beyond him the ground vanished, dropping precipitously down to the little valley where Naiche's people had camped these past few days. Across the valley to the west and to the north, red cliffs rose into pinnacles and slabs. To the south a small creek that arose from a tiny perennial spring trickled out of the valley and downslope, where it joined other streams. Naiche, with Jeffords stumping along stiff-legged behind him, drew up next to the great warrior, who stood motionless until the two men passed him. It was proper that Naiche, with his familiar friend Jeffords, should proceed first into his own camp.

There in the temporary lodgings among the tall pines, their wives awaited them, Naiche's, and Juh's favorite wife, Ishton, who had accompanied him from the Sierra Madres a month ago while huge with child. The child had been born here in the relative safety of the soaring ramparts of the Chiricahua Mountains, and in due course Juh would give it a name. Today, the cradleboard in which it would spend most of its first year was nearly finished. When the little boy child was placed in it, there would be a brief ceremony, during which time the demands of war and survival would be put happily out of mind.

General George Crook would have far preferred to spend the morning hunting, or fishing. Instead, up well before dawn, as was his routine, and working by the light of the oil lamp hung from one of the two-by-four wooden struts that supported his field tent, he had drafted his semiannual report to the Secretary of War. He wrote at a small portable escritoire, sitting on a wooden folding chair, one of two that shared the tent's limited floor space with his cot. On the opposite strut his dress uniform hung facing the wall as if banished, which in fact it was. Crook preferred his civilian suit of tan canvas, more comfortable in the dry heat of the Southwest than the blue woolens of the army, just as he preferred his white cork helmet from Africa over the pompous, cumbersome helmet of the U.S. officer with its silly and frail ornaments that were always falling off.

Similarly, Crook preferred sleeping in his field tent rather than the cramped, low-ceilinged, and airless adobe quarters tucked into the hills at Fort Bowie. He was well aware that his personal peculiarities set him apart from other officers in the United States Army and were a constant source of concern among his tradition-plagued superiors—in particular, General Sheridan. Crook also knew that those unimaginative gentlemen would wink at his eccentricities only so long as the untraditional manner in which he pursued his mission worked. And it did work.

The mule trains, for example. He had long since, in his first tour in the Southwest, recognized the folly of trailing wild roaming savages in this rugged terrain with great wagon trains of supplies. You might as well attempt to chase them down with giraffes and rhinoceroses. Mules, on the other hand, suffered less in the extreme heat of these desert lands, were far more surefooted in the mountains, and could carry more than horses. Crook himself rarely even rode a horse, preferring instead his powerfully built mule, which he had named Apache.

The men under his command knew him to be a martinet when it came to the proper packing of mules, a task he often oversaw with finicky care though it would have seemed beneath the attentions of a general.

Another practical tactic that raised the eyebrows of his superiors was the use of Apaches as scouts. Sheridan had harrumphed about this one time: "They are the most despicable savages on the continent," he had said. "I can't imagine that any one man among them can be trusted."

Yet no one—no military unit in the history of warfare—was as likely to be able to track down a renegade Apache as another Apache. When mounted—and Crook believed that mounted Apaches constituted the finest light cavalry in the world— an Apache would ride until his horse dropped, then eat it. Often, each rider ponied a handful of spare horses, even when in flight at breakneck speed, and when a mount flagged, it was replaced by a fresher one.

As for infantry troops, there was simply no role for them in this warfare. The savages could travel seventy miles a day on foot day after day with nothing but a few bites of jerky to sustain them. They could disappear, literally disappear, under the gamma grass on a flat plain. In even the most godforsaken wastes of the godforsaken dry lands that lay south and west of where he now sat, the Apaches could find a sustaining trickle of water, hidden from all other eyes and probably unknown even to God Almighty Himself.

So Crook confidently pursued his own tactics and strategy, based on his intimate knowledge of the land and his ever-respectful familiarity with his adversaries here. His tactics had, after all, worked splendidly in the seventies during his first tour in the Southwest. The task then had been to round up all of the marauding western Apaches—those who lived among the mountains and river valleys of central Arizona. It had taken two years, but he succeeded, placing these people on a reservation north of where he now sat at Fort Bowie.

Within the hour he expected the arrival of a detachment of B Company of the Ninth Cavalry, and he intended to be noticeably present to welcome them into the fort. Stroking his volu-minous side whiskers, he cast his eyes again over his finished report. He was concerned that certain passages be absolutely clear and unambiguous, because his superiors were easily con-fused by the situation on the ground here in Apache country. Sheridan, Crook mused with a certain maliciousness, would have been more at home massing troops like chessmen against Napoléon's legions on some broad, green Old World battle-field, while the women in their finery took tea under parasols and observed the day's fighting from a nearby hillside.

Sir:

I have the honor to report that during the six months just past, the condition of military affairs in the Department of Arizona has been eminently satisfactory. The White Moun-tain Apaches, those bands that roamed north of the Gila River, have long been sequestered on the reservations at San Carlos and Fort Apache, where they remain content and free of trouble. Since the successful campaign by Col. Hatch against Victorio of the Warm Springs Chiricahuas in New Mexico that resulted in Victorio's death in Mexico in 1881, those people (with an exception as will be noted) have also been peacefully removed from southwestern New Mexico and settled at San Carlos. In addition, the great number of Chiricahuas from southeastern Arizona (sometimes referred to as Cochise Apaches) have also been sent to San Carlos and Fort Apache. For the first time in the history of these fierce people, the Apaches are at peace.

Efforts were made in the early spring to put the Chiricahuas at work for their own living. The two chiefs—Geronimo and Chato, who last year were our worst enemies—have this year made the greatest progress and have the best-tilled farms. The other Apache bands continue to do excellently well . . .

I regard this as one of the most important features of any policy which has as its objective the advancement of the savage beyond a state of vagabondage. He must be made to work, and he will do that with full heart only when he sees that he can always find a ready cash market for the fruits of his labor . . .

The facts above cited speak for themselves. They demonstrate that with but little honest encouragement, this Indian will drop from the list of worthless idlers and relieve the Government from the responsibility of caring for him . . . Captain Crawford, Lieutenant Gatewood, and Lieutenant Davis, the officers having military charge of the Apaches at San Carlos and Fort Apache, deserve the warmest praise for the intelligent and conscientious manner in which they have performed their arduous and thankless duties, handled the most difficult questions, introduced good order among the Apaches, and placed them so far on the road to civilization and self-maintenance.

There have been no troubles with the Apaches during the past six months, either those on reservations (and this is true also for the Mescaleros in New Mexico) or the few remaining bands that still roam wild. These latter have confined themselves to Mexico, with no reports of their presence in this period on this side of the border. They consist for the most part of two small groups—no more than 50 or 75 each—of Warm Springs renegades under the leadership of an aging chief named Nana and of Mangas, one of the sons of Mangas Colorado; and the Nedenni band, which traditionally has dwelt in the Sierra Madres and concentrated its depredations exclusively on the Mexicans. This band, often associated distantly with the Chiricahuas, is reported to have become relatively quiescent, especially since the death by falling of its chief, Juh, last year. In addition, we believe that a small number of Cochise Apaches have joined the Nedennis in Mexico.

Even given the period of peace that has continued through six months, there is reason to expect that marauding will occur again on our side of the border by the remaining free-ranging Apaches. In this expectation, we are strengthening our existing troops at the forts and other installations along the border with the addition of members of the Ninth and Tenth Cavalry, of whose successful campaigns in Texas and New Mexico you are already aware. This and your timely diplomacy with the Government of Mexico, permitting our troops to cross the border when in hot pursuit of the enemy, should bring a successful and, it can be hoped, early conclusion to this long campaign, and render this region finally freed from the threat of the Apache under which it has labored so long.

General Crook blinked his eyes, rubbed a big hand over his forehead, and stood up, satisfied. He had, of course, made no mention of the Apache scouts in his report, not wanting to wave any red flag under the nose of an uncomprehending bull. In emphasizing the manner in which even the hated Geronimo was taking to the path of civilization, he hoped to gainsay the widespread pressure from the Arizonans that the Apaches should be exterminated. Crook could understand the hatred with which his charges on the reservation were regarded by the settlers—but he could not condone it. He was also aware that what in the 1870s had been called the Tucson Ring—local politicians, ranchers, commercial people, and some corrupt government agents, all of whose survival depended on supplying the army—still had influence in Washington and opposed extermination, for obvious reasons. For how would they support themselves then?

Crook shook his head at the complexity of politics and the venality rampant among many of the very people he was charged to protect, recalling the several occasions when he had thought the best course might well be to leave these unforgiving lands to the Apaches and the other savages whose codes of honor, however ugly some of the results, were at least recognizable as that—codes of honor. Shaking his head again, he stepped out of his tent into the sunlight.

Two

"I don't want you doin' any more of that work, Minnie, you hear me? We don't need the money now, as we own this place."

Joe Bignon sat across from his wife at a wooden table in the bar of the Bird Cage Theatre in Tombstone, Arizona, with one hand clasped firmly around a tumbler that was half full of the best whiskey in the place. Joe was a small man with a heavy black moustache that drooped lugubriously down the sides of his mouth. He rather fancied it made him look like one of the Earp brothers, the heroes who had left Tombstone just over two years ago. The bottle from which he had poured his finest whiskey sat on the table in front of him, and he looked past it up at the face of his wife, known by most as Big Minnie.

Big Minnie was in fact very big, far bigger than her husband Joe. She was not quite six feet tall and almost two hundred pounds of warm round flesh. She had clear dark blue eyes that looked innocent, a slightly protruding upper lip, and a slightly upturned nose, all of which contributed to what was a usually happy-looking baby face. Seated across from Joe, she wore a fancy purple silk dress with a modest V neckline and a little skullcap covered with pink silk flowers that resembled primroses. Like her husband, she clasped a tumbler of the whiskey in one hand and thought, not for the first time, that Joe's moustache made him look like a rodent gone to a funeral.

They had arrived by stagecoach in 1881 at the height of the silver boom, when Tombstone was the biggest town in all of the Arizona Territory, with four thousand people, six hundred houses, two churches, and even a newly built school. Fabulous wealth was being torn from the earth in more than a dozen major mines and more minor ones than the townspeople could keep track of, and things were so good that even some of the whores on Sixth Street were grubstaking men and getting rich.

Joe Bignon had soon talked his way into a job as night manager of the Bird Cage Theatre, which also meant he introduced the acts, which mostly consisted of dancing by some of the higher-toned prostitutes in town. His wife Minnie watched this dancing for a few nights and announced that she was going to have a turn, so Joe, getting into the swing of things, billed her as "Big Minnie, six feet tall and two hundred and thirty pounds of loveliness in pink tights." And Big Minnie was an instant hit. None of the men sitting around the tables getting drunk had ever seen a woman that big prancing around on a stage before with so much jiggling and swaying going on. They hooted and whistled and applauded, and Big Minnie, as she would henceforth be known to all and sundry, got a smile on her face that was pure love and satisfaction.

Joe was thrilled for her, but not quite so thrilled when Big Minnie, with considerable enthusiasm, took up some of the other work the other dancers performed. In fact, when he found out about it, Joe threw himself a fit, but there wasn't much he could do about it besides splutter because Minnie, he knew, could cause him exceeding pain by either of two routes— withholding these same favors from him, or crushing him. And, he had to admit, they could bank the money. Which they did, and when the founder and owner of the Bird Cage, Billy Hutchinson, decided to move on, the Bignons bought the place from him.

Big Minnie frowned now, her baby face becoming a pout from her eyebrows to her chin. "Joe, I don't need to remind you it was mostly the money I made that we bought this place with." She lifted her glass, tilted it, and drained the last of the dark brown whiskey. She put the glass down, poured it half full from the bottle, and put the bottle down in the exact center of the table. She leaned forward on thick arms and glared at her husband.

"Dammit, Minnie, that's my en-tire point that I am making here. We used that money that got saved to make this here investment. We are now the sole proprietors of the Bird Cage Theatre, which is the most popular place of entertainment in Tombstone, so what I am saying is that we don't need no more money coming in from you—uh, from that other source of enterprise."

Joe Bignon's eyes flickered back and forth nervously. The barroom was empty but for three men playing cards in the far corner. It was three o'clock in the afternoon.

"And what I am saying to you," Big Minnie said carefully, "is that business is down. Look over there, only three customers in the place and the afternoon's almost gone."

"It is not, it's only—"

"There should be more people in here. But people ain't got the money they had only a year ago. Ever since that damn strike in January when everything shut down, and then they get around to settlin' it four months later, and the price of silver goes down four cents an ounce, and then they hit water in the Emerald Mine, and you know that water's down there under every one of these mines and what does that mean, huh?"

"They're getting pumps, big pumps. They can pump the water out and keep going," Joe said, and finished his whiskey. He poured another glass. "They already got started in—"

"Sure, and they can pump the water out of the ocean and charge money to look at Neptune himself," Big Minnie said, glowering at Joe. "Don't tell me we don't need any extra money. Way things are going, we may have to find a sucker to buy this place." Suddenly she smiled. When she smiled, her slightly protruding upper lip was stretched back toward the rest of her face and she looked breathtakingly pretty, like a little girl. Joe loved it when she smiled. He noticed that she was looking over his shoulder at the table where the men were playing cards. He turned to see what had amused her.

"That Mexican girl, name is Margarita," Minnie said. "She's got a thing for Billy Milgreen over there."

"That tinhorn?"

"Yep. See, she just come in and she's struttin' around the table for him, see?"

Joe Bignon pushed his chair out and to the side to get a better view of the table. Margarita, a prostitute newly arrived from Mexico, was tall, dark, and willowy—very attractive, swaying her hips in a tight black dress that flared out at the knee—and she was very clearly vamping Billy Milgreen, who was a no-account trying to make a living as a gambler. As everyone knew, he was the special man of Little Gertie, another soiled dove from Sixth Street they also called Gold Dollar, because she was as tiny as the dime-sized dollar coins of gold the U.S. Mint had started producing.

"I don't see what she sees in that Milgreen," Joe said, and then, "Well, look at that!"

Margarita suddenly plopped herself down in Billy Milgreen's lap and took to kissing him all over his face, and he was flapping his arms around, holding his poker hand so nobody could see it and trying at the same time to shoo away the tall beauty draped in his lap the way a man would shoo a swarm of hornets off himself.

"Joe!" Big Minnie said. "Go get the sheriff."

"What for? She's just kissin' the man."

"Because here comes Little Gertie, that's why! Now do as I say!"

Big Minnie was now standing, her ample bosom heaving, as the diminutive figure of Gold Dollar, blond hair flying, raced past screaming, "Get away from him, you furrow butt! Get your greasy hands off him!"

She pulled up at the table, and the other two players were already out of their chairs. Gold Dollar grabbed a fistful of Margarita's long black hair and yanked it. Small as she was, she had enough vinegar in her that Margarita wound up on the floor, her feet kicking.

"You heard me, you Mexican bedbug! Get away!"

While Margarita was shrieking and trying to stand up and Gertie was kicking her, Billy Milgreen chose to open his mouth.

"This wasn't none of my doing, Gert, she just—"

And Gert spun around to Billy and shouted, "You shut your mouth, you faithless bastard! I ever catch you feeling up one of these whores, I'll scratch your damn eyes out!"

At which point Margarita got her feet under her, lunged at the little blonde and grabbed at her face with long red fingernails. They scrambled and scrabbled and screamed, while Billy threw himself out of his chair and crawled away as fast as he could on his hands and his knees. Little Gertie, in her fury, pushed Margarita into the table, and the Mexican upended and fell over it onto the floor, and before anyone could do anything, Little Gertie snatched a knife from her garter and drove it into Margarita's ribs.

Blood spurted out from the gash in Margarita's black silk dress and she shrieked in Spanish that she was dead, but she wasn't yet. She lay on the floor, and Billy stood about ten feet away staring, and Little Gertie stood over her, saying, "Oh no, oh no, what have I done?"

Margarita's blood was oozing fast, making a puddle on the floor, and Big Minnie bustled over, shouting, "Dammit, Joe, get the doctor! And *then* fetch the sheriff! Don't just stand there!"

Ten minutes later the doctor burst in through the doors, looking stern, but Margarita was dead by then. The doctor knelt down, quickly confirmed this fact, and left, passing a deputy sheriff on the way in, a man named Danny Kinkaid. Little Gertie, the Gold Dollar, was now slumped in a chair on the other side of the table from the corpse, white to the lips and trembling. The deputy put his hands in his back pockets and stood staring down at Margarita, who was also turning livid.

"What was this all about?" he asked.

Little Gertie opened her mouth but no words came out. She began to sob. Big Minnie gave her a motherly pat on the shoulder and told the deputy what had happened.

"So," Big Minnie concluded, "it was a fair fight, Danny. As fair as has ever happened."

The deputy nodded and looked down at the corpse again.

"Well, Gert, if I was you, I'd go back to your house over there on Sixth Street and pack up your things and go someplace else, maybe Tucson, or over to Bisbee. Things are startin' up over at Bisbee. But no man around here's gonna want to be with a whore that kills people. Not anymore at least. That's just how it is when a place starts settlin' down and gets civilized."

Nearby at the Apache camp in the Chiricahuas, among the aspen trees with their trembling leaves, the elegant woman named Lozen worked on a cradleboard for the little son of Juh. She wore the traditional deerskin skirt of the Apache woman, and a deerskin tunic embroidered with porcupine quills. Lozen was known to her people as the Warrior Woman.

Like all young Apache girls, Lozen had learned many of the warrior's skills, especially running fast and for long distances, and disappearing into the landscape. She learned this alongside her brothers, including the one who would later be called Victorio, and at an early age she was handy with both a bow and a knife. At age twelve she was a better shot with a rifle than any of her brothers.

The adults who taught Lozen these skills told her she would need them as a grown woman—there was no telling what she might run into when she was out gathering nuts or firewood. When the men were off raiding or hunting and the White Eyes came, only the toughest women had a chance of escaping rape or slavery—both worse than death. But Lozen, by the time she was thirteen, had a lot more on her mind than self-defense. Lozen intended to be a warrior.

At fourteen she sneaked out of camp when some men and a few boys her age were going off on a raid, joining them when it was too late for them to do anything but let her come along. She acquitted herself well enough that the men were amused, and so she was allowed to go on three more raids in the next year. After the last one, in which she laid out a Mexican rancher with a blow from her wooden war club and single-handedly made off with eight of his horses, she had been quietly and without ceremony included among the warriors. She was Warrior Woman, and her standing grew rapidly in the warriors' council over the next few years as she proved her mettle in the traditional manner—by killing enemies.

There was nothing a warrior could do that Lozen couldn't. An especially daring rider, she streaked and wheeled against enemies with an unbridled fury and a high, shrieking howl that made a man's flesh crawl. Whenever a battle went badly for the Apaches and it was time to scatter, Lozen was always among the last to go, seeking one more kill. It was as if she had a special protection, some power that shielded her.

And Lozen did in fact have a special power, one even more valuable than her skill as a warrior. She knew where the enemy was.

Countless times, before a party set out to wreak war or on a raid to capture livestock, or in a long flight across the mountains and desert, Lozen would stand in the middle of the warriors with her arms upraised, chanting quietly to herself. She would turn slowly around through a circle, and then again, until she stopped. Where she faced, that was where the enemy was, and she would say how far away.

Lozen had ridden with her brother Victorio after the last breakout in 1880, when he led the Buffalo Soldiers on their long chase around Texas and New Mexico, and her presence alone made it impossible for the Mexicans to kill Victorio. No one got that close when the Warrior Woman was present.

Like her brother, Lozen's brows were thick and nearly met above a straight wide nose whose nostrils could flare wide like those of an angry horse. And like Victorio, her mouth was wide, the lower lip forming a taut straight line across a strong but pleasantly curved jaw. Unlike her brother, whose right eye was slightly off, the black pupil always riding a little higher than the left one, peering out from a lowered eyelid and giving him a look of unpredictable wildness, Lozen's eyes were a warm brown, evenly set under the heavy brows and lustrous hair. At times they were filled with a tenderness some might find odd in a woman capable of such renowned ferocity.

Like most Apache women, Lozen stood with her back straight and her head held straight and high, and walked in a fluid, even stately manner in which her toes touched the ground before her heel. Now, in the aspen glade, she stepped carefully around some wood shavings and bent down to pick up a rectangular piece of red cedar she had fashioned earlier in the day. On the trek north from Mexico, before Juh and Ishton's new son was born, they had asked her to be the Cradlemaker.

Making the cradleboard in which a baby would reside most of each day until it could walk was a sacred task, always to be done with the correct materials by a woman who commanded respect, because her qualities would be imparted, via the cradleboard, to the child. The prayers she made during its construction would remain with the child throughout his life.

Throughout her fashionings of locust and cedar wood and buckskin, Lozen sang quietly. She sang of the baby and her hopes for a long life for it, of how it would be safe from lightning and other hazards. She sang of the Creator, Ussen, who had made everything in the world, including everything Apaches needed for their survival and enjoyment.

Finally her task was complete, and the sun was gone behind the crags that rose to the west, leaving a pink glow in the sky. Lozen the Warrior Woman carried the cradleboard back to camp.

The next morning, Lozen took the cradleboard to Ishton's shelter. Only Ishton and Juh and their baby were present, the other women of the family having remained in Mexico.

Outside the shelter, Lozen reverentially held the cradleboard up and out—to the east toward the sun, then south, west, and north. Tenderly lifting the naked baby from Ishton's arms, she held him out in the same manner to the four directions.

They went inside the shelter, and Lozen washed the baby's feet with water and, three times, held him out toward the cradleboard. The fourth time, she put him in it, and Ishton tied the laces over him. After Lozen touched the top of Ishton's head with yellow pollen of the yucca plant, Ishton stepped back to stand beside her husband Juh. Ishton's eyes strayed up to Juh's face and saw that his eyes were brimming, crinkled up with a smile.

Lozen, meanwhile, gestured with the pollen four times in the direction of the baby and put some on his lips. He stuck out his tongue, tasting the pollen, and wrinkled his nose. The ceremony was complete and the adults could eat. They went outside into the sunlight.

Juh ate silently, his mind full of prayerful hope for this new son. But also his heart again filled with sadness and a searing rage for the infant son he had lost only three years before. Images flickered back now of the awful events. He could have willed them away, but he had learned that it was better, even essential, that he look unblinkingly at what had happened that night:

In the cold silence of oncoming night the angry vermilion of the sky has turned to a small bruise of red below dark gray clouds . . . gunfire erupts from three sides, a deadly roar, starbursts of flame, bullets skimming up dust all around, the thunk of lead in flesh, cries, people falling. From the sound, American rifles. How many? Too many. What are they doing in Mexico?

Hemmed in. Scramble up through the rocks, bullets pinging back and forth, no time for a counterattack, just grab what you can, whatever you can, run, leap, up. Two dozen head of horses left picketed, people dead in the camp among the rocks. Faster, faster! Up into the cliffs. A searing flame of pain in his ribs, a long welt.

Juh reaches out, snatches his wife Ishton toward him. She is already exhausted, so recently delivered of their son. Juh clutches her desperately as she clutches the new cradleboard with the week-old boy child.

"Come," he says. "Farther up. There's no other choice." He pulls at her and she comes, her eyes white with fear, her teeth clenched in a grimace.

The gunfire ends. The oncoming dark of night is quiet. Cold

settles over the rocks like a blanket. The People reassemble among the fissures and cliffs like ghosts in the dusk, feet silent on the rock. Juh counts. They began the day with seventeen—ten warriors, four women, and three children, two of them infants in their cradleboards, the other a young girl. Now they are eight warriors, three women, and three children. They are at the northern end of the San Luis Mountains, not more than a mile or two from the border.

They are trapped, hemmed in up here. The American troops won't follow them up into the rocks in the dark, but they will wait below till morning.

To the south behind their perch in these low cliffs, two large detachments of Mexican cavalry—some two hundred men altogether—have been following them, guided by Tahuamara scouts, poor warriors but skilled trackers. Alerted by the gunfire that rattles through the night air, louder under the cloud cover, they will be moving closer now in the night along the mountain crest above and among the mountains' flanks.

Here then, here in the cliffs, they are trapped. Juh smells the fear among his people, and the distant rancid smell of the White Eyes below, the odor of stale milk, of fat. Behind them, below them—too many White Eyes. Their one hope now is stealth, to move more silently than bats in the blackness.

One of the infants whimpers in its cradleboard—not Juh's son, the other child, a girl.

"Hsst," its mother says. The baby whimpers again.

Juh glances up at the starless sky. Again the infant whimpers, cries out, and its mother hushes it. Then his own son whimpers too. Ishton lifts the cradleboard, puts her face against the baby's.

Juh's heart sinks, as if a hood of ice had suddenly grown over it. He peers at Ishton, only a shadowy silhouette in the dark, then the other mother. She stares back, eyes white in the shadow. White with horror.

"No," she whispers.

Juh holds his hand out.

"No," she whispers again.

He turns to Ishton, who still holds his son to her cheek. He hears her breathe in deeply, then exhale, and she hands Juh the cradleboard and turns away . . .

And so, that night, quickly and with his own hands, his own long fingers, Juh did the awful thing that had to be done. They found a crevice and left the two infants there covered with rocks, and slipped silently past the troops ranged at intervals around below, passing breathlessly within mere feet of them. The next night, under cover of dark, they reached the Chiricahua Mountains.

It was during that silent and mournful trek from the San Luis Mountains across the border to the Chiricahuas that Juh had seen clearly what now had to be done. With a clarity that rose out of a heart leaden with grief, a clarity lit by a simmering fury that would never disappear so long as he breathed, Juh had glimpsed the only true destiny for the Apache, the hardest course, that which risked the death of everything and everyone against the vibrant dream of freedom.

Now he paused in his silent feasting, swallowed a bite of venison, and looked over at this new son in the cradleboard made for him by the Warrior Woman, Lozen. The infant slept, one little red hand near his mouth, tiny fingers rolled into a fist. His beloved Ishton had paused too, and watched the infant with bright eyes. Nearby, the little stream burbled past, shimmering and dazzling in the morning sun, flashes of light hiding the dark water that issued forth from the earth not twenty yards away—a perennial spring that never failed.

"Call him Little Spring," Juh said. "It will do for now."

Three

Grim-faced as always, the man whom everyone called Geronimo stared gloomily across his field. The name, Spanish for Jerome, was bestowed on him decades earlier by Mexicans when he led an attack on their village on the day of the saint of that same name, and it had stuck with him ever since. All of his own people called him Geronimo and not his birth name, Goyakla—One-who-yawns.

The name—and the man—had become synonymous with the popularly held view, on either side of the border, of the Apaches as a race of vicious, bloodthirsty, dishonest, thieving savages incapable of any form of human decency and certainly no more likely to be civilized than a mountain lion is to be tamed.

There were some four thousand of these "worst of all" Indians disarmed and crowded onto the San Carlos reservation and north up to Fort Apache. Many of them, like the Tonto Apaches, had been on the reservation for nearly a decade, and these western groups and the Chiricahuas and other more easterly Apaches made uneasy neighbors—and for one reason: they hated each other. So they lived as far from each other as the limited geography of the reservation permitted. Most of the Chiricahuas had settled near Turkey Creek, west of Fort Apache and as far from the other Apaches as they could contrive.

Geronimo knew that if he were to be regarded as a "good" Indian now, he would have to do this contemptible work, and do it well here at Turkey Creek. So his fields were among the most productive and well tended on the reservation, and while he never would have admitted it to anyone, he took a certain pride in them.

He now contemplated the rows of melon plants that stretched out before him. He had dug all the rows by hand with a shovel a few weeks after arriving here in the spring. He'd already harvested more bushels of corn than he could count. He had given most of it away to his fellow Chiricahuas near Turkey Creek and sold the rest to the agent for what he thought a pittance, using most of the money to buy whiskey that was bootlegged onto the reservation by a White Eyes trader named Sweeney who lived near Fort Thomas along the Gila River.

Suddenly feeling profoundly sorry for himself in his new and discomfiting role as captive farmer, Geronimo had proceeded to go on a five-day drunk. He woke up in a dry irrigation ditch near his fields before dawn with no memory whatsoever of where or how far he had wandered. Asked the next day by the soldiers about his absence, he explained that he had been in the south of the reservation undertaking a ceremonial obligation for a nephew. That was two weeks ago, and since then he had made a great show of weeding his rows of melons, which he would not eat, having discovered that they gave him a mild but highly alarming form of diarrhea.

It seemed a long time ago to Geronimo, almost a lifetime ago, that he had been a free man.

He sat now in the shade, dressed in a white canvas blouse given him by one of the soldiers, a white breechclout, and his high deerskin moccasins with the typical "silver dollar" fold of deerskin on the toe, added protection against the spines of cactus and other warlike plants of the desert. He had lived almost a half century, most of it at war with Mexicans, and more recently Americans too, and the years of strain had begun to show. His hair, loose and cut off at the shoulders, was showing some gray, and his eyes—twin slits—were surrounded with multiple tracks. Deep seams lined his face below prominent round cheekbones. His mouth was a wide and cruelly thin gash in a large and pugnacious jaw. It was a grim face, familiar to even the most distant of Americans, for Geronimo had permitted himself to be photographed several times in the past, and artists' renderings of these appeared in virtually every perfervid account of the Apache wars. For all that the rest of the world knew, Geronimo was the most powerful, most feared Apache chief since the famous Cochise, but twice as ferocious.

He was presently engaged in eating piñon nuts from a supply in a pocket of his canvas blouse. He looked up and to his left, hearing the sound of a horse's hooves on the dry ground. It was Captain Emmet Crawford, resplendent in his blue uniform with its double row of shiny brass buttons and black leather belt, holster, and boots that gleamed in the sunlight. A Colt .45 rested in the holster from which Crawford had cut the flap, and from his other hip hung a long, lethal-looking saber. He sat comfortably on his mount, a powerful bay mare, approaching Geronimo at a slow walk.

Captain Crawford, commander of the entire reservation, was a tall man, slender, with a brow that was both high and wide over a narrow face made all the longer by a moustache and goatee lighter and a bit redder than his dark brown hair, which he wore short in the military manner. He looked out at the world from pale gray eyes that suggested a wisdom well beyond his years. At twenty-eight, he was young to have attained the rank of captain, and he was a great favorite of General Crook, whose knowledgeable respect for the Apaches he shared. Unlike his stern and taciturn mentor, however, Crawford was an affable man who enjoyed bantering with his Indian charges.

"Geronimo," he said, smiling and with the proper Spanish pronunciation. "Good afternoon. You've finished your work?"

Geronimo put a piñon nut in his mouth, bit down on the shell, extracted the little nut with his tongue, and spat the broken shell onto the ground in front of him.

"Farmer's work is never done," he said.

Crawford laughed and dismounted, tethering the horse to a branch of the mesquite bush. He squatted down on his heels a few feet from Geronimo, the saber pointing rearward, its tip touching the ground.

Geronimo glanced at the officer, then looked out over his fields. "Big sword," he said. "You ever kill any Indians with it?"

They had been through this several times, Geronimo thinking that a sword wasn't much of a weapon even though he had received a wound on his arm from one years earlier, a gash that left an ugly purple scar on his left bicep.

"No," Captain Crawford said. "It's just part of the uniform."

"Maybe I could borrow it," Geronimo said. "Use it to harvest them melons out there." He permitted himself the slightest of smiles. Crawford surveyed the field with its rows of green melon vines. They looked lush against the dry landscape.

"Probably not sharp enough for that. It's just for show."

The two men fell silent, Geronimo waiting to find out what had brought the captain to his neighborhood. It was surely more than just making a head count. Usually, the weekly count was done by a lieutenant or a sergeant.

"I was over at Chato's place yesterday," Crawford said. "His fields are like these."

Geronimo grunted, and ate another piñon nut, spitting the shell out on the ground. Chato was a Chiricahua, a humorless man not greatly liked by the others, but he had gained some respect a year ago. Finding themselves low on ammunition, the Apaches had sent him out from the Sierra Madres at the head of a war party. Two days later he crossed into the United States near the town of Bisbee and he and his band traveled four hundred miles in six days. In that whirlwind raid, they killed twelve people at three ranches, burning the buildings down and making off with a long string of horses, nearly two dozen, and almost a thousand rounds of ammunition, disappearing with their booty back into the safety of the mountains in Mexico. During the six days, mounted troops from Fort Huachuca and several other camps rode frantically around the landscape in search parties, but never managed to lay eyes on them. Catastrophic in its sudden fury, it called forth yet more strident howls from the sparse citizenry of southeastern Arizona, the Tucson *Citizen* claiming it as "the utterest of disasters, and one that can be laid squarely at the feet of General George Crook." To the Apaches, of course, it was the utterest of successful raids, with not a single warrior lost.

In spite of Chato's success, however, Geronimo looked upon him with disfavor bordering on contempt, and this judgment had now been more than borne out.

"I hear you made Chato chief of the scouts," Geronimo said. "Now he's wearing a blue jacket, huh."

Crawford's eyebrows rose. "Word travels fast," he said.

"How come you didn't make me chief of the scouts? I killed more people than Chato." Geronimo glanced slyly over at the officer. Crawford laughed uncomfortably, and was silent. He had no intention of justifying his choice to Geronimo or any other Apache on the reservation, and Geronimo did not expect an answer. He knew he would have to kill Chato. It was not something he looked forward to especially—killing one's own kind was not something Apaches did—but in this case . . .

"Geronimo, I've come to ask your advice, and to seek your help."

"Why?"

"Because," Crawford said, "you are looked up to by many of the people here for your wisdom. Many of them followed you here, came here only because you decided to settle down and learn the ways of the white man's world."

Geronimo grunted, pleased to be complimented, and pleased that this young officer knew to compliment him.

"There have been reports these past two months that some of the Apaches have been, ah . . . have used a great deal of physical force with their wives."

Geronimo nodded. Wife-beating, along with a number of other Apache ways, had been prohibited by command of General Crook. When Captain Crawford announced the prohibition, one of the old men had objected strenuously. "You telling us how to treat our women?" he had said. "I *killed* people before you was even born."

"It's the Apache Way," Geronimo said. "When your wife does something wrong, you've got to beat her."

"But some of the old Apache ways have to end," Crawford said. "You yourself have sworn to give up raiding and warfare, killing and robbing. And you have taken up the life of the farmer. Very successfully, I might add. Now, this is another thing the Apache must give up if they are to become civilized and take their place in the society of Americans. I've come here to ask your help. I would like you to talk to the men about this, explain that in the new life they are learning to live, women must be shown respect."

"Apache women have a lot of respect," Geronimo said. "We—us warriors—we go to live in their camp. It's them who tell us—"

Crawford cleared his throat. "I understand that," he said. "But in this new world of yours—"

"In this new world of ours," Geronimo interrupted, "us Apaches have to stop being Apaches, huh." He shook his head. "Dig in the ground, get money. All that."

"Will you talk to the men? I'd be in your debt."

Geronimo ate another nut, spat again. "Sure. I'll talk to the men."

Crawford stood up, rising in a fluid motion, and stepped over to his mount. "Thank you, Geronimo."

The Indian nodded, and watched Crawford mount up and ride off the way he had come. He was, for a White Eyes, a good man. It was a shame that he too would have to be killed.

In good time.

When Juh sent word.

But now Geronimo had to act on his own, take matters into his own hands, as he had often enough before. He was not and never had been a headman, though the White Eyes thought of him that way. He had always sat to the right of Naiche in council—just as Naiche sat to the right of Juh. But Geronimo was both persuasive and a shrewd and fierce warrior, and he had led more war parties than he could remember, along with two grand breakouts from San Carlos. What the White Eyes could not seem to understand was that any Apache could lead a war party if he could persuade others to follow him. Nor could they understand that the Apaches usually had no great chiefs, no overall leader of the People—except at certain times of great necessity when someone emerged whom all the bands could accept as one who could see far enough. Cochise had been such a man. And now that man was Juh, whom the White Eyes thought was dead: Juh, whose name meant "He-who-sees-ahead."

After each of Geronimo's breakouts from San Carlos and months of successful raiding, he had returned—once in leg irons, once on his own—and each time the White Eyes took him back and believed him when he said he was ready to take the path of "civilization." Geronimo could not understand the White Eyes. They couldn't be so stupid as they often seemed and acted. Why they hadn't killed him, he simply couldn't fathom. Enemies were to be killed. And who, except for Victorio, had made more trouble for the White Eyes—or the Mexicans—in the last ten years than Geronimo?

And now Chato, with his one successful raid, had no doubt persuaded Crawford that he was a big man, a chief, a headman, so they had made him head of the Apache scouts. They had turned Chato with promises of money, a fancy blue jacket, and authority. But it was an authority bestowed by the army, not the Apaches—not authority that comes naturally, like the waters of a spring rise naturally to the surface. It was, instead, an empty jar of an authority. Both sides were tricking each other, both acting on delusions.

Yet there was great danger. Chato knew all of the springs, all of the routes through the mountains, all—or at least most—of the strongholds. Worse, while Chato did not know of Juh's plans—and Geronimo was sure that no one knew *all* of Juh's plans—Chato did know that the stories of Juh's death were fabrications. He might also know that Victorio was alive still, waiting among the Mescaleros.

Had he told the White Eyes? There was no way of knowing that. Had Geronimo been in Chato's place, he would have kept that knowledge back until it could be used to his advantage—but Chato might not be so shrewd. He had to be killed, and the sooner the better.

Tonight, Geronimo decided. One of Chato's less important shortcomings would be his undoing.

The half-moon had swung well to the west now, a silver slice of light in the sky. Its light reflected faintly and silver from the mesquite branches and cast helpful shadows on the ground. Geronimo crouched in one of these shadows. He was still as a rock. For more than an hour he had sat in the shadow without moving, watching the low rounded structure of interwoven branches that was only twenty feet away in the dark—Chato's wickiup. He could sit this way for several more hours, never moving, but that would not be necessary. Soon, any minute now, Chato would wake up and quietly, so as not to disturb his wife, leave the wickiup and emerge into the night air to relieve himself.

In his long and versatile experience killing his enemies, Geronimo had disemboweled several men, though he had never paused to examine the contents that had spilled forth. But men, he presumed, had much the same organs as deer or horses, including a bladder where urine pooled. And Geronimo guessed that Chato's bladder was small for, unlike most Apache warriors, he could not make it through the night without peeing. Because of this, the others regarded him with some derision. How, at a perilous time when silence was the most important thing, when slipping like a wraith past your enemy was your only hope for a continued life—how could you trust the One-who-can't-hold-his-water? Chato was, of course, aware of this flaw and others, and his eyes reflected the hurt he felt at his imperfection. In Geronimo's mind's eye, he saw the man's face, the narrow mouth, the hurting eyes.

The silence of the night was interrupted only by the occasional call of a night bird off somewhere in the mesquite and the quiet rhythmic sound of two people breathing in sleep. Then there was only the one person's breath, and in moments a shadow appeared, stooped over to pass through the low doorway, and stood up.

With his quarry in sight, however dimly, Geronimo felt the familiar rush of blood pounding more insistently in the thin skin over his skull, the surge of anger, of hatred, of contempt that always greeted him when it was time to cut down a man. He watched as Chato stretched, yawned, and walked across the bare dirt around his wickiup and then between two scrubby bushes only a few yards away from the shadow in which Geronimo crouched.

Geronimo stood up noiselessly and waited. He heard the stream of water splash on the ground, and in three silent steps was behind Chato, reaching around the taller man to grasp his chin, pulling it to the side, and with the other hand drawing his knife across the taut flesh—a slicing sound, a burbling sound of blood set loose, and a low, gagging, hoarse gargle like a whisper in the night.

Hot blood spewed onto his hand and his wrist, a salty, fecund smell filling his head, and he let the sagging body down to the ground. Crouching over it, he listened as the corpse drained itself and, in the distance, the night bird called again. Then silence, except for the almost imperceptible sound of one person breathing, asleep in the wickiup.

Come morning's light she would wail and keen.

Geronimo permitted himself one long exhalation of breath through his mouth, and set off into the shadows, listening to the thrilling rhythm of his heart as it pounded within his chest.

Four

Downstream about a half mile from the little spring where Naiche's people had their temporary camp, the waters passed through willow-lined banks, fell prettily over a series of rocky outcrops that formed well-worn steps, and sluiced as a small waterfall into a wider channel. At the downstream end of the channel a pair of beavers had long ago erected a ragged dam, creating a large pool of dark water in which, each year, they raised their kits in a lodge made of sticks, a ragged dome that rose a couple of feet above the surface and looked not unlike an aquatic wickiup.

On this day, the beaver couple shared their pond with the women of Naiche's camp who had abandoned their endless chores to bathe and gossip in the cold, sun-dappled water. All around, willows and aspens shielded them from the rest of the world, and leaves whispered overhead in a breeze. In all, six women and four girls splashed and laughed quietly near the waterfall, including Juh's wife Ishton. Her son, newly named Little Spring, slept in his cradleboard in the shade of a large boulder at the pond's edge.

Ishton sat up to her neck in the water, facing the waterfall and only a few feet from the shore where the cradleboard lay. The current pulled her long black hair out into a floating silken delta behind her. Near her, Naiche's wife Kozineh stood up to her waist, splashing water on her chest and shoulders. She was a short, broad-shouldered woman, full-breasted, and now in her fifth decade.

"It can't be much longer now. A few weeks," Kozineh

said, and Ishton looked across the water to where Kozineh's daughter was cavorting with the other young girls. She was tall and slender like a lithe young tree, and her breasts had budded out now. Soon she would have her first blood, and they would have her da-i-da, the feast and four-day puberty ceremony, and she would be a woman. Kozineh smiled, watching her daughter dive under the water, kicking up a dazzling spray. But then she frowned.

"I hope it's very soon," she said, "or there won't be any time for the ceremony." She sighed. "We have to put off so many things these days. Or forgo them. All this moving around, place to place." It was as close as an Apache would come to complaining.

Ishton nodded her agreement. "These days we have been here," she said. "It's almost like the times . . ." Her voice trailed off. Her grandmother had told her of the times before the White Eyes arrived, when the Apaches could withdraw into these mountains or others, following the game and the ripening plants up into the heights, and be secure. None of their enemies ever ventured into these retreats, and they could hunt and eat and dance and frolic in the mountain waters.

"And Juh believes those times will return, huh." Kozineh was older by almost twenty years than Ishton. She had mourned the death of three children already, two of them young warriors, cut down by the big gun of the White Eyes, the gun they pulled behind horses. The other child she lost had been a daughter, caught in a surprise raid by a group of miners and ranchers from around Douglas, vigilantes who had attacked a camp of women and children, raping and mutilating those they caught. At the time, Kozineh's daughter had been the same age as the daughter they now watched.

"Juh doesn't *know* if those times will return. He hopes they will."

"Hope." The older woman snorted. "What is that?"

"Juh says hope is doing what has to be done because it is the right thing to do." Ishton's voice was soft, almost girlish, but Kozineh knew its innocent-seeming tone was belied by the sacrifice she had already made, handing her firstborn over to be strangled three years ago.

"I promise you only freedom and death," said a deep voice. They looked up to see that Lozen, the Warrior Woman, had materialized out of the trees onto the shore next to the cradle-board. She was mimicking Juh's voice as she untied the rawhide thong around her waist that held her skirt in place. "I promise you freedom and death. I cannot promise victory." Her voice changed to that of a woman. "That's what Juh says. Freedom to die like an Apache."

She stooped over, stuck a finger out and put its tip in the baby's lips.

"That's a lot to ask of a little one like this," she said, squinching up her face at the infant and suddenly smiling. Lozen's smile was a joyous thing, and few ever saw it without smiling too. The infant smiled and drooled.

"It's a lot to ask of all of us," Kozineh said sourly.

Lozen pulled off her deerskin shirt and stood naked on the shore, tall, graceful and strong like an elk. The young girls had ceased their splashing and giggling and turned to watch her. She stepped lightly off the shore and sank up to her waist in the black water, hardly causing a ripple.

"I'd rather die our way," Lozen said, "than be a slave on a reservation and get plugged by some smelly White Eyes with hair on his back." She ducked under the water and came up spluttering, shaking spray from her head. "I know," she said. "That's what happened to your daughter. Such things make our vengeance all the more necessary."

She pointed with her lips over to the young girls. "She was like that one, huh. The time of mourning was over a long time ago, but it still goes on, yes? I'll bring you one, Kozineh. One day soon I'll bring you a White Eyes of your own. You can strip him naked and tell him what they did to your daughter while you cut his balls off." With that the Warrior Woman smiled her radiant smile again, said, "It begins within the week," and dove under the surface.

She came up spluttering again and called out, "You girls!

Swim over here. Who can get here first?" The girls grinned and fell to thrashing their arms in the water. "Kick, kick your feet!" Lozen shouted, and watched, laughing, as the little flotilla of girls and spray reached her.

Ishton watched all this and said, "Do you suppose she'll ever marry?" It was a question often asked among the Apaches.

"What warrior can bring home more horses for bridewealth than she can herself?" Kozineh replied, dismissing the notion of marriage to Lozen as impossible.

"And she's so good at cutting off balls," Ishton said, giggling. "Now what is she doing?"

The four young girls had all ducked down up to their chins. Lozen the Warrior Woman stood with the water up to her waist, arms outstretched, eyes closed, and a shiny, round rock in her right hand. She began chanting to herself, a low humming sound, and turned slowly around, water streaming from her hair over her breasts. Abruptly she stopped, arms still outstretched. Her chanting ceased. She reached back with her right arm and hurled the rock she held into the trees, then vaulted out of the water in a shower of dazzling spray, yelling, and raced into the woods.

Tentatively, the girls began to climb out of the pond, peering after her, but leaped back in the water, shrieking, and submerged again up to their chins. Lozen appeared on the bank, her eyebrows knit into an expression of fury, the fingers of her right hand buried into the long black hair of a boy who hung limply at the end of her arm, his feet barely touching the ground. He had a large red welt over his left eye where Lozen's rock had hit him, and two long scrapes on his chest where he had evidently fallen after turning tail to flee the onslaught of the big, legendarily fierce and totally naked Warrior Woman.

Lozen shook the boy, whose eyes darted back and forth in fear. They carefully avoided falling on the naked woman who had him in her clutches. He wore a white breechclout and low moccasins. The son of one of Naiche's warriors, he was one of a small group of ten- to twelve-year-old boys in camp.

"I caught this brave one, peeping. Trying to catch a look at our tits, weren't you, brave one? What shall we do with him, girls?"

"Hang him upside down from that branch," one of the girls suggested.

"Cut off his balls," another yelled, laughing.

Lozen peered at the boy.

"You don't have any yet, do you, brave one?" she said with a big smile. "But surely you do have a little . . . maybe we can hang you from that." The boy's eyes widened in terror and he struggled in Lozen's iron grasp. She snatched at his breech-clout, spun him around and let him go, delivering a loud smack on his buttocks. The boy leaped off like a deer, disappearing into the trees.

"Go on, little warrior," Lozen called, waving the boy's breechclout over her head. "Come back when you've got something for *us* to see." She allowed herself to fall backward into the water, and when she stuck her head up from under the surface, the four young girls were still doubled up with laughter.

"One day," Lozen said, "one day before too long, he'll be a great warrior. Believe me." She laughed. "That took a lot of courage, sneaking up on me." She laughed again. "Now he can tell his friends I don't have a man's thing, the way the little boys like to say." Lozen stood up. "Five years from now, maybe I'll marry him. I'll be too old to fight anymore, and he'll be young, strong, big, always ready to . . ." She made a lewd gesture, laughed brightly, and sank under the water.

The young girls tittered. Ishton smiled and let herself sink into the water.

"If he's still alive," Kozineh said sourly to herself.

"No, no! Not that way!"

The young packer cringed slightly, then turned red when he saw that it was General Crook himself who had found his dia-mond hitch wanting. Bareheaded, side whiskers glinting in the sun, Crook was advancing on him and the mule that stood phlegmatically under her two-hundred-pound load—two identical mess boxes teetering on her back. One of her long brown ears twitched desultorily at a circling fly.

Fifty-two mules in all stood in the hot sun of the morning in the parade ground of Fort Bowie, tended by ten packers under the command of packmaster Manuel Lopez, a veteran of General Crook's campaign against the western Apaches in the 1870s. Lopez, a burly Mexican who had grown up near Tucson on one of the first American ranches, stepped aside with a familiar smirk, letting the general pass.

"Let me show you, son," General Crook said. "Watch what I'm doing. You bring this running rope *under* the pack saddle this way, not around the side. Then you loop it *around* the standing rope, not under it. There. See?" He yanked the running rope in his hand. "Beautiful," he said. He put a big hand on the mess box now tied firmly to one side of the mule's back and shoved it. "There," he said. "Perfect." He stood back and admired his work.

"Yessir," the young packer said. Crook nodded at Lopez, the packmaster, and began to stroll off, hands locked behind his back.

"You get that?" the packmaster asked.

"Yessir," the packer said.

"Good. Then undo it all and start again."

"Yessir," the packer said, dismayed.

Now some ten yards away, Crook smiled. God is in the details, he thought to himself, and we need Him on our side. He left the parade ground and began up the slope to the row of one-story adobe buildings. On most of the buildings the stucco that had been plastered over the adobe bricks a decade earlier was cracking, much of it badly.

The place is falling apart, Crook thought, but there's nothing for it now. Maybe in a year when this is all over, men can be assigned to . . . but then, when this is all over, perhaps Fort Bowie won't be needed any longer, and its mud structures can be allowed to melt back into the earth.

General Crook walked slowly, erect, his hands clasped

calmly behind his back. Crook never looked hurried, never looked harried. He was an enthusiastic poker player, never betraying even the most appalling or the most spectacular news to his competitors. In the field, he always found time to attend calmly to the slightest detail, such as the young packer's imperfect diamond hitch back there, even when he was in fact impatient and in a great hurry.

Something was telling him that he had very little time left. It was a mental itch that came, perhaps, with a nearly imperceptible change in the weather, a slight edge to the chill of the predawn. A sense of foreboding, perhaps, or was it a sense of excitement? A different rhythm in his heart.

Whatever it was, he sensed it. And he trusted it. It had served him well during the campaign in the Arizona mountains back in the seventies, taming the Apaches there. It had served him less well against the Sioux in their vast prairie lands that had seemed so monotonous to Crook. But here again in Arizona, though God knew it was a different Arizona here near the border, something in the landscape seemed to speak to him, and today it said: hurry.

Any day now the renegades would materialize on this side of the border, looking for livestock and ammunition, and blood. They had been quiet too long. Even the Mexicans had reported no Apache depredations in the past two months. In all, Crook had four thousand troops—virtually all of them cavalry—in the area from the Santa Cruz River to east of the Rio Grande; and from Fort Apache, to the north, down to the border. They were stationed in forts and camps and temporary camps that formed a ring along the border and, more important, lay athwart the traditional routes that Apaches took into the United States from Mexico along some eight hundred miles of border. These routes were dictated, of course, by topography and chiefly the availability of north-running mountains and springs.

Of the four thousand troops at his disposal, 450 were Apache scouts, mostly recruited from the western Apaches, but some from the Chiricahuas themselves, and a few Mescaleros.

Back in Washington, General Sheridan, Commander of the U.S. Army, had insisted on sending yet another thousand troops into the area. Knowing better than to protest—what was Crook to do with a thousand relatively inexperienced troops when the only hope of running down the renegades was the careful deployment of the Apache scouts?—Crook sent orders to the commands in northern Arizona and northern New Mexico to send men south, with the newer troops Sheridan dispatched to fill in those tamer regions.

In any event, within a few weeks five thousand men would be in the region—one-fourth of the entire standing army of the United States. And lurking out in the Sierra Madres south of the border were at most a few hundred savages, the last free-roaming Indians. They had to be aware that their days were numbered. The pressure from the Mexicans was increasing now, the two states—Chihuahua and Sonora—coordinating their patrols for the first time in Mexican history. Surely the Apaches knew also of the buildup of American troops along the border. And Crook was positive also that, in their madness, they were prepared to go down with the maximum violence they were capable of inflicting.

The Apaches, he thought, should be singing their death chant out there in the crags and canyons of the Sierra Madres. Sworn and determined to eradicate these last wild savages, Crook nevertheless admired their mad resolve, and knew it would not lead them to any futile heroics in the field. Apache warriors were not given to heroics, preferring to have the odds on their side or to flee and reassemble and fight another day.

In one of the adobe buildings ringed around the hillside ahead of him, Captain Emmet Crawford was making a last-minute check of his equipment and the few belongings he would take with him. Crook had recalled him from the San Carlos reservation, needing his experience in the field. The reservation had been left in the hands of Lieutenant Gatewood, a remarkably able young officer who, additionally, had the trust and even friendship of the Apaches there.

Crook had determined to send Crawford to reinforce Fort

Huachuca near the San Pedro River with a hundred Apaches and the hundred recently arrived black cavalry from B Company. It had been some time, almost two years, since any Apache raiders had crossed the border in that vicinity, and Crook thought it was a likely place now. Once the Apaches crossed, the several hundred troops already deployed there were to harass them into turning back, and Crawford's fresh troops were to greet them at the border and destroy them, or pursue them back into Mexico and destroy them. But this morning Crook had changed his mind.

"Sir!" Captain Crawford said, standing up as Crook's silhouette filled the open door.

"At ease, at ease," Crook said, and slumped into the folding chair that stood against the low partition separating the beds of two officers. Crawford had had the place to himself the last two nights. "I have new orders for you, Captain."

Crawford's eyebrows rose on his wide forehead. "Sir?"

"Most of the Apaches down there," Crook said, gesturing with his head to the south, "at least most of their leaders, are Warm Springs people. Mangas, Nana, them. They must have an idea by now of what we're setting up here, so when they come I would guess they'd stick to familiar ground."

Crawford looked to the east. "New Mexico," he said.

Crook nodded his head.

"There's Naiche," the young captain said. "He's from here."

"Yes, Cochise's son. But even after his brother Taza died—you remember?—he went with that agent Clum to Washington, D.C., and got pneumonia. Even with Taza gone, Naiche never has become the big leader for the Chiricahuas. No one has. They're still operating in bands. And except for Naiche, all those leaders are on the reservation. Geronimo in particular. By the way, did he kill Chato?"

"Not that we could prove, sir. It might as easily have been one of the western Apaches, given all the rivalry there. There's just no way to tell. Geronimo insists that he has reformed, wants no more fighting. He's tired, and I think he likes the money he can get for selling his corn and melons."

"Yes, well, my guess, anyway, is that they'll be coming up in New Mexico, so I want you over there."

"Yes, sir."

"When you leave here this morning, you go on south and west, as if you were going to Fort Huachuca. But when you get south of the mountains, turn east. I want you to establish a camp near that little ranching place, Cloverdale, over on the other side of the Peloncillo Mountains."

"I know the place," Crawford said. "A lot of scum around there."

"Curly Bill Brocius." A thin smile appeared under Crook's beaked nose.

"He's dead now. They say that fellow Earp came back and unloaded a shotgun in him."

"Good," Crook said. "If any of those thieves get in your way, shoot them. But remember, *our* outlaws aren't the army's business. Congress in its wisdom has decreed that we of the military can't assist in keeping the civic peace."

Captain Crawford smirked. In the widely held opinion of the military stationed in the Southwest, the local constabularies in the territories were hardly distinguishable in kind from the thieves they were sworn to control. Several U.S. marshals were, in fact, nothing more than semiretired criminals, and the notion, evidently held in Washington, that so small a handful of officers, even if they were honest, could keep the peace in these still uncivilized realms was simply absurd on its face. But because of trouble between the military and the carpetbaggers in the South, Congress had been pressured in 1878 to pass a law forbidding the use of the military in controlling civil disorders. The result in the West, of course, had been a six-year epidemic of robberies and killings more expensive in lost lives and treasure than all the depredations by Apaches since the Treaty of Guadalupe Hidalgo in 1848.

"Congress. How noble in reason," Crawford said, quoting Shakespeare.

"How infinite in faculty," Crook replied, not to be outdone in literary matters. "Well!" He stood up. "I'll wire ahead to

Fort Bayard, let them know you'll be in the area. You'll be moving out—"

"Right away, sir," Crawford said.

"Very good. Farewell, then, Captain." General Crook reached out, awkwardly patted the young officer on the shoulder, and stepped out into the sun.

Below, on the parade ground, twenty-five blue-shirted black troopers were standing by their mounts in three parallel lines heading east. The men were tugging on straps, adjusting tack, murmuring among themselves, flashing the occasional smile in the shadows under their white summer helmets. With them, already mounted, was the young white lieutenant who had led them here from Fort Stanton.

Behind the Buffalo Soldiers, the pack-train mules stood stolidly in two long lines under their loads, watched over by their packers, and ahead forty-three Apaches sat on horses in a loose semicircle. Expressionless and silent, they each wore the red headband of the scouts and a personally selected combination of government-issue blue and Apache deerskin. Many were bare-legged except for calf-high moccasins and breech-clouts. Each was outfitted with a .50/70 Springfield Trapdoor rifle and a canvas belt of ammunition that most of them wore around their waists, though several preferred to carry them looped over a shoulder.

Several yards to the east of the contingent, a young bugler sat erect on his horse, blond curls visible under his helmet. Next to him two horses stood motionlessly, one bearing a broad-shouldered veteran sergeant with a face tanned deep bronze and a long graying moustache drooping down below his chin. The sergeant held the reins of the other horse, fully outfitted in shining leather and awaiting Captain Emmet Crawford.

God knew, Crook was used to sending men off on missions of high risk and great peril, and he did so with no compunction, it being his—and their—duty. But this young man Crawford, with whom he shared so much, even a fondness for Shake-speare . . . He wished there were someone else. But Crawford was his best, and his hunch was that this time the Apaches would come through the Peloncillos.

Damn their eyes.

Tom Jeffords was sprawled comfortably in a wooden chair at a table near the entrance of the Bird Cage Theatre in Tombstone. It was only ten o'clock in the morning and he was the only one in the place, except for the bartender, who had put a bottle and a glass on Jeffords's table, raked up some coins, and disappeared into a back room. Jeffords hadn't touched either the bottle or the glass, and he appeared to be asleep, his narrow-rimmed hat low over his brow, arms folded across his chest, legs outstretched before him, booted toes pointing at the ceiling.

Jeffords was known in Tombstone—known as peculiar, and to be peculiar in Tombstone took some doing. There were all kinds of peculiar people in Tombstone—fops, fools, flimflammers, fighters. There were those who put on fine clothes and airs, brandishing the money they'd made, and others who talked big and fast and smiled a lot and tried to get by on charm. There was a Presbyterian minister who wore a black suit all the time and, whenever he emerged from the church they built him, looked like a man picking his way through the eighth circle of hell.

Tom Jeffords was peculiar by being simple in his tastes—he had but one suit of clothes he wore when he came to Tombstone, which he did only every couple of months—and by being something of a recluse. He lived out about forty miles east on a ranch in the western foothills of the Chiricahua Mountains, not far from the place where all the hoodoos and rock pinnacles looked like an army of ghosts frozen in place during the long march of death. His spread was right in the heart of the old Apache country where he ran a few cattle and did some hunting. Aside from a few prospectors looking for silver, the Chiricahua Mountains were a place most people shied away from still, but not Jeffords.

He was peculiar mainly, of course, because he was known to

have been a great pal of Cochise before working out there as Indian agent after Cochise's death. And then, when they decided to move the Apaches over to San Carlos, and Jeffords quit and all hell broke loose, with the Apaches regularly on the warpath, Jeffords had set himself up on that ranch over there, and never, not once, had any of the savages descended out of the crags and hoodoos and run off with his cattle or bothered a hair on his head.

Naturally, whenever he came into Tombstone, people would ask him what the savages were up to these days, and Jeffords always said he didn't know, not being involved with them anymore since he quit being agent. But nobody believed him. His was the only ranch for a hundred miles in any direction that hadn't been hit at least once by the Apaches, so it was assumed he must still have some deal with them. So people kept asking him what they were up to, and he kept saying he didn't know.

Outside of these denials, he never seemed to say much of anything. When he came to town, he would buy up his supplies, get himself a dinner at the Bird Cage, stay on for a few drinks, take up with one of the whores, spend the night with her, and leave the next day, not to be seen again for a month or two.

Jeffords's wagon was hitched outside the Bird Cage, loaded and ready for the forty-mile trip home, while he sat sprawled at the table, maybe dozing. His eyelids popped open and he smiled a little smile when Big Minnie Bignon came through the door behind the bar. She paused with her hands on her round hips, surveying the back of the bar like a gigantic schoolmistress seeing that all the children's desks were neat, then picked up a glass and held it up to the light coming in the door. Satisfied, she came around the bar toward Jeffords's table and sat down. She wore a pink silk dress that clung eagerly to her mighty frame, and the familiar silken skullcap, this one with roses on it made out of cloth.

" 'Lo, Minnie," Jeffords said, and tipped his hat brim up. "You look as sweet as a bowl of cream this morning."

Minnie blushed and smiled girlishly. " 'Lo, Tom. And you

look like one of them hoodoos out there that toppled over. Why don't you sit up and have a drink? You already paid for it."

Jeffords straightened up in the wooden chair and glanced at the long dark interior of the Bird Cage. At the far end in the gloom, the stage was only a black shadow. From a vest pocket he took a neatly folded wad of bills and slid his hand across the table. Minnie took the wad and slid it down into her bosom, while Jeffords filled each glass with three fingers of golden brown whiskey.

"How's business?" Jeffords asked, and had a taste from his glass. He made a face.

"Bad," Minnie said. "Unless something happens, and I don't know what it could be, the good times are winding down here in Tombstone. It's not just all the water in the mines, and the pumps breaking and all that. The territory's gone to hell. Thieves runnin' around as free as chickens in the farmyard, and these marshals . . ." She made a spitting sound. "Couldn't catch these robbers if they found 'em in the outhouse with their pants down. Last week a bunch of 'em hit the stage and run off with—get this—with twenty-six cases of whiskey. And most of it was mine. I'm down to this rotgut, for which I do apologize. But it's still better than milk." She smiled her girlish smile at Jeffords, who glanced down at the place where his wad of bills now resided.

"And what do you hear from the boys in blue, so far, far from home?"

Big Minnie's hand rose to her big babyish face and she pulled at her slightly protruding upper lip. The question, and what it entailed, always made her nervous. Eight months ago she and Jeffords had made an arrangement, a business arrangement by which Jeffords would pay Minnie fifty dollars a month and she would direct her extracurricular services toward any officers or veteran noncoms who strayed into the Bird Cage on leave. From them she would extract as much information as she could about troop numbers and troop movements and anything else they might reveal—even matters of morale, and especially any braggadocio about new weapons—in short, anything unusual.

Jeffords let on that he was gathering what he called "intelligence" for the Mexican government, whose interests were not well served by the contemptuous way in which the United States Army kept them in the dark about their plans, particularly now that the U.S. was empowered to cross the border as needed. Jeffords had made it sound unimportant, just another foolish way for the Mexicans to throw around unnecessary money.

Big Minnie knew little and cared not a whit about international matters, and she did know that there was no love lost between Jeffords and the army since they messed him up when he was Indian agent for the Apaches. So she willingly acceded, not unmindful that she would be getting paid twice for what amounted to the same thing. Even so, as simple as it sounded, it made her just a slight bit nervous. There might, after all, be penalties for passing on such information, though she wasn't about to ask what they might be.

"They say a thousand more troops are being sent into the territory. From up north."

"When?"

"Now. There's some other things. I wrote them down." From her bosom she extracted a few sheets of folded paper, pink stationery on which she had written in a delicate hand, and passed them to Jeffords. "Companies going to one fort and another. I write it down because they all sound the same to me."

Jeffords sniffed the papers and then put them in his vest pocket. "Rose?" he asked.

"Gardenia," Big Minnie answered, and had a big pull at her glass. "Are we gonna invade Mexico or what? There's nothing else for the army to do now they can't chase these damn outlaws. All your Apache friends are digging wells and eating melons on the rez is what I hear."

Jeffords shrugged. "Doesn't make sense, does it?" he commented, smiling. When Jeffords smiled, the one vertical crease on each side of his mouth became three, and Minnie thought it was just a beautiful thing to see.

"Tom," she said, "how come you never got married?"

Jeffords sat back and looked at Minnie over the edge of his glass as he took his second swallow of whiskey that day. "I never thought much about it till it was too late."

"Too late?"

"When I found the right girl, she was already taken."

Big Minnie's eyebrows rose with maternal concern. "Who was that?"

"Why, Minnie, it was you, of course."

Minnie spluttered and laughed, a big throaty laugh. "Tom Jeffords, you are full of . . ." She paused. A lascivious grin took hold in the corner of her mouth and spread across her lower jaw. Her upper lip trembled. "Why don't we just run upstairs and . . ."

Jeffords put his hands behind his neck, which had the effect of pushing his hat down over his eyes. "Well, Minnie, maybe it's best we keep ourselves on a business footing, you know what I mean?"

"What d'you think *I* mean?" Minnie laughed.

"You already got all my money," Jeffords said, standing up. "Anyhow, I'm all wore-out. That little Mexican—"

"I don't want to hear about it." She stood up. "You take care of yourself now, you old horse."

"Interesting times ahead, Minnie."

"Sure," she said to his back as he ambled toward the door. "Times are always interesting. That's not the question."

Big Minnie finished off her drink, set the glass down on the table, and patted the wad of money under her dress. There's a man, she thought, who keeps things wrapped up tighter than a wet piece of hide.

Five

They struck in the first days of October.

They slashed northward, shattering the crystalline days of south Arizona autumn.

They struck with the screaming fury of a hornet swarm, as though seeking a final vengeance for every Apache warrior shot and scalped for a paltry Mexican bounty or mutilated just for the sake of it . . . for every Apache woman raped and murdered . . . for every Apache infant savagely slaughtered . . . for every Apache youth cut down or lost to slavery.

They snarled forth out of thin air—a cloudless storm, a terrible clap of thunder at first light, or midmorning, or late afternoon—to unleash an instant of violence become eternity, flesh ripping, wails, shrieks suddenly cut off in a gurgle, the guttural roar of victory in the gold-lit dust . . . and silence.

Silence but for the frantic buzz of flies, the crackling of flame.

And across the land, a miasma of acrid smoke and the spreading stench of blood.

Shortly after dawn on October 3, three cowboys were up and about in a camp at the southern end of the Empire Ranch, which lay near Greaterville, a small but thriving mining town in the foothills of the Santa Rita Mountains. The ranch hands' camp was a few yards out into the stirrup-high sacaton grass from the thick stands of cottonwoods and willows that lined what they called Sonoita Creek. A pale yellow light lit the tips of the grass to the east, and caught the steam rising from a blue-enameled metal coffeepot that sat on a smoldering fire.

The three cowboys were complaining about one thing and another, when two of them heard an ugly sound, a *thunk*, and before they could turn toward it, they heard a scream. Their colleague lay crumpled on his back across the fire, still screaming, one hand clawing at his neck, the blue pot having rolled away on its side, coffee spilling in a puddle. From the side of the man's neck an arrow about three feet long protruded, and blood as dark as red wine bubbled from his throat into its own puddle.

They could see that the arrow had come from the woods near the creek, so the two cowboys turned toward the sun and the high grass and began to run. After three or four desperate leaping steps into the tall grass, they pulled up, frozen. In front of them in a tight arc eight Apaches rose up, faces and chests streaked with red and black clay, black eyes glittering like the coal fires of hell.

Before the cowboys could fall on their knees and screech for mercy or help or just in terror, they were brought down by wooden clubs they never saw crashing against their skulls. Still breathing, they were dragged by the feet through the grass, past their camp, and into the trees.

There the Apaches were joined by others, and they used the cowboys' own riatas to tie the two men's hands together behind their backs, then truss their feet. They threw the other ends of the riatas over a low-hanging branch of an old, twisted cottonwood tree and hauled the cowboys up till they hung upside down about four feet apart and with their heads two feet above the ground.

While two of the Apaches went off to collect the cowboys' horses, which were still hobbled and unconcernedly enjoying the grass, another two built fires under the hanging men, the first flames licking up a few inches toward their hair.

Towing the cowboys' three horses by their lead ropes, the Apaches waded through the cold water and trotted through the grass to their own horses, which they had tethered in a hidden swale a few hundred yards west of the creek. Mounting up, they headed north. Not a word had been spoken since long before the first cowboy fell with an arrow through his carotid artery.

The Apaches were almost a mile away when the skulls of the two cowboys exploded.

An hour later the Apaches struck at the headquarters of the Empire Ranch, a collection of corrals, two low barns, and a ranch house. Amy Kittredge, who was forty-three years old and the mother of three boys, saw them coming when they were five hundred yards away—ten of them riding hell for leather through the grass down the slope of one of the rolling hills that surrounded the ranch buildings.

Amy set up a howl to alert the men in the barns and the corrals, and grabbed her husband Geoffrey's Winchester, which she knew how to use. She burst out the wooden door of the kitchen into the sunlight and onto the sharp point of an Apache lance that pierced her right side under the rib cage and plunged upward into her heart. All she felt was the searing heat of it, and she died with the unholy sound of an Apache scream in her ears.

Over near the corrals, Geoffrey Kittredge and two of his sons burst out of the bigger of the two barns, guns blazing at the approaching horsemen, who had now spread out, each about twenty feet from the next, and were coming at a slow lope. The three men never saw the Apaches who materialized behind them from around the barn, never saw the arrows that struck them in the back from point-blank range with a force like a mule and knocked them forward in the dust, never saw the moccasined feet of the Apaches who approached them and finished them off with sharp blows of their wooden war clubs.

The only one who saw any of this was another of Geoffrey Kittredge's sons, a twelve-year-old who had been told to stay back in the shadows of the barn. From his perch on some hay bales, he watched the explosion of violence, saw his brothers and father clubbed, and ran out the back of the barn. Two horses had been saddled and readied for work and he vaulted up onto the nearest one, snatched up the reins, and thrashed the horse into a full gallop toward the low rounded hill that rose up ahead.

Two hundred yards farther, the ground a blur beneath him, he saw the Apache horsemen, each about fifty yards to the side, but riding ahead of him, curving in toward his path. He sawed at the reins, wheeling to his left, then was plunging through the air, writhing. He landed on his back and the air exploded from his lungs. He couldn't breathe, couldn't breathe!

He guessed that the Apache who appeared over him, his arm upraised, was only a few years older than him, a kid too, then the arm came down and his eyes filled with vermilion fires.

An hour later, in midmorning, the Apaches were ten miles south and west of the Empire Ranch's headquarters, which now smoldered and smoked, an awkward tangle of blackened beams and planks and ashes. Eight White Eyes had been killed, twelve horses added to the Apache war party's mounts, and not an Apache rifle had been fired yet. No one would know until the sun had gone down behind the Santa Rita Mountains that the entire Kittredge family and their three ranch hands had been killed, and by then the Apaches would have struck again, twice.

Sonoita means "a good place to grow corn" in the language of the Pima Indians, whom the Apaches had long since dislodged from the relatively lush, grassy areas west of the Santa Cruz River and north of the border, where creeks and spring-fed wetlands provided moisture for crops. But the same conditions evidently made it a "good place" for disease—particularly malaria—and several generations of American soldiers had found themselves shivering with the ague in this hot place once they were stationed in a succession of forts and camps established and soon abandoned in the area. Fort Buchanan, for example, was established east of Tubac on the right bank of Sonoita Creek in 1857, a sorry collection of adobe and wood buildings without a stockade. It was abandoned and burned in a Confederate attack during the Civil War, briefly rebuilt and reoccupied later, and then abandoned again in favor of a nearby encampment, Camp Crittenden, which itself was abandoned as unhealthful in 1873. Similarly, Camp Mason was established along the Santa Cruz River in 1865 to replace the inadequate facility at Tubac some ten miles north, only to be abandoned a year later for reasons of disease—malaria and tuberculosis. And so this otherwise salubrious area was without any permanent military presence.

In striking the Empire Ranch near Greaterville, the Apaches had begun their rampage almost exactly between the two nearest military installations—Fort Lowell, part of the old pueblo of Tucson forty miles to the northwest, and Fort Huachuca, about the same distance to the southeast. In other words, so far as the United States Army knew, the band of marauding Apaches was somewhere in an area a bit greater in size than the eastern state of Rhode Island.

The commandant at Fort Huachuca heard of the attack on the Empire Ranch just as the sun set October 4 over the Huachuca Mountains. A ranch hand from a neighboring spread had seen the smoke rising from the smoldering Empire buildings, ridden over to discover its cause, and hastened to the railroad a few miles south. There he had flagged down a train running east on the new line between Nogales and Benson, and the news was telegraphed to Fort Huachuca from the station at Fairbank, which itself had been established only two years before as a supply point for Tombstone.

According to plan, the commandant at the fort dispatched two companies of Buffalo Soldiers northwest toward Greaterville and one company, accompanied by Apache scouts, to the southwest. This latter group had instructions to alert yet another similar group temporarily camped in the malarial vicinity of old Camp Crittenden. Thus, some six hundred troops were fanned out in an arc from the east to the south of where the Apaches had struck. A similar arc was forming at the same time to the north and northwest of the area, four companies of cavalry having been dispatched from Fort Lowell near Tucson.

The troops moved during most of the night, all of them making some thirty miles through the valleylands.

No one of the officers—from General Crook, brooding over the entire region in Fort Bowie, to the field officers on the move toward the "good place to grow corn"—were deluded into thinking that so sparse a blue line was enough to encircle the band of Apaches in their midst. But it was assumed that the Apaches would take note of the movement of so many cavalry troops—in all, more than a thousand men. They would, it was devoutly hoped, permit themselves to be pushed southward by all this military activity and continue their rampage in the heart of the malarial region, there to be confronted by the force of mostly Apache scouts patrolling between old Camp Crittenden and Nogales.

After destroying the Empire Ranch, the Apaches had swung southward into the foothills, descending on two small mines where they left three miners dead and another with a leg that would subsequently need amputation but served to get him to the railroad tracks by virtue of a night spent stumbling and, finally, crawling painfully. There he flagged down a train, and the telegraph operator at Fairbank again telegraphed the commandant at Fort Huachuca. The Apaches, it appeared, were rampaging within the arc of troops, which could now tighten like a noose and force them south, back toward old Mexico.

It was an excellent plan, but for the fact that the next morning the Apaches did not take note of the encircling troop movements from a hideout in the southern Santa Rita Mountains. They had already left the area, having themselves ridden through the night to a rarely used stronghold in the Whetstone Mountains well to the northeast. And at midday of October 5 they swept out of the hills down onto the old ranches at Boquillas, leaving three people dead, several wounded, and running off with yet another dozen horses. Here the Apache band split in two, a smaller group of five running the horse herd, now swelled to more than two dozen, back into the Whetstone Mountains, while sixteen warriors headed directly south, covering the four miles to Fairbank before anyone at the lonely rail depot saw the smoke from the torched ranches of Boquillas rising into the shimmering blue sky to their north.

Aside from a few wooden shacks and a stable that was little more than a shack, the only building in Fairbank was a one-story rectangle built from rough wooden planks, covered with a roof of primitive shakes that was adorned, on its peak, with a sign supplied by the Santa Fe Railroad saying FAIRBANK, ARIZONA TERRITORY in black letters on a white background. Between the building and the railroad tracks was what was intended as a freight platform, made from the same rough wooden planks as the building—in fact, the leftovers. The platform extended from one end of the building only about halfway down its length, at best an afterthought now turning silver in the great kiln of the Arizona sun.

Outside this Fairbank "station," a ten-thousand-gallon water tank—round and constructed also of planks, with a conical shake roof—rose up on thick-timbered legs some twenty feet into the air. Telegraph poles, linked by a sagging wire, trailed the railroad tracks north and south, and a much traveled dirt track stretched away to the east across gently rolling grassy hills toward Tombstone. Beyond the hills, as well as to the west, were the jagged blue teeth of distant mountains.

It was a lonely and forbidding landscape and in the heartland of Chiricahua Apache country, but it had been a decade since the savages had perpetrated any depredations in this area. Perhaps they were put off by the presence of so many bustling, and well-armed, folk in nearby Tombstone. In any event, Charlie "Jawbone" Phelps, stationmaster and general factotum at Fairbank, was not concerned about Apaches on the morning of October fifth. The man who operated the telegraph key at the other end of the building, Oliver Fredd, newly arrived from the tame environs of Santa Fe, had shared the news of the Apache raid the day before over near Greaterville—and also the news that the savages were headed south and, in addition, were about to be hemmed in by U.S. troops and run back into Mexico or wiped out at the border.

So Jawbone Phelps, who had taken the job as stationmaster a year before mostly because he had only one leg nowadays— the other cut off by the sawbones in Tombstone when it failed to heal after being shot by that sonofabitchin' Clanton boy— had only to finish sweeping the floor of his end of the building, limping along after the broom on his crutch made from willow, and think about whatever came to mind in the silence and peace of the day. Outside the doors that opened up onto the half-done platform and the railroad tracks, in the yellowing land beyond, the heat was already making the ground shimmer as if it were alive.

Out of this shimmering ribbon on the horizon, Jawbone Phelps noticed a lone horseman approaching, maybe a mile off, maybe a little more, and within moments it resolved itself unmistakably into an Apache. Jawbone hobbled toward the open doors and peered out, seeing now a wider swath of horizon but still only one Apache.

"Apache," he said in a voice loud enough for the telegraph operator to hear, and hobbled toward his desk, behind which he kept an early model Springfield carbine loaded and ready at all times.

"Ah, Mr. Lo," Fredd said, and clucked several times like a brooding hen. In earlier years soldiers and settlers in the West had taken to referring to the Indian as Mr. Lo, because so many stories about Indians written in the softhearted eastern press began with the phrase, "Lo, the poor Indian . . ." But no one called Indians Mr. Lo anymore, and that was one of the many quirks and habits of this man that irritated the hell out of Jawbone Phelps.

"It ain't no Mr. Lo, you goddamn fool," Jawbone said. "It's an Apache savage and he's off the rez and that means he probably means to cut off your balls and feed 'em to his wives."

Old Fredd chuckled and pulled from under his table a long-barreled and little-used Colt .45. He spun the cylinder and put the pistol on his table with a loud clunk. Oliver Fredd was a gaunt man, a bit stooped, and lying before him, the Colt looked huge, even unwieldy. Jawbone Phelps snorted at the sight and hobbled out into the sun where the approaching Indian was now a thousand yards off, still coming at a gentle lope. Standing on the edge of the wooden platform, he leaned comfortably by the right armpit on his crutch and snugged the butt of the carbine against his right shoulder. Thus propped against both gravity and attack, he stared from a squinted eye down the barrel of his rifle at the approaching horseman.

"You don't ever, ever want to let these savages see you ain't ready for 'em," Jawbone said to Fredd, who had joined him on the platform when a blur descended before them, two blurs falling, lunging, a glint of sun from knife blades, black eyes flashing in whites, and a great agony exploding in their hearts, Jawbone Phelps thinking, In plain daylight, how . . . ?

His horse rocking smoothly beneath him as he approached the wooden building, Mangas saw the two warriors drop from the roof and slash the two White Eyes, saw them fall, saw a dozen other warriors on the roof raising their arms, weapons held high, then leaping off. Only then did the warriors' shouts reach his ears. By the time Mangas pulled up near the station, it was burning at both corners, flames licking avidly at the dry planks and timbers. Smoke, thin and yellow, rose into the sky. From the dark interior of the building a warrior emerged carrying a wooden box—ammunition—followed by another with another box. From the the west, their horses came, driven by two young warriors—boys on their first raid—and soon a great jumble of horses and men raised the dust before the burning building and the two bodies sprawled on the bloody planks.

Mangas noted that the wooden crutch of the one-legged man had flown several feet away when the Apache knife had plunged into his chest. Flames had crept from the door frame of the station to the crutch and it now burned gaily at one end. Mangas permitted himself the thought that soon enough all the White Eyes would find their legs gone, their crutches in ashes.

Off to one side another fire had begun to consume the timbers that supported the water tank. Mangas, heading north back the way they had come that morning, signaled the warriors to follow him. Some five hundred yards farther he pulled up and wheeled his horse around to watch the water tower slowly sag on its burning supports and then fall over, hurling a great wave of water on the dry ground. Mangas was leaner than most Apaches and wore a perpetually sad look, as if his eyes had seen too much of the world, but now a smile crept over his face. It had been a long time, more than a year, since he'd led a war party, since he'd smelled blood and seen the violent swirl of horses and men, the surge of flame and smoke, the ragged corpses of White Eyes and the ruin of their world.

North then, Mangas thought. We go north and then west—then east perhaps. We shall appear and disappear, strike and vanish, as wayward as lightning. Just as we used to. Just as we always have.

Still smiling, Mangas, the son of Mangas Colorado, the greatest of all the old Apache leaders, turned his horse north, back where fires still burned and smoke still rose from the ranches of Boquillas. His father, he thought, had been shot once in a battle with the White Eyes and saved by a doctor in Mexico. So far, no bullet had ever torn the flesh of Mangas, the son. He felt invincible this day, this promising morning of death. No bullet *could* touch Mangas, not on this war party, not on this exhilarating excursion. Had he not, for several seconds, perhaps longer, been right in the sights of the one-legged American? He felt his blood pounding again as it did only at such times.

But this was more than just a war party, Mangas knew. It was also a beginning, the first part of Juh's grander plan. And with Juh's plan begun at last, only two outcomes were possible: the freedom of the Apache people, or their oblivion. Perhaps it was knowing this that made Mangas's heart pound so thrillingly in his chest.

Six

For two more days Mangas and his warriors rampaged through the landscape, striking here, there, anywhere, like a lightning storm gone mad. They took twelve more lives, put five more lonely settlements to the torch, ran off several hundred head of cattle and almost a hundred horses. On two occasions detachments of troopers dashing madly about, chasing tracks, chasing reports, even chasing rumors, came within a few miles of Mangas's war party, but not a single U.S. soldier laid eyes on them. The company in charge of the realm between Camp Crittenden and Nogales, consisting mostly of Apache scouts, moved back and forth along the border with each report of a new Apache attack. On one occasion they reached as far as the ranch lands well to the east of Bisbee, ever hopeful of standing between Mexico and the returning marauders. No one among the scouts saw any of their rampaging fellow Apaches—or, at least, so they reported.

So rapidly and so erratically did the Apaches strike that one of General Crook's officers suggested there was not one but two war parties at work. Indeed, the army never found out for certain until long afterward that it had been only one, led by Mangas. All that the army knew after the four days of terror was that the final raid took place—contemptuously—at a large, Mexican-owned ranch only five miles from Fort Huachuca itself, and that the next day, according to terrified Papago tribesmen, a band of Apaches and a torrent of livestock had driven south into Mexico like a flooding river about thirty miles west of Nogales in the lee of the Baboqivari Mountains.

66

Even old Indian hands at Fort Bowie thought such a feat—driving that many livestock for sixty miles in less than twenty-four hours—was impossible. Within days newspapers in Tucson and Tombstone were screaming with outrage. With five thousand troops in the region—which was one-fourth of the entire standing U.S. Army—how, they howled, was it possible that two Apache war parties could wreak such wanton havoc at will and disappear without ever being seen by anyone who was still alive?

The editorialists demanded the replacement of General Crook. They suggested that Washington, D.C., was inhabited by prancing popinjays who preferred plush seats at the theater to seeing to the safety of the pioneers on the frontier and their helpless wives and children. They complained bitterly about the quality of the troops, pointing to the high desertion rate—something near twenty percent. With less than coherent logic, they demanded yet more troops be sent to the region and, yes, a large-scale invasion of Mexico, if that was what it would take to rid the planet of these last vicious, blood-lusting vermin.

They went still further—all three independent newspapers concluding similarly. It was high time, they trumpeted, that the army rounded up the rest of the untrustworthy, unredeemable savages known as Chiricahuas now festering and *breeding* on the reservation in San Carlos and put them in irons along with all of Crook's lying and chiseling so-called Apache scouts, and shipped the entire unworthy horde out of the territory. To the bottom of the ocean, one editorial fumed.

Several prominent citizens of Tucson, mostly merchants, but several with considerable landholdings outside the old walled town, got together and wrote much the same by way of suggestion in a stentorian letter to Philip H. Sheridan, renowned Indian fighter in the Western Territories, hero of the War Between the States, and now General in Chief of the Army of the United States. Taking advantage of the recent reduction in U.S. postal rates, they affixed a newly issued two-and-a-half-cent stamp to the envelope and consigned it to the Tucson post-master. From there the letter proceeded overland, and by the time it reached General Sheridan in Washington a week and a half later, the Apaches had struck again.

George Crook was not at all pleased to find that his sixth sense had been dulled somehow, that the first Apache war party in half a year had not, as he'd predicted, been launched into New Mexico. He wondered if all his senses might have been dulled—not so much by advancing years, and so many of them spent in the howling wilderness, but by the incessant, distracting insect buzz in his mind brought on by politics, most especially War Department politics. Crook was not about to admit that he might simply be getting tired—but of course he was.

The United States had already spent an estimated forty million dollars attempting to rid this godforsaken land of the Apache threat, and had already lost almost five hundred soldiers in the attempt—never mind the far greater number of settlers and miners from west Texas to Tucson. Several times now the thought had crossed his mind that perhaps the game wasn't worth the candle. There were other places in the vast territories of the West to dig precious metals from the ground, other places to run great herds of cattle, plenty of room for greedy and impetuous men to fulfill their destinies and make their fortunes. But he had kept such thoughts to himself, and he did so now, even as he bridled under the scurrilous and dyspeptic attacks of the local press. His duty was clear: eliminate the renegade Apaches still on the loose.

In the days after the shocking four-day raid, he rallied his officers and men to that task, insisting that the current strategy was a good one, a practical one, and would work the next time. And so, north of the Mexican border, posted in remote forts and camps from El Paso to Nogales, the thin blue line waited, measuring its days by the sounds of bugles and short, visible "scouts" around the countryside, while in the secret places in the mountain chains that ran like jagged compass needles across the land, Apache warriors in small groups watched carefully and carried messages in the night. In the higher reaches of these islands in the sky, where the nights turned chill, the trembling leaves of the aspen trees began to turn a bright yellow-gold in the year's early elegy for itself.

Chester A. Arthur was, as usual, suffering. His back ached chronically from the kidney condition the doctors had diagnosed and could do nothing about. Urinating was a painful trial, one he simply had to endure, just as he had to endure the last weeks of his nearly accidental presidency.

The President of the United States stood up now from behind his desk, vainly seeking momentary release from the pain in his back, and noticed that the hugely tall visitor in his office—the Arizonan—did not rise. Arthur reddened, but elected to say nothing of the breach of decorum. The man was a barbarian.

Arthur himself had emerged from the factional and patronage-ridden broth of New York politics as James Garfield's vice-president, a political hack put on the ticket only to assuage one wing of his disputatious party. No one at the time thought of him as presidential timber, but no one thought Garfield would be assassinated either.

In any event, as president, Arthur had surprised a few people by signing a law that sought to control the evils of patronage, but otherwise had surprised few by the lackluster three years of his administration. And now he was a lame duck. The conventions had been held, the nominees selected. Instead of Arthur, the Republicans had chosen James Blaine, the Democrats had chosen that other and better known New York politician, Grover Cleveland, and Cleveland had narrowly won. So Chester Arthur, at best a caretaker president, had now to sit in his office with both his pain and his embarrassment, feeling more powerless than ever, waiting for the interminable days to pass until March, when he could go home.

His visitor, the territorial governor of Arizona, was both crude and wealthy, like many of the people a U.S. president meets in the course of his duties, but this man was also presumptuous and not a little intimidating. It was not his sheer size—he was at least six-four—but his air of complete confidence. He spoke in a deep, drawling voice from behind a voluminous white moustache with all of the moral authority of an Old Testament prophet, if not Jehovah Himself. This despite the fact that, as Arthur and everyone else knew, the man was as venal a wheeler-dealer as could be found, having amassed enormous tracts of Arizona mining claims by means that would hardly bear scrutiny in the more civilized regions of the East. And since his appointment by President Garfield as governor, the man had exerted his office chiefly to consolidate, protect, and even increase his holdings and those of a few other rawboned cronies.

"No, sir," the Arizonan said, "there's still plenty of silver to be got from Tombstone. It ain't finished yet. But there's plenty of metal all over the territory just lying there in the ground, doing nothing. And honest, hardworking men can't get to it because the U.S. Army can't control the damned Apache savages. Just the other day—"

President Arthur sat down and sighed. "Yes, Governor, I heard about the raid. Outrageous. Regrettable. General Sheridan assures me that proper offensive action against the renegades is planned. And other troops—in all, a thousand—have been dispatched to the area. What more can be asked?"

The unremittingly tawdry and confusing affairs of the West both escaped President Arthur's full comprehension and bored him. Worse yet, the pompous little ambassador from Mexico took every opportunity to fuss and natter about violations of the sanctity of the border, as if the last of the Apaches weren't Mexico's problem . . .

"Mr. President, they need to be cleaned out. All of 'em. An honest man can't do an honest day's work for fear of Apache raids. Women and children live in terror. Women, the very backbone of a civilized society. It's not just the renegades, it's all of 'em there in our midst on the reservation. General Crook seems to think—"

Chester Arthur, the lame-duck president and never a man

given to taking a heroic stand, decided that he had no intention of being intimidated by this crude appointee.

"Governor, you aren't going to iterate all that slanderous gossip about General Crook being an Indian lover."

"No, no, sir. Just—"

"And surely, Governor, you are aware that the silver output from Tombstone was so great only two years ago that it helped plunge the country into a depression. A short one, thank God. And surely, Governor, you are aware also that the man who will succeed me in this office believes that an overabundance of precious metals, in particular silver, threatens the integrity of the gold standard. I don't agree, but he will be president. These are *national* concerns, Governor. I need hardly remind you of that. Now, of course, this administration has been and will continue to be committed to bringing peace to your region. And until General Sheridan tells me otherwise, I will assume that it is in good hands. Now, Governor, if you will excuse me . . ."

After the tall man closed the door, President Arthur stood up, stretched his back and sighed. It was a shame it had been a private meeting, he thought, for it might well have been one of his finest moments as president. Lord, how affairs of the territories annoyed him. So much carrying on, and for what, finally?

He sat again at his desk and penned a hurried note to the General in Chief of the U.S. Army:

> Sheridan:
> For God's sake, rid us of the Apaches. Use whatever force is needed. They are a swarm of gnats in the Nation's ears, and must be swatted away finally so that the Nation may think!
>
> C. A. Arthur
> 13 October 1884

They assembled with only the stars and the thinnest sliver of the moon to light their way. In this palest of light and in the knife-thin air in the lee of the highest peak of the Chiricahua

Mountains, they came in silence and shadow and found their places and sat, surrounded by spruces standing like silent sentinels in the night.

Not since Cochise and Mangas Colorado had brought their bravest and wisest together in council more than twenty years past had there been so potent a gathering of Apache leaders. Except for Geronimo, who remained in San Carlos, every successful Apache war leader, every warrior who had been accorded the mantle of leadership of his band, would sit tonight in this unprecedented council, taking a place in the circle on the ground that began—and ended—with the large, shadowed figure of Juh.

Juh had been among all these men before. He had trekked thousands of miles during the last half year visiting each of these men in their camps and strongholds, talking, explaining, persuading. These were the men who, independent of one another for the most part, had created more havoc among the invading whites than any other group of Indian leaders in the West during the past decade. They were also the only warriors anywhere on the continent who had not by now given way to the overwhelming numbers of white men, ceding freedom, honor, and pride in return for a continued existence—an existence as pariahs in someone else's world. And now these last proud men had assembled in grand council, in the manner of a great general and his officers.

In the mountain chill, none wore more than a breechclout, headband, and moccasins, along with personal amulets hung around the neck. No rank could be discerned from such simple trappings. But on arriving in the clearing, each had silently performed his own subtle calculus, based upon his own feats, an assessment of his own power, and on the known feats and power of the others. Then each had taken a place in the circle, each place a statement of rank. That so delicate a matter had taken place so smoothly was, Juh noted, a good sign.

Naiche, as leader of the local band in residence here in the Chiricahua Mountains, was host of the council meeting. Early on he took up a position six feet to Juh's left, leaving space for two more men. Out of the gloom, Nana appeared—shrewd old Nana, now in his eighties but still as fierce as any Apache and still able to make a day's trek on horseback. He sat down creakily in one of the two spaces, leaving room directly to Juh's left. Nana had led a large band of Warm Springs Chiricahuas on the warpath during the past two years while the great Victorio was absent.

Nana's old eyes twinkled in the moonlight as he looked over at Naiche. "This space is for Geronimo," the old man said. "He's not coming, but this way he'll hear we honored him . . . and we don't have to listen to him. He talks on and on like an old man."

Naiche smiled, and listened to the murmur of laughter from the other men in the circle. To Naiche's left sat Loco, a stocky, bowlegged Warm Springs leader who had long tried to live on peaceful terms with the White Eyes, agreeing to live on a reservation near Silver City after the death of Mangas Colorado. This willingness to try reservation life had earned him his Spanish name, which meant crazy. Finally seeing the light, betrayed by the very men with whom he had tried to cooperate when they insisted Loco and his people leave his ancestral land near Warm Springs and go instead to San Carlos, he broke out at the same time as Nana, rampaging through the mining communities in the mountains of southern New Mexico.

On one occasion Loco had been wounded in an incident that served to make his name all the more appropriate in the eyes of his fellows. After boldly running off with a small string of cavalry horses, he and his band of ten warriors were pursued into the parklike ponderosa woodlands high in the mountains north of Silver City. Among the stately trees, and believing he was beyond the range of the cavalrymen's rifles, Loco had bared his back end and waggled it at his pursuers in a common Apache gesture of contempt. But a lucky shot lodged a bullet in his left buttock, where it remained until Loco and his band managed to disappear that night into the wilderness.

Not without some humor at Loco's expense, his warriors gouged the bullet out with a bowie knife, leaving sufficient scar tissue that Loco would never again be comfortable on a horse. None of this had lessened Loco's newly minted determination to do away with the White Eyes, however; nor had it diminished him in the eyes of his comrades.

On the far side of the circle from where Naiche and Loco sat was a motionless figure, head bowed, eyes on the ground, lost in thought. It was Lozen the Warrior Woman, who had assumed her place among these men without a word. She had taken the least position, directly across from Juh—but they all knew Juh listened to her and put his trust in her words as much as those of anyone present.

To Juh's right was another space, and beyond that Mangas sat in the shadows, lanky and sad-eyed, prepared to tell the council the splendid details of his recent raid as a prelude to the final presentation and formal ratification of Juh's grand conception. Now they all waited in silence for the last man to arrive and take the place to Juh's right. They waited for the man whom few of them but Juh and Lozen had seen for two years, the man who had mastered the tactic of feint and attack, who, with only a hundred warriors or so, had exacted a terrible price from the White Eyes in west Texas and New Mexico as he led the hated Buffalo Soldiers on a bloody chase of two thousand miles in a few bloody months. They awaited the man whom all the White Eyes were convinced had been exhausted by the chase, disoriented, and died at the hands of the Mexicans in a final siege four years ago: Victorio.

The Mexicans were great liars, and none greater than Colonel Joaquin Terrazas, who said he killed Victorio in the Tres Castillos Mountains in the autumn of 1880. The idea that Victorio himself could be trapped by the Mexicans was laughable, and the more so since his sister Lozen was with him.

To be sure, the Buffalo Soldiers in Texas had finally taken control of the last water holes, and in that way forced Victorio and his warriors to disappear into Mexico. And to be sure, Terrazas did meet up with Victorio's group in the Tres Castillos soon afterward, and inflicted many casualties. But that silly rooster of a man then reported that he and his troops moved up into the mountains in the dark, surrounded Victorio's camp, and listened to the Apaches sing the death chant through the night. Then in the morning—on October 14, he reported later—the Mexicans attacked and killed sixty warriors and eighteen women and children, capturing the rest. Among the dead was Victorio. Terrazas embellished his story yet further, saying that his men heard Lozen screaming that she would eat her brother's body before she let the Mexicans get to it.

In reality, after the skirmish, Victorio—and Lozen, along with thirty-four warriors and women and children—made their way into the Sierra Madres and met up with Juh, whose camp no White Eyes ever laid eyes on. It was there, over the next months, that they looked carefully back on Victorio's experience and the experience of other battles, turning them like a crystal in the light to see each facet, to extract whatever wisdom shined forth. In these long nights, Juh's scheme began to take shape in his mind, and not long afterward the story went forth that Juh himself had died, the result of falling drunkenly from his horse while returning among the high crags to his camp.

Among the Mexicans and Americans this news was received with relish—for now both of the Apaches' most feared leaders were dead. Of course, Apaches who heard the story suspected it was false: everyone knew that Juh never drank either the white man's whiskey or tiswin, the Apaches' milder brew made from corn. Juh celebrated his victories—and passed the days between—without strong drink of any kind. Too many Apaches had lost their lives when, minds addled, they had allowed the White Eyes to surprise them in their camps. In Juh's presence no one, not even Geronimo, was tempted by that particular demon.

Now, striding from the tall trees into the clearing, came the silhouetted figure of Victorio. For a moment he stood still outside the circle, letting his tribesmen take notice. He was broadshouldered, thick of chest. In addition to the amulet around his neck, across his chest he wore a canvas cartridge belt he had taken from the corpse of a high-ranking officer he killed with his knife in hand-to-hand combat in the dry country of Texas— a colonel. Victorio rarely went abroad without the cartridge belt.

The whites of his eyes glistened, the irregularity of his right eye noticeable even in the pale light. This and his thick eyebrows and unusually wide cheekbones gave him a look of implacable and unchanging ferocity, as if the anger of an entire race had become solidified in rock. Wordlessly, he walked around the circle and, with the grace of a cat, sat down to the right of Juh.

Looking at the ground before him, Juh nodded, formally acknowledging Victorio's arrival, and at the same time smiled to himself. Victorio, Juh knew—fierce, brilliant, sometimes impetuous, still young at thirty-odd years, filled with contempt for his enemies and lithe with animal energy and a hunger for blood—Victorio needed special recognition. Juh saw no reason to begrudge him such moments. How long it had been that this fierce and impatient man, the very embodiment of the Apache way, had bided his time.

The council began. The warrior leaders made cigarettes from leaves and wild tobacco and smoked as they listened with grunts of approval to Mangas's detailed account. His had been not only a raid, and a highly successful one, but a probe, a test designed to reveal General Crook's current thinking. When Mangas was finished, each leader in turn explained the role he and Juh had devised, and as each element within the grand strategy was revealed to the others it became clear to all that nothing like this had ever been conceived before. Nothing so bold, nothing so exhilarating, so beautiful, had ever come into their minds. With the warriors in awe, and with Geronimo absent, Juh explained the final piece of the plan—Geronimo's part—and the discussion moved then to timing.

There were those—most of the men present—who wished to implement the strategy as soon as possible, to strike before the aspen leaves had fallen and the army could strengthen itself further. Reporting Red Beard's findings, however, Juh had explained that another thousand troops were already on their way into the territory.

He listened carefully to all the men and again spoke, reiterating first the events of the past, the triumphs, the losses, the lessons that could be learned. He spoke sympathetically of how many Apaches had seen their freedom to roam and hunt turned into a lesser freedom—that of running in front of the white troops. Many had seen the game—antelope, deer—grow few from the incessant appetite of the White Eyes. Even the forests had grown smaller to fuel the White Eyes' works. Many had seen their Apache women grow fearful and exhausted, and lose children in birth. Many had seen their children growing up in terror. So many had agreed to take up the lesser life of the reservation. There were, many had concluded, simply too many White Eyes, and too many more coming—an endless river, an infestation.

Many of them now knew from personal experience that this lesser life, however, penned up by the White Eyes, being counted each day, grubbing in the ground, and lining up for rations that often were not provided—all this was worse than death, worse certainly than an Apache death, which was to die while inflicting death on the enemy.

But, Juh explained, his plan relied in part on the arrival of yet more army troops, not fewer. The more the better.

It took several hours to make this strange idea clear to men who knew the odds, who had spent their lives gambling that a handful of Apaches was superior to ten times the number of White Eyes, and all of whom at one time or another had been overrun, had been worn down, had barely escaped.

With this astonishing notion understood, however, it was soon clear that Juh's strategy would be best implemented after the first snows came to the mountain slopes and canyons. Lozen, the Warrior Woman, pointed out with sarcasm that even the seasoned army troops, those who had fought for years in this region, had not learned how to dress properly. They were always too hot in summer, too cold in the harsh winters. And at that time when the year was turning to winter, when the sun was moving away, it still burned hot in the valleys by day while life froze on the higher ground. A bad time for seasoned troops, it would be yet worse for the newer ones.

So it was agreed. Not long before the first light of dawn, all those in the circle drove their knives into the ground before them, stood, and retired from the clearing. In the morning the others would come to the clearing and see that there had been agreement among the warriors at this great council—thirteen knives driven to the hilt in the hard soil.

Ishton smiled and held Juh to her warm body, welcoming him into her and responding with an enveloping, dreamy in-dolence, joining him in his rising tide and following him as he ebbed into lassitude. Outside the entrance to their lodge the eastern sky began to lighten, and Juh's entire being let loose. It was only here—between Ishton's thighs, wetnesses mingling, his face buried in her flowing hair and the warm musk of her neck—that Juh had ever been able to relax completely, to es-cape the urgencies of the world. Her fingers lay soft as butterfly wings on the small of his back, and he sighed in contentment.

Presently she felt the ropy muscles along his spine begin to harden again, and only then did she utter a questioning sound from deep in her throat.

"Yes," he said. "It is done. It is all agreed now. When the first snows come to the foothills, we begin."

Her fingers kneaded his back muscles while he lapsed into silence again, his breathing deeper, regular as in sleep.

"It will not ever be the same," he said, whispering into her neck. "Whatever happens, we will not recognize the world."

Ishton waited.

"Who knows what it will be like—to die and join Ussen? That awaits us if we fail. All of us. You, and Little Spring. All of us."

The baby slept noiselessly beside them in his cradleboard. Ishton smiled.

"And if we succeed?" she asked.

"It will never be what it was. We will live on an island in a river. Our island. But surrounded with water. The water shapes the island."

Juh breathed on in silence.

At length he spoke again.

"Victorio. He is sure we will succeed. I wish I were so certain. And once we have succeeded, he thinks that the world will again be like it once was for us. No White Eyes will be found in our ancestral land. We will go back to the old ways, all of them. Hunting in the mountains and the valleys, gathering food as we always have. Left alone to be Apaches."

"When were we like that?" Ishton said with gentle mockery. "Left alone?"

"In the dreams of old men, old women," Juh said, laughing quietly so as not to wake the baby. "And maybe when we go to be with Ussen."

∽ ∾

Seven

From Black Point, the highest and one of the most southern of the Peloncillo Mountains, the Animas Valley was visible in its entirety, stretching northward, a vast sea of stirrup-high grass now a dull yellow with the onset of the cold nights and shorter days. East of the valley, the Animas Mountains rose up, sharply delineated in the thin air but a softer, more rounded presence than the violent blue silhouette of the Hatchet chain that lay farther east and visible on the horizon. To the west beyond another huge grassy plain lay the grand fortress of the Chiricahua Mountains, rising with massive defiance into the air.

From his perch on Black Point, Loco could see all of this and, by turning south, a good deal of old Mexico, as well. From hour to hour nothing in the vast landscape could be seen to move, except the occasional herd of pronghorns in the far distance, or the occasional handful of cattle strayed from the main herds of Cloverdale, a collection of ranch buildings almost directly below Black Point. Silent, still, and mostly a tawny gold, the lands below were nonetheless a vital crossroads, a remote thoroughfare of mostly illegal activity. It could be said that no one had any legitimate business in this isolated chunk of the territories.

Through this part of the Peloncillos, small wagon trains occasionally brought smuggled silver from Mexico into the United States, headed for Tombstone to the west, where the coins or bars would magically be alloyed to the legitimately dug tonnages of that town to increase the fortunes of all involved. It was in one of the canyons nearby that the Clanton brothers, local "ranchers," had intercepted such a shipment, shot down all the Mexican drivers from the rim of the canyon, and somehow lost the silver. This was before several of the Clantons lost their lives at the hands of the Earps outside Tombstone's OK Corral.

It was here where Cloverdale ranchers turned outlaw by night, where outlaw preyed on outlaw, and where Apache bands had long plucked their own booty as the notion struck them. Here in the vast and lonely stillness where almost no one chose to live, and few even chose to pass through, the ground was nevertheless much bloodied and grievously defiled by several generations of mayhem. This was perhaps the most lawless place in the United States. Even northeast in New Mexico's Lincoln County, where young Billy the Kid had made an international, if overblown, reputation for himself as the West's preeminent killer, the Buffalo Soldiers at Fort Stanton maintained a certain order, and the law had, after all, prevailed in the name of Sheriff Pat Garrett, who had blown Billy the Kid into the hands of God three years earlier. Down here, in the New Mexico boot heel, a patch of the territory that jutted down into old Mexico, there were no laws and no lawmen—only a few men.

It was here also that an increasingly impatient Loco waited, eyeing the landscape and telling the thirty-odd young and even more impatient warriors under his leadership that they simply had to wait for Juh's signal before satisfying their desires to prove themselves again by bringing death to the hated invaders.

Loco had agreed with the others at the grand council and, by plunging his knife in the ground, had formally, ceremonially, attested that he would adhere to Juh's plan, Juh's timing. But Loco was not completely satisfied. For one thing, he had led Apaches on many raids since Victorio had disappeared into Mexico. He had lost several of his fellows to enemy fire and been wounded himself. But Victorio, who had not raised an

arm in vengeance and anger for three years, was unquestion-
ingly assumed to be the leader in the east during the coming—
and final—initiative against the White Eyes. Loco had been
given a secondary role—that of decoy. He understood the
strategy, even approved it, but bridled inwardly at playing the
role merely of a jackrabbit.

Loco had quietly been planning to augment his role in Juh's
strategy. He would play the jackrabbit, yes, but it would be a
lethal jackrabbit. It was, he satisfied himself, not so much a
matter of personal pride, but a necessary addition of responsibility, without which his young and hungry warriors might
well bolt, might ride out on their own with blood in their
eyes. Juh was wise, yes, but his wisdom did not extend—could
not extend—into every detail, into the hearts of every Apache band.

And, also to the point, Loco's warriors had brought along
with them from the south a supply of tiswin, as well as a few
bottles of the White Eyes' stronger drink, and during the idle
nights of their vigil they took to using these spirits to invigorate
their own spirits, to stoke their own vengeful fires. Indeed,
now—two weeks after the grand council—his warriors were at
the flash point, and Loco had been hoping that some opportunity would present itself soon in which he could release some
of this pent-up fury without damaging Juh's overall scheme.
They had ventured north across the border with this in mind.

Several miles off to the east, where the ridge of the Animas
Mountains dipped gently down to form the pass the Spaniards
had named for their San Luis, some movement caught his eye.
A small flurry of dust from a dry patch in this otherwise thickly
blessed grassland. Loco's gaze fixed on the small point of
movement, seeing it resolve itself into wagons—four wagons,
each drawn by a team of four. That suggested a heavy cargo.
Mexicans. Four horsemen rode guard. His eyes moved over
the rest of the landscape below; the valleys and the mountains
were silent, still. A herd of pronghorns that had been grazing
five miles off near the Animas Mountains had disappeared, no
doubt into higher ground. A lone vulture dipped and soared on

its shallow V of wings, far off against the blue sky. Loco made a whistling sound in the back of his throat, like the alarm call of a quail, summoning the warriors from where they idled nearby.

Sergeant Jeremiah Danforth was used to discomfort, but the sun's heat, beating down on the oversize canvas shirt he wore over his uniform, was worse than usual for this time of year, and the broad-brimmed hat he wore was a size too small and had given him a headache. He was riding picket, about twenty yards out in front of the wagon train, eyes sweeping the landscape before them, listening to the old iron wheels grind and clank over the ground, the horses snorting dust from their nostrils. Out ahead, the grassy valley stretched away and to the north for miles, and to its west the Peloncillos rose up beyond rounded, rolling foothills. Distantly, Sergeant Danforth could make out a few of the buildings in the little settlement called Cloverdale—a meek sort of name, he reflected, for a nest of vipers.

It was the third time in a week that Sergeant Danforth had led this wagon train across San Luis Pass and into the Animas Valley. He had instructed two of his fellow riders to stay close beside the wagons and the third to allow himself to drop well behind them. They straggled on, down the ragged slope to the valley.

An hour later, with the sun as high in the sky as it would go that day, the wagon train was nearly halfway across the valley, making its way laboriously through the dry grass miles from any protective feature of the land. Danforth was not surprised, but almost relieved, to see the Apaches coming at them now through the grass—about thirty of them, he guessed, two miles off to the southwest.

"Here we go!" he called out, his voice very much like the croak of a frog ever since he had taken a blow in the larynx from a Sioux warrior whom he'd proceeded to drag off his pony and slice open from sternum to crotch in enraged retaliation.

The wagon train continued along its course, the four out-riders ambling along in position. When the Apaches were within a mile, the outriders' horses wheeled and pranced, Frog Danforth galloping back toward the wagon train. The drivers stood and whipped their teams in tight turns and the wagons began to move off, two heading back where they had come from, the other two going off in opposite directions, clearly in panic.

Loco, flanked by fifteen warriors on each side in a tight line, squeezed his calves into the horse's flanks and it picked up the pace even more. Soon he would signal the warriors to spread out and encircle the fleeing wagons. A bullet whipped by his head, a wild but lucky shot by the Mexican who had been in the lead, shooting a pistol. Now the four mounted men were racing this way and that, trying not to present easy targets. Loco fired his rifle and heard the thunder of others from each side. The wagons . . . they were stopping, the four guards racing toward them. The four wagons were equally spaced apart in a line. Suddenly, what had been each wagon's cargo, covered with canvas and lying low in the beds, was transformed. The wagons bristled with rifle barrels, ten bluecoats in each, and orange flame erupted—a trap, a trick! Loco heard bullets whirring past like angry hornets, heard an Apache to his left scream. He saw an explosion, a burst of flame, from beyond the farthest wagon, and a cloud of black, greasy smoke rose quickly up in a column. The four mounted guards were now behind the wagons, safe, adding their fire to the fusillades.

The explosion's clap of thunder reached Loco's ears and he shouted, wheeling his horse. The others turned in a melee of hooves and tossing heads and, clustered in a loose bunch, plummeted southwest across the valley toward the mountains and Mexico.

To their left, more than a mile off, Loco saw horsemen pouring over the low rise that was San Luis Pass, a stream of bluecoats, half of them with the red headbands of the Apache scouts, thundering southwestward too, bent on outflanking them. As if on a signal, Loco's band broke into five separate groups, each heading off at a different angle to the west, out of range of the riflemen in the wagons. The ground was a blur under him, and Loco's buttock, with the scar tissue of his earlier wound, was a fountain of agony, worse than ever, the pain reaching up even into the flesh above his hip. He looked down—no, not the old wound, but a bloody tear in his side. He squeezed his horse into greater effort.

Off to his left the scouts were careening across the valley, closing the distance to the southernmost splinter of his fleeing war party. He saw one, then another warrior fall, spinning across the ground and disappearing into the tall grass. His ears were filled with a loud roar.

Fanned out behind him and the other Apache warriors, racing at breakneck speed, were at least a hundred bluecoats, perhaps a half mile away. Like the other warriors nearby, Loco had slid backward on his horse, his head down almost to its withers, keeping as much of himself as possible out of the way of bullets, and his weight as far back as possible over the horse's pounding hind legs. The horse surged through the grass, and Loco's mouth was dry, a metallic taste on his tongue.

It was the taste not of fear, which Loco had never known, but of humiliation.

Captain Emmet Crawford was by no means a religious man in any sectarian sense, but miracles he relegated only to the hand of God. Since God, in Crawford's estimation, could hardly desire to lend His hand to such thieving, murdering savages as the Apaches, their disappearance into thin air once they achieved the rounded foothills of the Peloncillos could not be considered miraculous. Nevertheless, once Crawford's cavalry—both Negro and Apache—breasted the first tier of these hills not more than a thousand yards behind the fleeing savages, the Apaches were nowhere to be seen.

They had melted off in various directions, probably each man for himself. This was the usual Apache pattern. But how had they done it? Crawford admired their craft even as he deplored their criminality. He urged his Buffalo Soldiers south through the foothills, and ordered the Apache scouts to comb through the higher ground as they too went south. Surely the renegades would head for Mexico, only a few miles away, and Crawford vowed to himself to pursue them as far into that country as needed.

Three hours later, and several miles into Mexico, Crawford's scouts picked up the trail. The renegades had begun to reassemble into small groups, and all were hastening southwest into a land of rises and dips where the thorny plants of the desert were replacing grassland. By nightfall they would reach the mountains now lurking in a mild haze on the horizon. Crawford knew he had lost ground on them—they were probably five miles ahead of his advancing cavalry—but he was confident he would find them and engage them with his superior force.

Each rise they breasted promised a glimpse of the fleeing Apaches, but each rise delivered disappointment, and the lowlands between were beginning to fill with a mist that glowed a curious bronze color in the midafternoon sun. They pressed on, a hundred strong, into the mists in this foreign landscape, and, for all Crawford's confidence in his hot pursuit, he was aware of an occasional shiver somewhere deep inside—a shiver of foreboding.

Three hours later they rode across the pebbly ground of a flat valley in mesa country. All around, in the distance, low flat-topped tablelands emerged from the valley floor like mastless yellow ships immobilized in a solidified brown sea. Around the base of each mesa, slabs and scree extended out, sloping down to the desert floor—rocky necklaces the Spanish called *bajadas*.

As if they had been looking for just this place, the Apache scouts wheeled off toward one of the mesas and raced around its prow, continuing along its western face to a great gash where it looked as if the mesa had been split in two by a giant god's axe. On the ground the gash presented itself as a wide-mouthed canyon, littered with immense slabs and boulders of yellow rock that had tumbled down in some ancient rockfall. The canyon widened, then narrowed as it led finally up into the sheer side of the broken mesa.

The black cavalry followed the scouts into the broad open mouth of the canyon and, dismounting, took up positions in the cover of the ragged, loose rock. They saw the scouts scrambling for cover behind boulders ahead of them as rifle fire spattered everywhere, sending rock fragments slicing through the air, dust spurting up from the pebbly ground. The sun, now low on the horizon, lit the canyon like a cosmic searchlight, and the Apache renegades, perched behind boulders and natural breastworks above the canyon mouth, enjoyed the added advantage of being in deep shadow cast by their rocky defenses.

After the first intense fire, the crack of rifles became sporadic, each side trying to pick off individuals as they moved among the rocks. The Apaches were moving up, slowly backing away into the craggy gash in the mesa itself, while the scouts darted back and forth among the rocks in relentless pursuit. Crawford had signaled the Buffalo Soldiers to stay fanned out behind the advancing scouts when suddenly, dismayingly, gunfire broke out from the sides of the canyon, from behind rocks on the *bajada*'s slopes. One after another several scouts, lit from behind by the glowing light of the sun, writhed and fell.

From his vantage point Crawford saw this was not another band of renegade Apaches, arriving to defend those who had fled up the canyon. It was Mexicans!

Mexican soldiers firing at the Apache scouts, thinking they too were renegades. The *idiots*!

Crawford swore as he urged his horse up a rocky promontory and screamed out in Spanish: "Stop! Stop shooting. This is the American army! Stop!"

By now the scouts, believing themselves under attack by yet other hostile Apaches, were firing back at the Mexican riflemen, and the sound of gunfire drowned out Crawford's shouts. To his right, far to the west, the sun winked out below the horizon, leaving a dull glow in the sky. Crawford leaped from his mount and scrambled up onto a huge flat-topped boulder, shouting, "Americans, Americans!" and waved his sword over his head frantically, assuming the Mexicans would take note of his blue uniform.

"Americans!" he shouted again, and his voice ended in a harsh gurgle as a bullet struck him in the temple and his head exploded with blood. He toppled and fell off the boulder, fetching up like a broken doll among the slabs and scree below. From above and from behind men were shouting oaths in two languages, and then a silence descended over the battlefield as if, in a flash, it had suddenly become clear to everyone that they were engaged in an unspeakable mistake.

Commands to cease firing were heard echoing among the rocks, and Crawford's second in command, a lieutenant named Kraus, drove his horse up the scree through the boulders to the top of the *bajada*, waving his blue helmet and shouting imprecations. Meanwhile Loco and his band, now only fifteen strong, slipped farther up the mesa in the deepening gloom and vanished, delighted by the rare spectacle of their two enemies killing each other with such gusto. What stories they would be able to tell one day to wide-eyed women and children around the campfires of the night. How they would all howl with laughter at the foolishness of the White Eyes.

That night, Lieutenant Kraus remonstrated with his opposite number, a surly captain named Vargas who was almost twice Kraus's age, and finally extracted from the man a not altogether penitent apology. When the sun rose the next morning, the Mexican detachment had left the premises, perhaps to avoid any further anger and contempt that still might flash from the venomous blue eyes of the American lieutenant, and the Americans began the sorry journey north, bearing the body of their commander to Fort Bowie, where he would be buried with honors, the first member of his class at West Point to die in battle. In later reviews of the battle and the war of which it was a part, Captain Emmet Crawford would, in the full sourness of history, be denied the Congressional Medal of Honor that his commanding officer, General George Crook, would recommend from retirement.

Two days later, while the bugler played taps over Emmet Crawford's final resting place at Fort Bowie and eight funereal rifle shots pierced the thin air of early morning, Juh awaited the arrival of Loco, whom he had sent for, requesting that he and two of his warriors come to the camp in the Chiricahuas for a meeting.

Loco arrived soon afterward, having made the journey across the valley from the Peloncillos under cover of the night. Clouds had come into being, enveloping the upper reaches of the mountains where they met. The sky was uniformly gray, the temperature dropping.

After the formalities of greeting, Loco and Juh sat down near his lodge while the other adults in camp, including Naiche, Lozen, and Ishton, stood nearby, alongside the two warriors who had acompanied Loco. The children were sent away, disappearing into the surrounding trees, but soon sneaked back to the edge of the clearing in hopes of hearing the talk.

In great detail and with many flourishes in his strong voice, Loco described the events that had occurred, making his case that without some such diversion as an attack on the Mexican wagon train, his warriors might well have bolted out of impatience. His two companions remained expressionless through this account, as did Juh, who wore the perpetual frown that was etched into his face. His black eyes looked straight ahead, rather than at Loco, who sat directly to his right.

Loco continued, dwelling only briefly on the manner in which the wagon train had turned into an armed force, spending more time on the nature of his and his warriors' splendid escape from the hordes that had poured over the pass, including some fifty traitorous Apache scouts. And when Loco explained how the Mexicans had begun firing on the Americans, killing several—maybe as many as twenty—of the traitorous scouts, even Juh smiled. The smile persisted through the rest of Loco's recitation, heartening him, and when he finished, saying that it would be a good story to tell around the campfires of the Apache, he spoke his humble thanks to Ussen that he and most of his warriors had been spared.

Juh's face resumed its usual expression and he nodded, saying, "Yes, and there will be other tales to tell around the fires." He was silent for a long moment, staring at the ground before him, and Loco scratched at his chin, locating an errant whisker that would need tweezing out.

"And four of your warriors were lost," Juh said.

"Five," Loco corrected him, and looked downcast. Juh's eyelids closed over the slits of his eyes.

"There have been times," Juh said, "when I have had to find some excitement for the warriors with me, when their eyes grew red and their muscles twitched to show their prowess. Times when, as leader, I had to change my own plans to make them happy . . ." Juh paused, and Loco nodded his head solemnly.

"It is," Juh continued, "the Apache Way. Each warrior has a say, each can choose to fight or not, each can choose his own path. It has always been thus."

Loco nodded again.

Juh's eyes opened and he looked up at his wife Ishton standing ten feet away. "When you came in the morning to where we held our great council," he asked her, "what did you see?"

"A circle of knives," Ishton said. "Thrust into the ground."

"How many?" Juh asked.

"Thirteen."

Loco scratched again at the lone hair on his chin.

Juh switched his eyes to Lozen. "Who was present at the grand council besides yourself, Warrior Woman?"

She mentioned ten names. "And you," she said. "And Loco. Thirteen."

The wind had risen, blowing colder out of the darkening gray sky. Loco fidgeted, and his forehead creased over his eyes. "I could wait no longer," he said, spitting out the words. "As leader, I needed to move. I changed the plan. As we always have done when needed. But—"

"Your knife was in the ground. It spoke your agreement in the new way we agreed on—the circle of knives."

Loco sprang to his feet. "And I had to change—"

"There is another way to settle a dispute," Juh said, "to remind the rebellious—"

"Let me do this," Lozen said, and rose to her feet with the quickness of a serpent.

"Sit down, Lozen. I have more to say. Loco, in the grand council we spoke of how some of the old ways needed to change. How new ways were needed if we were to succeed against the soldiers. You recall those words?"

Loco glared down at him and said nothing. Juh rose and stood facing him.

"And you agreed with them with your voice and with your knife," Juh said. "But not in your mind."

Loco glared up at him. "I listened to my warriors," he said, "and I led."

"You made a lie of the circle," Juh said, and as his hand swung upward, a knife appeared in it, the blade almost instantaneously disappearing under Loco's ribs. Juh held it there as Loco's eyes widened, then wrenched it out, and Loco pitched over, falling sideways to the ground, a gobbet of blood suddenly erupting darkly from his open mouth.

"Go back to your group," Juh said to the two young warriors who were standing frozen, gaping at Loco, whose body twitched and went still. "Tell them you will all join Nana now. He is a wise old man, and you'll prosper by doing as he says. And," he added, nodding toward the corpse on the ground, "tell *this* story too around the campfire."

He turned and strode toward his lodge, stooping to enter through its low doorway. A few specks of snow began to ride on the wind.

Eight

General Crook was outraged. Nothing outraged him more than incompetence, and for two days his mind had been full of imprecations calling, at their mildest, for the wrath of God to descend painfully and early on every man jack who wore a Mexican uniform. Because of the sheer stupidity, the abject incompetence, of the ragtag fools that comprised the Mexican military, he had lost his finest officer and fourteen of his best Apache scouts. Two others were missing, probably escaped into the mountains to join the renegades, and Crook could hardly blame them if that were the case.

Once he had enough of the melancholy facts in hand, he fired off a telegram to Washington, to General in Chief Philip Sheridan, demanding that the Secretary of War raise holy hell with the Mexican government. Crook wanted a public apology, yes, but he also suggested firmly that the Mexican troops were hopelessly ill-led and that, if they were to remain in this theater at all, they be put under American command. Without such coordination, they were apt to continue creating havoc.

When a sergeant brought him Sheridan's response in his tent, Crook waved the man away and, donning his metal-rimmed spectacles, read the handwritten message twice. Anyone watching would have seen red rising up the general's neck like mercury in a thermometer, his face soon suffused with the crimson of anger.

"Sergeant!" he barked. "Come back here!"

He threw the message down on his escritoire and stood, hands on hips. The message read:

> Secretary War seeks apology. American command of foreign troops impossible. To avoid further incidents, remove Indian scouts from all duty. War Department has authorized two more cavalry divisions to be sent to your command. Details follow.
>
> Sheridan

"More?" Crook fumed to himself. "More green troops? Good God, what *fools*!"

The sergeant appeared at the entrance of Crook's tent and coughed. "Sir?"

Crook snatched up the message, held it out to the sergeant, turned away, and said, "Take this reply down, Sergeant: 'Added troops unnecessary. Must request order to dismiss scouts be rescinded.' Signed 'Crook.' "

The sergeant scrawled Crook's words down on a notepad and stood at attention in the entrance of Crook's tent. The general turned to face him, a look of nonrecognition on his face.

"Sir?"

"Sergeant, do you have any ambition to become an officer?"

The sergeant flushed and stammered something unintelligible.

"If you do have such an ambition," Crook said, "then put it aside. You might succeed. You might become a general, a field general. You might then be promoted to high office in Washington. And there, Sergeant, your brains would turn to porridge, you can take my word for it."

"Yessir."

"Very good. Dismissed."

Crook watched the man march away, and smiled for the first time in two days. It was a thin, grim smile. He gazed out at the parched landscape. Off to his east were the carefully surveyed and constructed rows of military buildings flanking the parade ground—so neat and orderly, so full of confidence. It was an

engineer's geometry imposed upon a wild and disorderly landscape, a violent landscape that was formed from, and had
always known, chaos and upheaval. How puny is our geometry
of straight lines and right angles, Crook thought, and he
glanced southward to the soaring tangle of turrets and cliffs
that comprised the Chiricahua Mountains. He pondered the
titanic events that must have occurred in bringing about so
grim and hostile and beautiful a place, and he wondered too
whom Sheridan would pick to replace him.

A week later George Crook stood in the pale light of the
midday sun, at Steins, where Southern Pacific trains took on
water. The railroad had erected a single wooden structure to
serve as quarters for men who from time to time arrived to
check the two large water tanks and the windmills that filled
them. The windmills were now idle, not even the slightest
breeze blowing across the flatland that stretched away in all
directions to far-off mountains. To the east lay several dead
white stretches lower by mere inches than the surround, what
the Spanish-speaking locals called *playas*. Here water from the
seasonal rains lay on the land, slowly evaporating, leaving an
alkali film in which no form of life could gain a toehold. The
playas shimmered now in the thin light, ghostly presences.
Beyond, some twenty miles farther east, lay the settlement of
Lordsburg, where train passengers from Santa Fe could catch
trains headed west to Tucson and beyond.

Across the *playas* and the tawny flatland beyond, Crook saw
black coal smoke rising in an elongated funnel, and he signaled
to the sergeant who, with a small detachment of riders, had
accompanied him to this desolate spot. The sergeant saluted,
took the reins of Crook's mule, Apache, and motioned his men
west. They would reach Fort Bowie before dark, while Crook
would arrive there in time for a late lunch.

Out of courtesy, Crook waited at Steins so he could accompany General Nelson A. Miles the last thirty-odd miles to Fort
Bowie and his new command. Crook stood now in his usual
tan canvas suit and white helmet, hands clasped behind his

back, his expressionless face as still as the far-off mountains, disguising the gall he felt at being replaced by such a pompous coxcomb as Miles, whom he knew all too well.

He could hear the train now, its great pistons driving, easily pulling the few cars that carried Miles and his entourage. A vast machine this iron horse, but it seemed puny far off across the flatland with its dead alkaline *playas*.

Within minutes the locomotive began to slow for the stop at Steins, a great clattering of pistons and shrieking of steam and black smoke. Once it had shuddered to a halt, Crook swung up into the forward car and the train lurched forward with a shriek of metal on metal, paused, and lurched forward again. In the back of the car in the small wooden seats, each with its open window through which tatters of coal smoke and soot blew, sat several officers of varying rank, all resplendent in their uniforms. In their midst sat General Nelson Miles, whose blue jacket and white cap with a black visor were so adorned with gold braid, gold epaulettes, and gold insignia that he looked, Crook thought sourly, like a bejeweled gigolo in some European court.

"George!" Miles called out, and smiled beneath his perfectly trimmed moustache. He held up a white-gloved hand. Crook winced inwardly: no one called him George. To his intimates he was known simply as Crook; his inferiors called him General. And Crook counted this popinjay, who so far was only a brevet general, among his inferiors.

"Gentlemen," Miles said as Crook reached the cluster of officers, "this is General George Crook, Indian fighter and hero. I will have a word with him."

The officers stood and wobbled into the car to the rear, leaving the two generals to themselves. The train was picking up speed, nearly at the thirty miles an hour that would deliver Crook's replacement to Fort Bowie in less than an hour.

"Sit down, George. Here." Miles scooted over in his wooden seat, but Crook perched on the seat across the aisle. "Kind of you to meet us. I know this is an awkward moment in your career. And what a career it's been, eh?" He flicked a large piece of soot from his sleeve and grinned self-consciously. "Well, now, that's pointless, isn't it?"

"There are a few things it might be useful to know about this new assignment," Crook said.

"Yes, of course. Glad to have you fill me in."

Crook gestured out the window. "As you can see, this is nothing like the country you're familiar with. And the Apaches are nothing like the Indians you have fought. The Sioux? We both know about the Sioux, great horsemen, yes, but these Apaches may well be the finest light cavalry in military history. And on foot—"

"Yes, George, I've read the reports. Very illuminating. But we will simply run them down, overpower them with superior numbers. Just as I did at Red River. And with the Nez Perce. Two more cavalry divisions are being sent—"

"Beyond the thousand men who just arrived?" Crook asked, incredulous.

"Exactly. We'll wear them ragged, camp in every mountain pass, surround every water source, keep them on the run. Everywhere they turn, they'll see more U.S. troops. All these savages think alike, George."

Crook stared at the man. His sideburns were carefully trimmed, descending below his ears, and his moustache drew one's attention away from a softness of features on a face that was running to jowls. It was a handsome enough face, the face of an egotist, and Crook was aware that Miles had his eye on one day, after concluding a brilliant military career, becoming President of the United States.

"And of course, George, both Sheridan and I are of the opinion that your Apache scouts should be just that, scouts. Not fighting men. Have to trim their ranks, demote them a bit. Can't fight savages with their own kind. They're all mendacious, totally untrustworthy. Worthy opponents, some of 'em, but not reliable allies."

Crook's neck began to redden slightly. He put his tongue between his teeth and held it there. Then he spoke.

"Is that how you found the Crow warriors who helped you run down the Nez Perce? Mendacious? Unreliable?"

"Oh, yes, the Crow. They were helpful, of course, George, but not crucial by any means. They detest the Nez Perce. And the Sioux. But using Apaches against Apaches—"

"General Miles," Crook said. "I will tell you this one thing this one time. One day, historians of our conquests on this continent will overlook the fact that most of them have been achieved as swiftly as they have only by pitting Indian tribe against Indian tribe. But here, this is of no use. There is no tribe anywhere in the West that has inflicted anything but minor pain on the Apaches. Even the Comanches have been little more than an annoyance to these people. You will find, *General,* that the Apaches are a fighting force superior to anything you have ever seen or read about."

He leaned back in his seat and stared out the window at the featureless plain of the San Simon Valley hurtling by.

"I do not think, General Crook," Miles said, visibly miffed, "that a few hundred renegades can outrun seven thousand fighting men of the United States. No matter how superior they may be to the other savages whom we have so successfully subdued."

Pompous ass, Crook thought, and he began the nearly impossible task of putting the Apaches—and this godforsaken, thorny, unforgiving, beautiful land—out of mind. And this soft-featured popinjay of a general too. Oh, he would learn, he would learn, now, wouldn't he?

But George Crook could not have known how soon the Apaches would administer their lesson—or how devastatingly.

Nine

After a night that brought a new chill to the mountains in southern New Mexico and Arizona, with vast damp clouds building rapidly over their upper reaches, the dawn of December 7, 1884, arrived under lowering gray skies that shielded the land from all but a faint smudge of light in the east. The sun was too weak to cast its usual fingers of gold and saffron into the sky, and tiny crystals of snow that had already blanketed the mountaintops began to fall in the foothills. Color left the world, but for black, white, and gray.

A mile west of the railroad's way station at Steins, three figures rose in the gloom from a depression that ran along the railroad tracks. Overhead, the telegraph wires sagged limp and inert in the windless chill, the poles marching off east and west as far as the eye could see, a single file of blind sentinels linking outpost to outpost, fort to fort, and this remote land to the rest of the world. Between the poles, the black wires undulated into the distance like the flight of a woodpecker.

One of the three figures put his arms around the nearest telegraph pole and began to scramble up. From below, the two others watched as he alternately pushed upward with his feet, reached up with linked arms and pushed again with his feet, finally reaching the point where the wire was linked to the pole.

The man on the pole, like those on the ground, was barechested, clad in only a breechcloth and high moccasins. His

98

cheekbones were streaked with a greasy black, and red had been daubed down his cheeks in rough lines. Leaning out as far as he could from the pole, he took from a deerskin pouch hanging on his belt a long string of rawhide and knotted it to the wire. Drawing its other end toward him as tightly as he could, he knotted it again to the wire, and from his belt drew a knife. He slipped the blade between the rawhide and the telegraph wire and, with a violent upthrust, severed the wire.

From his pouch he pulled another piece of rawhide, this one longer and wider than the other, and wet all through. This he wrapped around the severed telegraph wire and the rawhide string that held its two severed ends together. The wet rawhide would dry within an hour, shrinking and tightening crushingly on the wire, a poultice that would both hold the separate wires firmly and apart and be almost invisible to anyone riding along below, trying to find the break.

The man on the pole nodded to those below and began to shinny down. This was Juh himself. It had been a simple task, one he might have assigned to any young warrior. Indeed, the same procedure was being performed on the White Eyes' magical wires at five other places between Fort Stanton in New Mexico and Tucson. It would be days—two? three?—before the soldiers could converse again across the distances, depending on how sharp were the eyes of their patrols, now diverted to riding the telegraph poles instead of looking for Apaches. Juh smiled inwardly.

Juh had wanted to execute this task not because it called for special talent or bravery, but because it was the first step in what he knew would be—regardless of outcome—the last Indian war. Mangas's violent raid in the autumn had been a preliminary, a successful one. Had not the White Eyes sent for yet more troops? And Loco's foolish outbreak, itself a failure, had also served notice on the White Eyes that the remaining Apache renegades would not be easily run down. And again, had the White Eyes not called for yet more troops—two thousand? And a new general, the man Nelson Miles?

Red Beard, whom white men called Tom Jeffords, had

passed along these numbers to Juh, and also the news of Miles's arrival. Miles, Red Beard had said, was a famous killer of Indians, but he was no Crook. And the Sioux and the Nez Perce whom Miles had subdued were no Apaches. But that all would be seen now as true or not—now that the soldiers' voice was silenced and for two days at least they would be in the dark about the mayhem about to descend on the land, not like a lightning storm, but like the end of the world.

As unobserved as a desert lizard, the three Apaches slipped off to where their horses had been hobbled and, once mounted, they headed eastward under the pewter sky toward Steins. There they would plant the fire sticks that the miners used. Then, while the water towers and the station house flew into the sky in splinters and the iron rails writhed like worms exposed to the sun, they would slip into the foothills of the Peloncillos, joining Lozen the Warrior Woman and sixty-five warriors from Juh's own band, the Nedh'nis, the Enemy People only lately arrived from old Mexico.

By the time Juh and his two companions reached Steins, it was snowing even there in the valley. Dead white flakes had begun to scatter invisibly into the dead white alkaline *playas*, blowing in now, silent and secret on a morbid northern wind. And by the time the installation at Steins was a fiery ruin and Juh and his band were poised in the Peloncillo foothills for their part of the region-wide assault, the entire floor of the valleys east and west of the Peloncillos lay under an inch of snow.

At ten-thirty on the morning of December 7, one of the two Apache scouts with Sergeant Jeremiah Danforth's detachment of cavalry came across the tracks of three horsemen moving south into the foothills. The scout, under orders now, as they all were, to wear the blue uniform jackets, saw at once from the hoofprints in the snow that these were Apache riders and signaled to Danforth, who held his gloved hand up, bringing the detachment—in all, ten blacks from the Ninth Cavalry and seven horsemen from the newly arrived Fifth—to a halt. As Danforth approached, the scout looked up and said, "Apache."

Danforth looked down at the tracks, which clearly showed that three riders had moved at a lope across the ground, and looked up at the scout, a man with an unpronounceable name— something like a double cough—whom the troops called Peaches for his yellowish red cheeks.

"How do you know they're Apaches?"

Peaches pointed to his head and grinned. Danforth glowered at the Indian, who grinned again and pointed down and motioned with his hands, as if putting one down after the other.

"All three the same," he said, still pretending his hands were the feet of horses. "White men don't know how to do that." His hand gestures changed into an ungraceful, choppy gait. He slipped off his horse and approached some dark, still-damp horse droppings among the hoofprints. He drew his knife and pried one of them open.

"Grass from the mountains," Peaches said. "Not hay." He pointed south into the Peloncillos, where the tracks evidently led. "An hour ago. Maybe less."

"Okay, Peaches," Danforth said, shaking his head. "Let's see if we can find 'em."

The detachment followed the tracks at a gallop; they led into the western foothills, rising and falling but moving steadily upward over the snow-dusted land and into a wide draw between two rounded hills. All around them the ground was speckled with colorless sagebrush and the inky scrawls of mesquite bushes. At Danforth's signal the horsemen slowed to a trot, spreading out into a phalanx like the tip of an arrow. The Apaches, Danforth knew, rarely assaulted a body of troops greater than ten. There was nothing cowardly or craven about these savages—they were merely cautious. All the old hands in this campaign knew that an entire war party of Apaches, fifteen or twenty of them, would watch a handful of soldiers, even as few as two or three, throughout most of a day's march, waiting for the moment when their guard was down before attacking. If this were an attempt to lead them into an ambush, Danforth welcomed the opportunity.

The rifle fire came first from the rear. Two men on the right flank spun off their horses and had fallen to the ground even as the crackle of guns sounded in the crystalline air. Danforth wheeled around, saw nothing, heard nothing, just sagebrush and a moment of horrible stillness.

Gunfire broke out again, this time from his right, and another horseman toppled off, the horse screaming as it fell on the rider and scrambled to its feet. Springfield Trapdoor rifles, the sergeant thought, knowing the sound—nothing like the troops' Winchester seven-shots—when a flaming pain seared through his side and wrenched him around in his saddle.

Where are they? he was screaming to himself. *Where are they?*

More gunfire from his rear, horse churning under him in a tight panicky circle, he was falling, numb. Numb on his right side. Sergeant Danforth found himself looking dumbly at the snow inches from his face now, cold, icy cold, seizing him even as his side flamed.

God *damn*, there must be a hundred of them.

He tried to roll onto his other side, aware of gunfire, shots, screams, a chaos of horses, men, some naked to the waist, oh shit. He heaved up on his good arm, struggled to his knees in the snow. His arm hung limply at his side, and he reached down with his left hand for the Colt, drawing it from the holster across his body, so far across his body; it felt cold in his hand. One of the savages was racing at him. He could see only the face in the tunnel of vision still afforded him, painted red and black, contorted, teeth bared and the blackest eyes, arm upraised, and the eyes, the *eyes*, her eyes like burning coals . . . Her? A woman?

Sergeant Danforth raised the Colt in his left hand, trying to force its weaving barrel into the narrowing tunnel, and entertained his last thought—I'm killed by a woman, a damned *woman*—and the sunlight burst forth in his skull and the world went black as the woman's war club drove the crushed bone of his forehead three inches into his brain.

Five minutes after the death of Sergeant Jeremiah Danforth, the clouds over the valley began to dissipate and sunlight, weak at first, fell on the small valley between the two round hills. It fell on the bodies of seventeen cavalry troopers lying awkwardly on the ground, and that of a single Apache warrior. Presently, the eighteenth trooper, horse missing—no doubt scattered off with the others—noted that the Apaches were gone and slowly pulled himself to his feet. Maybe he could get to Steins, get word through . . .

The sun—stronger now—caused the snow to disappear in the flat, empty reaches of San Simon Valley, the glistening white vanishing as if it had never been, leaving a trackless waste of dun-colored sand, gray-green sage, and the contorted black branches of mesquite under the silent sky.

At about the same time the snow vanished from San Simon Valley, far to the west, a patrol out of Fort Lowell in Tucson stopped when the scout at its head pointed to a line of what looked like large black birds emerging from the cottonwoods lining the banks of the Santa Cruz River three miles north of the old mission and abandoned presidio at Tubac. What at first appeared to be six birds—maybe ravens or vultures, but walking in single file—were seen on second look to be humans—women. Sisters. Nuns. They were followed out of the brush and barren woodland by three more women in long skirts of homespun, each carrying a bundle of some sort, and three children on foot.

The cavalry patrol wheeled in their direction and approached at a lope, crossing the distance in a matter of minutes. As they approached, the procession of women halted and bunched together nervously, herding the three children into their midst. The young officer, a lieutenant named Bixler, dismounted and announced his rank, name, and unit, asking what the women were doing alone out in such a place.

One of the nuns—an older woman, judging from the seams that lined her face, and a woman accustomed to command, judging from her nearly military bearing—cut off the other women's murmuring with a gesture of her hand.

"Apaches, Officer. They destroyed the mission. It's a smoldering ruin. Father Pio is dead, collapsed when he saw the three *brazeros* fall in the gunfire. His heart just stopped, may he rest in peace. The savages set upon us at first light, appeared out of nowhere ... I don't know, Officer, perhaps fifteen or twenty of them ... It was horrible, horrible. They, they ... God have mercy on poor Father Pio ... I ordered the women—these women here with the infants, and the children—all of them into the basement, where we listened to the gunfire, the shots, the screams. And one of us, one of the babies, cried in the pitch-black, and the trapdoor opened and his horrid face, black and red striped it was, peering down at us like a wild animal ... Yes, yes, in Spanish, he told us to come up, and we prayed as we climbed the ladder, and the savages, oh Lord, ten of them stood grinning at us, yes, in God's own house, the stink of them! They led us out of the mission—on our way to be slaughtered, we were perfectly sure—and into the woods by the river, and all but two of them left, disappeared. One of the two pointed to himself, said he was Mangas, said he was letting us go. He pointed north, this way ... Yes, Officer. Why, sir? Why were we spared? Oh, sweet Mother of us all, poor Father Pio ..."

Three hours later Lieutenant Bixler and his patrol, all now on foot and each leading a mount carrying a woman or child, neared the low adobe walls of Fort Lowell, where he soon learned from his superior that the telegraph lines were silent, severed no doubt by the Apaches. The women were taken into the protection of the fort, young Bixler was ordered back on patrol, this time to track along the telegraph lines to the east, and his commanding officer—a brevet major named Hapgood, who was a veteran of two years in Arizona—wondered why the Apaches had chosen the Santa Cruz River as the path for their war party. There were other places along the border that were more remote, where fewer might notice their arrival from the wilds of old Mexico, where the cavalry patrols were more spread out in lands where concealment was easier ...

The major had never heard of an Apache raid where they let anyone go, even women and children.

By the time daylight had dwindled on December 7, and clouds had begun to build up over the mountain ranges, sixty-seven enlisted men and three officers of the United States Army had lost their lives between the Hatchet Mountains in New Mexico and the Santa Cruz River in Arizona. The old friar, Father Pio, and the three *brazeros* at the Tubac mission brought the total dead up to seventy-one.

In all, over a region that was two hundred miles in breadth, only five Apache warriors lay dead where they had fallen. By morning, December 8, their corpses had vanished, taken in the night to secret places of burial in the crags and canyons of their ancestral lands, their names not to be mentioned again among their tribesmen lest their spirits be reluctant to go on to Ussen and instead stay nearby to do evil things to the living. The world was, once again, still.

At Fort Bowie, north of the towering Chiricahua Mountains and overlooking Apache Pass, General Nelson Miles knew only that a war party had surprised and massacred one of his detachments in the foothills of the Peloncillos. One enlisted man—one man out of eighteen—had managed to escape the onslaught of what he reported were at least a hundred of the savages, and made his way to Steins, finding it a still-smoldering ruin, the water tanks demolished. After struggling westward along the railroad tracks for three miles, he had been picked up by a patrol sent out to find where the savages had cut the telegraph lines. The break was found just before dark and repaired, but the lines were still dead. It was apparent that this had been something more than the usual rampage.

Not until the afternoon of the following day, December 8, would General Miles learn the extent of the disaster—that five separate war parties had struck the day before like a rank of lightning storms, only to disappear into the vast silence of the landscape. It was an unprecedented onslaught, obviously a wholly new strategy. Reports from the few addled survivors were probably exaggerated, but it seemed that somewhere in the neighborhood of five hundred warriors had rampaged through the two territories in one day.

But to make matters worse—far worse—word came that night once the telegraph was working again that Geronimo and some two hundred Apaches had broken out from the San Carlos reservation, leaving four soldiers and eight scouts from the Western Apache bands dead, along with the roundly hated Indian agent. Geronimo and his followers had managed to disappear into the night, mounted on U.S. Cavalry horses, and fanned out in practically every direction, no doubt to meet up later at some appointed spot, as was the Apache Way.

Hearing all this, General Miles experienced a twinge of fear, an ominous, premonitory pang, the first he had felt in ten years fighting Indians, as if something had clutched his shoulder with an icy-fingered hand. Shaking the sensation off, he pondered the map pinned to the plaster wall of the adobe building in which he stood alone, hands clasped behind his back.

The building had recently served as quarters for four officers, but soon after his arrival, Miles had appropriated it for his command headquarters. Cots and bed stands had been taken out, replaced by two desks and a collection of uncomfortable wooden chairs. The old corporal who served as Miles's valet and factotum had, after an oath guaranteeing his absolute secrecy, sawed a quarter of an inch from the front legs of all the chairs but Miles's own. The general detested long meetings and preferred that even his most trusted officers not settle in, even during times of relative informality. Unaware of the slight tilt to their chair seats, men tended nonetheless to grow restless quickly, feeling the urge to stand up.

The general had visited the San Carlos reservation only once and only for three days, soon after his arrival in Arizona. He realized that he—and the officers he had brought with him from the north—were at a distinct disadvantage not knowing the land around San Carlos with any intimacy. He crossed the room, put his head out the door, and summoned the old corporal, telling him to bring to his headquarters a grizzled sergeant of the Ninth Cavalry, a man named Jenkins whose face was as black as anthracite and who had patrolled this region for nearly a decade. When Jenkins arrived, he saluted smartly and told the general that the telegraph lines had gone dead again.

ᖆᖇ ᖇᖆ

Ten

Grover Cleveland, the Democratic governor of New York who a little more than a month earlier had won election as the next President of the United States, had never been so uncomfortable. Or so terrified. Or so humiliated.

Clutching the side of the stagecoach as it hurtled over the rough, rutted track fifteen miles south of Tombstone, he crossed his legs, clamping his ample thighs together to hide the small damp stain that had just erupted.

He had thought that, as President-elect, it would be politic if he toured some of the places in the nation with which he was unfamiliar, particularly the territories and states west of the Mississippi. As an antisilver Democrat, he knew perfectly well that many of the senators and others in the West were not his friends, but Cleveland was nothing if not brave. Best to go to the lion's lair and speak frankly, the better to deal with the beast later.

Two days before, he had arrived by train in Tucson, where the townspeople made a proper fuss over him and his small party, greeting him with flags and bunting and martial music at the railroad station, wining and dining him at the hotel. Cleveland had not been impressed—by the hotel, which was an adobe building of only two stories alongside a main street of dirt; or by the food, which was far too spicy; or by the wine, which was raw; or by the women, who all seemed a bit bovine. The territorial governor, a tall and Jehovan-looking man without a shred of manners, had then hauled him to Tombstone the day before. Tombstone was the territory's largest settlement, hardly what Cleveland would have called a city, and was given over to the production of inappropriate quantities of silver, but it had been entertaining enough. In all, however, Cleveland was not much taken with the West, confirmed now in his earlier opinion that it was full of badlands and uncouth ne'er-do-wells.

This morning they had boarded a stagecoach, just the two of them, to make the journey south to Bisbee, which the governor seemed especially anxious to have Cleveland see. Now almost fifty, just a bit portly from the fine food a New York politician had access to, and accustomed to a mostly urban life, Cleveland had grimly and uncomfortably sat on the hardwood seat as the godforsaken contraption rattled through this appalling brown wasteland, making his emergent jowls quiver unpleasantly. They had pulled the leather curtains over the windows, but this did little to keep the chill out, and Cleveland shivered even under his heavy black woolen coat.

Miserable on several counts, he was listening with half his mind as the governor carried on about the territory's mineral wealth besides silver, and cattle, and the future, when the first gunfire sounded. Cleveland snatched the leather curtain aside and was stunned to see a man hurtle past the window. It was the man "riding shotgun," and he flew past like a rag doll.

The governor lurched across the seat, stuck his head out Cleveland's window, and bellowed in biblical fury, pulling a long-barreled Colt from his holster and firing off three rounds with a series of monstrous explosions, the shock of which Cleveland felt slam into his head as he tried to get out of the wild-eyed governor's way on the narrow seat.

"What is it, for God's sake?" he shouted.

"Outlaws! A holdup. But not if I have . . ." the governor said, the rest of his words being lost in two more violent explosions from his Colt.

It was then, hurtling across the ground in a wooden coach that squealed and groaned in agony itself, the sound of gunshots echoing painfully in his skull, that President-elect Grover Cleveland realized he was very likely about to die in the wilderness, and also realized that, in utter terror, he had wet his pants. So he crossed his legs and prayed in earnest for the first time since he had been a youth. With his considerable weight thus off balance, the next seizure on the part of the stagecoach as it leaped out of a rut in the dirt track sent Cleveland rolling over on his side on the wooden seat while the territorial governor shouted up at the driver, his words being torn away by the wind. The coach began to slow.

"They gave up, Billy!" the governor shouted out the window to the driver. "Scared the manure out of 'em. Damned if we didn't. Oh, my God. Oh, my *God* . . ."

He pulled his head back in the window as Cleveland managed to regain his seat. The governor's face had gone ashen beneath its coppery burnishing from the Arizona sun.

"What is it?" Cleveland asked, his voice little more than a croak.

"Apaches. A damn war party!" The governor began reloading his Colt, fingers fumbling. The President-elect watched dumbly as a .45 caliber bullet in a brass casing fell on the floor and rolled back and forth between his feet while the coach began again to pick up speed. Outside they could hear the driver's high-pitched appeal to the team of four, and the cracking of his whip.

The governor swung around and put his head through the other window, looking forward, backward, then forward again.

"Holy Jehosaphat, there's a hundred of 'em. We're in for it now, Mr. President." Grover Cleveland tightly recrossed his legs and stared wide-eyed at the wooden planks in front of him. The coach slowed, came to a stop, and he ventured a look out the window. On horses that pawed the ground and snorted steam in great plumes into the icy air, dark-skinned, bare-chested men with faces horridly painted and rifles held at the ready pranced around kicking up dust. There was a terrible noise, a high-pitched liquid baying, and Cleveland watched as the savages, for all the world like wild and predatory beasts from another world altogether, looked back at him from black eyes set in ferocious slits. Suddenly, unexpectedly, a strange calm came over the President-elect, perhaps arising from the sure knowledge that his time on earth was now as good as over and the only worry he had was whether there really was, as guaranteed from every pulpit in the land, some kind of existence on the other side of the Stygian murk of death.

A grim-faced savage with hair down to his shoulders stared through the window at him, his nearly lipless mouth set in a thin line, jaw protruding, eyes gleaming like black glass.

"It's Geronimo," the governor whispered. "The worst, basest, cruelest, meanest-tempered—"

But Grover Cleveland didn't pause to hear the rest. He had seen pictures of the man, drawings in the newspapers back East, and had heard the stories. He was sure they were exaggerated by a perfervid press, as everything was. But he was also certain he was about to die, and he was damned if he'd die sitting on a hard wooden bench in an ugly, uncomfortable, unseemly Arizona stagecoach. He struggled with the handle of the door, opened it, and stepped down onto the ground, pulling his black woolen coat around him.

"Sir," he said. "You are Geronimo, the great Apache leader? What do you want?"

The savage turned almost sideways on his horse and looked out toward the ring of warriors around them now. He said something that was both guttural and lilting, and turned back to look down at Cleveland. The warriors were still as statues, leaning toward the coach on horses that were equally immobile. They all held rifles of one kind or another; bows and arrows could be seen over their shoulders.

"I am Grover Cleveland, the next—"

Geronimo pointed a dark finger at Cleveland's chest. "You are a lucky man, Cleelan," he said. His voice was oddly soft and musical.

Cleveland waited, hearing nothing but his own heart beating in his ears. Geronimo leaned back on his horse, slumping comfortably.

"Dangerous road," the Apache said with a predatory smile, gesturing to the north, then to the south. "Robbers. A lot of robbers in our country. Bad men. We killed them." The black eyes seemed to gleam with a savage happiness. "You go now."

With that, Geronimo wheeled his horse off to the right, waved his rifle toward the southwest, and led the Apaches up a low hill covered with dead grass and scrubby bushes. Cleveland watched them disappear as magically as a band of centaurs where the breast of the hill met the leaden sky. He turned to the stagecoach and heard a long breath escape from the governor inside.

"Well, I'll be God damned," the governor said. "We were dead."

"What happened?"

"Beats the hell out of me, Mr. President. But you are one brave man." As Cleveland heaved his bulk up into the stage, the leathery Arizonan poked his head through the window. "Billy, turn this thing around. Take us back to Tombstone."

"No no, Governor," Cleveland said. "We were going to Bisbee, were we not?"

The following day, when the two political leaders returned to Tombstone, they learned that not only had Geronimo broken loose again from the reservation—which they, of course, knew—but also that the entire region had suffered the rampages of at least five renegade bands of up to a thousand Apaches and maybe more, a day and a half of madness and savagery, after which the Apaches had simply disappeared.

Under what was thought to be the first modern banner headline in journalism—TERRITORIES SAVAGED!—the newspaper at Tombstone announced all this in as much detail as they could muster from accounts ranging from actual to nearly mythological, and screamed in editorial outrage. The writer demanded protection from the Apaches at the same time he leveled every conceivable charge of incompetence at the United States Army and speculated venomously that the powers in Washington— and particularly the "great" Indian fighter Philip Sheridan— had become too happily cozened by the ribbons and salons of the capital with all its eastern pretentions and blandishments and, with judgment thus impaired, sent the wrong general to head the troops whose absolute duty—whose first and only reason for being—was to protect the good people of Arizona from . . .

On and on the editorialist raged, even suggesting—in a wholly unself-conscious lapse of memory—that what was needed was the return of General George Crook to the scene, a man who at least knew the difference between Apaches and such second-rate and half-tame feckless savages as the Sioux and Nez Perce.

For his part, President-elect Grover Cleveland decided to cut his visit to the West short and return as expeditiously as could be arranged to the East. He groaned to himself when he learned he would have to make the first leg—to New Mexico—by stagecoach since the railroad tracks beyond Fort Bowie had been sabotaged. He wanted to go directly to Washington itself, where he intended to discuss an idea with Chester Arthur, a long-term political adversary—but a fellow New Yorker—who had little to do these next three and a half months but keep the presidential chair warm for its new occupant.

Later in the morning a detachment of seventy-five troops from the Ninth Cavalry at Fort Huachuca arrived in Tombstone to escort the President-elect out of the territory and into New Mexico, where he could board a train at Deming. Cleveland, who preferred to travel more anonymously, acceded to the escort when the captain of the detachment explained that another two hundred Apaches had broken out from the reservation. These were Mescaleros, from the reservation near Fort Stanton.

According to Colonel Hatch at Fort Stanton, who was in charge of the reservation savages, they had all scattered westward into the badlands of the Jornada del Muerto, Journey of the Dead Man, a place of knife-sharp, black lava fields and dead white sand dunes that stretched for miles up the middle of the New Mexico Territory east of the Rio Grande. The half of the Ninth Cavalry not on duty elsewhere in the territories—the Buffalo Soldiers—was in pursuit, but in the three-hundred-year history of the Apache wars, no Spanish or American troops had ever succeeded in running down an Apache band in that accursed wasteland.

Victorio agreed with Juh's plan. It was brilliant—and partly Victorio's, after all. The two of them had hatched it over several months in Juh's stronghold in the Sierra Madres while the world believed both men were dead. And having listened to Juh describe its final details this past autumn at the great council, Victorio had wholeheartedly plunged his knife into the ground, making his oath.

Now the lands of the Apache were under full siege, seven bands on the rampage all at once. Never had anything like it happened before—not even in the days of the great leaders, Cochise and Mangas Colorado. Victorio knew that once, shortly before the White Eyes troops had abandoned the forts to go fight each other in their Civil War, the two great leaders had assembled nearly two thousand warriors to assault Apache Pass. But such was not the Apache Way. Massed together in the manner of a white man's army, they had failed, losing warriors to cannons for the first—and last—time.

But now the world was exuberantly alive again with Apache war parties, leaving behind an enemy bewildered and fearful, thousands of troops rushing this way and that, not knowing where death would come from next. And the death-dealing Apaches were always on the move like butterflies, alighting here and there, striking, scattering, vanishing. Scorpions, not butterflies.

But scorpions with selected prey. Juh had explained the value of swooping down only on American troops, or American bandits, or the Mexican ranchers who lived north of their border. It was, Juh had said, necessary to show the White Eyes a new and more lethal warfare, but one they could understand, a warfare they would think of as civilized, and thus let their better instincts betray them.

Victorio stood in the shadow of a jagged outcrop in the southern peaks of the San Andreas Mountains. From his perch he could see, eastward across the white sands, the windblown dunes marching overland like white crescent moons in a white sky. Beyond and to the north lay Sierra Blanca, the great peak rising above the world, glistening white with snow. Turning, Victorio could see westward as well, across the tawny flatlands between him and the silver ribbon of the Rio Grande. Victorio was exhilarated, standing here in the cold wind, long hair snapping at his neck, astride the world. For how long now he had lived disguised and hidden among the Mescaleros—relatives, yes, but not his people. His task had been to persuade them of the rightness of Juh's vision, persuade them that they should take to the warpath this one final time. The reward: freedom— or an Apache death. But not the slow death of the reservation, the humiliation of digging in the ground for things only the basest animals ate. Of being counted every week. Of suffering men in their midst who talked of alien gods.

In disguise, Victorio had bowed low to the White Eyes, and the memory of it strengthened him. But those whom he had persuaded had lived many years under the White Eyes' "peace," without fighting, without the taste of blood. Victorio watched the land below, hoping for an early test. They had done well enough in the breakout the night before, arising like wraiths in the dark, silently killing the White Eyes who guarded the reservation and the others who guarded Fort Stanton's livestock.

Now, like columns of ants, the troops from Fort Stanton could be seen emerging from the canyons far across the white dunes—six tiny columns some three or four miles apart, inching across the lifeless land toward Victorio's mountains. Victorio amused himself for a moment, thinking about ants. The black ants were venomous, the white ants less so. But neither were a match for the red ants now assembling in the highlands. Even so, these Mescaleros needed testing. Victorio would fight the ants later. He had his mind on simpler prey. It was the day of the week the White Eyes devoted to their god.

The town known as Mesilla, "Little Table," had been settled by Mexican farmers thirty years earlier, and one of the first things the devout folk of Mesilla had done was build a small church to which a priest was soon enticed. Over the decades, every niche in the interior walls of the church had been filled with carved wooden saints, some of them dressed in finely sewn clothes. The walls nearly glittered with pewter *milagros*, little fetishes of gratitude for favors divinely granted. Behind the altar was an elaborately carved screen of many colors and nearly sublime innocence, the work of two generations of a family of wood-carvers, and along the walls of the nave were loving representations of the twelve stations of the Cross.

Over the years, as the settlement of Mesilla prospered, a small plaza came into being, dominated at its southern end by the church that rose two stories above the adobe buildings around it—a general store, one given over to tack and feed, a modest saloon, and two buildings that served as warehouses. Outside the plaza were the adobe brick homes of most of the settlers who went from these humble dwellings each day out into irrigated fields where, among other crops, they grew fine, even legendary fields of chilis, which in season they exported widely throughout the region.

Every home in Mesilla, however humble, every building on the plaza, and of course the church itself, sported cheerful bunches of red chilis—called *ristras*—dried and strung on long loops and lending a festive appearance to the town throughout the year. The *ristras* were more than decoration. As needed, dried chilis could be plucked and cooked, and there were many among the townspeople who shared the belief that the *ristras* served to ward off certain forms of evil from one's house and hearth.

Throughout each week for almost a thousand weeks now, all the townspeople of Mesilla but a few storekeepers on the plaza had toiled faithfully in the fields or tended to the other, unceasing chores of rural life, but every Sunday the settlement was utterly deserted. The people came from all around to attend the church that had been named three decades earlier for San Miguel, the archangel.

It could have been construed as foolish to leave no sharp-eyed watchers on the periphery of a settlement located in so dangerous a part of the world given over to both roaming savages and roaming outlaws. Foolish or not, it was for the townspeople a form of defiance—the faithful meek believing they would at such holy times enjoy the protection of the saints and of the Lord whose praises they congregated to sing. And for three decades they had in fact been spared.

On the morning of December 9, the mass had reached the point when, accompanied by a guitar, the assembled townspeople were singing a hymn that signaled the imminent arrival of the season called Advent. On the roof of the church, three Apache warriors could hear these voices raised in unison, an outlandish sound that made the Indians smile.

The warriors, along with fifty others led by Victorio, had entered the town on foot, the rest remaining with the horses far beyond the outermost house in an arroyo that led to the Rio Grande, now merely a slow trickle through the wintery land. While the three warriors ascended to the roof, others quietly sealed the doors of all the church's entrances but the main one—a splendid arch of heavy, carved doors with thick strap hinges forged locally, which opened out on the plaza.

Below, the Apaches waited in the shadows of the plaza, while on the roof one warrior with a burning branch lit a bundle held by the other two—a cloth bundle full of wood chips and chilis that had been snatched off one of the plaza's portals. When gray smoke began to rise from the bundle, the warrior put down his smoldering branch and pulled open a wooden cover panel. The sound of a hundred voices rose through the opening, and the two warriors let their burning bundle fall into it, closing the panel and sealing the church as acrid, throat-searing fumes billowed throughout the nave.

In a matter of moments the warriors heard screams and bellows replace the singing, and soon they heard the thump of people hammering on the doors on the sides and the rear of the church. Anxious to be an even greater part of this raid, the warriors moved quickly to the front of the church, where, from behind a large wooden cross, they could see the townspeople begin to erupt into the plaza, pouring wildly out of the church, stumbling on one another, coughing, eyes streaming.

And then came the gunfire, and more screams. From above the three warriors loosed arrows into the melee and watched their targets fall. Victorio had said to kill only men. Before long, smoke from the rifles rose in clouds above the plaza, the smell of gunpowder filling every nose, and any man of Mesilla who had issued forth from the church lay dead in the dust. A few women knelt over them, moaning, while others fled back into the church. The smoke of the chilis rose greasily from the church's main entrance, driving even the three warriors back from the edge. Hastily, they descended from the roof and joined the others, slipping triumphantly out of town to the horses in the arroyo.

Ten minutes later, his heart pounding joyously in his chest, Victorio led his two hundred escaped Mescaleros north toward the badlands. There in the mountains they would patiently watch and wait in order to wreak havoc on the approaching columns of ants before disappearing maddeningly into thin air.

When hunting, Victorio knew, it is often best to let the game come to you.

Eleven

After the Apache marauders disappeared, the territories were left to an ominous and terrifying period of anticipation. General Nelson Miles placed the region on a full-scale war footing. He declared martial law over an area of six counties, his officers taking over all civic jurisdictions. The U.S. marshals, territorial and county sheriffs were all put under military command, as were the courts. Travel in the region without a military escort was forbidden. With the telegraph lines now fully restored, Miles called for a thousand infantrymen, who were promptly dispatched from various northern forts where the Indians seemed to be under control. Useless on an active campaign against the Apaches, they would be assigned to maintain around-the-clock patrols of the railroads and all population centers, most notably Tombstone.

To deflect the men under his command from immoral distraction, the young officer in charge of the troops that suddenly appeared in Tombstone ordered the bawdy houses and saloons closed. At the same time, troops were summarily billeted in Tombstone homes, causing various leading citizens who considered themselves to be the town's "upper crust" to complain that they shouldn't be inconvenienced when the bawdy houses would presumably be happy to house the troops. The newspaper, taking a higher road, fumed about constitutional rights. Meanwhile, in sympathy for their fellow retailers, all other commercial establishments in Tombstone closed their doors. The young officer relented with regard to the bawdy houses and saloons, and by way of saving face, ordered the emergency conscription of the paper's presses to print army documents instead of newspapers.

Elsewhere, a group of laborers sent by the Southern Pacific Railroad to repair the mangled rails at Steins and two other sites thought to hold out for better pay and found themselves promptly ensconced in irons in a windowless blockhouse outside of Fort Bowie. There, the laborers' resolve soon withered, and within twenty-four hours they were at work.

By now eight thousand troops were in the region or on the way. More than one-third of the entire standing United States Army would spend Christmas in the lands of the Apache. The military presence, having doubled in a period of two months, put a severe strain on local resources such as food and firewood. General Miles put several of the newly arrived infantry companies to work guarding companies of citizens conscripted to scour wood from the mountains, those woodlands near the forts being already seriously depleted.

Local food reserves were quickly seen to be on the path to depletion, and mule trains were now too few to carry supplies to all of the outlying locations of cavalry in good time. Some suppliers from Tucson attempted to raise the price of such staples as corn in response to the shortage, and found their warehouses taken over by the military in return for hastily contrived—and probably worthless—promissory notes. In the field, daily rations fell to two meals a day, mostly hardtack, and rations at the forts themselves were severely cut.

The new troops—officers and men—had never experienced any action in so thorny and unforgiving a place nor against an enemy so endowed with nearly magical powers to appear and disappear. Veterans of the Apache wars found the new arrivals to be nuisances at best, cluttering up the area, and took to describing to these tyros the most outlandish Apache habits they could imagine, including that of taking prisoners back to camp where the Apache women delighted in carving small pieces off of them over several days: just before the hapless captives finally lost consciousness and joined their maker, they were treated to the sight of their very own genitals raised high before them.

As for the five hundred Apache scouts General Crook had recruited, General Miles had of course demoted them upon his arrival, though still expecting to use their services, despite his agreement with General Sheridan back East that they were not to be trusted. The scouts themselves, however, now began to vanish, drifting away from the forts and encampments, first in New Mexico and then to the west. Word spread among them that it was none other than Victorio—unmistakably Victorio—who had led the breakout from the Mescalero reservation and the subsequent rampage that had wiped out the men of Mesilla and sixty-seven troopers, including half of the Buffalo Soldiers' Company B.

Some of the deserting Apache scouts were simply making a practical choice about the changing fortunes of war. But most of them were struck with abject awe at the thought that a dead man, Victorio, had been somehow restored to life. Ussen had to have intervened directly for such a thing to have occurred, and only a foolhardy warrior would oppose a man with such unheard-of powers. And as the word spread also that it was none other than Juh whom Victorio and the other leaders were following—Juh alive, also magically returned to life—the die for all but a handful of Apaches was cast.

Those few Apaches who did remain in the service of the army, though servile, still possessed sufficient pride to detest the Navajos from the north in New Mexico and the Papagos from over near Tucson who were hastily conscripted to fill in as Indian scouts. These other Indians were immediately greeted with Apache condescension and hostility, with fights breaking out on the spot, several with homicidal results. The scouts were hurriedly separated from each other on a tribal basis, the newcomers showing little aptitude and less heart for tracking the lethal renegades anywhere, much less into their impregnable and probably witch-infested strongholds in the alien lands of Mexico.

General Miles, stunned by the size and swiftness of the

Apache rampages and puzzled by the sudden quiet, was also greatly preoccupied with sorting out such matters as logistics. It seemed imprudent, in his view, to mount any active campaigns—for example, trailing the savages into Mexico, where no doubt they had fled, and pursuing them in some cat-and-mouse game. So he ordered his troops, reinforced and spread out across the landscape in two tiers north of the Mexican border, to act the spider instead. To await, for now, the dropping of the next shoe.

Even had the United States government seen fit to send the remaining twelve thousand troops under its army command into the region, the nocturnal spread of information among the Apaches, now mostly tucked away in various mountain fastnesses in Mexico, could not have been stopped. Unobserved, secreted in the landscape, lone warriors stealthily tracked the comings and goings of the White Eyes with the sure-eyed vigilance of jaguars on the prowl. No troop movement, no patrol, no shipment went unobserved by at least one pair of black eyes, and all this information came on silent feet in the night to the encampment where Juh sorted it, for the most part a solitary figure among the rocks some distance from his camp in the Sierra Madres not far across the border into Mexico. There he sat by day, still as sculpture on the parapet of the mountain, hunched over, not unlike a mythical beast-man, brooding over the details of his people's destiny.

On this day, the third since the attacks ended, he was joined by two of his fiercest—and most widely feared—lieutenants, Geronimo and Victorio, as well as his most trusted lieutenant, Naiche, the quiet son of Cochise. The four of them sat in a circle facing each other, except for Victorio, who sat partly sideways in the circle, his off-center eye restlessly searching the distant lands below.

"We were riding a fast horse," Victorio said. "When you are riding a fast horse, you do not get off and walk. You ride it till it drops."

Geronimo snorted. "That has always been our way," he agreed. "And once the horse drops, you are on foot anyway. Perhaps in the wrong place at the wrong time. You are too impatient, Victorio."

Little affection existed between the two men, as Juh was all too aware. Victorio was pure warrior—impetuous, throbbing with anger and an unslakable desire for vengeance. He had paced like a caged animal while disguised and hidden among the Mescaleros. Now, recently blooded again, he was driven by the killing urge.

Geronimo, on the other hand, while capable of stunning feats of warfare, was a man of cunning, a sly man with other powers besides those of the warrior. As a war leader, he bowed always to Naiche, but his people regarded him with the respect, and fear, they felt in the presence of all with the talents and powers of the shaman. Geronimo could see things; he could persuade the powers of the universe to heal. But it was suspected of him, as it is of any shaman, that he could also harness those same powers to cause harm.

"While we wait here," Victorio said, "the White Eyes gather strength. This is what you have told us, Juh."

"The enemy gathers in numbers. Strength is another thing. The enemy is never as strong as you think," Geronimo said, citing Apache wisdom.

"Nor are you," Victorio replied testily, completing the adage. "We should strike again, strike now, hard, strike while the enemy is unready." He stood up and glared angrily to the north.

Juh sat silent as the two men argued. Anger, Juh had learned, was like the wind that could blow out the firelight of the mind. Yet it could be usefully employed. Both of these two fierce men, like the Apaches before them, had always responded to an invasion or an attack like a hornets' nest—with sudden, raging, indiscriminate fury that sought and got immediate vengeance, but often died in the process, as a hornet loses its sting.

"Vengeance," Juh said, interrupting. When he was explaining his vision to people, his minor speech defect—a hesitation between some words—vanished. He spoke at such times in a voice so soft that his listeners had to lean closer to hear.

"Vengeance is a matter of the heart. It is one's own. And we will have it. But taking vengeance all these years since before our grandfathers' time has not returned our land to us. Why do you suppose the American soldiers have come?" He turned to Naiche. "We have talked often about this. Why do these people fight us?"

"For our land," Victorio said.

"For money," Naiche said. "They make money from the land, and money makes them rich. They do nothing except for this money. If they couldn't turn our land into money, they would go away."

"Victorio, we have talked about this before. Let me speak plainly. How many horses did you give your father-in-law to marry your wife?"

"Thirty."

"That is a great many. She is a valuable wife. What would you have done if he asked for sixty?"

"For her?" Victorio said, the beginning of a smile tugging at the corners of his mouth. "I would have told him that is too many."

The four men chuckled.

"And would you have stayed in his camp? Would you have fought with him?"

"No. If he wouldn't take thirty for her, I would have looked for another woman somewhere else."

"And that is just what the father hoped. He wasn't angry at you. He just didn't like you. He didn't want you in his camp, in his family. So he asked for far too many horses. And suddenly his daughter didn't look so beautiful anymore. It's like a game, isn't it? That is what we are doing. We aren't looking for vengeance now. We are asking for so many horses that the land is suddenly not so beautiful anymore."

Victorio frowned. "So we have to play this White Eyes game. This money."

"All games are really the same thing," Juh said. "Aren't they?"

Juh knew that the place called Washington was somewhere far to the east—how far, he had no idea. On the other hand, he had seen money—pesos, dollars—and the notion was not entirely foreign to him of it changing hands in return for something real. It was, he realized, like a language. If an Apache wanted to talk with a white man and neither understood each other's language, a Mexican could translate the Apache words into Spanish, and the white man, knowing that language, would understand.

Tom Jeffords—Red Beard—had tried to explain all this. He had also tried to describe Washington, but there was nothing in Juh's experience to which he could refer the idea of a legislature, or a treasury. The American leader, the President, a man called Arthur, lived in a white house and did what a legislature told him to do. Soon another man named Cleveland would live in the white house and be President. It wasn't clear to Juh exactly who the leader was, or how many there were. But as vague and unseeable as these things were in his mind, he understood whom the game was being played against and what the opponent believed the stakes were. The soldiers and the ranchers and miners who were massed in the Apache's ancient lands were just the markers.

The meeting was held not in the White House but across the street in the Blair Mansion, in an enormous room that had served at one time as a ballroom. Above, a gilt cornice set off the ornately wallpapered walls from the ceiling, from which three spectacular lead crystal chandeliers hung, dazzling in their own candlelight like a trio of starlit firmaments. A mahogany table thirty feet in length took up about half the room's floor space, and around it, in matching Hepplewhite chairs, sat twelve of the most influential men in the United States House of Representatives and the United States Senate:

President Chester A. Arthur, three members of his cabinet, and three elaborately uniformed generals of the United States Army, including Philip Sheridan, a man with features as fierce as his reputation and short gray hair that never seemed to have learned to obey orders.

Sheridan was profoundly uncomfortable. His discomfort was not because he was especially in awe of this company of men, none of whom he considered to be his equal in matters that counted. He was uncomfortable because he suffered fools lightly and a man he believed to be one of the greatest fools ever born of a woman's loins was now holding forth with his usual orotund hypocrisy. Sheridan believed he could stand no more of it.

". . . and furthermore," the senior senator from South Carolina was saying, "we are required by the faith vouchsafed us by the American people, the sacred trust of the people themselves—this trust demands that we weigh carefully the value of the lives that have already been lost and those that will be lost in this endeavor. We must weigh them, too, against what might be gained. These are *American* lives, gentlemen, the lives of young men, our finest flower—"

"Senator," Sheridan interrupted in a voice like the crack of a rifle. Fingers fluttered and throats rumbled with phlegm at this rudeness. "I understand that what we are discussing here is more than a military question. And I will speak only to its military aspect, which you have just raised. First, the soldiers engaged in this particularly difficult war are proud to do their duty, and in doing it, they compute the value of their contribution and even of their lives in the coinage of professional honor. Secondly, about a third of them, and the ones who have seen the most combat against the Apaches during the past three years and more, are from the Ninth and Tenth Cavalry. They are what you, Senator, refer to as 'nigras.' I happen to know that you don't give a damn for the life of such people, so please spare us what I can only consider the most transparent hypocrisy. No, Senator. Please sit down. I *will* finish.

"The bare *military* facts are easily summarized. In the last outbreak—an unprecedented, concentrated outbreak of seven separate bands all at once—the Apaches lost five men. The United States Army lost seventy-five, and altogether forty civilians were killed, chiefly at the village of Mesilla."

The senator from South Carolina was looking at Sheridan with undisguised detestation.

"So what you are saying, *General*," the senator said, "is that these Apache savages are fifteen times better fighting men than yours."

"No, Senator, that is not what I am saying. I am saying that we have eight thousand troops in the area now, and I believe it will take even more to put an end to these savages. They are fighting a new kind of war."

"Maybe if you put more of your reliance on white—"

"Senator, you may not—"

"Gentlemen," the President interjected. "Gentlemen. May we put our own sectional rivalries behind us? Along with the past? Let me remind you that all of us here in this room are from east of the Mississippi. We have that in common, eh? And all of the states east of the Mississippi have somewhat different needs than our countrymen in the territories of New Mexico and Arizona. It is these needs we must weigh, as always keeping in mind that the federal treasury is not a fund without limits."

President Arthur sat back and crossed his hands over his chest. He frowned, not so much at the gravity of what he had said but because his back ached, thanks to his ailing kidneys.

"Sir," the senator from Illinois said. He was a man known to speak bluntly, which he considered a Lincolnesque trait. "Are you suggesting that the territories be abandoned to these savages?"

"Of course not," the President said. "But we need to evaluate the worth of some of the territory at issue—what I believe are six really quite thinly populated counties—against what will be required to civilize them."

"Ridding ourselves of the Apaches and civilizing the other

people out there are two different tasks altogether," the Secretary of War said to a round of guffaws.

"The howls from my western colleagues—" began the senator from Illinois.

"How many are there now, Percy? A handful, all of whom owe us in the East a great many favors," the President said.

"What about your successor, Mr. President?" asked the senator from Illinois. "After all, in three months—"

"Yes, in three months I will be a private citizen, quickly fading into what you Democrats believe to be a well-deserved obscurity . . ." Arthur paused until the ripple of laughter died down.

"In fact, I have discussed this with Mr. Cleveland, along with other matters, of course. I have a letter here from him on just this topic." He fished a paper from his waistcoat pocket and unfolded it, placing a pair of gold-rimmed spectacles on his nose.

"I quote: '. . . and if your administration and the generals of the military conclude that this game is not worth the candle, and if the distinguished leaders of both houses of the Congress are similarly disposed, I would, as an incoming executive, not find it appropriate to express any opposition.' "

The President folded the letter and held it in his hand.

"Mr. Cleveland had a most extraordinary experience there only last week. In Tombstone. You have all heard about it, I imagine. I wouldn't be so pusillanimous as to say that it colored his thinking, but you gentlemen are all no doubt aware of Mr. Cleveland's opinions about the value of silver."

"So, you are saying . . . ?"

"I am saying that this is a matter we should all think about with great seriousness. I would appreciate it if you would let me know your thoughts in, shall we say a week's time? Now, gentlemen, let's adjourn. I'm sure none of you wish to be missing when they put the capstone on the Washington Monument this morning."

The President flipped open the letter again and let his eyes rest on the final paragraph, one that articulated a sentiment he had chosen not to recite to the assembled leaders. In it, President-elect Grover Cleveland expressed his expectation, were the Apache matter to be resolved prior to his taking office, to provide his fellow New Yorker and honored political rival with a lifetime appointment to the board of any one of three important and well-paying federal commissions located in the city of New York.

If he'd waited a day more, Joe Bignon might well have shaken the hand of the next President of the United States. That august figure had spent his last evening in Tombstone at the Bird Cage Theatre, admiring the swaying frame if not the singing voice of Big Minnie Bignon, who had to perform on stage three times that night. This was because of the last minute cancellation by Angelique Pettifleur, the "French Queen of Balladry," who, while not precisely a Frenchwoman, was no fool and wasn't about to place herself and her entourage of two slender young men into any danger of being massacred by Apaches suddenly on the rampage. So Big Minnie was the sole act that night, and later, upstairs in her voluminous bed above the stage, she literally charmed the pants off the President-elect.

Joe Bignon would no doubt have considered this an excellent move had he been in town, but, with much the same reasoning that had persuaded the French Queen of Balladry to proceed no farther into Apache country than Tucson, he had himself left town, left the Bird Cage Theatre, and left his wife of seven years, Big Minnie. Joe had been listening to old Apache hands, sitting drunk at his tables in their blue uniforms, discussing the fine carving techniques of Apache women, and Joe, given to vivid nightmares, couldn't take it anymore, not when he heard that Geronimo was out again and some other Apache savages were on the warpath. Without so much as a word to anyone, but with a satchel of cash and a change of clothes, Joe Bignon slipped out of town on a stagecoach headed for Tucson and was never seen or heard from again in Tombstone or any other place in the territories.

It was not Joe's departure itself that put Minnie in a mood to exact her own pound of flesh, but the discovery that he had run off with the family cash—in all, some twelve thousand dollars. So Minnie let the word go forth that Joe had gone back to St. Louis to care for his mother who was dying from the very same venereal afflictions that had evidently at birth rendered her only son as impotent as a dishrag his whole life.

But, in the days before Christmas of 1884, Big Minnie was despondent. Replacing the cash the little rodent had run off with looked like an impossibility. People were not coming to Tombstone. More specifically, people were not spending money in the Bird Cage Theatre. Joe had not been the only one to leave now that the entire territory was waiting with dread for the next assault by the Apaches, who, it was clear, were fighting a wholly different sort of war.

In spite of the infantry patrols through the streets of Tombstone, the citizens of the town did not feel safe, never mind that the last time the Apaches had attacked a town anywhere near the size of Tombstone had been over a century ago. The troops living among them looked pretty green, and all the second-guessers had reduced the chances of Nelson Miles accomplishing anything worthwhile to nearly zero. To make matters worse, two of the mines had flooded again when the pumps froze up and broke, and one of the companies concluded that it was not worth fixing them. The laid-off miners chose not to hang around waiting for work and drinking up their nest eggs, but instead went searching for a steadier life somewhere else, where at least the damned savages had all been wiped out. But even without the renewed Apache threat, it looked like Tombstone's heyday was past.

Big Minnie helped herself to three fingers of whiskey at the bar and sat down at a table. It was four o'clock in the afternoon and the place was empty. Outside, a thin snow had begun to fall into the muddy street and she heard the clump of boots on the wooden sidewalk. She looked up as the doors swung open, expecting to see the pair of peach-fuzzy privates who were on patrol, but her eyes brightened appreciably when she saw that it was Tom Jeffords stomping the mud off his boots in the doorway. A smile crept over her girlish face. Jeffords shucked his long duster, looked around the place quickly, and sat down.

"Hey, Minnie. These winters seem to be gettin' colder every damn year. What d'you hear?" From a pocket in his leather vest he took out two crisply folded bills and placed them on the table.

"I don't hear much of anything, Tom. These little boys they got patrolling town don't know anything, and the officers . . . prissier than schoolmarms. Tombstone's dyin'. You can almost hear the death rattle." She pushed the two bills back across the table. "I can't take this."

"I heard Joe left."

Minnie's face clouded over in a pout. "The little runt ran off with our nest egg. Scared of the Apaches, I reckon. Good riddance." She smiled. "Now we can get married like you always wanted."

"I'm beyond all that, Minnie."

"You could let me be the judge of that," she said cheerfully, but her baby blue eyes were not smiling, and her round rosy cheeks were a bit pale under their light coating of rouge. "Tom, what's going to happen?" She reached out and took one of his hands in hers. "People are leavin' town like there was the plague. There's only three saloons still in business, and I'm one of 'em, and you look around—there's no one here, there's no one next door. All the French whores've left, said they was gonna open up a say-lon in Leadville, Colorado . . ."

Tom Jeffords stood up and picked up the two bills from the table. He reached over and tucked them down into Minnie's bosom.

"If I was you, I'd wait awhile," he said. "What with everybody leavin.' "

"Wait for what?"

"From what I hear, the town's gonna need a mayor."

"What, has that overweight tinhorn Fitzhugh run off too?"

"Not yet," Jeffords said, and turned to go, plucking his

duster up with one finger from the back of his chair. "Merry Christmas, Minnie."

Minnie shook her head, confused, and watched the tall man leave, tears in her eyes. She'd forgotten it would soon be Christmas. She'd be alone for Christmas. She'd wake up Christmas morning and there wouldn't be anyone there, any presents to open, and she'd surely feel sick to her stomach just like she had every morning for the past week . . . She'd heard all about morning sickness. She wouldn't be completely alone, would she?

It looked like after all those years of Joe Bignon shooting blanks and of Big Minnie taking a few prudent precautions on other occasions, she had gone and got herself pregnant. And by none other than the next President of the United States.

Not that anyone would ever believe that.

∽ ∾

Twelve

In a second meeting in the Blair Mansion across the street from the White House two days after Christmas, 1884, a decision of state was made—secretly for the moment and on almost purely pecuniary terms. The men assembled there under the three grand chandeliers of lead crystal concluded that the $45 million already spent was enough to persuade any critic, including future historians, that the United States had made every effort possible. They concluded as well that the estimated ten million more that would be needed was simply too much to ask, never mind the additional cost in human casualties.

Additionally, they concluded that while Mexico might well object, it had no say in the manner by which the United States disposed of land it had acquired from Mexico four decades earlier in a transfer ratified by both sides in the Treaty of Guadalupe Hidalgo.

All things considered, they concluded with satisfaction that it was well within the national interest to lop off some five thousand square miles of mostly useless wasteland in southern Arizona and New Mexico and deed it to the Apaches to do with what they wished.

Of course, there would be conditions. For one, the Apaches would have to agree that existing railroads would continue to enjoy safe passage through the Apache lands. For another, existing mining interests would be able to negotiate royalty terms to extend over a period of, say, thirty years of continued mineral extraction.

The Apaches would have to permit safe passage out of the area of any settlers who wished to leave. Each such settler would receive, oh, say, $250 as a resettlement fee from a generous United States government. Most important, the Apaches would have to relinquish forever any claim on any other lands in the United States over which they might once have roamed, and agree to stay put within the new boundaries. Their lives would be carried out henceforth and in perpetuity without any further call on the resources of the United States. They would, in reality, be their own principality, their own nation.

These principles having been found agreeable to the men at Blair House, a thick black line was drawn on a map of the region by President Chester A. Arthur himself. Once all of the assembled had nodded in approval, he presented the map to the Secretary of War and instructed him to put it and the terms it embodied as expeditiously as possible into the hands of whomever was the responsible leader of the Apaches and see to it that they agreed. Congressional ratification, the President said to the accompaniment of unanimous nodding, would be swift.

Two days into the new year of 1885, three men on horse-back—followed by a train of four mules—crossed the border into Mexico and proceeded on their way to the Sierra Madre Mountains. Two of the men were Apaches, chosen from among the few remaining scouts because, in the complicated way of Apache kinship, they were cousins of some kind to Geronimo. The third horseman was a young lieutenant named Charles Gatewood, who had served under General Crook and had evidently gotten along well with the Apaches at the San Carlos reservation.

General Miles had assigned Lieutenant Gatewood to carry out the details of what Miles considered the greatest travesty of national honor he could ever have imagined. The news that the land he had been charged with liberating was to be, instead, ceded to the savages—*surrendered*—struck an insuperable blow to Miles's ambitions. How could anyone who was the general in charge of a *loss* of United States territory ever expect to be elected President? By choosing Gatewood, Miles sought to put as much distance as possible between all this and himself, rather like a man asked to remove another man's urine bottle from a sickroom.

It was only later that infuriated hard-liners in the territories, including the editor of the Tombstone newspaper in his last fulmination, would see a biblical parallel for Miles and tag him, however unfairly but for the rest of his life, as the Pontius Pilate of Arizona.

As the three horsemen began to wind their way up into the Sierra Madres, they were closely observed, deemed harmless, and finally approached. They made it clear that they had a proposition for Geronimo, and within an hour they were seated in the shaded bottom of a dry streambed of flat red rimrock high up in the crags, in the presence of Geronimo and several others whom the grim-faced warrior introduced as Mangas, Naiche, and Victorio. There was another warrior, a large man whom Geronimo did not bother to introduce, who sat slightly apart from the others and reminded Gatewood, for some reason, of a brooding gargoyle. Above them the banks of the streambed were lined with Apaches standing with their rifles held ready.

Juh listened without expression or apparent interest to the elaborate courtesies the two sides exchanged, and only once looked over at the young officer—when he said the President of the United States had asked him to bring this new, generous, and final peace proposal to the Apaches. And Juh remained still and remote even as his heart began to pound furiously in his breast while what the President had to say began to unfold.

As the officer's recitation went on, Geronimo, Naiche, and the others occasionally glanced over toward Juh, their eyes gleaming, burning. It was dawning on these men that they had won.

Won.

It occurred to them that they were sitting in the presence of an Apache they had all known for years, the one to whom they had given their respect, yes, and the one Apache warrior, among all the others in three hundred years of conflict, who had produced victory: who had won freedom for the Apaches, freedom to roam and hunt on their own land, to come and go as they pleased.

Juh.

Juh, whose name meant "He-who-sees-ahead."

When Gatewood pulled a map from his saddlebag, unfolding it and putting it on the ground before Geronimo, Juh signaled with his hand—the first time he had moved during the entire colloquy—and a warrior on the bank above disappeared.

Moments later the men in the streambed looked up as a few stones rolled down onto the rimrock and a tall rangy man with gray hairs streaking his unruly red beard began the descent.

"You're Charlie Gatewood, aren't you?" the man said. "You were with Crook. I'm Jeffords, Tom Jeffords. Agent with these folks a bit before your time. My friends here aren't all that familiar with the nature of maps. They asked me to look this over for them."

Jeffords reached the streambed and stood before the young officer. He stuck a big hand covered with liver spots out. Gatewood rose and shook it.

"Not that these people have any reason to mistrust you," Jeffords added wryly. "Well, now, let's have a look." The two men sat dawn. "This black line here—this is what you propose for an Apache nation? Wait a moment, wait a moment." Jeffords turned away.

"Before we get to settling all this, I think you'll want to make the acquaintance of another of my friends here. Lieutenant, this here is Juh. He's what you might think of as the Apaches' Gen'l George Washington . . ."

The talks went on well into the night, the men adjourning with the onset of dark to conclude the parley around a fire that burned high in the middle of Juh's camp, the first time in months that an Apache fire had been visible in the mountains.

Sometime after midnight, the fire still burning, Tom Jeffords guided Juh's hand as he wrote his name on the map and on the bottom of the sheet of paper which, Jeffords assured him, said what Gatewood claimed it said.

And thus, on January 3, 1885, to the sound of a drum in the thin mountain air, the independent nation that would soon be known as Apacheria was born.

In the firelight, the Apaches danced until dawn, joined by eight fierce-looking figures with faceless black heads that emerged from the surrounding dark—the Mountain Gods, come to dance, undulating in the firelight, to seal the victory, to ratify the glorious destiny of the Apaches, and to bring the blessings of Ussen.

By dawn the Mountain Gods had receded to the heights, the fire was allowed to die down, and the Apaches, having greeted the sun, went off to sleep.

In his lodge, Juh lay on his back beside his wife, Ishton. She lay on her side, a hand on his thick chest, watching him with her black eyes. Behind her, in his cradleboard, their son slept.

"It's over." Ishton sighed. "Now you can rest."

"Rest?"

"You can sleep."

Juh's smile, so rarely seen, was like a small sun in the shadows of the lodge.

"For a while," he said. "For a short while we can sleep."

He glanced over at Ishton, who looked puzzled.

"My father told me," Juh said, "after a victory it is time to sharpen your knife."

And Juh, the one who sees ahead, closed his eyes.

BOOK TWO

⤳ ⤳

The Apache Nation

The whore and gambler, by the state
Licensed, build that nation's fate.
—William Blake

Thirteen

AUTUMN 1894

An hour after sunrise a party of Apaches eighty strong set forth on horseback through the San Luis Pass. They were armed only with bows and arrows, and all were dressed in traditional moccasins and breechcloths—all but the ten women among them, who wore buckskin shirts decorated with beaded latticework that gleamed gaily in the early morning sunlight. No one spoke.

Ahead of them was a gradual two-mile descent through sagebrush, the occasional cactus, and scattered clumps of bear grass whose long fronds, clattering lightly together in the morning breeze, would later in the year be plucked by the women to be made into brooms.

Beyond lay an enormous gold prairie. Early autumn blossoms of goldeneye, now concealing the blades and seed heads of the other grasses, stretched westward for miles to lavender mountains—the Peloncillos and, more distantly, the Chiricahuas—far enough away and low enough on the horizon to seem tame under the mountainous white clouds that rode above them in the vast blue crystal of the sky.

Among the large band of Apaches were several youths, one of whom was mounted on a mare sired by a gigantic black stallion which for two years had borne none other than Colonel Edward Hatch of the Ninth United States Cavalry, and which had been stolen out from under him in the last raid in the last Indian war by Lozen, the Warrior Woman.

Lozen was astride that stallion now, riding beside the youth on the stallion's daughter. The youth, dressed like all the men in the party, was tall for his age and lithe, not yet into the period of rapid growth where he would become disjointed, even clumsy. This was Little Spring, the son of Juh, in his tenth year and the final days of his annual stay among the Warm Springs people in the eastern realms of the nation of Apacheria.

Wordlessly, Lozen pointed to a place ahead of them, and Little Spring spotted the small round depression an antelope had pawed into the ground among the withering grasses, depositing a dozen dark pellets. The youth's stomach fluttered with nervous excitement. He looked over at Lozen, who smiled at him. It was a dazzling smile, transforming a face that in repose still retained the fierceness of her warrior days—high cheekbones forming a ledge under widely spaced obsidian eyes and heavy dark eyebrows. No longer did Lozen wear her hair in the manner of the warrior; instead it was pulled back from her face and held by a beaded barrette behind her head, streaming down from there in a shiny black tail that reached nearly to her waist.

Aside from his mother, Lozen was the most beautiful woman Little Spring had ever seen, and the sight of her, these days, had begun to fill Little Spring with an uncomfortable and wholly incomprehensible yearning. She rode beside him, her back straight, her eyes glinting with the gold of the prairie they were entering, her coppery knee and leg riding lightly against the stallion's black flank as eighty horses picked up the pace, breaking into a slow trot. Keeping Lozen in the periphery of his vision, Little Spring stared ahead and matched her gait.

For as long as Little Spring could recall, Lozen had been his companion in the summers, his teacher and goad. "Your greatest allies," she had been telling him since before he could remember, "are not your people, not your family, not me, but your legs." Always she had challenged him, urging him to run farther, faster, to keep up with her, to outdistance her, and at the end to spit out his mouthful of water and wait ever longer before drinking. She had taught him to ride, to cling to a horse with his legs, to shoot an arrow at full gallop, to leap from a racing horse and hit the ground in a somersault, coming to his feet in a crouch exactly on a spot marked earlier.

Little Spring was a good pupil in the arts and skills of the warrior and the hunter, and no one thought it strange that he was taught each summer by a woman when it was traditionally one's uncles from whom one learned such things. For it was Lozen, as able as any male warrior when she was young, who had also crafted Little Spring's cradleboard when he was only days old, thus becoming his spiritual parent. To be taken in hand in so many things by so powerful a being as Lozen— Lozen, sister of the great Victorio; Lozen, who had never been bested, even blooded, in battle, who could see a distant enemy, who it was said could reach into the world of the spirits—to have such a teacher conferred upon the son of Juh the highest of expectations.

And so each summer, Little Spring had grown stronger, faster, more able, more accurate. He knew in his muscles the feeling of perfect motion; he could guide a horse or an arrow without thought—only intention. He could see the passing of an animal or a man in the bending of a grass blade. He knew with his back and arms how to wrench a sapling from the earth, knew how to run without a sound, to disappear, to catch a squirrel without a weapon, to skin a deer. He knew the exhilaration of being free under the immense sky, free to roam, to dream.

And now, at the end of this season among Victorio's people, he had been asked to join the hunt.

Far off to the north, some two miles away, the Apaches saw the herd of antelope—perhaps a hundred of them in several bunches, grazing on the sage that was sprinkled here and there among the golden flowers a half mile from the flanks of the Animas Mountains. Without any signal, the Apaches began to lope out onto the prairie, forming two lines, one line a half mile behind the other. In minutes the lines extended a mile out, some fifty yards between each horseman. Little Spring and

Lozen were among those on the far western flank in the forward line, and they began to move toward the antelope herd in a lope that soon merged into a gallop and then a breakneck race across the golden land. The antelope looked up, startled, and began a chaotic dance, racing back and forth, heading away from the advancing horses only when it was too late. The two wings of the Apache lines swung ahead of the herd and closed in toward each other, the antelope leaping and running in erratic circles. The ring of horsemen tightened, and Little Spring's heart pounded in his throat at the sight of the antelope, a maelstrom of tawny plunging . . . black horns and gaping eye whites, rump patches of white leaping, high-pitched whistles—*whiieeuuuuu*—from the terrified creatures, and the staccato thunder of horses' hooves on either side of him.

Arrows like hornets seared into the plunging, sunlit mass, his own arrow streaking toward a white-striped chest, embedded, the antelope falling in a cloud of dust, another streaking toward him, panicking, black-pronged horns blurring past in a twenty-foot leap, animals falling, bewildered, more of them coming his way, racing past, leaping, an arrow flying off, his arrow, and an antelope diving into the gold, flopping over, more flying past . . .

Then only dust and carcasses in the golden yellow, the tang of blood, horses snorting, his own wheeling under him now in the excitement, and Lozen's black stallion rearing, Lozen's grin shining white and triumphant through the dust on her face, and Little Spring feeling himself grinning back.

All around, the Apaches whooped in delight, and overhead, so soon, so quick of eye, two vultures were gyring up into the blue, silently summoning the others as they always had, since long before memory.

Little Spring's eyes followed the circles of the vultures, watched a third materialize in the sky like a mote in one's vision, and he imagined himself soaring with them, when his horse lurched with a great impact, plunging sideways and down, the ground coming up, horse neck rearing up under his hand, down, spinning. Little Spring launched himself to the side and away, hitting the ground on his side, a sharp pain slicing deep into his pelvis. He scrambled to his feet, the pain stabbing down the length of his leg, and saw his horse standing a few yards off, legs splayed apart, staring at him with eyes white and wild. Little Spring turned, crouching, and a horseman was silhouetted above him, black in the glaring sun. In the silhouetted face he could see two eyes glinting, one of them awry.

Victorio.

The great Victorio, looking down at him with . . . what in his eyes? Derision?

"You dream too much, boy," Victorio said in a voice that rasped like the sound of women grinding dried corn on a stone. "The vultures teach you nothing except to claim your kill quickly. Keep your eyes to the ground or you will fall off the earth."

Little Spring, hip throbbing with pain, pride crushed by falling from his horse before so many, and his mind swirling with confusion, said nothing. An Apache, he knew and had known for years, never complains. He couldn't imagine what Victorio, who had now ridden off, was talking about, and he felt hatred for the man rising in his throat. He turned to his horse, which was snuffling among the yellow flowers for grass, and clicked with his tongue twice. The mare looked up and walked toward him, trailing her rope lead. Together they walked to the antelope Little Spring had brought down, the second of two kills on this day of his first major hunt, and he wondered if he were strong enough to heft the carcass up onto his horse's back.

He glanced up as Lozen approached, high on the black stallion, and gritted his teeth to disguise the pain he felt.

"The eagle doesn't hunt flies," Lozen said in a quiet voice, leaving the youth all the more bewildered. He wondered if he would ever understand adults. Ignoring the pain in his hip, he leaned down, grasping a pronged horn in one hand and a fistful of loose skin and fur with the other. In a burst of fury he hoisted the carcass that weighed as much or more than he, swung it backward, and hurled it up onto the horse's back. Without a look behind him, he led the horse toward his other kill, spine straight as a rifle barrel, head high in defiance—though defiance of exactly what he didn't yet know.

From the Peloncillos north into the grander and more rugged wilderness of the Gila Mountains, Victorio's vision had held sway over Apache hearts for ten years since the great and sudden triumph over the White Eyes. Here in the eastern lands of Apacheria, the People lived again much as they always had before the arrival of the Americans. In these vast stretches of valley and mountain, the only reminder that the Americans and the surrounding United States existed was the presence in Silver City of the mines and the miners, who still groveled under the ground for silver and other metals, and shipped the ore out on the railroad.

The mines and the railroad paid tribute to the Apache nation for the right to continue this work, but the Apaches who lived in this part of the nation cared not at all for such considerations as tribute, money, or the trappings of the white man. They were happy only to be left to themselves, living the old Apache ways, arranging their lives around the turn of the seasons, gathering wild foods, hunting, moving into the cool mountains in summer, down on the warmer plains in winter. They were happy recounting stories of Apache origins and Apache triumphs around fires in the night, teaching the younger ones about the victories of the Twins against the Monsters who had ruled the world in earlier times, and those of the People against the despised Mexican invaders, and the grand triumph of Victorio and Juh against the Americans. And inviting the Mountain Gods to dance in their midst.

Elsewhere in Apacheria, in the nation's west, some Apaches were less given to the purity of the old ways. There, somewhat to the contempt of Victorio and others of like mind, they claimed to hold on to the old truths of Apache while living different lives, taking on some of the trappings of the white man. The mines at Tombstone had revived, some of them, at least, and two companies paid unimaginable sums to the Apache nation in return for taking the ore away and selling it in the United States. Cochise's son Naiche spent most of his time there, among the white people hired to keep the town open, and they had built a school. None of this meant much to the eastern Apaches, now so comfortable leading proper lives under the vast skies. They knew Ussen shined mostly on them, and they thought rarely about their fellows to the west.

Of course, Victorio and his followers had not forsworn *all* the trappings of the white men who had for so long been in their midst. Each Apache man had at least one rifle among his possessions, and they were all free to obtain ammunition from the tribal stores of such things. There they could also obtain the white man's tobacco, and the young braves had no trouble putting their hands on bootleg whiskey when they found the old corn-based tiswin too tame.

And all of this, of course, could sometimes combine with a certain nostalgia and produce an old-fashioned raiding party that would slip undetected into Mexico. There, under cover of darkness, the braves would practice the ancient Apache art of stealth and rustle some cattle or horses from the contemptible Mexican ranchers. Over the years, as well, it seemed that Mexican nationals would occasionally and for reasons unknown undertake to cross over the border into Apacheria—perhaps, the Apaches shrugged, they were unaware it was no longer the United States—and wind up shot.

Added to this sport, the Apaches played their old games of ball, and raced in footraces and on horseback, and gambled mightily. It was a good life.

Now in his mid-sixties, Geronimo remained a vigorous if not athletic figure. His legs had bowed outward with age, giving an exaggerated sideways roll to his gait, and his hair—still worn in Apache style, cut off at the shoulder with bangs hanging an inch down over his forehead—was streaked with coarse gray. Time had etched yet further canyons into his face, rendering it all the more fierce-looking at times, but a decade without war had also etched something new into his visage: the unmistakable lines around the eyes of a humorous view of the world. The ferocity of youth and adulthood had given way to Geronimo's natural craftiness, and this now served him in especially good stead in his position as Apacheria's ambassador to the United States government in Washington, D.C.

The old warrior cut an exotic figure in the ornate drawing rooms of the national capital, where, he had found, he was most effectively deployed. In public he was never seen without the Apache warrior's red headband, a soft buckskin shirt bedecked with turquoise fetishes around the neck, and knee-high moccasins. His one sartorial bow to civilization was to wear a pair of loose-fitting white trousers that he kept tucked into his moccasins, and on state occasions he wore, over these trousers, the traditional Apache breechcloth.

The women of Washington's rather desultory social whirl were especially taken with Geronimo. He provided the tingle of knowing a savage who had massacred hundreds—once the most feared and dangerous man in the country—with the comfort of knowing the old boy was now tame as a lapdog. Also, Geronimo had an eye for ladies, particularly older ones, and much to their delicious amusement openly teased them about matters their own late-Victorian society had long since discouraged them from contemplating. No bosom, however properly layered over with high-necked lace or silk, went unogled.

Geronimo had arrived in Washington in 1889 a month after President Grover Cleveland handed over his office to Benjamin Harrison, and it had not taken the old warrior long to determine where the power lay. The so-called Great White Father—the President—had far less to do with the great decisions of the country than the large group of men in Congress. Congress remained pretty much the same year in and year out even though some of its members disappeared once they lost the respect of their own people—for reasons Geronimo could never fathom. The President, it seemed pretty clear even in so confusing a world as that of Washington, could do nothing of any importance without the approval of Congress.

The men in Congress were for the most part preoccupied with matters that had little to do with the fortunes of the new nation of Apacheria, and were too busy to spend much time with Geronimo. The old warrior also thought they were mostly too stuffy to be seen with a savage, and, of course, those congressmen from the western states still detested Geronimo for all the depredations he and all his Indian ilk had perpetrated on the frontier.

In any event, he soon fastened onto Washington's women, and congressional wives in particular, as his best source of information. And information—any hint of a changing attitude on the part of the White Eyes to Apacheria—was what he was charged with finding out. But with the coming of Grover Cleveland's second term beginning in 1893, Geronimo discovered he had a friend indeed in the White House.

President Cleveland prided himself on shooting straight in matters of politics and government, and as a result had offended most of his own party, the Democrats, on numerous occasions—and without gaining any favor among Republicans. It suited this rebellious streak in the man to present himself as a friend of Geronimo. With an arm around the savage's shoulders, he would stand at a reception in the White House and regale those present with the dramatic tale of his rescue from a horde of stage-robbing bandits by Geronimo and his renegades. European ambassadors and their entourages particularly loved to hear of such derring-do, but representatives of the western states deplored these moments. The two men came to enjoy each other's company, finding much in common, including the enjoyment of Irish whiskey.

One evening in the early autumn of 1894, Cleveland summoned Geronimo to his office in the White House, greeting him with a serious look on his face. The President's wide-set light eyes looked troubled. He poured Geronimo a glass of Irish whiskey and one for himself, and gestured to an overstuffed sofa into which Geronimo promptly sank.

"I had a visit today," the President began, "from that awful man de Vargas. The Mexican ambassador. The man's a ridiculous peacock, always taking offense at imagined slights, but today he ruffled his tail feathers with unusual ferocity . . . and some justification."

Geronimo's eyes smiled mischievously at the image. He put his hands under his armpits and flapped them, making a soft bugling sound. "That man de Vargas, he was a soldier. Led some Mexicans against Loco and his people when they was runnin' away down there. That Captain Crawford, your man, he was chasin' Loco too, with his Apache scouts. They all come together at one place down there and de Vargas and all them Mexicans began to shoot all of your Apache scouts. While that was goin' on, Loco, he just went on up in the mountains and laughed."

Geronimo had a long, lubricating swallow of his Irish whiskey. "I can tell you lots of stories about Mexicans, Cleelan. I bet I killed four, five hundred Mexicans."

"I don't want to hear about it," Cleveland said. "I've had a serious complaint from Mexico, never mind that the messenger is a popinjay."

Geronimo sipped again at the whiskey and sat quietly. He had seen peacocks in some of the fancier gardens in Washington, strutting around in their astonishing finery. He had, on several occasions, swiped some of the feathers and sent them back to his people. But a popinjay must be some eastern bird he hadn't heard of.

"Apparently some of your people have been raiding again," the President continued. "In Mexico. The Mexican government has asked me to use the influence of the United States government to see to it that it is stopped."

Geronimo sat back in the sofa. "You know those stories about Mexicans comin' over into Apacheria, how they ended up gettin' shot?"

The President nodded.

"It don't happen anymore. Mexicans stay real far away nowadays. Even *banditos*. Some of Victorio's people, they still like the old ways, sometimes the young ones go over the border"—Geronimo held up a gnarled hand and put the tips of his thumb and forefinger an eighth of an inch apart—"just a little ways. Scare 'em." He giggled.

"That's exactly what de Vargas is complaining about."

"We don't have any Mexicans crossin' over anymore. But you do, Cleelan. Over around El Paso, them places. Smugglers, *banditos*. Maybe the U.S. should hire us Apaches. Scare the shit out of 'em for a while."

"Geronimo!"

"Sorry. Manure. Droppings." Geronimo giggled again. "Peacock droppings."

President Cleveland allowed himself to laugh, a peculiar barking sound. "I'll think about it. Quite a compelling idea—an Apache border patrol. And what should I tell the peacock, Geronimo, to keep his tail feathers in place?"

Geronimo, feeling the buzz brought on by the President's whiskey and looking forward to more, said, "Tell him he should come see me sometime. Tell him I won't hurt him any. We can sign a treaty. All us Indians love treaties." The old Apache's thin lips pulled back in a wondrously predatory grin.

Cleveland smiled. "You will take care of it, won't you, old friend?"

Geronimo nodded. The old warrior knew that while the Apaches had won their independence from the giant that was the United States, they were not outside its shadow. There was no point in offending the Americans . . . unless it was a matter of necessity. Victorio and his people had their eyes on living the old ways, never mind what was going on elsewhere around them. Maybe . . . maybe it could be done, but how long could anyone ignore the rest of the world where things were always changing?

Geronimo had visited the great golden-domed building of the Smithsonian, where they kept stuffed animals and old artifacts, and full-size figurines dressed in Indian costumes. Maybe Victorio would turn into that—a museum exhibit, a living exhibit for people to come and stare at.

But such a life was not for Geronimo. More than any of

his tribesmen, perhaps, he knew the outside world, knew that one could be an Apache, truly Apache, and still take what one wanted from the white man's world.

Juh knew this too. Geronimo knew he would have to talk to him about Victorio and the trouble he was becoming. Juh would take care of it.

Geronimo nodded again as President Cleveland filled their drinks.

"I'll talk to Juh. Goin' back there next month."

Fourteen

Of all her accomplishments as the mayor of Tombstone, Big Minnie Bignon was proudest of the school she had started in the two-story white clapboard house on Sixth Street that the French whores had abandoned just a few weeks before Independence nearly ten years ago in 1885.

With life stirring in her womb—or, if it wasn't exactly stirring yet, it was making her pretty sick every morning—she had found herself preoccupied with matters that had never much impinged on her mind. Mainly, she didn't want this precious child growing in her to grow up as she had—meaning mostly uneducated except by harsh experience in raw frontier towns. She wanted there to be a proper school up and running, with all the kinks worked out, by the time this child of hers was ready. Big Minnie had learned to read and write, of course, but for the rest she was self-taught, and she wanted more than that—a lot more than that—for this child who was, after all, the offspring of the President of the United States. So, a fine school was already on Big Minnie's list of priorities when Tom Jeffords showed up on a cold and overcast afternoon a few days into 1885 with an Apache named Naiche in tow.

Naiche was the first Apache that Big Minnie had ever seen close up. In those old days, the savages didn't come into town much, and when they did, they lurked around the outskirts, looking uncomfortable, trading things. But then into the Bird Cage Theatre walked Naiche with his red headband, a deerskin shirt and leggings, and those moccasins high on his legs. He was about five-ten, almost as tall as Big Minnie, and he had

153

long, shiny black hair that glistened. She watched in fascination as a few flakes of snow evaporated from his hair, and she was reminded of how stars fade in the dawn sky. He had a typical Apache face, high cheekbones and those black eyes in triangular slits, and while Big Minnie knew he must be uncomfortable standing there in the Bird Cage Theatre, he exuded an unmistakable pride, like that of a stag elk or a mountain lion. And while he looked as fierce as anyone could imagine one of these savages, there was something in his expression—a sadness, a fineness . . . Big Minnie couldn't put her finger on it.

But Big Minnie was shocked by the fact that she knew, and freely admitted to herself, that this Apache was the most magnificent man she had ever laid eyes on. Suddenly having trouble breathing, she smiled her prettiest, most girlish smile at the Indian and looked politely away, having heard that if you stare at a savage, he thinks you're either angry or trying to insult him.

What Minnie didn't know at the time, couldn't have known then and only found out a few weeks later, was that Naiche was equally stunned. Accustomed to the broad shoulders and narrow hips of classic Apache beauty, a beauty tempered by the athletic exigencies of war and always chastely enveloped in deerskin, Naiche had never seen anything like Big Minnie. Everything about her bespoke softness, lushness, to this battle-hardened warrior's eyes—the luxuriant bosom that seemed poised to escape from the shiny purple silk, the rounded hips, the pink mouth with its welcoming smile and protruding upper lip, the rounded cheeks . . .

In any event, matters proceeded so quickly that day that Minnie's head was left spinning. It seemed that Naiche was an emissary of sorts from the main Apache leader, Juh, but also more than an emissary. Naiche, she gathered, was in some way in charge of the western part of the new Apache country, maybe an overseer of sorts, and it was the intent of the Apache leaders that Tombstone continue on much as it had before.

Mining would continue, and all the other businesses. They would pay what Tom Jeffords explained was a royalty to the

Apaches and be subject to Apache law. Tombstone and, to a lesser extent, towns like Bisbee would remain mining centers and places where outsiders—that is, whites—could continue to work and visit and spend money. The hotels, the saloons and eating places, the whorehouses—everything would go on as before. The one thing that the Apache nation would not tolerate was banditry. The outlawry that had been a scourge to the region, largely beyond the control of the few United States marshals, the local sheriffs, and the army, was simply not to be tolerated. The law would be enforced by the Apache warriors, in the traditional manner.

But, Jeffords explained, the Apaches recognized that they knew nothing about how a white man's town worked. They required someone to run Tombstone for them, and Jeffords had brought Naiche to the Bird Cage Theatre so that he could meet Big Minnie and decide if he agreed with Jeffords that she would make a mighty fine mayor.

"Why not you?" Big Minnie asked, and Jeffords replied something about how he didn't have the knowledge to run a saloon much less a town, nor the patience to spend that much time with his fellow man. That was all true enough, but what they discovered six months later was that already, at the time of Apache independence, Jeffords was dying from some internal thing that was slowly eating him alive. When he did finally die, the Apaches fetched him from his ranch over near the Chiricahuas and took him to old Cochise's stronghold in the Dragoons. Apaches came from all around to honor him, and you could hear the wailing from a long way off, echoing through the mountains. It lasted for two days and nights, continuing well after a few men, including Juh himself, took Jeffords's body off into the rocks and left it in some secret place.

In any event, Naiche did approve of Big Minnie being appointed mayor of Tombstone—which he did just that very day. And Big Minnie was suddenly launched into a new life, one that suited her in every way. From the child growing within her she took a newly found, calm strength, a sense that anything she needed to accomplish, she could, and would. She became a whirlwind of executive energy. With a view of the life she wanted for her child, she ran a tight ship—always mindful, of course, that if it were a ship, it was designed as a pleasure cruiser.

She saw to it that the dirt streets were regularly cleared of horse droppings, the sidewalks kept spotless. She brought in an engineer she had read about from Cornell University back East and had him design an up-to-date water system for the town. She persuaded all but a few flowers of the night to join a cooperative savings plan that would provide each with a bit of a nest egg against the day that their petals faded, and had the local doctor provide them with regular and free medical attention in lieu of his paying any of his profits to the Apaches.

Tombstone began to look spiffy, and act spiffy, and the hospitality it afforded visitors soon became well known. People who had left or stayed away out of fear of the bloodthirsty and pitiless savages, soon began to return and spend money in the old freewheeling manner. Business thrived again. That the town and the lands around it were largely free of outlawry was part of its attraction: few places in that part of the world were.

In February 1885, just after Apache independence, a dozen bandits had thought to rob a stagecoach running between Bisbee and Tombstone. They were intercepted by a party of eager Apache warriors at about the place where Geronimo had earlier killed the bandits who attacked Grover Cleveland's stage. Those thieves who weren't shot off their horses on the spot were led off, on foot and trussed up like sides of beef, to a fate that was left to the public to imagine. The word got out that in place of lackluster sheriffs, disorganized posses, and corruptible judges, outlaws faced a new kind of justice, administered swiftly and without any hope of appeal by savages who considered simple hanging too fast a way for a miscreant to die, and furthermore, no fun for the executioners. Subsequently, few criminal incidents were reported in the area; robberies, rustling, and other forms of mayhem fell off to nearly zero within three years. The only violence in Tombstone itself was the uncontrollable sort that breaks out from time to time between men in saloons—the sort of excitement that Big Minnie thought added zest to life.

As for zest in her own life, Big Minnie soon had more than she'd bargained for. Before two weeks had passed after her appointment as mayor, she and Naiche recognized and managed to confess their still-astounding feelings for each other, and sealed what would turn out to be a lifelong mutual admiration with a joyous and memorable night cavorting in Big Minnie's plush bedroom one floor up above the stage at the Bird Cage Theatre. The next morning, Big Minnie discovered, much to her amusement, that a good deal of her upper body and her neck sported bright pink hickeys, administered there during the repeated heights of Apache-style passion, and she thenceforward took to wearing colorful silken scarves much like a trademark or badge of office.

Naiche's Apache wife, the dour Kozineh, who remained in Naiche's camp in the Chiricahua Mountains, was not at all put off by his liaison with Big Minnie. Polygamy was not infrequent, after all, among the Apaches, and this arrangement—wherein Big Minnie was never in Kozineh's way and kept Naiche occupied a good part of the time—suited her just fine.

On September 15 of the first year of Apache independence, Big Minnie gave birth to a son who weighed just a bit over nine pounds—the largest newborn the Tombstone sawbones had ever seen. A week later she drove the infant, all bundled up in an Indian blanket in a buckboard, out to Jeffords's ranch, where the old man lay dying in the care of an ancient Apache woman who was bent over like a hairpin and looked just as fragile.

Jeffords looked when he heard Minnie come in, looked from dimming, watery eyes at the baby, and said, "So this is the President's kid. Fine-looking boy, Minnie." His voice was little more than a whisper.

"You and I know about that, Tom, but the life this kid is gonna have here with me owes as much to you as it does to Grover Cleveland. So I named him Thomas Jeffords Cleveland

Bignon. I didn't ask your permission, I just did it. I hope you don't mind."

Jeffords, for whom talking was increasingly painful, merely beamed—a wide, long-lasting grin filling his gaunt face in a way that Minnie would never forget. He crooked a finger at the old Apache woman and mumbled something in her language.

She shuffled out, returning with an old, well-oiled holster on a dark leather gun belt. The holster held a shiny Colt .45 with a six-inch barrel. On the ivory panels on the handle someone with a steady hand had etched *TJ* in elaborate filigree script. The old woman handed the gun belt and holster to Minnie, and Jeffords, before he drifted off to sleep, gave Minnie a big wink.

Before many months had gone by after little Tom Jeffords Cleveland Bignon was born, Big Minnie began to visualize in her mind the kind of school she had in mind to found. Tombstone Academy was what she would name it, and by damn it would be the finest school south of Denver. She wanted it to be a school for Apache kids and white kids alike. There wouldn't be any of this nine-hours-a-day stuff with tiny little kids chained to the books by some overbearing prison guard of a schoolmarm, learning their boring lessons like a catechism.

She wanted little kids to spend most of their time playing, and in the process, learning each other's language, the way kids do so easily when they're little. And not just each other's language, but each other's ways. When they were about ten, that would be plenty of time to teach them how to read and write and figure, plenty of time for them to learn all those things like geometry and geography, which would get them ready to go on to college. She was sure that her boy Tom Jeffords Cleveland Bignon was destined to go on to a university, one of those places back East in the United States like Yale or Princeton, the best, and she didn't see any reason at all why there shouldn't be a bunch of Apache kids doing the same thing. They were going to have to live in two worlds, whether they liked it or not.

So Minnie did her planning and her figuring, and one night in January 1886 explained her idea to Naiche while the two of them were huddled together under a snow-white down comforter about a foot thick that Minnie had ordered from Switzerland. An icy breeze blew in the window overlooking Main Street, chilling the tips of their noses, which was about all of them that stuck out from the comforter and Minnie's pillows. Naiche was pleasantly nestled among the grand softnesses of Minnie's frame, but he listened carefully as she outlined her plan.

"I figure it'll take five thousand dollars of tribal funds to get started," she concluded, "and about twice that to run every year, once it's up and runnin'. What with the money comin' in from Tombstone nightlife alone, never mind all the mining royalties from here and Bisbee and that safe-passage money you savages extort from the railroad—hoo, I mean take for bein' helpful—this doesn't hardly seem like a drop in the bucket. What do you think? No, no, Naiche darlin', what do you think about my idea? None of that till you think about this, you hear?"

And so it came to pass that in the autumn of 1895, Juh's son Little Spring, now ten years old, returned from the wild prairies and mountains of eastern Apacheria to begin learning the three R's, an experience he looked forward to with less delight than killing two antelope from horseback with a hundred tribesmen, or overtaking Lozen after a daylong footrace. But he did look forward to spending time with his friend Big Ears.

Big Ears was the Apache name Naiche had given to Thomas Jeffords Cleveland Bignon, whom he had taken on in the manner of a stepson. Big Ears did have big ears, and also a streak of mischief in him that was wide as a river in spring flood, and the two boys laughed a lot when they were together, pulling pranks on the grown-ups, especially if they didn't get caught.

There is no impetus to vengeance more potent than moral outrage, and there is no sense of morality more acute—especially when it comes to fair dealings—than that of a ten- or eleven-year-old boy. A great deal of what is called adult behavior can strike a boy of that age as patently unfair, and no amount of explanation, no attempt to palm off an unfairness as a misunderstanding, will alter that perception or dampen the seething, and usually unfulfillable, desire for retribution. More often than not, it is only the notoriously short attention span of boys that keeps the peace.

It could well have been a misunderstanding, but it might as easily have been a case of breach of contract, a matter of downright chiseling on the part of Homer Nye, that led to what came to be known in Tombstone as the Sour Ball Fracas. Homer Nye ran a small and gloomy general store called Tombstone Sundries about two city blocks west of the string of whorehouses on Sixth Street, along with Nye's Stable next door, which, with six stalls, was the smallest of six stables in Tombstone proper. The westernmost of the whorehouses on Sixth Street was now, of course, the Tombstone Academy.

Homer Nye was a dour and homely man who kept pretty much to himself, his side of a conversation always kept to the barest practical minimum to accomplish whatever transactions were called for in his store or his stables. He was about six feet four and couldn't have weighed more than 150 pounds, a man so lank it was said that if you came upon him standing sideways, he wasn't there. He was short-waisted to boot, meaning that his legs—always encased in a pair of black canvas trousers—looked like a couple of charred drainpipes that had fallen off some house.

No one in Tombstone knew much about Homer Nye, except that he had arrived during the first of the town's boom years, set himself up in business with cash money he brought with him, and lived by himself in a shed attached to the back of his store, where he kept a lot of books that he read.

Usually, a customer going into Tombstone Sundries would catch Homer standing behind the counter like a stork peering at the pages of one his fat old books, and Homer would look up with the exasperated air of a man rudely interrupted. He'd always close the book and put it down behind the counter, so no one knew what was in those books, but the rumor was that

Homer was a student of strange European politics like anarchism, whatever that was.

It was also known that Homer Nye didn't like the school kids playing around out behind his corrals and often went after them with a broom, which of course most kids took as a challenge, so Homer was always being pestered by kids.

Among the shelves of dry goods and canned food and nostrums and so forth that sat on Homer's shelves, he also kept a gallon glass jar full of brightly colored sour-ball candies—five for a penny—which also attracted kids. Little ones who were penniless would sometimes come in and stare at the glass jar longingly, and Homer would look up from his tome, annoyed, and shoo them off, telling them to come back when they had the money. This was taken as a pretty harsh lesson by many kids, who, when they grew a little older and braver, would try to sneak into the store when Homer was in the stables and snatch a sour ball. The kids knew that Homer kept count of the sour balls, so he would know he had been robbed, but not by whom, and that was a pretty good form of revenge for a kid to perpetrate on so mean-spirited an adult.

Of course, the kids kept an eye on Homer Nye in the same way a wolf pack keeps track of the behavior of a herd of deer, so they all knew Homer's daily schedule, which he adhered to with the precision one would expect of a storekeeper who was also a recluse.

What ignited the Sour Ball Fracas in the autumn of 1895 was the notion Tom Jeffords Cleveland Bignon got in his head as he thought about the imminent return of his pal Little Spring from the wild Apache life in the east. Tom wanted to welcome this best of friends back in some special way, and it occurred to him that Little Spring would appreciate being greeted by the sour balls he had had to go without during the summer. Maybe ten sour balls, which they could then share, having apportioned them out by color. But Tom didn't have the two cents to buy them, and he didn't see how he would be able to swipe this arbitrary number of sour balls that had settled into his mind. So he did the next best thing: he offered his services to Homer

Nye. Specifically, he offered to muck out Homer's stables, knowing that Homer had been kicked on the elbow by one of the horses the other day and was out of action.

Ever suspicious, Homer took Tom on and they agreed on a price. Or at least they thought they had agreed on a price. One sour ball per stall, Homer later said they agreed on, but Tom heard it differently. He envisioned two sour balls per stall, which would have added up to twelve sour balls, two more than he needed. Why, he asked later with outraged logic, would he have agreed to do a whole lot of work that was going to net him only about *half* the sour balls he required?

In any event, the day before Little Spring was to arrive back in Tombstone to begin learning how to read and write, Tom Bignon labored mightily and mucked out all six stalls, only to receive half of what he thought was coming to him—that is, Homer Nye doled out six sour balls, two red, two yellow, and two green. Tom's remonstrations did him no good, and he was shooed away with Homer saying, to his satisfaction, that "a deal's a deal, young man."

The next day, Little Spring rode into town with his father, Juh, and a group of other Apaches, some of the kids who'd spent the summer like Little Spring out in the wilds to the east. They were greeted by Naiche and Tom's mama, the mayor, and some others, including two teachers from Tombstone Academy, and they all stood around talking. Soon enough, Tom got Little Spring off from the crowd and gave him the six sour balls, explaining the malevolence of Homer Nye. It was quickly and eagerly agreed that Homer should receive his just desserts, and Tom explained the plan he had hatched lying in bed the night before, unable to sleep a wink, so great was his moral outrage.

That very evening, then, on the principle that justice should be rendered swiftly, Tom and Little Spring were hidden by some sagebrush behind Nye's Stables a few minutes before six o'clock, which was exactly when Homer Nye closed Tombstone Sundries—every day without fail—locked the front door, carried whatever book he was reading at the time around back, and entered the outhouse next to the stables, where he always remained for at least ten minutes and often more. In this, according to Tom Bignon, he was as regular as a clock.

"Ten minutes?" Little Spring asked. "What's he do in there for ten minutes?" The sun had set over the western hills and the stables were now in the cold shade of oncoming evening.

"I don't know," Tom said. "I guess he reads them books of his."

"Why would anyone want to sit in a shithouse that long?" Little Spring asked. In fact, the very idea of an outhouse with its concentrated fumes rather sickened Little Spring. It was a White Eyes notion that he simply couldn't fathom.

"Here he comes," Tom hissed. They watched as Homer Nye came around the stables on his storklike legs. Under his arm was a fat book with reddish brown covers, and in his hand he carried a candlestick with a thick, short white candle that was unlit. Homer passed by the stalls and stooped to enter the outhouse that stood some five feet back from the stables. Homer's outhouse was a flimsy-looking affair, its wooden planks silvery dry with age. It had a crescent moon cut into the door, which now closed behind him. The boys heard a match being struck on the planks, saw a faint glow from the crescent moon, then heard a few thumps as Homer got his gangling long legs all arranged in the outhouse's narrow confines.

Tom Jeffords Grover Bignon hoisted a three-foot-long timber that had fallen off one of Homer's corrals and nodded his head. Little Spring crouched over a little pile of twigs they had gathered earlier and struck a spark from his flint. Before long the twigs had begun to burn, and into the flames Little Spring thrust the end of a dry branch of desert cedar. With this aflame, the boys moved silently toward the outhouse, Little Spring moving around to the rear.

Seconds later there was the sound of a night bird calling, and Tom Bignon stuck one end of his timber firmly into the ground, shoving the other end against the outhouse door, precisely as Little Spring lowered his desert cedar torch and lit a sizable pile of dried wood chips and twigs they had built earlier against the outhouse wall just where one of the old planks curled out away from the others.

"What's that?" they heard Homer Nye call out as they tiptoed away, back into the sagebrush beyond the corral. Tom Bignon couldn't suppress a giggle that arose in his throat at the picture of old Homer with his black pants around his ankles, long skinny legs all folded up in the tiny place.

"What's that?" Homer shouted again. "Who's that? Holy Christ! Fire! Fire!"

The boys ducked down behind the sage and listened to Homer bellow and curse and heard his knees and elbows thumping against the old planks, everything getting more frantic as the flames appeared now, having licked their way rapidly up the back of the outhouse to dance gaily on the ragged shake roof.

Homer was really setting up a clatter in there by now, and swearing like a cavalryman between shrieks of "Fire!" and the boys suddenly got worried.

"Can't he get out?" Tom asked. "What if he can't get out?"

"We best go tip it over," Little Spring said, standing up, but just then the whole outhouse seemed to rise up a foot or two off the ground, and it began to fall into pieces, planks splitting off the sides while the fire burned brightly on the old shake roof, and suddenly the outhouse simply exploded outward as if a bomb had gone off inside it, and Homer Nye stood there in his collarless white shirt and his black pants down around his ankles, a stricken look of horror on his face.

Flames were burning on the planks around his feet on the ground, and he stooped over, scrabbling around in the dirt, and picked up his book, which was smoldering, and grabbed at his pants, which got stuck on his ankles, with the result that he began to topple. Dropping the smoldering book, still yelling fire, he righted himself and started hopping out of the fiery arena on his skinny legs with his skinny bottom bobbing up and down like the white flag of a deer or an antelope, and the two boys doubled over with laughter.

Homer disappeared around the stables, hopping, and evidently managed to get his pants organized, for a few minutes later he came flying back around the stables, fully clad and waving an old saddle blanket with which he beat out the flames on his ruined outhouse, tears all the while streaming down his cheeks. Finally, the last smoke rising around him as the embers died, he reached into the wreckage and picked up his book. The edges of the pages were charred, the boys could see, and the red covers were all black, and Homer was still weeping as he thumbed through the volume.

Tom Bignon and Little Spring, using all the Apache wiles they knew, slipped silently and unseen away through the sagebrush, headed for their respective homes, suddenly feeling awful.

It was a long walk the next morning from where Juh had set up his camp outside of town to the front door of Tombstone Sundries. In fact, it was only about a mile, and it took only a few minutes, but to Little Spring it seemed like an eternity.

He had wakened after the sun was up and went off to the creek to make water, and when he came back to camp, he saw that Big Ears—Tom Jeffords Cleveland Bignon—and his mother Minnie Bignon were standing there outside his father Juh's wickiup, talking to him. That seemed ominous, and Little Spring thought about taking off, but he made his way up to the others in time to hear Big Ears explaining that he never would have undertaken such a labor if he hadn't been promised at least ten sour balls.

Big Ears's mother stood next to him, her arms folded under her enormous bosom, a pink silk scarf around her neck, wearing one of those long dresses that came almost to the ground. It was the color of the asters that had already started to come out in the sagebrush and in corners and nooks around town. She had a frown on her face, her big upper lip like an upside-down crescent moon. Little Spring's father stood erect as a fence post in his breechcloth and moccasins, his arms folded across *his* chest, his face expressionless and therefore frighteningly fierce. To Little Spring, he seemed immense, looming up in front of him.

Juh turned his head slightly and his black eyes flickered down to catch Little Spring's.

"You did this thing?" Juh asked, though it sounded more like a statement than a question.

Little Spring glanced up at his father's eyes, then away. He nodded. He was caught—caught!—and he began to sweat.

"They will come with me," Juh said, and Big Minnie put a hand out onto Tom's head.

"Now, it didn't turn out that serious—" she began, and Juh cut her off.

"A fire near horses is serious," he said. "And they burned a book. You're the one who takes reading books so seriously. Now these two will come with me."

The three of them marched off, the guilty boys a few paces ahead of the leader of the Apache nation. The boys, out of pride, kept their heads up, their eyes straight ahead, and so they did not see the twinkle in Juh's eyes as he turned his head to look back at Big Minnie, nor did they see her round baby face break into a mischievous smile in return.

When the threesome arrived outside Tombstone Sundries after what seemed an eternity of a walk, they found Homer Nye awkwardly sweeping off the sidewalk with a broom with his one good arm. The door to his emporium was open, and inside it seemed darker, gloomier, than ever. Homer looked up at them and an expression of what might have been fear flickered over his face and then fled, leaving him with a sour expression.

"You know who these boys are?" Juh asked sternly.

"Yeah, and I know what they—"

"They have something to say to you."

"They think they can get away with anything, being the sons of—"

"They have something to say to you."

Homer Nye closed his mouth and held his broom in one

skinny hand. The boys, speaking one after the other, stammered out that they were sorry they had burned down Homer's outhouse and they were sorry for all the trouble it caused, and they were sorry that they didn't think about how close it was to the stables, and they hoped it hadn't hurt Homer none, and they were sorry about the book getting burned, and they certainly would help him build another outhouse today if he wanted them to. These lengthy apologies were followed by a strained silence, during which Homer shuffled his feet and kept glancing at Juh's implacable face and then away.

"And you have something to say to them," Juh said.

"Huh? I . . . I do?"

"About fair pay."

Homer's long face turned red and he cleared his throat. "I . . . I . . . just a moment." He turned and fled into his store.

A moment later he returned with a small brown paper bag in each hand. He held them out to the boys, but Juh interrupted.

"Let me see," he said, and took the two bags from the storekeeper. Peering into the bags one after the other, he shook his head, and handed one of the bags back.

"Too many. You only owe six to this boy here." He handed the other bag to Thomas Jeffords Cleveland Bignon. "These boys will muck out your stables for a week. Your arm will be healed by then?"

"Yes."

"And you will pay them twelve of these sour balls each time."

"Oh. Yes, yes, of course."

"And they will muck out your stables for another week for no sour balls." The boys' heads jerked up. "That is because they burned your book."

"It . . . it's really only charred. Still readable," Homer croaked.

"Good. Maybe after they have learned how to read in school, you will let them read it." Juh turned away and walked down the dirt road toward Tombstone Academy without another word or backward glance.

∽ ∾

Fifteen

"Maybe Geronimo has spent too much time in Washington among the White Eyes. Maybe he has forgotten he is an Apache."

The orange light of the council fire gleamed in Victorio's eyes. He alone among the six men sitting cross-legged at the council was bare-chested. The others wore blankets over their shoulders to keep the night chill from their backs. The fire burned in what was still referred to as Juh's stronghold, a campsite high in a relatively inaccessible part of the Chiricahua Mountains, the same site at which Juh had explained a decade ago how the Apaches would defeat the White Eyes, and the site, also, where a small spring-fed creek had inspired the name he gave his infant son.

In the Apache way of things, the words Victorio had just uttered were tantamount to offering a mortal challenge.

"Perhaps," he added, "in his old age, Geronimo has given up being an Apache."

But for the crackling explosions of burning wood, Victorio's words were greeted with silence. Earlier, Geronimo had reported President Cleveland's concern about raids in Mexico by the Apaches in the eastern part of the country. With cheerful hypocrisy, he had also suggested that the young Apache braves who engaged in these raids might be inspired by too much tiswin, but in any case their energies should be directed elsewhere. He had pointed out that there was little to be gained by annoying the great colossus of the United States.

"The President," Geronimo explained, "he told the Americans that they already have enough land. They don't need any more. There are some people from Cuba—Cuba is a country in the water, south—and they want the Americans to take over their country. But Cleveland says no, the United States is big enough. But there'll be another President, and a lot of those people in Congress think the United States isn't big enough. They want to take this island, Cuba, and some other places. Some of them think they never should have given us our land."

It was at that point that Victorio had erupted.

"They didn't give it to us. We took it," he said. "We fought for our land, all of us here around this fire. We fought and we won. We fought so we could be Apaches in our own Apache country, not like the others, like those Navajos and Sioux and all those, living on reservations, taking what the White Eyes give them, going to the White Eyes' churches, forgetting, forgetting . . ."

He fell silent. His right eye had, with age, strayed slightly more, giving him a wilder look than before. He glanced around the council at the five leaders, all of whom looked straight ahead into the flames.

"All those other people," he said. "Those other tribes, they are asleep. They are dead. Only the Apaches . . ." And then Victorio began to lay down his challenge to Geronimo.

Juh listened, motionless, along with the others. If his old friend Geronimo, whose explosive temper had often gotten him into trouble in his long life, took the bait, then one of the two men would have to die. And there was no telling what Geronimo would do, though he was no longer up to a fight with the younger Victorio. Victorio might be partly right too; Geronimo might well have grown soft during all his time in the white man's city.

The council watched tensely as Geronimo grunted and rose up onto his bandy legs. He approached the fire and drew the remains of a branch from it, now merely a straight stick with a glowing end. He held the ember up to his face and blew on it till it erupted in flame. Turning the stick downward to preserve the flame, he reached into the recesses of his blanket and withdrew a greenish tube-shaped object, stuck one end of it in his mouth, bit down and spat into the fire. Then he lit the other end, letting smoke issue forth from either side of his mouth.

"That place Cuba I was telling you about," Geronimo said. "These come from there." He dropped the stick back into the fire and took another pull on the cigar, letting the smoke drift from his mouth.

"Cuba cigar. The best. The Americans make these things too, but the best ones come from Cuba. The Americans bring these from Cuba. They bring the best whiskey from another island, way far east. Eye-er-land. I learned to smoke these cigars last year. President Cleveland smokes them. After they all eat, he and the other men go into a room and smoke these. They make the women go in another room. So I smoke these cigars and listen to the men. I tell them stories about us sometimes."

He twisted the cigar in his fingers, looked at the ash.

"You smoke these real slow. They taste a lot better than our tobacco. Real sweet. Soft. Gentle. Cost a lot of money." He snapped the cigar in two and threw the two pieces into the fire. "One of the White Eyes' things that Apaches don't need." Geronimo grinned widely, and looked into the fire. "Those people have a lot of things an Apache doesn't need."

Suddenly he whirled around. A flash of light sped through the dark and hit with a *thunk*. Victorio looked down, and between his crossed legs he saw the well-worn handle of Geronimo's bowie knife. It was buried up to the hilt in the earth.

"I got that off a bluecoat, an officer," Geronimo said. "Thirty years ago, maybe forty. I killed a lot of White Eyes with it, used it all that time. Was I an Apache then?" The old warrior grinned down at Victorio. "I killed Chato with it too. When he decided to go against us. I don't keep that knife with me all the time in Washington, where I am among our old enemy. Do I need it here among my own people?"

Slowly, Victorio reached down and removed the knife from

the ground between his legs and, holding the blade in the flat of his hand, offered it back to Geronimo.

"Geronimo suffers," Victorio said with a smile that showed his teeth in the firelight but did not reach as far as his eyes. "He suffers in Washington so we can be free."

Juh breathed out through his nose, realizing that he hadn't done so since Geronimo had hurled his knife. The flare-up was over, a fatal duel averted. But the difficulty was not solved. There had always been Apache men who were hunters, not warriors, who knew that killing enemies would also kill their special ability to find and kill the deer, the antelope. But there had always been Apache men who could measure themselves only by the killing of enemies. Without killing enemies, without plundering their enemies' horses and cattle, how were they to stand before their women? What were such men to do with themselves now?

It had been better when Mexican bandits still ventured across the border into Apacheria. But now not even a madman would try such a thing. And certainly it had been simpler when the Apaches were at war with the world, as they always had been. Without allies, without need of allies, everyone was an enemy. Simpler too, probably, before the Americans had come and there were only the Mexicans to kill, and the other tribes to raid. There was no one alive now who could remember the times before the Americans came. There were just stories.

And now, Juh thought, the world has changed again, just the way a river can change course.

How can you be an Apache without an enemy to kill?

Juh glanced over at Victorio, staring contemplatively into the flames. Beyond sat Naiche, whose eyes had a vacant look in them. Naiche, who spent more and more of his time in Tombstone, less and less in the mountains with his ugly wife Kozineh. Who could blame him? Naiche seemed comfortable taking care of the towns—Tombstone, Bisbee—watching the mining companies, seeing to the stores, the whores, keeping track of the money. Naiche had learned about money, counting it, making it grow, like plants, apparently.

Naiche also was comfortable lying with the enormous white woman, Minnie. Juh was not interested in white women. They smelled wrong to him. But he didn't begrudge Naiche his pleasures the way Victorio did. Victorio held Naiche in contempt, Juh knew. Victorio had told his sister Lozen that Naiche caught the white man's disease of greed from lying with the fat white woman—and Lozen, of course, passed this on to Juh. Eventually, everything got passed on to Juh.

Who was right? Victorio riding free in the plains hunting antelope, living the past and wishing for enemies? Geronimo with his cigar from Cuba, his hotel room in Washington, and his Irish whiskey with the President? Naiche, collecting the white man's money for the tribe, building schools and plugging the fat white woman?

They each followed their own path. And they all looked to Juh. But only the future would tell what was right, what was the Apache way in a new world that had changed course. And Juh knew he could not see that far. It made him tired.

Juh had reached a point in his life when, in earlier times, he could have relinquished his leadership to a younger man, perhaps a son, perhaps the son of another. Only old Nana, who had finally died three years ago in his nineties, had remained a leader—a war leader—for so long. But the decades of war, the intensified wars against the bluecoats, had taken a terrible toll on the People. Many Apache sons had been killed. In all, during the decades from Cochise's death till independence, half of all the Chiricahua Apaches had died, killed. Three of Juh's own sons by his first marriages had been killed—and of course the infant son of his with Ishton. Those first of Juh's sons would be in their thirties and forties now. The only son who remained was Little Spring.

Few men among the Apaches were of the age, of the inclination, and of the character to take on leadership. So it is left to old men like us around this fire, Juh thought. We will have to stay on until the ones like Little Spring are grown and are tested.

But what tests?

What tests would face Little Spring now, his son who burned down the white man's shithouse, who spoke English as if he had been born to it, and who would learn to read and write that language? Little Spring, who also knew the ways of the Apache, the hunter, who had killed two antelope from his horse.

But the warrior? Juh wondered how his son Little Spring would learn the way of the warrior. For surely the Apaches would always have enemies.

Sixteen

SPRING 1900

On a Sunday afternoon in late April, with the sunlight beginning to shade from a thin silver to a more robust gold, a single passenger alit from the stagecoach before the Tombstone Hotel, cradling a much used Winchester carbine in his right arm. With his left hand he deftly caught the big duffel bag the driver threw down to him, and stood for a moment in the yellow dust kicked up by the wheels of the stagecoach as it jerked into motion and moved down the street toward the company stables.

The man was about six feet tall, thick of chest, and dressed in worn buckskin shirt and leggings, a pair of calf-high boots tightly laced, and a wide-brimmed Stetson hat that appeared to have been dragged along behind a horse, or maybe a train. The man looked around him, bright eyes carefully taking in the empty wooden sidewalks and the three saloons across the dusty street, all with swinging doors, and all open, which was not usual in the man's experience. Sunday was respected as the sabbath throughout the American West nowadays.

The man had no quarrel with the Lord, quite the contrary, and he thought that on balance it was a good idea to close saloons one day a week in His honor, but there was something about getting off a stage in a western town and finding the saloons closed that depressed him a bit. It was surely a sign of the passing of the Old West that he had, almost too late, come to love. It struck him as pleasantly ironic that the wide-open,

174

rip-roaring free-spiritedness of the American frontier survived perhaps only in a foreign country—Apacheria.

The man grinned—both at the irony of it and also at the prospect of a tumbler of whiskey—and his smile revealed a wide, almost ferocious set of white, square teeth. He turned and lugged his gear into the hotel and approached the desk behind which a balding, gray-haired man in a white shirt and a red brocade vest sat on a stool.

"Yes, sir?" the clerk said.

"I'd appreciate it if I could obtain a room in this establishment," the visitor said in a loud voice with an unmistakably eastern accent. Across the lobby another old man looked up from his newspaper and shook his head. "I'll be staying for two nights, and perhaps more. Hope to do a little hunting."

The clerk fumbled around behind the desk and pulled out a registration form, which the visitor filled out and signed with a flourish: *T. Roosevelt*.

The clerk turned the form around and peered at the signature, then up at the grinning face for a moment. He reached around behind him and produced a key. "Room fourteen. It'll run you four dollars a night, Mister, uh, Rooze-velt."

"Splendid, splendid. Tell me, old-timer, which of those saloons across the street do you recommend?" Roosevelt, who was at the time the governor of New York State and whose face was known to virtually everyone in the United States as the grand, swashbuckling leader of the heroic Rough Riders, found it altogether charming to be in a place where he was evidently just a stranger in town. He had left his entourage in Tucson, hoping for just this kind of anonymity, the solitude denied public men.

"Prob'ly you want to try the Bird Cage Theatre," the room clerk said. "Big Minnie's the proprietor and she can fix you up with, uh, with a good huntin' guide. She's the mayor too."

And so, within the next hour, the governor of New York got his tumbler of whiskey and met Big Minnie Bignon and was in turn introduced to a sixteen-year-old Apache boy who, Big Minnie assured him, was as good a tracker as anyone could ever need. If it was a mountain lion he wanted to bag and only had three days to do it, then this was his best bet. No one, even the boy's father, was as likely to spot a big cat in these parts, she said. Why, this boy had even seen them in broad daylight.

The Apache boy's name was Little Spring. He was nearly six feet tall, slender, and he wore his shiny black hair pulled into a tail behind his neck. Soft-spoken, with black eyes gazing calmly out from Mongol lids, the boy gave off a sense of self-possession that Roosevelt had encountered in few adults. Indeed, "catlike" was the word that came to Roosevelt's mind when he first saw the boy walk through the swinging doors into the Bird Cage Theatre, and during the next two days, Roosevelt, who thought he knew something about horsemanship and woodcraft, was stunned.

On the ride over to the Huachuca Mountains, the leader of the Rough Riders was hard put to keep up, and marveled that a human and a horse could become so close to being one entity. It was like seeing a centaur loping along ahead of him over the grassy hills.

They camped to the east of the Huachucas, and the next morning Little Spring led the way up a steep canyon down which a creek tumbled and roared like a symphony in water and rock until they reached an upland covered with woods, mostly thick oak trees. Underfoot, the ground was sprinkled with oak leaves, and Little Spring led his horse through the forest as deliberately as if he were on his way to a prearranged rendezvous. At one point in the early afternoon he stopped and gestured toward a spot on the ground under an oak that stood alone, a bit separate from the rest of the trees. Roosevelt saw nothing on the ground but leaves. The boy squatted down and pushed the leaves aside from what Roosevelt could now see was a slight mound. Underneath were the remains of a deer, a young one.

"Mountain lion," Little Spring said. "She'll be back sometime. Maybe two, three days."

"She?" Roosevelt asked.

Little Spring turned and pointed off to the side with his chin. There Roosevelt could now see that the leaves had been disturbed, lightly scraped away, and in the dirt was a print about three inches wide and three inches long. "Males are bigger." The boy held up a hand with thumb and forefinger about a half inch apart. Roosevelt peered at the four toe prints and the heel, a perfect track. In all his experience, he had seen only one other mountain lion track, in Idaho, and the hair stood up on the back of his neck.

Later in the day they reached an upland area of high meadows, rolling hillocks of ocher grass like unkempt hair overseen by patches of dark oak forest, and Roosevelt found himself daydreaming that he was the first white man ever to see this place. He half expected to see a herd of woolly mammoths over the next rise. At one point their horses bore them past a wooded edge where a small herd of mule deer, about a dozen, were browsing no more than fifty feet away. They looked up, unconcerned, at the passing horsemen and returned to browse.

Roosevelt legged his horse abreast with Little Spring. "They aren't scared of us?"

"We don't hunt 'em on horseback," the boy said. "If we were on foot . . . ?" He made a quick gesture of flight with his hand.

Later, as the sun began to set, they made camp in a copse of oaks, and Little Spring led Roosevelt over another hillock of dry grass into a woodland patch from which they could hear the sound of water trickling. Plunging into the trees, they soon came to a stand of marsh grass and horsetails. Beyond, water moved, flickering in the saffron light as it passed slowly over rocks green with moss and slick with algae. The boy walked silently back into the trees and squatted down on his heels. Roosevelt followed suit, realizing that they were in a natural blind formed by two boulders. He could smell the sweet aroma of moisture carried on the breeze that blew lightly into their faces from the west.

"We wait," the boy said.

Roosevelt's mind wandered, noting sometime later that the western sky had gone a brilliant orange with long streaks of purple-gray cloud drawn across like curtains that had been violently torn. Some of the streaks glowed with intense golden edges. The world seemed ready for a musical crescendo, a grand finale from a full orchestra, but all was silent around him except for the lightest trickle of water and the almost inaudible hiss of the breeze in the oak leaves overhead. Next to him, the Apache youth was as still as the boulders in front of him. He hadn't moved a muscle for God only knew how long, and Roosevelt began to feel a distinct ache in each knee. He longed for the pleasant sensation that would attend him if only he could simply fall lightly back on his rump and let his legs stretch out before him. But he remained squatting, not to be outdone.

Roosevelt didn't hear it. He saw the Apache's head turn slightly to their left, and his eyes followed. The orange light seemed to pick up some motion in the underbrush about thirty yards away, but then it was gone, the world returned to stillness. He kept his eyes fixed on the point where he had seen something—what?—and presently he saw motion again, a slight movement of tawny yellow in the gold-dappled shadow. Twice it disappeared again and then he saw it emerge, as if from the night air, an enormous yellow cat spotted with little roseates of black. It turned its head toward him, and Roosevelt stared at two green eyes, eyes that suddenly seemed oceanic in their ancientness, in their mastery—and he gasped. The cat turned its head away and, as suddenly as it had emerged, vanished into the shadows.

"*El tigre,*" the Apache whispered.

"A jaguar," Roosevelt said under his breath, rather like a prayer. "My God. A jaguar." He looked dumbly down at the Winchester in his hands. He hadn't thought of it, hadn't thought to raise its sights to his eye. He looked over at Little Spring, whose teeth gleamed in what appeared to be a triumphant grin.

"Apaches believe *el tigre* can't be killed with a gun. Bullets go through him without making a hole. We believe you get good luck if you see him."

Roosevelt let himself fall back on his rump and stretched his legs out before him. He set the carbine down in the leaves, and his big square teeth gleamed back at the Apache youth.

"That's grand," he said. "That's just grand. We're both going to have good luck, are we?"

"*El tigre*, he doesn't come any farther north than here, Apache country," Little Spring said. "My aunt Lozen told me that's why only Apaches have their own country and the other Indians don't."

"Your aunt must be right. Good luck never hurt anyone."

"She is right. She knows all the Apache ways. Even the warrior ways. She says there are other things Apaches have to know now. She says I have to go to the white man's college."

Roosevelt's eyebrows rose and danced briefly over his eyes.

"Did you go to college?" the boy asked.

"Yes, a place called Harvard. In Boston."

"Is that the best?"

Roosevelt laughed. "I think so. But there are others that are very good. Yale. Princeton."

"Boston. That's a big city, huh? They all in Boston?"

Roosevelt laughed again. "No. Yale is in the city of New Haven. Princeton is in a town called Princeton. In New Jersey."

Little Spring sat thinking about this. "A town?" he said.

"It's a place about the size of Tombstone."

"Good. That's where I'll go."

That night, sitting at the campfire, Teddy Roosevelt engaged in a long monologue in which he talked with growing enthusiasm about such things as the geography of the world, about the ancient Greeks, about astronomy and Shakespeare and Michelangelo, about warriors and scholars, the things that Little Spring would learn about when he went to college. Little Spring listened, enrapt. He was caught up in the man's enthusiasm, though for the most part uncomprehending. And as they turned in for the night, Roosevelt said he would help Little

Spring when it came time to go to college. It was the least he could do, he said, for the man who had shown him a jaguar.

The same day that Teddy Roosevelt appeared in Tombstone, another man arrived in the hills outside what had once been Silver City but now was an abandoned ruin. He called himself Nakahyen, "Keen-sighted," and told the few people who asked that he was an Apache. His mother had been an Apache who was carried off into slavery by the White Eyes when she was pregnant, and escaped with her infant son a few years later into Comanche country, where she promptly died of the coughing disease and where he had been raised by the Comanches.

When Nakahyen was still a boy, he had begun to experience dreams and visions that called him back to Apacheland—disturbing dreams and visions of old men calling to him, explaining things to him, speaking to him in Apache, which he found he understood. Among the old men who would come to him in these visions was Mangas Colorado, the great leader of the Warm Springs Apaches, and on one occasion Mangas Colorado had reached out across the void between the living and the dead and vouchsafed to the boy Nakahyen a deerskin pouch which he now wore around his neck. In the pouch, along with other medicine that belonged to the leader, was the bullet that had wounded him, the one the Mexican doctor had plucked out of Mangas's body and which Mangas kept to ward off other bullets. He had wrapped the bullet in a piece torn from his red shirt.

Nakahyen let a few of the Apaches look on this talisman, and before long the word began to spread in the eastern part of Apacheria that the young man who had arrived in their midst—the son of an Apache woman who some of the older people recalled, and a man capable of speaking their language even though he had been raised among the Comanches—was someone who bore listening to.

He was, it seemed, in touch with some of the Old People, the ones who had long since gone off to the Red Ground Country.

He was, he had to be, a man of special power. He was, it seemed, a prophet.

Nakahyen preferred to live off by himself in his own wickiup near the headwaters of a spring that ran close to the old stone ruins, the place where earlier people had lived before the Apaches came. People visited him there, brought him food, though he hunted for himself as well. At such times he was sociable enough, talking and laughing with the others, eating mescal, drinking tiswin into the night, gambling, listening to the old stories of war. But there were times, moments, when he seemed to be taken away from them. His eyes would go dull and his breath became so slight as to have vanished altogether. And when he returned, he would speak but with a different voice of an unnamed evil, an unknowable evil that was loose among the People. He would speak calmly, slowly, in ominous riddles, and then his eyes would clear and he would look around him like a man who had just woken up. More and more of the Apaches came to listen, fascinated, horrified, enchanted.

Of course, Victorio heard about the prophet newly arrived in their midst. He remained aloof, but from afar he too listened.

Every year in the autumn they came south from somewhere, in high-flying V's and ribbons, a liquid burbling sound overhead. They came over days, weeks, in the thousands, and they found the places alongside the river where the water stood still all year in shallow pools and the ground was always damp. By the time they all arrived, the leaves were gone from the cottonwood groves along the riverbanks and the skies were sometimes gray with the promise of winter. In the marshlands, in congregations too great to count, they strutted and mingled in the grasses, these great and dignified birds—the pinkish gray cranes and the snowy white geese.

At any time of day some signal might set the geese off—the passage too close of a coyote, a sudden rustle in the grasses, who could say?—and the sky would suddenly fill with wings, white wings gathering whatever was left of the sunlight, the entire sky filled overhead with thousands of white birds wheeling. And then they would settle down, quibbling, swooping back down to the earth and the marsh grass to strut and mingle again.

When Victorio approached the marshes on horseback at the beginning of a day in late November, the geese took nervously to the air, filling the sky with great wheels of wings while the sun put its forehead above the eastern horizon. Victorio was with his sister, Lozen, she on the big black horse she still rode when speed was not needed and nothing was at stake. The two Apaches sat their horses on the edge of the marshlands and watched the spectacle overhead. On the ground the cranes, who were less excitable birds, perhaps because of their greater height and size, proceeded on their errands in the grass.

Brother and sister watched in silence, trying as they always did to spot the leader, the bird who passed the signal to the others that the alarm was over and they could descend. There was, of course, no way of telling. It might have been possible a long, long time before, at the beginning of things, when the birds and the four-legged animals were more like people—or the people were more like them—and all spoke the same language. But no more. Perhaps it was no longer needed that all the creatures speak the same language, now that the world had been ridded of the monsters who had also been present at the beginning.

The monsters were gone, Victorio thought to himself, long gone, but the People had always had enemies, had always been enemies with the rest of the world. Chosen by Ussen to oppose the world, and now living in a time of peace—perhaps a false peace. Perhaps the Apaches had all settled down to the ground, like the geese, when they should still be on the alert, wheeling in the air, ready.

There was this new man, Nakahyen, who preached that there was evil loose again. Today Victorio and his sister who feared nothing in the world had come to watch. Nakahyen had invited people to join him in the river where the waters flowed slowly out of the marshland and mingled with the faster waters of the channel. Here, standing in the water, they would pray and listen.

Victorio and Lozen turned their horses south, circled around the marshland and the birds, and climbed the low bank between the marsh and the river. Before them the river swept to the southeast, wide and shallow, its slowly drifting waters smooth and reflecting the sky. Fifty yards offshore, some sixty Apaches stood up to their knees in a great half circle in the shallow water. Some of them were women, but most were men— younger men—who stood naked but for their breechcloths in the icy water. Their eyes were closed and they all chanted, a low sound whose words were indistinguishable to Victorio and Lozen. They all faced inward toward the lone figure of Nakah-yen, standing in the water facing the east, his arms upraised. Slowly Nakahyen began to turn in the water, to face the north. He too was chanting.

"Can you hear?" Victorio asked.

"He's looking for the enemy," Lozen said. "The source of the evil he sees is loose."

They watched Nakahyen turn, facing west, then south, slowly turning in a complete circle two times, three times, and then stopping, facing west. Facing Victorio and Lozen.

"Us?" Victorio said, his brow creasing with incipient outrage.

"No, no. Beyond. To the west of here. In the place named for the dead. That is what he says."

"What place? We have no place named for the dead."

"You forget," Lozen said. "The place we call White Metal. Tombstone."

"Are we to believe him—this prophet?" Victorio asked. The old warrior knew the danger of prophets, of course, the challenge such a man might pose to his own influence and leadership in eastern Apacheria. Such a man could unleash uncontrollable energies among the people, particularly the younger people. And yet, to Victorio, the purist, who sought only to maintain the old and true way of the Apache, the town called Tombstone was where the Apaches of the west pandered to the White Eyes and profited from their immoral ways, their forms of gambling, their disgusting prostitutes . . . a place of corruption.

It galled him to think that Juh put up with its presence in the land of the Apaches. Juh, never a friend of the white man and his ways, preferring to spend more and more of his time alone in the Chiricahua Mountains, believed he was straddling two worlds. Using the white man's world, he said, to save the Apache world.

Since the time of independence, Victorio had believed the white world could be ignored by those who wished. He had believed that he and his bands in the east of Apacheria could be sealed off from its corrupting influence. But perhaps not. Perhaps Tombstone was a sore from which the pus would inevitably spread.

Perhaps, he had begun to think, this prophet could be put to good use.

Victorio looked directly at his sister and repeated his question. "Are we to believe this prophet?"

Lozen shrugged. "Aren't most prophecies about the past?" she answered.

Seventeen

On a breezy day in December 1900, Big Minnie Bignon and her consort, the Apache leader Naiche, arrived by buckboard in front of the Ruby Star Saloon on Maiden Lane in Tucson. An afternoon shower had left the sweet smell of moisture in the air and had tamed the dust of the street. Big Minnie was resplendent in a vast purple dress with her signature silk cap with flowers perched on her head, and the buckboard strained downward on its iron springs and sprang up six inches as she disembarked. Naiche, bareheaded and dressed in a black worsted suit with a black string tie, with his hair in a long braid that hung down his back, handed the reins to an obsequious young man who appeared from within the saloon, and stepped down after her.

The Ruby Star was, of course, more than a saloon; it was a gambling hall with the most up-to-date and fanciest roulette wheels and one-armed bandits in the Arizona Territory, and some said that this was as it should be in the territory's largest city. Now with a population of some six thousand souls, Tucson had begun to grow again after a decade when its fortunes had lagged. In 1900 it was even greater than the Apache's chief tourist attraction, Tombstone, and it was reexperiencing growing pains.

There were many in Tucson who believed it looked forward to a grand and glittering future as the cultural capital of the West, what with the newly established university and the newly refurbished opera house with its ornate lobby complete with two breathtaking chandeliers of lead crystal. Such refined boosters—the self-appointed first families of Tucson—no longer looked kindly on the activities that took place around the clock in Maiden Lane, for the saloons were more than gambling dens. They were also—most of them at any rate—whorehouses, to boot.

On the other hand, there were many in town, including some of the city fathers, who openly supported the saloons as a crucial source of employment, as well as much-needed municipal tax revenue. Among these supporters were the Sons of Rest, a group of men constitutionally opposed to work of any kind who were given money to sit at the gaming tables to create an atmosphere of sociability. These helpful souls were loosely organized under the leadership of old Frying Pan Charlie Alzamorra, a severely cross-eyed man who, while frying some eggs in the saloon's kitchen in the 1880s, heard that a game of poker had gotten under way and raced avidly off to watch, frying pan still absentmindedly in hand.

The various Sons of Rest now lolling about in the Ruby Star all took cheery note of Big Minnie's arrival when her wide frame momentarily darkened the open doorway.

"H'lo, Big Minnie!" Frying Pan Charlie called.

"Darn if it ain't the S.S. Minnie," remarked a man with a nautical background. "Heave to there."

"Hail to the Queen of Tombstone," said another.

Yet another sang the first few bars of "She's Only a Bird in a Gilded Cage," while Big Minnie found a seat at one of the round poker tables and sank happily into it. Naiche, meantime, leaned against the wall near the door, his arms folded across his chest. His eye fell on a row of new slot machines, elaborately wrought and gilded, that stood sentinel under an enormous painting in an ornate gilt frame. It showed a fanciful scene in which a conquistador in full regalia peered around the folds of a voluminous curtain at a reclining nude woman of heroic voluptuousness whose eye, evidently, had been caught by a cherubic winged baby, also nude and armed with a tiny bow and arrow. The painting was locally quite famous, and Naiche, still a prisoner of Apache prudery in such matters, studiously avoided looking at it.

"Boys," Big Minnie said affably, "it's always a pleasure to come in here and see what the devil has thought up lately for idle hands. Now where'd those new one-armed bandits come from?"

"They make 'em over at Kansas City," one of the Sons of Rest explained.

"Now, Minnie," said another, "don't you be tryin' to fool us. You're here on a recruitin' trip, ain't you?"

In fact, Big Minnie always had her eye out for new talent she could entice into working in Tombstone. It was not merely a matter of commercial rivalry, though that existed, to be sure. But Minnie also firmly and devoutly believed in the core of her large and generous heart that, thanks to her enlightened policies in such matters, a working girl enjoyed a better life in Tombstone.

She was about to reply to the Son of Rest's accusation when all heads turned toward the swinging doors of the saloon. From outside in the bright afternoon sun they could hear a voice raised, a voice of piercing certitude like that of a preacher at full Sunday-sermon bore, and the sound of feet, many feet, marching resolutely in the dust of Maiden Lane.

"What the hell is that?" Big Minnie exclaimed, and heaved herself to her feet. She came up behind Naiche, who was peering out the door, and looked over his shoulder. "Who in the *world* is that?" she asked, and the several Sons of Rest arrived at the door, unable to see over her or around her.

"Get out of the way, Minnie!" one of them called, and Minnie went out through the swinging doors onto the wooden sidewalk. Before her in the street stood a crowd of women, well dressed in long-skirted dresses of muted colors and proper hats, with expressions that combined a stiff-jawed resolution with a glint of what could only be called elation. Standing between them and the sidewalk, glowering at Big Minnie, was a woman in black—black dress, black hat, black shoes—carrying a black-bound Bible in one hand, and in her other hand—of all things!—an axe. The woman in black was easily six feet tall, square-shouldered, and erect as the steeple of a church.

"Are you the proprietress of this iniquitous den?" the scowling woman demanded. "You bring shame upon all womanhood."

A buzz arose from the crowd behind her, some saying "Amen, amen, yes, shame," while a few were saying "No, no, that's not the owner," and Big Minnie felt herself being jostled from behind as the Sons of Rest and the few other patrons of the Ruby Star emerged from the dark of the saloon into the sunlight.

A grin crept over Big Minnie's face and she laughed out loud. "Who are you? I thought the angel of death was a he; thought he carried a pitchfork, not an axe."

Up and down the sidewalk and across the street, people were emerging into the light to learn what this unusual disturbance was. The woman in black stepped up onto the sidewalk and stood, chin out, staring into Big Minnie's face. She held the axe handle in her left hand, its shiny head at shoulder height, as a medieval knight might have held his lance. She brandished her Bible under Minnie's nose.

"I am Carrie Nation," she announced. "And I come bearing the enlightened message of temperance in support of these good and *civilized* Christian women who stand here before you. We will shut these saloons, mark my words, shut their doors, and Demon Rum will no longer prey on the citizens of Tucson, turning its men into . . ."

As Carrie Nation continued her message of temperance, her voice growing louder with each orotund phrase, she somehow inched closer and closer to Big Minnie Bignon, until the two enormous women were bosom-to-bosom, nose-to-nose. The men on the sidewalk watched in fascination.

Big Minnie put a hand out on the shoulder of the still-preaching Carrie Nation, who stopped, mouth agape, and shuddered as if touched by the serpent.

"Don't . . . don't . . ." she said.

"I agree," Minnie said, smiling with the innocence of a gigantic baby.

"What?" The furrows in Carrie Nation's angry brow changed into puzzlement. Her ice-blue eyes darted back and forth. "What did you say?"

"I agree with you and these good Christian ladies here. I'm not who you think I am. I'm not the proprietor of this den of iniquity and shame, this cauldron of sin and degradation. I fervently do believe that this saloon and all the others here on Maiden Lane should shut their doors. They should destroy their stores of Demon Rum . . . and Demon Whiskey while they're at it. And lead away the poor women who have been so badly shamed by the liquored-up appetites of these weakling men . . ."

By this time, the sidewalk had erupted with guffaws and Carrie Nation had begun to perceive that she might be the butt of some kind of prank. She turned angrily to face the good Christian women of Tucson and saw that some of them, too, were tittering behind their hands.

"Mrs. Nation," one of the ladies said. "That's the mayor of Tombstone."

Carrie Nation turned back to face Minnie, only to find the huge woman standing with her arms spread wide, a beatific look radiant on her round baby face.

"All you sinners, all you poor victims of John Barleycorn, all you fallen women, you sadly used, you storm-tossed, you'll all find a welcome in Tombstone."

Amid the cheers and laughter that filled Maiden Lane and echoed off its ornate facades, Carrie Nation stood nonplussed, her face reddening.

"Barbarians!" she shouted, her voice as deep as a man's. She spun on her heel and marched off the sidewalk into the street, where several of the women of Tucson patted her apologetically on the shoulder. She turned to face the grinning and guffawing crowds, and raised her axe.

"You'll see," she shouted. "A tide is rising in this nation, and it will flow even to this benighted backwater. It will drown out this place of sin and degradation! These saloons will be closed!" Again she spun on her heel and marched down Maiden Lane, head up, shoulders back, proudly leading the contingent of Tucson's first ladies out of the doomed and sun-drenched precincts of hell.

Later, seated at a quiet table in the Ruby Star, Big Minnie turned to Naiche, who had been staring off into the distance for the last couple of hours while she spoke with some of the whores. Now they were alone. He was a handsome devil, Minnie thought, age having improved him the way a good oak barrel improved good bourbon. There were squint lines around his eyes that looked like twin knots on a fine tree, and little vertical fissures that ran down the hollows of his cheeks, emphasizing his high cheekbones and his potent jawline. She smiled her girlish smile and put her hand up between Naiche's eyes and the place, God knew where, that he was seeing somewhere in his mind.

"What are you seeing, darlin'?"

His black eyes refocused as he turned his head toward her. He grinned. "You made a fool of that woman," he said. "But she didn't care, did she?"

"Not for long she didn't. You can't embarrass anyone who's that righteous."

"That's what I been thinkin'," Naiche said. "That axe woman, you can't shut her up. Someday them White Eyes're goin' to shut all the saloons. All these people here in Tucson—what are they gonna do then?" He waved his hand in a grand sweep across the north from west to east. "All those people—they can't all fit in Tombstone."

"So what are you thinking?" Big Minnie asked.

"Maybe we need another Tombstone."

Eighteen

1906

Only one of the nearly one hundred windows in the facade of Nassau Hall was lit, and this would soon wink out, leaving the oldest building in Princeton, New Jersey, dark and silent under a velvety April sky. The days were balmy now, the excitement of seasonal change was borne on the gusty winds, and the nights themselves had begun to soften as well. It was a night without a moon. Clouds obscured the stars. From the parkland of grass and spreading elms that stretched between the old stone building and the dirt thoroughfare called Nassau Street, the high gilt cupola atop Nassau Hall's tower was lost in the darkness.

It was a perfect night for what the two young men had in mind to do.

They stood on the steps below the long flagpole that angled out over the grass. They were invisible even to someone passing a few feet away in the gloom, thanks to the black pants and black shirts they wore. But there were no passersby at this time of night—just after midnight—and now the last light had gone off. The university's president, Woodrow Wilson, had put in another long night, and the two young men lurking in the dark were impressed. This was the tenth night in a row that President Wilson had worked this late. It was also the tenth night in a row that they had stood here, waiting for Wilson to give it up for the night and go home.

"Okay," whispered the shorter of the two young men. "Let's

go." He cupped his hands, fingers laced, and the other young man put his foot in the cup and vaulted upward into the dark.

"Got it," he said, and swung up onto the flagpole with the agility of a tumbler. Straddling it, he inched outward toward the gilt wooden ball sixty feet away . . . or, to be precise, fifty-five and a half feet away. On each of the previous nine nights, these two young men had managed to remove the gold ball and the pulley at the flagpole's end, saw six inches off the pole, and restore the ball and the pulley. Their bet—that they could remove six feet of the flagpole without anyone noticing it—had been accepted, and five hundred dollars was theirs if they won. In addition, a number of side bets by other students at the university brought the total wagering on this prank to nearly four thousand dollars.

Down below, Tom Jeffords Cleveland Bignon stood watch, rubbing his hands together at the thought of the $250 that was his if all went well tonight and the next two nights. Something was in the air this night, something that made Tom Bignon's throat a bit phlegmy and gave him the urge to sneeze. Above, Little Spring—whom Princetonians called Patch—made his way silently out and up. The gold ball at the flagpole's tip was more than a foot in diameter and more than twenty feet above the ground, a heavy and cumbersome object. Suspended in the gloom, the Indian worked mostly by feel. As the work progressed, the two whispered in Apache, and Little Spring said he was ready to lower the ball and the pulley down on a rope when Tom Bignon made a hissing sound.

"Someone's coming," he said. He faded back into a doorway under the flagpole and stood breathing silently through his mouth as footsteps approached from the right along the broad flagstone walk. Two men. He could hear their voices murmuring now. He prayed he wouldn't sneeze.

"My dear Wilson," a voice said, now only thirty feet away. It was the voice of an old man. "I hardly need to tell you that the majority of the trustees of this university are men with their heads buried firmly in the past, their notions of excellence measured in purely pecuniary terms. These ideas you have for reform will not go down easily in such old-fogeyish gullets."

"But you will talk to them, my dear Cleveland. A former president carries some weight, after all, even with gentlemen of the Republican persuasion."

"You don't have to be a Republican to be an old fool," Cleveland said. Tom Bignon, standing only five feet away in the dark, suddenly realized that this was Grover Cleveland, former president not of the university, but of the United States, now a lecturer and a Princeton trustee. Tom's mother had told him years earlier that she had named him for two admirable men, one of them being President Cleveland. So this was he, his namesake, standing now only a few feet away in the dark.

Tom Bignon was suddenly overcome with a sensation of great urgency, and he sneezed.

"What's that? Who is that?" President Wilson barked.

"Er, um . . ."

"Speak up!"

"It's Bignon, sir. Tom Bignon, class of aught-six."

"What are you doing, lurking about out here in the dark at this time of night?" President Wilson's voice softened, as if relieved. "Come forward so I can see you."

Tom stepped toward the shadowy figures. "I was, er, thinking," he said. "About Tennyson, sir."

"Tennyson?"

"Yes, sir. Professor Van Dyke was discussing Tennyson today and something, some lines, caught in my mind. I couldn't sleep thinking about them, so I, uh, took a walk . . ."

"What lines were those?" Wilson asked, and Tom wished he could sneeze again. Or better yet, vanish into thin air. His mind spun.

"I never could stand Tennyson," Grover Cleveland said. "It's like suffocating in a cloud of perfume."

In the silence of the night there was a faint tremulous sound that Tom knew at once was Little Spring suppressing something, perhaps a laugh, out on the end of the flagpole. Hastily he began to recite: " 'O well for him whose will is strong! He suffers, but he will not suffer long . . .' "

And President Wilson said: " 'He suffers, but he cannot suffer wrong.' Yes, a strong little poem. 'Will,' isn't it?"

"A lot of treacle," Cleveland said. "Bilgewater."

"And those lines puzzle you, Mr. Bignon?" President Wilson asked. Tom heard another muffled wheeze in the dark.

"Suddenly, sir," he said quickly, "I think I see what the poet was driving at. Man is man, master of his fate. That sort of thing. Does that seem right, sir?"

"Quite," the president said. "Where are you from, Mr. Bignon?"

"Tombstone, sir. In Apacheria."

"Ah, one of our foreign students."

"I was there once," Cleveland said. "A long time ago." His voice seemed almost dreamy. "Before your independence. Before you were born, I expect. Remarkable people, you Apaches. Splendid to have you at the university. Well now, my dear Wilson, it's long past my bedtime."

"Yes, yes. Come along. I'll walk you home. And you . . ." President Wilson said. "Mr. Bignon? You'd better be getting to bed, hadn't you?"

"Yes, sir."

Tom listened to the two men stroll off and heard Cleveland say: "Bignon. Bignon. Something familiar about that name, but I can't recall . . . Age. A terrible thing. Now, about my fellow trustees. I think . . ."

The voice trailed off in the distance and the gloom and Tom Bignon breathed in deeply. Presently he heard the sound of a saw. He strode out into the darkness and stood below what he guessed was the end of the flagpole.

"You certainly weren't much help," he hissed. "Spluttering up there while I had to fend off—"

" 'O well for him whose will is strong, he will not suffer long,' " Little Spring said, his voice soft and velvety with mockery.

Fifteen minutes later, the night's vandalism complete, Little

Spring landed like a cat on the grass. "Only another foot to go," he said. "Come on, Big Ears. It's time for a bit of tiswin."

"Tiswin? I don't want—"

"White man's tiswin, compliments of Monsieur Courvoisier."

"That's more like it."

Little Spring, now a young man of twenty-two, in his final year of studies at one of the leading universities in the United States, his mind full of Homeric poetry, English literature, and the canons of political science, felt almost as at home at Princeton as he did astride a horse in pursuit of pronghorn antelope in the high plains of Apacheria. Here he was "Patch," an object of fascination and a certain awe, as well as affection, to his friends, all of whom were white, eastern, and wealthy, and all of whom loved to hear him talk of the ways of the Apache, their legendary bloodthirstiness, their prowess in war. He moved easily in their company, wore their same clothes—the white flannel trousers, the fine silken cravats—but knew he cut an exotic figure by virtue of the glossy black hair he wore long, sometimes loose, sometimes in a single braid down to his shoulder blades. He excelled in their game of polo, was unbeaten as a wrestler and a long-distance runner, and had a legendary capacity for brandy and Scotch. Brought up listening to old stories told around a campfire, he was able to repeat many lectures almost verbatim several weeks after hearing them, and he found some of the university's intellectual offerings—and in particular, political science and European history—of great fascination.

Little Spring glided with the ease of a man on skates between the world of Apacheria, where he spent his summers in breechcloth and moccasins, and the rarefied and high-toned world of eastern university society. He nevertheless remained provincial enough—naive enough, perhaps—to take it for granted that he had gone hunting with one President of the United States, Theodore Roosevelt, the current officeholder, and had just perched in the dark on a flagpole some twenty feet above another, former, President. He lived, in fact, in two very small worlds, and had little idea how vast and how complicated and how frightening most of the world really was.

Almost everything he had encountered in his life gave him delight, but little surprised him. The world—indeed, both his worlds—seemed to have been made expressly for him, a continuing feast for his enrichment. Only one thing he came across in his twenty-two years had left him surprised, unsettled, with a feeling of desperate unfulfillment, indeed, a kind of panic. That was the personage of Muriel Freeman, age twenty-one.

Miss Freeman was a swan-necked young woman with flashing brown eyes and black hair swept up on her head whom he had met two weeks earlier when one of his classmates, Puffy Vanderbilt, took him and Tom Bignon home for a weekend at his parents' home in New York. A small but lavish afternoon tea dance in the mansion on Fifth Avenue had been planned as a highlight of the weekend. There, 150 or so guests and family members represented almost half the accumulated wealth of the city. They gathered in a ballroom that, by itself, had cost upward of a million dollars to build. It was, one could easily have argued, the most beautiful place in America, but little of this registered on Little Spring's brain because, in one of those miracles of perception, the first thing his eyes fell upon as he entered the room was the face of Muriel Freeman standing in a group across the ballroom some forty feet away.

All else was suddenly distant, a kaleidoscopic blur, while his hunter's eye bored in on this visage that he could see even at that distance in every detail—the slightest upcurving of her lips at the corners, the shell-like perfection of her ear, the delicacy of eyelash . . . He had no idea how long he stood transfixed, heart and lungs at a standstill, in a form of suspended animation during which time simply was not a coefficient. He saw her deep brown eyes sweep by him, stop, and return for a fleeting moment to his, saw an expression of . . . what?—surprise, maybe?—flutter briefly over her face, saw her turn to her friend, a woman with yellow hair, and whisper something. Did she laugh? White teeth dazzled briefly. Little Spring shuddered.

He found himself propelled across the gleaming parquet floor, found himself standing only a few feet from this woman now turned toward her friends, seeing her face in profile, long ivory throat rising from ivory lace and lavender silk. He watched as her eye flickered and she turned her head to look at him quizzically.

He introduced himself by his Apache name. "We haven't met," he went on. "They call me Patch."

He saw her eyes widen. She smiled briefly up at him. She was a head shorter than he. He put out his hand and said, "I should have waited for someone to introduce us, but . . ."

"But?" she said.

"But I didn't." He smiled apologetically.

She put her hand out and he shook it, feeling the fingers cool on his palm. "I'm Muriel Freeman," she said. "You're . . . Patch?"

He nodded, and began to feel dizzy. She was still looking at him.

"What *are* you?" she asked. "Oh, that was rude of me, wasn't it?"

She had withdrawn her hand from his.

"No, no. I'm Apache. A friend of Puffy's. From Princeton. I'm, uh, I'm not sure what . . ."

Her eyes glanced over his shoulder and he heard Puffy Vanderbilt.

"Oh yes, Muriel Freeman, this is my friend Patch. He's an Apache warrior. Wonderful chap. I see you've met already. He's full of the most terrifying tales of life on the frontier. You must get him to tell you about it. But, I say, we should all have some champagne, shouldn't we? Here, let me introduce you to the rest of these people . . ."

So Puffy Vanderbilt introduced him to the others, and had he paid much attention, he might have noticed that he was being treated, ever so slightly, as if he were some form of exotic trophy, something Puffy had managed to bring from the wild that was tame, yes, but still perhaps just a tad . . . dangerous? But Little Spring paid no attention, only mouthing the needed courtesies and formalities, recalling no one's name he met that day and registering no faces he saw that day other than that of the astonishing Muriel Freeman.

Though the occasion was called a tea dance, and a small orchestra played gaily through the afternoon, there was actually little dancing—which suited Little Spring, who had mastered the waltz but few others of the dance steps that were popular. On one occasion he did glide with Muriel around the dance floor in a spirited waltz and was filled with joy at the sensation of holding her lightly in his hands while the room swirled around them. On another occasion he stood expressionlessly and inwardly fuming while a cherubic young man with a shock of blond hair took Muriel off to hop around to a new Scott Joplin piano tune. Afterward, Muriel led her dance partner back to where Little Spring was standing; one look at Little Spring's face and the blond man excused himself.

Muriel laughed. "Poor Geoffrey," she said conspiratorially. "He thought you were going to kill him. Such a scowl! You can stop scowling now."

He grinned. "Was I scowling?"

They spent the remainder of the afternoon in a long conversation while seated on a damask-covered divan at the far end of the ballroom or walking outside in the Vanderbilts' extensive gardens, where thousands of bulbs were making their early spring appearance. She listened with an intense directness to his description of life in Apacheria, raising her eyebrows only when he mentioned—albeit briefly—the attractions of Tombstone, and with a dreamy look in her dark eyes as he talked about riding in the high forestlands, seeing jaguars, coming on a herd of elk.

In the garden toward the end of the day, she rested her hand on his forearm as they strolled, and he felt his spirit soar. Little Spring had never felt so comfortable with a woman, any woman, or for that matter with any white person. He was in a state of euphoria unmatched in his life. All his senses seemed heightened, honed, and all the world seemed new. So the descent—sudden, unexpected—was all the more severe, leaving him bereft, as if his soul had been wrenched away.

She was on her way to Europe.

Her father, Abner Freeman, was a businessman of some sort in Chicago—something to do with the cattle business and real estate. He was taking her and her mother on a European tour for two months. They were in New York, staying with her aunt this past two weeks, all of their clothes and other necessities already repacked in a vast array of Louis Vuitton steamer trunks ready for sailing the very next morning at dawn for Le Havre, from which they would go by train to Paris. Muriel seemed excited at the prospect—she had been to Paris once before—and her delight was, of course, the exact measure of Little Spring's dismay.

Of course, he didn't protest, or complain. Apaches never— ever—complained.

Abner Boniface Freeman was living proof that if you had enough money, you could buy your way into any social strata you wanted in the United States of America, and probably any place in the world. Abner Freeman's parents had abandoned him in New Orleans when he was an infant, leaving him to be brought up in a Catholic mission by the Sisters of the Mournful Blood. He had no known antecedents, no pedigree of any sort. Like many such young men, he had gone West once he was old enough, which was when he was fourteen, and wound up working on cattle ranches in the Dakotas and then in Texas. He participated in some of the first long cattle drives, saw men in places like Kansas City making what seemed to be a fortune from the sweat on his brow and the saddle sores on his posterior, and by the time he was twenty-six, he was an entrepreneur, buying and selling cattle and soon real estate as well, putting together princely fiefdoms from the failed claims of sodbusters. When he was thirty-three, he moved eastward to Chicago, married a socially prominent young woman there, had a daughter whom he named Muriel, and continued to amass several fortunes—some of them open and aboveboard, and some a bit less so.

One of the things that had struck Abner Freeman growing up an orphan in New Orleans and had stuck in his mind after all the years of hard work in the West, was the warmth, the sparkle, the camaraderie, the cheerful music, and the sheer gold and crimson beauty of the New Orleans bordello. So, once established beyond a doubt or query at the top of Chicago society along with people like Mr. Montgomery Ward and other commercial geniuses, he began to live his dream. He opened a string of New Orleans–style bordellos in some of the better sections of the city.

These were altogether different from the scandalous panel houses and creep joints of Custom House Place and the other brothel streets for which the city was infamous. Those low-life operations were already being closed down with almost the speed with which they proliferated, largely due to the efforts of a single policeman named Clifton Wooldridge. Panel houses were as given to robbery as to prostitution, designed with panels in the doors so that an unwary customer's wallet could be lifted while he was busy with the prostitute. They were worth a million and half dollars a year in theft in Chicago alone. The prostitutes, of course, could claim to be innocent, and any victim foolish enough to complain would find himself summarily ejected onto the sidewalk with only, if he were lucky, a broken nose. It wasn't until the legendary Officer Wooldridge took to arresting the landlords who rented properties to the panel-house operators that business began to fall off.

Abner Freeman's bordellos were a wholly different affair. It was his intention to bring "class" to Chicago, just as he and other local millionaires brought culture in by generously financing opera houses and museums and establishing funds for the arts. Abner's bordellos were fine residences of which he was the untraceable owner. They were discreet, dignified places taken to be men's clubs—places for elegant dining, for example, and evenings of drawing room music, even the discussion of literary or scientific affairs. They were just the thing for a growing upper middle class in Chicago that aspired to elegance, and they flourished.

While Muriel's mother—a woman of frail beauty and fragile constitution—never did learn much about any of her husband's businesses, by the time their daughter Muriel was fifteen, she had a pretty good idea what her father's regular trips to New Orleans were in aid of. They were more than a hobbyist's interest in strange new forms of music. She knew, in a general sense, what a bordello was, knew that the best ones were in New Orleans, where, along with everything else, an exciting new kind of music was evidently coming into being.

It was called "jass," a Negro word that evidently also alluded to a bordello's main business, just as the music called jass derived from Negro spirituals. Young Muriel learned this from a man named Charles "Buddy" Bolden, a cornet player her father brought to Chicago one spring to perform in one of his "clubs," and who took an avuncular shine to the girl. By the time Muriel was eighteen, Buddy Bolden had gone insane and was locked up in an asylum back in New Orleans, but other musicians like him were imported to Chicago, and Muriel had come to know them, as well.

As a result, Muriel was a pretty worldly young woman by the time she was twenty-one, and her father decided to take her and her mother on the tour again, including a two-week stint in the rarefied high life of New York City Society. What with an adventurous spirit received directly from her rawboned father, and her own passing acquaintance with Chicago's low life, Muriel found society in New York City pretty tame. The young men—like Puffy Vanderbilt, for example—seemed to have all been cut from the same cloth, an expensive but boring flannel, and Muriel found that she yearned for more exotic fabric.

So her heart skipped a beat when she looked across the Vanderbilt ballroom and saw a fierce, coppery-skinned young man staring fixedly at her from black eyes behind cheekbones that looked like ledges on a mountain crag. He was, to someone as open to the world as she, stunningly attractive. His shiny black hair appeared to be pulled back tightly behind his neck. He stood a bit apart from the others, reminding her of a wild animal poised between attack and flight. She turned to point him out to her friend and—what was this?—he, this exotic creature, was walking straight across the parquet floor as lithe as she imagined a panther, coal-black pupils flashing as if lit from within, looking directly at her.

He spoke in a quiet voice with a strangely gentle lilt, and she was both embarrassed and amused to discover that she had blurted out the question, "What are you?"

All she knew about Apaches was that they were terribly dangerous Indians, and had fought off the entire U.S. Army years ago and established their own country where they lived like savages still. But here was one, speaking perfect English and perfectly dressed, but with an animal elegance that made the other men in the room seem porcine . . . Here was an Apache Indian, of all things, who was clearly intent on spending his time with her. Inwardly, Muriel preened, and knew that her last day in New York before she set sail for France would be a memorable one.

But, as it turned out, it was more than that. She found herself nearly mesmerized by the soft-voiced man with the ferocious expression on his face. She was delighted when the foppish Geoffrey—one of the Astors—fled from his scowl. She felt transported by his tales of life in the mountains and on the deserts. And when he was clearly crushed by the news of her impending trip, she was surprised to find herself deeply moved, almost wishing that the journey could be postponed.

They sat in a gazebo in the Vanderbilts' garden at day's end. Around them were flagstone walks and a maze of hedges and the sound of voices. He was still as a rock, sitting beside her, his black eyes staring ahead.

"I'll be coming back in the early days of June," she said.

"To Chicago," he said, and stood up.

"We spend a week in Washington first. My father has business there."

The Indian paced back and forth, restless, his face expressionless and fierce. She wondered if he were going to pounce on her, or if he were going to vanish into thin air.

"People in there," he said. "They seem to be leaving."

She smiled. "Yes."

She was never quite clear in her mind about what happened next. Suddenly he was bent over her, suddenly she sensed that he held a knife, sensed his hand behind her ear. She gasped, flinched, and he held his hand up. A lock of shiny black hair was in his fingers, her hair. His white teeth flashed in a wolfish grin. The knife . . . no longer in sight.

"What . . . ?" she said. Her heart was pounding audibly. Was it just relief that she hadn't been scalped by a Red Indian?

"A keepsake," he said. "Isn't that what you call it?"

She felt herself grinning from ear to ear.

"I'll keep this until you come to Washington. June. I'll go visit old Geronimo there."

Muriel stood up. "What about me? Do I get a keepsake?"

He took her by the arms and pulled her to him, bending his head down slowly, and kissed her. He stopped, lifted his head, and his anthracite eyes bored into her. He kissed her again, then let her arms go. He stood before her, then turned, and she watched him walk around the hedge and disappear.

Two hours earlier he had stridden across the parquet floor and introduced himself by his Indian name, a collection of syllables both liquid and guttural that she could neither pronounce nor remember. His friends called him Patch, he had said. That was all she knew.

Patch from Princeton.

An Apache.

My God.

Nineteen

The trouble started in late spring of 1906 in the mining country around Silver City in the eastern part of Apacheria. It couldn't have happened at a worse time or in a place more fraught with tensions—tensions that had been roiling in the Apache nation like water coming to a boil.

Mining in the southern foothills of this vast mountain wilderness region had long been a sore point for Apaches, going back even before the days of Mangas Colorado. A good deal of the distrust between Apaches and Americans had arisen early here, when the newly arrived American miners—whose presence was at first tolerated by the local bands—turned on their hosts. Every Apache knew the stories of the massacres that followed. After that, there was no trusting these people, whose word was no good in the first place, and who, in the second place, did the contemptible work of taking things from under the ground. But the violence had mostly ended with Apache independence in 1885, and the mining companies remained in place by virtue of the agreement Juh had made with the United States government. The miners were restricted to certain places, most of them living along with a handful of whores in Silver City, in a few outlying camps near the smaller mines, and in the narrow ribbon of the Southern Pacific Railroad whose tracks crossed the new nation. The mining companies paid a handsome royalty to the Apache nation—in all, twenty percent of the value of the refined ore taken from the ground.

In the early days of Apache nationhood, the miners were

well aware of the animosity the Apaches bore them—after all, most of them had experienced that animosity in the form of wounds and dead comrades. They were careful not to antagonize their hosts in any way, and company foremen enforced this discipline with a sternness born of fear. So an uneasy truce had existed in the environs of Silver City for nearly two decades after independence.

But as the nineteenth century melded into the twentieth, and the old miners who had lived through the Apache wars died of lung disease or retired, they were replaced with a new generation from other mining regions in the United States—Colorado, Montana, Nevada—men who had grown up in the intense and highly politicized beginnings of the American labor movement.

In the United States, in particular in railroading, but in other industries as well, strikes had become commonplace by the turn of the century, as had their summary quashing by federal troops. Laboring men were used to a new kind of violence, that between the worker and management, between labor and capital. The new miners who began to appear in Apacheria in the late 1890s were steeped in—or at least danced to the tune of—these new ideologies, and they had a newfound if half-baked pride, and a sense of their own rights as workers and individuals. Thus self-absorbed, they more easily overlooked the courtesies, the self-effacing behavior that would make them, if not welcome, at least tolerated by the tradition-minded and still angry Apaches who dwelled in eastern Apacheria and who firmly and jealously believed that they kept the ancient flames of the Apache Way burning.

Yet here too were members of a new generation—young Apache men who knew the pride, the satisfaction, the heady rush of the warrior's way . . . but only from stories told to them by their fathers and uncles. These were young men of high spirits and animal energy, imbued with a sense of their own grandeur and of the glory of Apache history, but who at the same time had very little to do.

They could hunt as always, and some had taken to running

their own herds of cattle in the grasslands. But one could no longer prove oneself by the crafty and bold raiding of live-stock, no longer show one's prowess with the weapons of war, no longer stand before the tribes' women as a whole and worthy man. Who performed the war dance anymore around a fire blazing defiantly in the night? Who sang the songs of war? Who could look forward to the death chant and a noble Apache end to life?

Many of these younger Apache men drank too much, as Apaches always had, and fought among themselves, and occasionally, out of boredom and restlessness, encouraged trouble with the miners in Silver City, taunting them outside the few gaslit saloons there and brawling in the dusty streets in the darkness of night.

And into this already dangerous mixture, the prophet Nakah-yen had over the years since his arrival been feeding the Apache youth in particular with an ominous sense of apocalypse, a feeling that a hostile world was still, as ever, arrayed dangerously against the true and rightful Apache Way. Only evil and disgrace, he taught more and more openly, could come from the White Eyes, the white man's greed, his slovenly and despicable grubbing for money, his mines, his railroads, his whores, his diseases, and the acrid stink of his presence in the Apache midst.

On May 28, after a weekend of openly defiant meetings, the 112 miners in the employ of two mining companies with long-term contracts in the Silver City area—Phelps-Dodge and the Santa Fe Metals Company—went on strike. Their demands included a raise of ten cents an hour to thirty cents, eight-hour shifts instead of the current twelve, and a handful of other benefits of a technical nature. These demands were formally forwarded that Monday morning by telegraph by the company representatives on the scene to the executive offices of the two companies in question, where the demands were already known. That the strikers would not under any circumstances be allowed to win, that their demands would not be met, was not at issue in the companies' headquarters. The only matter of dispute was the manner by which the strike would be ended and the miners taught a lesson they would not soon forget.

One of the largest shareholders in the Santa Fe Metals Company was the Hearst family, in effect the two sons of George Hearst, former gold miner, western land baron, and U.S. senator from California who had amassed a fortune before dying in 1891. The Hearst sons, William Randolph and George Jr., had both learned a handy ruthlessness from their father, a man reputed to have been so mean that one time while patrolling some of his holdings in the Arizona Territory he was bitten by a scorpion and the scorpion died.

While son William headed off on a career in journalism and publishing, young George continued in the family's mining tradition and it was he who, in the days just before the strike was to take place, suggested that he go talk to Victorio, whom he had met on earlier mining explorations, about these upstart strikers. In this, the Phelps-Dodge people quickly and eagerly colluded. George Hearst Jr. boarded the train that afternoon in Santa Fe, where his company's headquarters were located, and headed for what was still shown on U.S. maps and train schedules as Silver City in the eastern heart of Apacheria.

He arrived there alone on the very morning the strike took place, Monday, May 28, just as it began to rain. He was covered with soot from the coal-fired steam locomotive that spewed black smoke and cinders through the open windows of the carriages, and beneath the soot he was dressed in clothes that resembled the uniforms worn by Teddy Roosevelt's Rough Riders during the Spanish-American War eight years earlier.

George Jr. was an impressive figure of a man, nearly six feet tall, broad-shouldered, with a trim military-style moustache and long sideburns—nearly muttonchops—that drew attention away from the thinning of his once luxurious brown hair. He was greeted at the ramshackle station by his company's representative on the scene, a dour young man with a harelip, and was immediately taken to even more ramshackle stables, where he commandeered a large roan mare and set off through Silver City's three streets. He was eyed curiously and sullenly by the idle miners, standing around in the muddy streets uncertain of what they were to do to advance the justness of their cause now that their demands had been tendered and the mines were, effectively, closed.

"That's Little George Hearst," one of the few remaining old-timers said. "They say he's as mean as his old man. What the hell is he doin'?"

"Let's go ast him," offered another man, a younger one.

"You ast him, sonny. You just do that. Get your damn head taken off one way or another."

"Hey, you! Hearst? How about our demands?" the younger man shouted. Hearst, mounted on his roan, turned his head, smiled broadly, touched a forefinger casually to the brim of his campaign hat, and rode on wordlessly out of town in the direction of the northern foothills and the green-carpeted peaks that lay beyond.

Two days later, during which time it had continued to rain intermittently, turning Silver City into a quagmire and causing flash floods in the arroyos outside of town, George Hearst Jr. rode silently back into town just past noon. As he passed a large group of idle miners sitting outside the Fat Chance Saloon, he again smiled and casually saluted, touching the brim of his campaign hat with a forefinger. Reaching the stables, he turned his roan mare loose in the corral and was met there by the two company representatives. The three men proceeded to the ramshackle railroad station and sat without a word on the rickety platform for an hour until the eastbound train arrived. All three boarded the train without so much as a look back at Silver City, and the striking miners watched it disappear around the bend east of town, a smoke-spewing dragon impervious to the urgency and importance of the events it was leaving behind.

That night, the frustrated strikers met again in the Fat Chance, drank much of the saloon's most inexpensive whiskey, and argued aimlessly about what it all meant. Many brave things were said, along with many foolish things. The miners did manage to conclude that the company stores of food were dwindling rapidly, were hardly likely to be replaced, and would have to be supplemented. It was agreed that the miners would have to resort to hunting, and a hunting party was appointed.

Before dawn the following morning four of the six men appointed as hunters set off on horseback into the hills, the other two men being unrousable, owing to the effects on their bloodstreams and nervous systems of the Fat Chance saloon's least expensive whiskey. Of the four active hunters, two had done some before, one of them being the old-timer who had recognized George Hearst Jr. when he rode into town.

"Do you suppose that boy Hearst was goin' off to talk to the damn Apaches?" one of the less experienced hunters asked of the older man.

"Maybe he was, but he went in the wrong direction," the older man said. "They down in their summer camps now, not up here."

The hunting party made its way up through the piñon and juniper woodlands and then into the more open, parklike forest of tall ponderosa pines, some of which reached as high as a hundred feet into the emerging light of the day. At this point, the horsemen spread out about a hundred yards apart and continued upward, moving slowly and as silently as they could manage over the blanket of pine needles, each man catching only the occasional glimpse of a companion off to the side.

The old-timer, who had worked on the big sailing ships out of San Francisco in the Pacific trade before turning, for reasons he could no longer recall or fathom, to the grimy work of mining, allowed his eye and mind to wander. He looked long and aimlessly at a delicate splash of color on the ground, a wildflower that looked like a tiny halyard strung with bell-like vermilion pennants. He thought about the sailor's life, that it had been just as hard and unrewarding as being a miner, and he heard a bird chirping—a rasping sound somewhere up ahead breaking the peace of the morning. And he responded too late.

The arrow pierced his chest just above the lower right-hand

rib, a searing pain like being kicked by a horse, and he toppled off his mount cursing to himself, watching the pine needles on the forest floor rush up at him as the world turned black. He became aware of lying on his back with a horrid pain in his side, and he opened his eyes. Above him stood the Apaches. How many? Four. Stripped down to the waist, painted black and red, blood in their eyes, staring at him . . . Oh, God, oh, no . . . and for the first time in more than a decade he prayed to Jesus Christ to intervene, to take his soul, please, now, Jesus, *now* please.

Just before noon most of the miners were sitting in the town's three saloons when someone ran into the Fat Chance and reported with alarm that fifty or a hundred Apaches were headed into town from the north, coming out of the woodlands on horseback, all bare necked and painted like the savages they were. In fact, that was an exaggeration. As the miners poured out onto the wooden sidewalks, they saw there were only twenty Apaches, but they were indeed stripped to the waist and painted, and in their midst were the four horses that had carried the hunting party out of town that morning.

As the phalanx of Apaches rode closer, a silent horde with implacable black eyes looking straight ahead, the miners could see that the four horses had been stripped of saddles and other tack. They were being led by simple rope leads. And across each of their backs, arms and legs dangling down, lay a corpse. The miners watched in horror as the Apaches drew nearer, turned the four corpse-bearing horses loose, and moved off twenty or so yards down the street, where they turned around and looked back at the miners. No one said a word.

Something was wrong with the corpses. Their heads and shoulders were charred, blackened. The skulls were misshapen. Charred and broken. Gray goo was dribbling from the cracks. There was a retching sound, a splatter, and someone said, "Sweet Jesus!"

One of the Apaches' horses moved forward a few steps, and the rider pointed at the four corpses.

"These men," he said, "try to steal our game, hunt our deer. You go back to work and your company feeds you. You go back to work, dig in the ground." The warrior paused to spit in the street. "You finish your work."

With that, the Apaches wheeled around on their horses and loped down the street, out of town, heading south. The strike was over. The sorry, charred corpses of the hunting party were quickly buried, and the men went back to work.

About the same time the last shovelful of dirt was dumped on the graves of the four hunters, George Hearst Jr. sat on one end of a comfortable settee in the headquarters of the Santa Fe Metals Company located on Palace Avenue east of the historic old plaza in Santa Fe. Hearst was no longer dressed in his field uniform, and his brightly polished visage was free of coal soot. He wore a finely tailored black worsted suit and a silk cravat and matching pocket handkerchief of crimson, and he pulled comfortably on a cigar that had cost two dollars and come from Cuba. The other three men in the office were similarly attired and had their own Cuban cigars. They listened with increasing happiness to Hearst's account.

"I told Victorio—he's getting on now, gray in his hair, but he still looks plenty fierce. Glowers out at the world with that one eye askew and he looks like he'd as soon slit your throat as give you the time of day. Of course, Victorio hates the mines, hates the miners. Those people still don't believe it's right to dig things from the ground. Some kind of pagan religious notion. Won't plant corn. Won't dig silver. Well, of course, they don't think any kind of work is proper for a man to be caught doing. God, what savages they remain. At any rate, I told old Victorio that I knew as well as he that the Apaches hate these mines, I sympathized with that. But the Apaches *did* have these contracts, I said, they were like treaties that shouldn't be broken by honorable men. And then I told him that we knew better than anyone there was only a certain amount of silver in the ground there, that we had been mining it a long time and it would run out one day. I pointed out to the old man that the sooner it ran out, the sooner all the miners would pack up their tools and leave, gone forever. So I wanted old Victorio to help us persuade the miners to go back to work."

"Brilliant, George, brilliant," one of the men guffawed.

"I told him," Hearst went on, enjoying the moment, "that how he did it was his affair entirely. I did say that I wondered from time to time if some of the younger Apaches didn't get bored these days, restless. Maybe, I said, they could help. And, gentlemen, we just received this telegram from that fellow with the harelip, what's his name, Jenkins. I sent him back there from Soccoro; I figured that Victorio wouldn't waste any time." He flourished the yellow paper. "Gentlemen, the men are back in the mines."

"Bravo," the senior officer of Santa Fe Metals Company said. "Bravo. That calls for a bit of brandy all around."

Several years earlier, one of the leaders of the Navajos had ridden down into Apacheria from the barren sheeplands to the north where they were sequestered on their reservation. Manuelito his name was, a man who had gained some renown as a warrior before the Navajos finally gave up and, so far as the Apaches were concerned, stopped being real People. Manuelito brought gifts, which was proper, and one of these was a red and black chief's blanket his wife had woven. Juh took an immediate fancy to the blanket, and nowadays wore it over his shoulders at all times except when it was too hot for such things. And these days, even in the early part of the summer, it wasn't too hot for Juh to wear his chief's blanket.

It was a sign of age, he knew, this feeling of constant chill, but he said nothing of that and let everyone believe that he kept the blanket on even when the weather was quite balmy as a badge of office, a recognizable sign of his leadership. But that being the case, Juh was often reminded by his blanket to think about the day that would come before too long when he would go to the Red Ground Country and someone else might want to wear this same blanket.

Perhaps it would be his only remaining son, Little Spring,

the old man thought as he rode along the flatland with its white *playas*, toward the green mountains on the horizon ahead. Who could say? Not Juh. He knew that was not how things happened among his people. After he was gone, someone would emerge to be leader. Juh had done everything to see to it that Little Spring was prepared for such a role. His son knew the Apache ways as well as any man, and he was in the college called Princeton, where he was supposed to learn enough about the white man's ways not to be fooled by them. It was all a father could do. That, and hope. That, and pray.

It was about the time of year for Little Spring to come back from the college in the East. Any day now, the old man thought. He looked forward to their reunion. He wished he had had more time himself to instruct his son over the years, to spend time with him. But he had needed to put him in the hands of Lozen, and the teachers in Tombstone, and then the teachers in Princeton for all his educations.

But at last Little Spring was finished with Princeton. They would spend more time together now. That would be a good thing. Better to know that than to regret the time they had not spent together. Juh allowed his mind to go blank while his horse made its way confidently toward the higher ground on a familiar path. He slumped a little on the thick saddle blankets under him and his mind drifted into a state akin to sleep where he could forget everything, even the pain in his joints—his knees, his shoulders, his gnarled old knuckles—that was a nearly constant companion these days.

Later, with the sun more than halfway down the western sky, Juh heard a whistling, something like the call of the night bird, and he came alert, listening. His horse was plodding through some willow trees alongside a creek that ran quickly and silver with the last snowmelt of the year. Up ahead he heard the sound of a horse's hooves, moving ahead of him, and soon he heard several horses, now coming his way. In a few minutes the horsemen appeared, standing on the edge of the creek on a pebbly spit of land. The riders, three young Apache braves, saluted him and grinned. They exchanged the courtesies of the

Chiricahua and the additional courtesies due a Chiricahua leader and fell in behind the old man. Before long they came into a large clearing where Victorio's camp was pitched, in all a dozen wickiups made from willow branches housing his three wives and his extended family of children and cousins.

People stuck their heads out of the wickiups, mostly women, and Juh, remembering the gravity of his mission after a long ride and a long meditation, remained expressionless as his horse walked among the lodges toward the eastern end of the clearing, where Victorio's wickiup sat. The women murmured greetings and little children ran naked and careless in the grass, darting here and there and laughing. Juh smiled at a naked little boy with a fine round belly, perhaps three years old, who ran up, wide-eyed, as he rode in. The old man then slowly and painfully dismounted and stood next to his horse, his hands on his knees. Slowly he straightened up while the boy stood staring at him not more than three feet away.

"Am I the oldest one you have ever seen?" Juh asked with great gravity.

The little boy shook his head. He bent over in a fair imitation of a very old person and said the words for "grandmother."

"Your grandmother looks older than me?"

The boy grinned and nodded.

"But she's a woman. I have one of those," Juh said, pointing at the little boy's tiny penis. "Like you. I am a man."

The little boy looked stunned. His eyes widened again and then he grinned and fled around the wickiup nearby just as Victorio, stooping, came out into the sunlight.

The necessary formalities were lengthy, and when they were complete, Victorio murmured some orders and his wives began to bustle about, making food available. The two men ate in silence and then retired to the edge of the camp near the trees and sat down.

"Your little grandson thought I was an old woman," Juh said. He laughed. "A time comes when it is hard to tell. And when it makes little difference."

Victorio frowned.

"You disagree, Victorio?"

"Juh speaks of wisdom? How it comes to all old people?" Juh nodded.

"Old people don't always agree," Victorio said. "Where then is wisdom?"

"It is there. Among them. Some here, some there." Juh sat silent for a time, and then spoke again. "You must tell me the wisdom of killing those miners."

Victorio explained about the visit from George Hearst, who had come alone on horseback to Victorio's camp, just as Tom Jeffords had come alone into the stronghold of Cochise so long ago. Hearst had asked for the Apaches' help so that the mining could end sooner and the White Eyes would leave the country.

"And you believe this man, Hearst," Juh said. "That they will dig out all the white metal and then leave."

Victorio said nothing, and Juh nodded.

"So now the miners work harder, faster," Juh said. "I understand. I see the wisdom you have learned, Victorio. You too are growing wiser as you grow old."

Victorio looked up, sensing mockery in Juh's line of talk, and the older man smiled briefly at him.

"Sometimes," Juh went on, "to keep the Apache Way safe and pure from the ways of the White Eyes, you have to do the White Eyes' bidding. Is that not so?" He nodded, a man suddenly seeing the light. "And so the White Eyes are now happy because the Apaches killed some of their people." He paused.

"You see how much the world has changed, Victorio? Since we were young warriors, since it was only us, the Apaches, against the whole world? I wonder how you explain this to the young men, now that they've smelled the blood? What are they to think?"

The men sat silent. Off to the west the sky had turned red, and three dark birds with white patches on their wings soared and swooped overhead.

Juh realized he was exhausted—tired from the long journey, to be sure, but exhausted by his responsibilities, the need to chastise his old ally, to try to hold the world in balance. Now, having delivered his warning to Victorio, he had to restore the warrior's pride, his authority.

"You will know what to say to them, to the young men. They will need your wisdom now." Juh yawned. "These days," he said, changing the topic, "these days I find I need to sleep earlier. Has this happened to you yet? No, you are younger. Was that your grandson I talked with, or was that a son?"

Juh rose slowly to his feet.

"My son," Victorio said, and gave his name.

"A fine-looking boy." Juh stretched, and Victorio stood and led the way to one of his lodges, where Juh would spend the night.

The following morning Juh's heart stopped.

The old man was wearing his red and black chief's blanket and sitting on his horse, half asleep as he crossed the San Simon Valley. Ahead of him the craggy ramparts of the Chiricahua Mountains soared up into the sky. All around Juh the midmorning sun had bleached the world into colorlessness, but the mountains ahead remained defiantly red. It was then that Juh's seventy-six-year-old heart fluttered violently a few times and went still. For just the slightest interval, he knew what was taking place, but it all happened too quickly for him either to welcome it or regret it.

His body slid sideways off his horse and landed sprawled on the ground. The horse stopped, turned, and looked at the body, puzzled. It snorted once, twice, and stood there for a while, indecisively raising and lowering its big head. It was June 1, 1906.

Twenty

The two men formed a strange cameo, standing in the middle of the marble floor of the cavernous hotel lobby on the first day of June. Around them, green-and-gold-liveried Negroes went back and forth on innumerable missions, taking luggage out the bronze doors onto the sidewalk, returning with yet other bags, other visitors in tow. The hotel's departing and arriving guests were almost entirely men in fine dark suits and carefully brushed hats, and women in long pastel dresses and hats festooned with white egret feathers. As each set of guests departed or arrived, they looked with either amusement or mere curiosity at the two men standing as still as boulders amid the bustle and swirl under the vast chandelier that hung thirty feet overhead.

One of the men was tall—a young six-footer—dressed in a black suit and a maroon cravat against a soft white shirtfront. There was nothing unusual about that, but what caught people's attention was the brownish, almost coppery tint to his skin, the narrow Oriental eyes, and the anthracite braid that hung down his back. The other man, far shorter, had a red headband over his long white hair, and a leathery brown face seamed with age. His old eyes were sunken and watery, his jaw thrusting forward with a steady belligerence. He wore a loose white tunic, and white trousers that were tucked into moccasins that rose up his bowed legs almost to his knees.

These two men were not at all what one expected to see in the lobby of the Willard Hotel on Pennsylvania Avenue in the capital city of the United States. Indeed, most of the hotel's guests had never seen what they quickly realized were Red Indians anywhere. Few among them, however, knew they were looking at Apaches, though one man, a large and prosperous-looking man with a gold chain hanging across his ample stomach, leaned over to the woman whose hand was on his forearm and whispered, "That old fellow, Alice. Do you see? He looks a bit like that Apache warrior, Geronimo, doesn't he? Couldn't be Geronimo, though. That old savage would have to have died by now."

The two Indians stood, oblivious to the passing stares, keeping their eyes fixed firmly at the top of the red-carpeted staircase that descended grandly into the lobby.

"There," the younger man said. "That's her." The old man, who was in fact Geronimo, squinted up the stairs. At the top, standing still for a moment as she surveyed the lobby, was a white woman with dark hair swept up on her head, dressed in a white blouse with long sleeves, and a full, floor-length skirt that was the yellow of daffodils. In one hand that hung down at her side, she held a yellow hat with yellow feathers.

The young man watched a smile come over her face, and saw her lips form the word "Patch" before she began to descend. He stepped over to the bottom of the stairs and watched her come down, only vaguely aware of the tall figure that descended behind her. He stood grinning and speechless as she reached the bottom stair and put out her hand.

"Patch," she said again, her eyes level with his. He reached out and took her hand. Green flecks seemed to dance in her brown eyes, and he felt his heart flutter a few times in a staccato rhythm.

"You got my message," Little Spring said. "The hotel gave it to you?"

"Yes. That you are whisking us off somewhere for lunch. Where are you taking us? Oh, yes," she said, "this is my father, Abner Freeman. Father, this is Patch."

Little Spring felt his knuckles squeezed almost painfully by the big florid-faced man. Abner Freeman was broad-shouldered and thick-chested, and had thinning hair of a nondescript color, nothing at all like the ebony mane that his daughter Muriel wore swept up from her neck onto her head. But he had the same dark brown eyes, which studied Little Spring with what the young Apache thought might be mirth as the two men exchanged courtesies. Little Spring introduced them both to Geronimo, who nodded happily as he shook their hands. As the foursome made its way across the marble floor to the hotel's huge bronze doors, Geronimo made a point of taking Muriel Freeman's arm in his gnarled old hand, and he scuttled along beside her like a triumphant old rooster.

Fifteen minutes later Abner Freeman and his daughter Muriel were surprised to see that the driver was turning the black brougham into the semicircular drive on the north side of the White House. They were astonished, even momentarily dumbfounded, to see that awaiting them as they stepped down from the brougham, standing grandly in the entrance of the presidential mansion, was none other than the President himself, beaming broadly, his big teeth gleaming and the noon sun glittering from his rimless spectacles.

"Aha!" the President boomed. "Geronimo! And Little Spring. Splendid, splendid!" He stepped forward with a big paw outstretched. "Welcome, welcome."

Muriel turned to Little Spring with a quizzical smile. "Little Spring?" she said.

"That's what my Apache name means. It's the place where I was born." Muriel smiled enigmatically, and Little Spring said, "Sir, this is Muriel Freeman, and her father, Abner Freeman. They're from Chicago."

The President welcomed them and drew them into the White House, escorting Muriel across an anteroom and down a long hallway, while Geronimo scuttled along close behind. Little Spring was aware that Abner Freeman was glancing at him curiously as they followed the other three down the hall.

There was a series of loud, high-pitched whoops, and a heavy wooden door swung open ahead of them. Two boys about eight years old raced across the hall into a room directly across the way, pursued by three others who wore feathers jammed in headbands and carried what looked like small hatchets. The second door slammed behind them.

President Roosevelt laughed loudly. "My son Quentin and some of his friends," he explained. "Playing cowboys and Indians, it looks like. Looks like the Indians are winning." He cleared his throat and changed the subject.

"Let me tell you, Miss Freeman, I asked Geronimo to drive in my inaugural parade. It was a terrible mistake. I was completely upstaged. Everyone along Pennsylvania Avenue was so impressed to see the great Apache warrior that no one—I assure you, no one—noticed me at all. I might as well have stayed home." He laughed, a booming sound. "And Little Spring . . . my dear, I notice that you smile in a what—mischievous way—when I say Little Spring. You'll have to tell me why that is. At any rate, Little Spring—you see? There you go again. He showed me my first and only jaguar. *El tigre*, right?" he said over his shoulder. "Now, lunch is served, I believe. Follow me this way."

Once he discovered that Abner Freeman had started out, so to speak, in the cattle business, President Roosevelt regaled his guests with tales of the West, his own experiences ranching, then stories of hunting and fishing, returning at one point to Little Spring's jaguar.

"There was something so astonishingly pure about that—the magnificent animal with its green eyes staring at me for a moment, the eyes so wise, so ancient . . . It stuck in my mind and I began thinking about the places in our West where such a sight is still possible. I began to realize that those places needed protection. They needed to be set aside as refuges, wildlife refuges. So that is exactly what I have done." He grinned broadly around at his guests.

"So, you see, young man," he said, his eyes resting on Little Spring, "you are one of the inspirations for the American system of National Wildlife Refuges. Here's to you and to the Apache people." He held up his wineglass in a toast.

Abner Freeman gasped slightly and raised his glass. Muriel Freeman smiled beautifully and glanced at Little Spring under long dark lashes. Geronimo's knife-edge lips pulled back into a vulpine grin, and he raised his glass with a flourish, eagerly downing its contents. It was a moment of almost total triumph and joy for Little Spring, which is why he found it not just odd but terrifying when a deep and clammy cold fell over him, as if some icy claw had grasped his shoulder. For a moment, while the deadly chill lasted, he sensed himself being wrenched toward a glowing orange light surrounded by blackness.

The vision left and he was startled, almost frightened, by what he suddenly perceived. As if he were standing aside, he sensed himself sitting at the lavishly set table with its white linen tablecloth and gold service. He was dressed in a black suit with a soft white shirtfront and maroon cravat, seated among these people, these friends. How was it he felt comfortable in this room? There were, he suddenly understood, two Little Springs, two versions of himself, both true, both valid.

He shuddered and looked up like a man suddenly coming awake. He smiled at his friends, then looked down modestly at the gold plate of mixed, exotic greens before him on the table and wondered what spirit had paid him so abrupt, so alarming, a visit, and brought with it so peculiar a truth.

The following day, at the invitation of Abner Freeman, who was deeply impressed by Little Spring's "credentials" in Washington, D.C., the young Apache and Princeton graduate boarded Freeman's personal and private Pullman Palace Company car. Freeman, who was something of a brigand, as were most of the American captains of industry and enterprise, rather admired what he knew about the Apaches in general—they were winners to begin with, and outstanding raiders who were not above taking what they wanted from the less apt.

And there was something about this fellow Patch: some steel in there, is how Freeman put it to himself. The son of the Apache nation's president or leader or whatever they called him—sachem? Probably inherit the mantle. Useful chap to know.

Abner Freeman also rather liked it that his daughter Muriel

often came up with these interesting, rather than conventional, swains. They came and went, of course, and Lord knew whom she would eventually settle upon. Certainly not this Indian fellow. But he was an interesting young man, and certainly well connected. God bless America, he thought.

Freeman's Pullman car was a shiny green with bright crimson fittings around the windows, and the door was lettered in gold. The interior was spacious, plush, like a slightly over-crowded hotel lobby filled with furniture that appeared to be European. The windows were curtained in lavender damask, and a single Oriental rug covered the floor. Brass lamps and glass, lots of glass, shimmered yellow in the gaslight. It was a world unto itself.

As the train lurched twice at 3:03 in the afternoon and began its slow departure from Union Station, a Negro in a white jacket with red trim arrived through an ornately carved door of walnut with a silver tray bearing assorted fruit juices and a decanter of sherry, along with three silver cups. Little Spring watched the black man carefully pour amber liquid from the decanter into the silver cups and hand them to Muriel Freeman, her father, and to him. He again had the fleeting sensation of somehow being outside himself. He looked deep into the silver cup with its amber fluid and realized that nowhere in his country, nowhere in the land of Apacheria, did one see anything exactly this color.

At the same time, two thousand miles to the west, the people of Apacheria began to assemble, trekking upward in family groups and in whole bands, streaming up into the steep vastness of the Chiricahua Mountains like a great seasonal migration. No one of them spoke. Even the children were subdued and silent, aware that the moment was one of gravity, though not understandable in its details. Juh, they knew, had died, and everyone had fallen silent, hissing the little children into silence too. Exactly who Juh was, most of them didn't know, but they all could see that his death was the most momentous event so far in their lives.

Through the day and into the night, from all directions, the People streamed up into the mountains along old and familiar trails through the rocks and cliffs, and when they reached the height where the low piñon and juniper forest began to give way to the taller ponderosa pines, they could hear the wailing that was already under way. The sound—both low and high in pitch, and continuous—descended the ravines and arroyos like tendrils of mist, filling the world with an opaque sadness, and it rose high into the sky like the howling of wolves—how far into the heavens, no one knew. It was punctuated with the violent high-pitched trill only the women made, a terrifying sound of pain and loss and fear and defiance that carried far, especially in the stillness of night.

Juh's body lay wrapped in his blanket in his camp near the small spring-fed creek that flowed perennially. He was watched over by a few nephews and his wife Ishton, and various Apache leaders as they arrived in the light of an intensely burning fire, Juh's last. From above them and all around the wailing came, pouring forth from nooks and crannies and echoing in the surrounding crags, and when one group somewhere in the dark paused, another took it up.

The lamentation rose and fell like an ocean tide, consuming the mountains and filling the sky, continuing through the hours of the night and past the first glimpse of the sun in the east, when the ocean of sound . . . ceased. Silence fell over the mountains—an awesome stillness. Juh's nephews stood up as one, carefully placed the body on a litter, and carried it away beyond the trees that ringed the camp to a secret place in the rocks above, a cave that they sealed with boulders and left, never to be mentioned to anyone.

Throughout the morning, the People remained silent, only the occasional voice murmuring among the rocks, more often than not to summon a small child, restless with hunger, back from some mindless distraction away from the adults. The high mountain chill soon left the air, and the People warmed themselves like lizards in the rocks and the clearings of the Chiricahuas around what had been Juh's camp. As the sun rose higher, food began to appear—jerky, nuts, traveling fare the mourners had brought with them. Tendrils of blue smoke rose here and there, disappearing into the air like prayers—small fires sparking into life.

The wailing was over, the spirit of the dead man presumed gone. One remained quiet nonetheless lest it be tempted to return—this was a necessary precaution—and no one mentioned the name of the onetime leader—this was an absolute taboo. But the pulse of life was returning, along with the warming sun.

And so through the morning and afternoon, the People remained in the mountains, quiet, respectful. A death had taken place, and any death was troubling, bringing to the fore, as a death always did, the hidden world of spirits, the dark and dangerous mysteries. But there was a silent rejoicing too. In all, more than five thousand Apaches, most of them children, had made the sorry trek to the mountains and had wailed and mourned and now warmed themselves in the sun, and without being completely aware of it, they enjoyed the simple presence of so many of themselves gathered in one place. A sense of utter safety, a sense of power, of a muscular hope, was arising unspoken among the People. They all felt it, this great gift of the leader whose name they would not mention again for a long time, the one who had wrought the great victory, and the independence that had followed for more than twenty years.

An air of tense, urgent expectation hung over the mountains, old matters as always making way for the new.

Ishton felt it, alone as she was, watching the last embers of the fire die away. She sat wrapped in a blanket, part of her mind still far away, part of her vision seeing not dying embers but small features from another part of the world, the past she had shared with her husband. She knew she should not let herself see these things, let her nose recall old scents, her ears hear murmurs from long ago, but they called to her, beckoned to her, and she let them have their say, off to the side, the way one glimpses little shapes against one's eyelids when they are closed and it is dark. If she didn't look directly at them, didn't have them directly in her mind, they would not interfere with the proper passing of . . . things.

Her voice had risen with the others through the night, over and over, from deep within her, her whole body shuddering with the force of it. It had come like a river in flood, an overwhelming, roiling rapids, thrashing her, shaking her, drowning her in wave after wave of ecstatic pain, seeing nothing, leaving her finally exhausted.

Now she would have to let them go, these warming glimpses, and let them take away with them the awful weight that lay on her. Maybe the weight would go with them. But perhaps she could let them remain with her—these dear, tender glimpses—just for a while longer. They were so little. So little. So fragile.

And the world was so cold.

She felt a hand touch her shoulder, and without looking up, she knew it was Lozen, the Warrior Woman now long past those things, her old friend, and the one who had taught the skills of the Apache to her son. Her son who was not here to mourn the death of his father. Who was somewhere in the East and didn't know his father was dead.

Another thing to grieve about.

Lozen let herself down on the ground beside Ishton with a grunt. The two women sat silently for several minutes, cloaked in blankets. Then, without any of the formalities that might normally have passed between them, Lozen began to speak.

"My husband died when he fell from his horse, you remember?" She pointed to the west with a puckering of her lips and a tilt of her head. "Over there. But he was drunk when he died. Fell off, fell down the cliff and froze to death before anyone found him. He was a brave man. He killed a lot of enemies. Not like . . . your husband or my brother Victorio. But many."

She fell silent.

"More than me," she said when she resumed. "He was a warrior. Not a hunter. He had nothing to do after independence, so he drank, and he left us. Look over there, Ishton." She pointed again. Across the clearing, Victorio stood glowering at the water in the little creek, his arms folded across his chest. Around his neck he wore an elaborate necklace of porcupine quills and the teeth of a mountain lion. Under a thin and softening layer of skin, Victorio was still a hard man of muscle and sinew. Above his breechcloth his stomach was flat, and his legs were planted straight and far apart like young trees.

Here and there small clusters of people stood or sat on the ground, many having taken positions in the shade. On some high ground in the sun at one edge of the clearing, several young men sat watching. Among them was Nakahyen the prophet, lank and grim-faced, his face a mask of perpetual contempt. From time to time his mouth moved, and the young men around him turned to listen.

Fifty yards downstream from where Victorio stood alone, the creek dropped into a channel that ran through the trees. A few people stood idly there, talking quietly among themselves, then took a few steps backward, as if to make way. Lozen and Ishton watched as Naiche emerged into sight with his sad face. Behind him out of the shadows a wide-brimmed hat of plain black appeared and then the rest of Minnie Bignon, enveloped in a plain black dress. She was holding one corner of its long skirt up to permit her to step over the rough ground, and now she let it go, her bosom rising and falling hugely with exertion. In her other hand she held a handkerchief with which she lightly touched her forehead. Her eyes darted around the clearing and came to rest briefly on Ishton and Lozen. She glanced in the direction of Victorio, still motionless by the creek. From behind her three other women similarly dressed in black emerged from the trees. Together they slowly followed Naiche as he began to walk across the clearing toward the white ashes that were all that remained now of the fire that had burned through the night. A light breeze was lifting some, floating them up in little puffs.

Lozen and Ishton watched Naiche step around the ashes and walk toward them slowly, with the huge white woman and the other three behind him. Naiche's face was drawn and dark pouches sagged under his eyes like bruises. The slightly startled look he had always had on his face was gone, disappeared into the deep vertical lines that descended from his cheekbones to the bottom of his jaw. He was getting old, Ishton thought. They were all getting old.

She listened with only half her mind as Naiche's soft voice spoke the elaborate Chiricahua courtesies that were due a matriarch. The thought flickered that no longer would she be a matriarch, a woman of power. Just another old woman of the tribe. But no, she was the mother of Little Spring.

Who was not here. Not here while the People sat expectantly, wondering who among them would emerge as the leader. Would anyone? Or would the People split apart into small groups again, like splinters from a fallen tree, the way they had lived before ... before the-one-who-was-gone-now had brought them together into one?

If only Little Spring were here, Ishton thought. He was too young, too fresh, too untried for the People to accept as their leader. But even so, if only he were here, perhaps the People, seeing him, would know to wait.

Wait? For what? How could an Apache—any Apache, even an Apache so well trained in so many arts—call forth the respect and loyalties of the People without having led men in war?

And here was the greatest remaining warrior, Victorio, striding past the ashes toward them. His crazy black eye was flashing like obsidian in the sun, the other nearly vanished behind its eyelid. His jaw was set like rock. He moved like a great lion on the hunt.

He stopped before the two Apache women who were seated cross-legged on the ground and, without a look at them, addressed himself to Naiche in a voice that was quiet and harsh as a knife cutting deer hide.

"Why is she here? Why have you let her and these whores come here? This is a sacred place, a sacred time. It shouldn't be defiled by White Eyes." Victorio was staring, glaring into Naiche's eyes, compounding the insult of his words. Naiche looked back, his mouth sagging in what might have been seen as sadness. Minnie Bignon's softly protruding upper lip which, even after all these years, added so to the innocent appearance of her baby face, began to tremble visibly. Her eyes widened with a distraught look.

"These women came to express their respect—" Naiche began, and Victorio shook his head impatiently.

"The whores don't belong here. They foul this place." His words, like hammer blows, resounded in the silence that had fallen over the clearing.

"I'll go, we'll go," Minnie said, her eyes filling with water.

"No!" Naiche barked, turning momentarily toward her, then back to Victorio. "They will stay, Victorio."

"These are not their people here," the warrior insisted. "They meant nothing to the man who is gone. Only to you, Naiche. You. A onetime Apache who writhes in the rolls of white fat, who counts the White Eyes' money."

Ishton leaned forward, putting her hands on the ground before her, and pushed herself upward. She rose from her cross-legged position to her full height. Her eyes looked past the people in the clearing.

"This," she said, "is my camp. It is my camp until I have it burned down and nothing is left. And then I will go away from here and cut my hair off. Until then, it is to me to say who may come and who may go."

She looked into Victorio's eyes.

"You, Victorio. You were his rival but also his friend. You were loyal to his vision." She looked at Naiche. "You Naiche, you too were loyal. We all were. We were all enlarged by his wisdom. He let us be one people the way we were a long time ago, before anyone can remember. All of us."

Ishton put a hand out toward Minnie. "She and these others who have chosen to live among us, they are our people too. That is what he said many times." She turned, tugged her blanket more tightly around her shoulders, and walked the twenty feet to her wickiup, stooping to enter it.

No one spoke, no one moved for several moments. Then Lozen, the Warrior Woman, grinned savagely.

"Why don't you two warriors go squat down in the creek and dunk your balls in the cold water. We women need to get to work."

She stood up with a grunt, and a titter rippled around the clearing.

By the time night fell, and food that seemed to appear from nowhere was being prepared, and numerous fires were crackling cheerfully in the mountains, everyone among the Apaches had heard about Lozen's comment, and the tensions and the sadness of the day were, at least temporarily, eased by the restorative medicine of laughter.

Twenty-one

For all the lavish craftsmanship and money expended on the construction of Abner Freeman's personal Pullman Palace Company car, including its highly engineered wheel base and system of springs and suspension, it remained a railway carriage being towed by a vast iron horse over steel rails laid on wooden ties that stretched across an uneven landscape. No engineering known in 1906 could eliminate the slightly arrhythmic clatter of steel wheels over rails or the subsequent buffeting of everything in the railroad cars—however subtle a buffeting it might be. The effect of this, coupled with the more rhythmic snorting of the distant engine, had a highly soporific effect on many railroad passengers, and one of these was Muriel Freeman, who spent most of the day and a half the train took to reach Chicago either dozing gracefully among some large pillows on a settee in the drawing room or sound asleep in one of three small but comfortable compartments.

This threw Abner and Little Spring into a situation where they were largely alone together for longer periods than either of them had counted on. For a good part of this interval, Abner excused himself, pleading the press of business, and sat at a small escritoire with curvilinear legs decorated with gilt curlicues at one end of the drawing room, writing letters with a gold pen. Abner was a tall man, slightly over six feet and big-boned, and it looked to Little Spring as if the delicate table would crumble under his elbows at any moment.

For his part, Little Spring spent his time looking at Muriel dozing on the settee, thinking about her while she was in her sleeping compartment, watching the farmlands of Pennsylvania and Ohio and Indiana blur endlessly past the window, and trying to remain relatively still while every fiber in his frame screamed at him to move, to walk, run, even break the window and jump—anything to escape what pressed in on his soul as an overly ornate cage. While in Washington, waiting for Muriel and her father to arrive, he had visited the newly built zoo set in the steep valleys of Rock Creek Park, and quickly left in horror. Now in the Freeman's palace car, he felt exactly as he imagined the zoo animals must feel. One of them, an African doglike animal of some sort, had worn a deep path in the dirt pacing back and forth before its bars.

At one point in the late morning of the day after they had left Washington, Little Spring was idly wondering how long it would take a man—him, for instance—to wear such a path in the Oriental rug in the parlor car, when Abner Freeman capped his pen, turned in his tiny curlicued chair, and said, "Boring, isn't it? Seems endless, traveling across this country all cooped up. Let's have a drink. Do Apaches, uh, ever have a drink before noon?"

Little Spring smiled. "Yes. Whenever the spirit moves us." Both men laughed lightly at the witticism.

"Scotch, then?"

"Thank you."

At another delicate table against one wall, where several crystal decanters and some glassware had been laid out, Abner made two drinks, still wearing the spectacles that rode low on his large red nose, and handed one to Little Spring.

"You Apaches beat the tar out of half the U.S. Army back in the eighties. That's a hell of an achievement." He took a drink from his glass and said, "Aahhhh!" and resumed. "Outwitted all those pompous fools in the general command. Miles, his name was, wasn't it? I met him back then. I don't mean to take away from your achievement, but the man was a popinjay. His favorite work of art in the world was his own reflection in a mirror."

Freeman laughed and took another swallow. Little Spring sipped from his glass and smiled.

"Nothing like a little whiskey to loosen things up a bit," Freeman said. "It's the oil a lot of society runs on, bless it. For example, you and me, here, we've got ourselves a situation that could be, well, awkward. Socially, I mean. There were quite a few times when I was younger, about your age, when I had to protect myself and I wound up shooting some of you people. Indians. Not Apaches. Mostly this was in Wyoming and Montana.

"And you Apaches killed your share of us white people, that's for damn sure, and here we are, the two of us, sitting in this parlor car together twenty years after you people beat the tar out of us and started your own country. Now that could be awkward enough . . . You finished there? I am. Let me make another for you . . . But then to add to that, it's not hard to see that my daughter has taken a shine to you. Here. Damn good Scotch, isn't it? Now Muriel is a free-spirited little thing, and this isn't the first shine she's taken, but it is . . ."

"I'm her first Indian shine?"

Freeman laughed, and applied himself to his glass of Scotch. It was either the Scotch or the man's forthrightness, or both, but Little Spring began to feel comfortable.

"You don't have to worry," he said. "Not until I show up at your doorstep with a string of horses for you." He explained the Apache custom of bride price.

"How many horses?" Freeman asked with a grin.

"Thirty?"

Freeman shook his head.

"Forty?" Little Spring said. "Forty is a lot of horses."

At this moment Muriel appeared in the doorway that opened into the narrow hall down which the three sleeping compartments were located. She had a sleepy look on her face and she grasped the doorjamb as the train bumped and lurched.

"What's this about horses?" she asked.

"Well, darlin', Patch and me, we're just comparing the value we each put on things."

Muriel looked puzzled, smiled, and raised her hand to cover a yawn. "Excuse me," she said. "I'm going to fall asleep again. It's the train." She turned and walked down the hall.

Both man sat silently for a few moments, each slightly embarrassed. Finally, Little Spring spoke.

"I'm just very lucky that your daughter includes me among her friends. Many people don't think of us Indians that way. As friends. Especially Apaches."

"Yes, well . . ." Freeman said, and cleared his throat. "None of those other Indians have their own country. That's a big difference. A real difference. You know, I'd like to hear about Apacheria, how it works down there. You don't really use horses for currency, do you? What do you do for money? I'm always interested in that sort of thing."

Little Spring explained that the Apaches used both American and Mexican currency, mostly American, and that most of the American money came from mining royalties. Abner Freeman nodded his head and looked startled when Little Spring explained how every member of the tribe received a monthly stipend from these royalties, the remainder going into the tribal accounts to build schools, a few medical facilities, to pay the doctors, and other such expenses.

"That sounds like socialism," Freeman said. "What some of the radicals like that man Eugene Debs are talking about." They discussed the differences for a few minutes.

In all, Little Spring's account of modern Apache economics used up an hour of the train ride, and the two men consumed half of the decanter of Scotch.

Abner Freeman nodded with some enthusiasm when Little Spring explained that most of his people, maybe three thousand out of the total of about four thousand, preferred to live the old way, hunting, following game on its seasonal migrations up and down the slopes of the mountains, collecting wild food, living simply.

"Sounds damn fine, a life like that. Free of worries," he said. "But can it last?"

"Last?"

"My guess is that you got more people now than you did before, what with no one being killed in war and all. Is there going to be enough game for everyone if you keep growing?"

But he was particularly interested in the tourism to Tombstone, drawn there by saloons and bawdy houses. He asked a number of trenchant questions about their operation and management, some of which Little Spring had no answer for.

"Now let me get this straight," Freeman said at one point. "You have these American companies doing the mining and they pay you a royalty. But you own and operate the saloons and the bawdy business in Tombstone and take all the profits, pay the salaries. How is that? Why the difference?"

"We don't dig things from the ground. It's part of our religion, I guess you'd say. Some Apaches don't even believe in planting seeds, in farming."

Abner Freeman's eyebrows rose on his forehead. "But gambling is okay? And liquor? And—"

"Apaches haven't got anything against drinking." Little Spring laughed. He held up his glass in a small toast. "As we were saying before. And everybody in Apacheria gambles. Everyone. Women, children. We bet on anything, everything. But our rules of marriage, chastity, all that—they're very strict. But we don't care what other people's rules are."

"It's their business?"

"Yes."

"So it's okay to make it your business."

"Yes."

"That seems very enlightened," Freeman said. He laughed. "Wish I could say the same about certain segments of American society. These days everyone's coming up with a blue nose." He went on for a while about the temperance movement and how several states already had voted in prohibition, and some of them had outlawed gambling, even the one-armed bandits that were a fixture in any self-respecting saloon. And now there was a lot of political clout behind the criminalization of all forms of prostitution.

"See," he said finally, "I'm in that business myself. Along

with my cattle business and other investments, I run a string of private clubs, we call them, very high-toned places but the same thing really that you've got in Tombstone. Would you be interested in seeing them? I mean," he said, "from a purely operational standpoint, of course."

"Yes," Little Spring said. "I would."

The doorway to the narrow hall opened and the black attendant entered, bearing three leather-bound menus. He handed one to each man and paused.

"The lady?" he said.

"It will be just the two of us for lunch. The lady is catching up on her sleep."

"Very good, suh."

Packard House, site of meetings of the Chicago Literary and Debating Society, the Chicago Naturalists, and also home of a little-publicized organization of local millionaires known as the Patrons of Chicago, was located on the western side of Grant Park, which extended out into the waters of Lake Michigan. Packard House was a four-story mansion of gray stone that had once belonged to the founder of the Chicago *Tribune* and now, on paper, to the Patrons of Chicago and, through various layers of syndicates, to Abner Boniface Freeman.

On the ground floor, Packard House housed two separate libraries, a large music conservatory, an intimate lecture hall, and a restaurant and kitchen that served the best food in Chicago—all, of course, for members only. The fourth floor was given over to the quarters of Packard House's permanent domestic staff and its administrative offices. In the elaborately remodeled basement lay the largest and most ornate gambling casino in the nation, enlivened nightly by the playing of a continuously revolving string of musicians from New Orleans. Finally, on the middle two floors were what connoisseurs of such things generally agreed was the most elegant brothel in the world. Those members of European royalty who were fortunate enough to have a friend among the Patrons of Chicago had been entertained at Packard House in the six years it had existed in its present configuration.

Packard House was the crown jewel in the small diadem of five such places that Abner Freeman had built up, each with its own character, each with its own membership requirements, each designed for a different strata in the increasingly wealthy upper end of society in this booming central hub of American commerce. Astounding fortunes were being created almost overnight in turn-of-the-century Chicago, but even with all the newfound wealth in the world, one could not count oneself at the pinnacle of Chicago society until one was admitted into the select membership of the Patrons, which conferred as its only benefit access to Packard House.

For all that most Patrons of Chicago knew, Abner Freeman was simply another of the fraternity who paid annual dues of fifty thousand dollars. His role as founder and chief officer of Packard House was known only to the five-man syndicate that shared comfortably with him the annual profits, which, while not great compared to their other businesses, produced for each member of the syndicate several times his annual dues. To achieve such a return from the mere exercise of harmless vices appealed to these grand and self-made panjandrums of commerce in a way that nothing else could or did.

Sunk in the comfortable leather seat of Freeman's hansom as the two men were driven north on Lake Shore Drive from Packard House to the Freeman residence, Little Spring was lost in thought. He was trying to think how he might describe the multifarious levels of elegance of Packard House to his father, Juh. The old man's English was serviceable for many things, but hardly for discussing such matters as roulette and baccarat, black walnut paneling and odalisques, a word new to Little Spring himself.

Part of the second floor of Packard House was set apart and decorated as a Europeanized version of a Turkish harem, and as Freeman led him through this perfumed place in midafternoon, the heads of every languid flower had turned appreciatively to look at the exotic young visitor passing through. It was presently beyond Little Spring how he would explain the difference between the brassy, no-frills strumpets of Tombstone and the refined odalisques of the Packard House seraglio.

On the other hand, the numbers, the ratios, and the odds that Freeman had explained to him—these were more easily translatable into terms that both Juh and Naiche could understand and appreciate. And a bit dazzled by all of it—odds and odalisques alike—Little Spring was beginning to glimpse a possible future on the Apache horizon.

They had left the women—Muriel and her mother—to oversee the servants unpacking all the clothes and souvenirs from the European trip while the men went off to have lunch and "survey" some of Freeman's enterprises, as he put it. Now, as the hansom pulled through the tall wrought-iron gates of his home, a mansion of the same gray stone as Packard House though only half as large, Freeman broke the silence.

"Mrs. Freeman—" he said all of a sudden, and cleared his throat. "Mrs. Freeman is not especially interested in my business affairs, which is just how it should be. She looks after several charitable matters when her health permits. She's a bit frail, the poor dear."

Little Spring glanced over at Freeman. The big man had his arms crossed over his thick chest, which made him seem even more robust. His eyes caught Little Spring's for a moment and flickered away.

"I see," Little Spring said. "And like the rest of Chicago, she knows Packard House as a men's club."

"Exactly. Patch, you are the very soul of tact."

"What about your daughter?" Little Spring said. "If I may ask."

Freeman waved a gloved hand. "Oh, she's of a different generation altogether. Enlightened. I don't think she approves of the bawdy business especially, but she knows there's always going to be a bit of sin in the world. Certainly she knows that Packard House—and the others too—aren't just meeting places for old men with nothing on their minds but the latest stock market reports. None of that is part of her world, of course. But Muriel loves the new music from New Orleans—jass, they call it. Cheerful. Makes you tap your foot. She's made the acquaintance of a number of the musicians I've had up here. Bring them over to the house every now and then. I daresay that's as close as she's ever gotten to the, ah, demimonde. Well, here we are."

The hansom's wheels came to a smooth stop on the gravel driveway, and Freeman consulted a gold watch he extracted ceremonially from his vest pocket. "The ladies'll be having tea, I expect. Let's join 'em."

Muriel Freeman loved her parents without any reservation. It never occurred to her that any other feeling about them could exist in her breast, but this did not mean that she was unable to make rational and objective judgments about them. Her father, she knew, had the soul of a buccaneer and both the cruel streak and the ebullience that went with it, but to his friends, his wife, and Muriel, he was protective and openly affectionate. And while he made every attempt to "fit" into the society of the wealthy, there was no cant in him. In an era given over more to polite circumlocution than frankness, especially between men and women, Muriel always knew she could be honest with her father—and with herself. And so she was free. It was a gift she treasured.

Muriel's mother, on the other hand, tended to be preoccupied with the form of things—from the right furniture to have in one's house to the proper behavior of people. At the same time, she was too sweet-natured, too timid perhaps, to try imposing all her views on her small family. It was as if she stayed meekly in the shade of a porch, watching with a continuous series of wondering sighs as her husband—and her daughter—performed unpredictable exploits in the sun. Muriel loved her mother with all the patient affection one has for a good-natured invalid.

"He's so well mannered," her mother had said about Patch

that afternoon when Muriel asked playfully what she thought of him. "Of course, they teach that at Princeton."

"But what do you think of his looks, Mother?"

"He's an Indian, dear. They all have such high cheekbones, don't they?"

Muriel doubted that her mother had ever seen an Indian before, maybe just some photographs. And she doubted that her mother had seen much beyond "Indian" when she first met Patch.

Muriel laughed. "But Mother, haven't you noticed the way he moves? Like a lion. Or a great tiger."

Her mother reddened slightly and pursed her lips. "No, dear, I haven't noticed that."

Yes, Muriel thought now, when he turns his head to face you, there is the look in those coal-black eyes that he has seen you, seen all he needs to know about you, seen deep into you, the way a tiger might look at any other passing denizen of the forest: Do I want this one? Or shall I let it pass?

Lying beneath the eiderdown that lay across her canopied four-poster bed, with a cool breeze blowing gently in the window from Lake Michigan, Muriel thought about the way he walked across the floor, as he had the first time she saw him, in New York two months before. Was it really that long ago? When he walked across the floor with slow, lithe, sure steps, it seemed he could suddenly launch himself into the air in a powerful, all-encompassing, explosive lunge from which there was no escape . . .

What have those eyes seen, those eyes so black and unfathomable, so mirthful, so transfixing?

She put her hands behind her head, crossed her ankles under the eiderdown, and imagined the two of them walking through some woodland, a bright sun shining gold through the trees, casting black shadows on the ground, stripes lit between with gold . . . *She can see both of them as if she is somehow outside herself, following. They are talking. She can hear his voice, quiet with that odd lilt, and she can hear her own voice. She can hear them laugh. She can't quite make out their words. In a clearing, she sinks down on the grassy floor in the golden light, her skirt flowing out around her, and he stands between her and the sun, dematerializing in the glare . . . She blinks as the sun bursts yellow, and he is before her, black eyes glittering from a shadowed face, hands grasping her arms above the elbow . . .*

Once before, she had been to the brink, had stood on the precipice, impelled to dive over the edge, to reach out into the mystery, but no, no, she kept her footing. Would she now? Or would she leap, would she open herself to the wind, to the magical heights, and soar?

And where would she land?

She smiled to herself in the dark, and in her mind she recalled the scent—like a hint of wood smoke—that hung about this man, this Indian, this lithe descendant of marauding savages, with such good manners, this Apache man with the knowing, mirthful obsidian eyes . . .

Was she asleep when she heard the ticking sound, like a piece of paper falling on its edge onto the floor?

The sound came again.

Oh no, she thought. Oh yes. Oh no.

She slipped out from under the eiderdown and stepped into the middle of the room. But for the breeze that tugged lightly at her nightgown, it was silent in the dark familiar room. Had she imagined a sound? Dreamed it?

Yes. Maybe. No. She took four steps, feeling the tight-woven Turkish rug under her feet and then the doorknob in her hand. Was it warm in her hand? Should it be cool to the touch? She stood still.

Slowly, as quietly as she could, she turned the knob and pulled the door toward her. The scent—smoky the way tea was smoky.

The strange Apache syllables. His name in Apache. Had *she* whispered his Apache name?

"Muriel." It was not a question.

"Oh, yes," she answered, and found his wrist. She drew him

into the room. "Oh, yes," she said again, and her mind reeled, dizzy for a moment. They would have to fly.

Necks arched, chests heaved. Nostrils flared wide with eager intakes of breath. The world seemed to shudder and fill with electricity and oncoming thunder, rolling thunder. It was a sound no one had heard on Lake Shore Drive for a decade or two, and people in their mansions along the drive, including those not otherwise engaged in the inner rooms of Packard House, all leaped to the windows to see what they knew it couldn't be—not here on Lake Shore Drive among the elegant mansions of Chicago's wealthy—but it sounded just like . . .

Many of them had led lives in which they had never, in fact, heard such a thing at all, but there it was—the wild, erratic drumbeat of horses, dozens of them, racing by at full gallop, a herd of horses, too many to count—and they marveled at the elemental roar of so many hooves, the exalted snorts, the enormous, supple bodies heaving like a writhing tide of muscle and bone . . .

What was going on? What the *hell* was going on . . . ?

Abner Freeman heard it. He was sitting in the sun in a wicker chair with a huge circular back, a chair made in the Philippines and brought by boat and train along with three others that sat in a ring on the grass next to a rose garden where he liked to doze a bit on a summer Sunday afternoon with a book open in his lap and a silver bucket of ice and a crystal decanter of Irish whiskey on the wicker table next to him.

For a moment, time went backward in a rush, and Abner was in the midst of a dust cloud, with a wiry mustang between his legs, and a thousand cattle thundering across a dead plain under an enormous blue sky. He heard the whoop of a vaquero, and another, and the thunder of the hooves, and woke up, and heard the whoop again.

He leaped out of the wicker chair and ran around the hedge of rosebushes, entering onto the front lawn through two huge oak trees that were nearly as old as the city of Chicago itself. Between Abner's mansion and Lake Shore Drive a hundred yards across the greensward was a high wall of stone quarried in Vermont, and a pair of stone pillars hung with wrought-iron gates formed the entrance. Real dust rose in a cloud, moving along behind the stone wall, and the sound that had inspired Abner's dream filled his ears.

He stood dumbstruck as the first of the horses—five? six?—plummeted through the open wrought-iron gates, kicking up gravel. More followed, urged on by high-pitched whoops and the very joy of the pell-mell race, horses pouring through the gate out of a sharp turn and leaping forward with a renewed burst at the sight of the straightaway before them. They came endlessly, it seemed, a roiling stream of horses, magnificent, the ones in the lead pulling up uncertainly where the drive bent around past the great porte cochere with its dark gray stone steps—what the *hell*?

And another outlandish whoop, and through the gate a man riding bareback, black hair streaming out behind him—for Christ's sake, what is he wearing? Nothing. A white thing. Patch. Grinning like a wolf, pulling up, trotting over.

Abner found himself laughing, guffaws heaving up from his stomach, pummeling his diaphragm, while the herd of horses reared and snorted nervously in his driveway, and the Apache slid off his horse while it was still trotting and stood before him like something out of prehistory, a big grin on his copper face, and Abner couldn't stop laughing.

Finally, he caught his breath. "I'll be goddamned," he wheezed. He glanced at the wrought-iron gates a hundred yards away and saw a handful of people peering into his estate. The sight, and the thought of what they might be thinking, started him laughing again. Again he caught his breath. He looked over at the horses, now beginning to calm down. Several had begun grazing on his close-cropped grass.

Abner turned back to face Patch, who stood expressionless and still as a post before him, holding a rope lead in his hand. His horse stood beside him, a muscular black animal with the look of something from a storybook.

"How many?" Abner asked.

"Forty-seven," Patch said. "Counting this one."

"Forty-seven," Abner repeated. "Including this Arab here."

"That's a lot of horses," Patch said.

"It sure as hell is."

"We thought it would be good if she visited my country. See what . . ." The Apache shrugged. "If she doesn't . . . well, you get to keep the horses."

"You Apaches certainly are a fair-minded crowd. I've got only one question."

"Sir?"

"What are you going to do about that bunch of horses that're heading for the gate?"

Patch spun around and streaked across the grass to outflank the four errant animals. Out loud, Abner said, "My God, I believe I'm the first man in twenty years who's been raided by the Apaches." He began to laugh again.

When the meaning of this astounding gesture became known to Muriel's mother, she was overcome with shock, dismay, and outright horror at the thought that her place in Chicago's world would be forever tainted, if not destroyed, by the fact that her daughter—her *only* child—was running off to an untamed wilderness with a Red savage. She took immediately to bed, from which she arose three hours later with her jaw uncharacteristically set, and explained to her husband Abner that the entire idea was ridiculous and she would not permit it.

Abner, who was not about to deny his daughter anything that she was clearly set on having or doing, saw the matter differently. In actuality, he rather liked this young man, seeing in him some of the bravado of the frontier that he so sorely missed, and he could certainly understand why his daughter would find him more interesting than the foppish nitwits that milled around uselessly in Chicago and New York social circles, trying to sound like English gentlemen.

"My dear," he told his wife, "this man is not a *Red Indian*, like all the rest of those people. He is the son of the leader of a foreign nation. Would you object if he was a prince of, say, Spain or Portugal or one of those places?"

"Yes, I would. All those people are swarthy foreigners."

Realizing that persuading his wife was hopeless, Abner did what he usually did when they disagreed. He overruled her. But realizing that she did have a point after all, he told her he was assigning an employee of his, an experienced and mature female employee, to accompany them and see to it that Muriel was treated properly and was promptly brought home if anything, anything at all, did not seem right.

Unappeased, Muriel's mother took to bed again, and developed several ailments that kept her there for several days. Meanwhile, Abner did appoint one of his employees to dog the couple's every move. She was Adelaide Buchanan, who, as a freckle-faced and lissome woman, had arrived in this country from Scotland and wound up one of the favorites at Packard House, where she served enthusiastically for a decade. Then, as Adelaide began to assume more Rubenesque proportions, she was assigned more administrative duties, and three years ago had become the club's executive director, which is to say, its madam.

Adelaide Buchanan was fond of her employer's daughter and an adventurous sort at heart, so she welcomed the opportunity to accompany her and her amazing, no, astonishing and, yes, *delicious* Red Indian prince into the wilds of the West.

≈ ≈

Twenty-two

In the days following the death of Juh and the wailing at his camp in the Chiricahua Mountains, the mind of the prophet Nakahyen seethed with visions and grotesque omens. His dreams were filled with black wings. Nakahyen was like a man being twisted to death as one might twist a rope until the strain was so great that it broke. The dozen young men who accompanied him to the place of the stone figures noted, of course, these moments when Nakahyen wrestled with his internal furies, for he would lie with his eyes rolled back, the horrid dead whites staring. His face contorted into a grimace, and his body trembled with greater and greater violence, like someone afflicted by miasmas or the White Eyes' smallpox.

Nakahyen lay shuddering on bare rock in a narrow grotto among enormous pinnacles and columns of dun-colored stone that rose into the sky all around. Thousands of these sentinels stood on the northwestern edge of the Chiricahua Mountains, as if placed there by an earlier race of giants. Their surfaces were blotched with yellow lichen and many had heads perched precariously on narrow necks. All were motionless, but poised to come to life when whatever had made them dead summoned them forth again.

Presently, the shuddering subsided and Nakahyen was calm, breathing lightly as if asleep, but with the whites of his eyes still staring blankly heavenward. His companions sat in fascinated fear nearby, not knowing with any certainty whether the spirits with whom Nakahyen communicated at such times came to him, or if he went far away to them. They did all know that such times were perilous, that not only Nakahyen but they themselves were close to the edge of a cliff over which they could all be tantalized.

Outside the grotto the sky had begun to darken, a metallic gray, and a wind had begun to whine through the pinnacles of stone, causing them to sing. The first raindrops landed with loud slapping sounds on the rock, and in moments small rivulets began to run along the crevices and cracks. The world suddenly flashed white and thunder exploded overhead, and the sentinels of stone shrieked in anger and despair.

As suddenly as it arrived, the storm passed, hurtling to the east and leaving the rocks dripping, glistening with moisture. Throughout, the prophet lay staring upward and breathing lightly. In the metallic purified air, he was seen then to close his eyes, and a smile crept over his thin lips as he crooned wordlessly to himself. He sat up, looked about like a man waking from a long sleep, and, from the deerskin pouch that hung around his neck, took a small, worn piece of pink cloth and rubbed it between his thumb and forefinger.

Nakahyen's companions sat as still as the surrounding rocks, holding their breath. It was Mangas Colorado who had come to Nakahyen. They waited.

"They shall live among us," Nakahyen murmured. He repeated the words several times and his voice gained clarity. "Yes, they shall live among us, they will be us, they will be Apaches. And they shall live our ways," the prophet said, his voice rising. "They will abide by our custom, live by our law! They will marry the ways Ussen has taught, and their noses will breathe deeply the purified air of Apache! Their faces will be open to the sun, and that is how they will be known!"

Nakahyen paused and looked slowly around the circle of his companions. Quietly, he said, "This is what should be. It is our way."

The men in the circle remained still, and the only sound was a throaty murmur of assent.

Over the years, the many-faceted daily round of activity in Tombstone had settled into a largely predictable pattern, much of it centered around the town's six saloons and three brothels.

The saloons were unchanged physically from their earlier days when Tombstone was a raw boomtown: the swinging doors were open twenty-four hours a day, the wooden floors were still covered with sawdust. The long bars with brass railings were the original ones; the mirrors behind the bars and the tables and chairs had often been replaced because from time to time men still breathed too much of the old frontier spirit, drank too much of frontier spirits, and engaged in minor brawls that were harder, usually, on the furniture than on the men themselves. But they were replicas of the original mirrors and furniture, and this was all part of Tombstone's charm, part of its draw for tourists and people from Tucson and other rapidly civilizing places who missed the boisterous life of what they thought had been the Old West.

The days of the blazing six-gun, however, the quick draw over too slick a dealing of the cards, were long gone. Such weapons were barred from all the saloons in Tombstone. This restriction, and the few other rules deemed necessary lest the tourist trade be discouraged, were enforced by a group of Apaches loosely organized into what could be thought of as a police force. These men—mostly in their twenties and thirties, and mostly members of Naiche's extended family—numbered about forty at any given time. They were rarely seen patrolling Tombstone's dusty streets and wooden sidewalks in the manner of police elsewhere, but turned up as if from thin air whenever a fight broke out or serious violence threatened.

Usually dressed in a military-style tunic over traditional Apache breechcloths and high moccasins, they carefully observed exuberant barroom brawls, intervening only when a life was threatened, and they were quick to enforce a certain amount of decorum in the brothels on Sixth Street whenever summoned. These were still housed in the original Victorian-style wooden buildings, but they had been thoroughly modernized inside with up-to-date fixtures, and they operated in a far more high-toned, by-appointment-only manner. While no Apache was known to have availed himself of any of the brothels' services, a mutual understanding—even a fondness—existed between the Apache "police" and the whores. The flowers of the night were widely considered, by whites and Apaches alike in Tombstone, as artisans if not professionals, and they enjoyed the esteem due anyone with a socially valuable skill.

In the rare instances in Tombstone and its environs of crimes such as theft, the Apaches rode down the perpetrators gleefully and in force, and, more often than not, the hapless thief was never heard from again. As a result of all this, by 1906 Tombstone was one of the few places left where one could experience some of the boisterous, bare-knuckle days of the Old West, while at the same time it was far and away the most crime-free town of its size anywhere in North America.

Tombstone's white population—mostly the operators of the tribally owned saloons, hotels, and brothels, along with storekeepers, schoolteachers, and a variety of artisans and craftsmen—mingled comfortably with the Apaches who chose to live in the town or on its outskirts. Many of these were families whose children attended Tombstone Academy from September through May but who spent the summers in traditional campsites in the hinterlands, living traditional Apache lives. Much of the town was residential and thus largely quiet.

The commercial center of town, on the other hand, quieted down only at about three o'clock in the morning, when all but the most resilient drinkers and poker players folded up and the prostitutes sent their customers off into the night satisfied and spent. From then till midmorning, most of Tombstone slept.

One of the few citizens who was typically up and about at this peaceful time of day was Homer Nye, operator of Tombstone Sundries and the adjacent stable located on the western edge of town on Sixth Street. The commercial bustle of modern Tombstone had pretty much passed Homer's store by. Its inventory had hardly changed in years and was only gradually dwindling. Sales, and the use of the stables, were winding down, as was Homer himself, now in his late sixties and suffering from numerous bothersome ailments including arthritis, chronic heartburn, and myopia.

But every morning at dawn Homer pulled himself out of bed, put an overcoat on over his long underwear, and groped his way out to the stable, where he fed the three horses that lived there now, effectively in retirement. On the few mornings when Homer had overslept, one of the horses—a twenty-six-year-old gray that tried to bite anyone who approached her—began rhythmically kicking the wall of her stall and kept this racket up like a metronome until Homer appeared with her breakfast. The arrogance of this summons was so annoying to Homer that thereafter he was rarely late again lest he have to confess to himself that he was, after all, subservient to an ill-tempered old bitch of a horse.

It was Homer Nye, then, who was first to notice about a dozen horsemen riding into Tombstone from the west at dawn one day in June about a week after the death of the old Apache leader, Juh. He had just finished tossing hay into the three stalls when he heard the gentle clip-clopping of a lot of hooves, and he guessed they were Apaches because, from the sound of it, they were unshod. Coming around the corner of the stable, he saw a blur of horsemen walking past, certainly Apaches, but which ones and exactly how many were questions that lay behind the resolution of Homer's failing eyesight. He wondered what they were doing—this was not the usual time to see anyone moving about in Tombstone—but he shrugged and put them out of mind, returning to the stables and his few equestrian chores of the morning.

Thus engaged ten minutes later, it was also Homer Nye who was among the first to hear the screams.

Belle La Fleur was a nine-year veteran of Tombstone's bawdy business, and nearing the time when retirement from the life was indicated. She spoke most of the time with a rich French accent that was oddly given to the occasional guttural, and this was because she had arrived a decade earlier in her early thirties straight from Germany. She cheerfully gave up her real name, Hilda Bergenstrohman, along with any mention of her Teutonic origins or the errant Herr Bergenstrohman, as soon as she learned of the Francophile preference among the patrons of Tombstone's most ornate whorehouse, known far and wide and simply as Mam'selle's.

At dawn Belle slept the deep sleep of the just and hard-working, having entertained the mayor of Tucson that night with more than her usual athleticism, he being an important man as well as one possessed of vigor surprising for his age. She slept now on her back, reddish blond hair in a grand rococo tousle around her face, her mouth open slightly and her breath taking auditory form as a light snore while her dreams played out pleasantly somewhere before her.

But something, perhaps the sound of her door opening, interfered with whatever dream was entertaining her and the story went sufficiently awry that Belle La Fleur woke up from her slumber to see three dark-skinned faces with glittering black eyes staring down at her. One face peered down from the right side of the bed, the other two from the left. They were extremely angry, these faces, the brown skin taut over their cheekbones, their mouths set in horrid straight lines. They were angry Apache faces, Apache men she had never seen, and she felt hands pin her arms down onto the counterpane of her soft bed, another on her forehead pressing her head deep into her pillow. The hands were tight on her arms, squeezing, hurting her. She opened her mouth to scream out for help but before she could utter a sound, she saw a flashing motion and felt a searing tug, as if her nose had caught fire, and the faces disappeared behind some blood—her blood—in her eyes, hot on her face, salty in her mouth. She gagged and finally screamed.

As she screamed, Belle put her hand over her face and felt that it was not her face any longer, not the familiar touch, and she screamed again, louder, a wordless agony rising deep from her soul. Against the palm of her hand she felt something like a chicken bone protruding from where the tip of her nose had once been. Her scream turned into a long moan, and she clutched her pillow to her face to stanch the blood, and tried to get out of bed, only to collapse on the floor, where she sobbed for her beauty, now lost forever, for the face she dared not look at.

She heard, then, the others screaming down the hall.

And then she heard the shots.

In spite of the house rule at Mam'selle's that customers could not spend the entire night there regardless of how much they paid or carried on, Thomas Jeffords Cleveland Bignon had spent the entire night in the bed and arms of a young Mexican recently arrived from Casas Grande via four months' employment in Tucson. Her name was Inez, a tawny and lithe eighteen-year-old with a luxuriant mane of shiny black hair, and she was one of Big Minnie Bignon's acquisitions, per-suaded over to Tombstone from the Ruby Star. Inez was happy to express her gratitude for this fortunate rise in station by breaking the house rules to accommodate Big Minnie's son in a small but comfortable bedroom located on the first floor behind the kitchen. Tom Bignon had spent most of his nights there since returning from the East.

Both of them woke with a start when they heard screams issuing forth from upstairs, screams of a pitch neither had ever experienced.

"Jesus Christ, what's . . . ?" Tom exclaimed, spilling out from under the covers onto the floor, where he groped on his knees for his clothes. Finding his trousers, he soon located the gun belt he often affected, and the Colt .45 his mother had given him on his fifteenth birthday, a gift from his namesake, then long dead.

"Get under the bed," he barked in Spanish, and charged through the door into the kitchen, screams still shattering his world. He heard a woman's voice cursing in French—Mam'selle herself—and he burst out of the kitchen and ran through the dining room, dodging past tables covered in white linen, realizing he was naked as a newborn and beginning to panic.

Through the high arched doorway that led into the vaulted front hall, he saw three Apaches appear, then two more, evidently having come down the grandiose paneled staircase. Bare-chested, with black paint daubed on their chests, they all spun and glared at him. He noticed vertical red lines of ocher on their cheeks—they were wearing war paint, for God's sake!—and the red ocher on their hands . . . no, that was blood!

"What have you done?" he shouted in Apache. He pulled the heavy revolver up and pointed it through the archway. "Stop! What have you done?"

Tom recognized one of them through the war paint. It was Nakahyen, that lunatic prophet from over near Silver City. The Apaches in the hall began to move—toward the front door—and Tom shouted at them again to stop. Nakahyen did so, turning again to glower at Tom, his eyes embers of manic intensity.

"We have treated these harlots like all adulterous Apache women," he said, his voice a knife edge of righteousness.

Tom's mind reeled. Apache husbands, he remembered, could either kill an adulterous wife or slice off the tip of her nose. No one did either anymore that he knew of, but he had seen a few old women in some of the more remote camps wearing the awful badges of their shame—elongated nostrils like pig snouts.

"Christ!" Tom croaked. He gagged at the thought and the Colt exploded in his hand, kicking upward. Through the smoke he saw an Apache lunge backward and fall. He heard the Colt explode again and saw plaster raining down on the Apaches in the hall. He jerked his pistol down, fired twice more, and through the smoke saw an orange flame and felt the impact, like a horse kicking him in the leg. As he hurtled backward, the back of his head cracked into the polished chrome ornamentation of the gigantic wood stove and he blacked out.

A block and a half east of Mam'selle's, three of the Apache police force raced from a bunkhouse onto the street, wakened by the distant yelling and the louder reports of gunfire. The first one to emerge from under the portal onto the street was struck instantly by an arrow in his throat and fell without a sound into the dust, his long-barreled pistol firing once aimlessly into the sky, which was now lightening into blue. The other two leaped back under the portal, one of them staring dumbfounded at the dozen Apache horsemen breaking into a gallop and heading their way. The other, one of the older men of the force and the youngest son of Naiche, emptied both barrels of his shotgun into the mob as it thundered past, kicking up swirls of yellow dust, and he saw two warriors flail the air and topple before a bullet struck him in the left cheekbone, knifed through his brain, and shattered the back of his skull.

The younger man leaped over his dead companion and, kneeling in the street, emptied his pistol at the fleeing horsemen. Only ten minutes elapsed from the first scream—Belle La Fleur's agonized realization that she had been horribly and irreparably disfigured—to the moment when Nakahyen and his warriors—now only nine—vanished around the corner of Sixth and Clum streets, headed east toward the Dragoon Mountains.

But at the end of that ten minutes, three of Tombstone's honored prostitutes had been maimed, the tips of their noses sliced off like pieces of pork, two Apache lawmen lay dead along with three of Nakahyen's fanatic followers, and Tom Bignon was unconscious, his skull fractured on the stove and a bullet hole in his thigh. With an eerie symmetry that sometimes characterizes such moments of horror, the oldest of Victorio's grandsons lay sprawled in the dust of Sixth Street, his chest mostly pulp from a blast of the shotgun of Naiche's youngest son, also dead in the street.

In the immediate aftermath, Mam'selle raced into the street, a hastily donned negligee whipping around her legs, howling for someone to fetch the doctor. Several members of the Apache police arrived on horseback, but seeing there was nothing they could do, joined the others giving chase to the east. The other two whorehouses emptied, the women flocking into Mam'selle's with whatever they could find by way of bandages, joining the moans when they saw what had been inflicted on their sisters. The doctor arrived, an old man of long tenure in Tombstone who had seen just about everything in the way of maiming and wounding. But nothing so purely awful, he said later, nothing so grotesque, had ever occurred in Tombstone, even back in the autumn of 1881 when five bank thieves, two of them cousins of the Clantons, were dragged through the streets behind their horses and then, bloody but still conscious, their eyes open and pleading, were hung one after the other from lampposts, to the applause of everyone in town.

The doctor, sick at heart and his hands trembling, did his best to patch up the three girls, but he knew, as did everyone in Tombstone before noon that day, that their constant companions for the rest of their days would be a wholly undeserved shame and despair.

It was only when the doctor ordered up some boiling hot towels from the kitchen that they found Tom Bignon unconscious and bleeding on the kitchen floor. He regained consciousness about the time the old doctor finished up as best he could with the three disfigured women, and while the old fellow dug around in his thigh for the bullet, between shrieks and curses at the pain, Tom kept yelling something garbled that sounded like "patch."

"That's what I'm gonna be doing, goddammit," the doc shouted back at him. "Patchin' your leg. Then I'll patch your goddamn skull. Why don't you just bite down on this here rag and shut the hell up." Tom bit down on the rag someone jammed into his mouth and blacked out for the second time that morning.

It had taken only ten minutes of unspeakable violence on an otherwise innocent morning in early June 1906 to tear apart the fabric of accommodation and understanding that existed in Apacheria from the time of independence until the passing from the scene of the People's greatest leader. As soon as they heard of the awful events in Tombstone, everybody experienced the same foreboding, the same certainty that life in Apacheria was about to fall into chaos.

Now, so soon after the People had gathered as one to mourn the death of Juh, the sound of wailing and the smoke of watch fires rose over separate Apache camps. In the east, in Victorio's camp, the mourning for two fallen grandsons continued through the night, and angry young men began their preparations. The smell of blood was in the air, and the next night, yes, perhaps as soon as that, they would perform the war dance around yet another great fire. Moccasins would pound the earth and bodies would writhe in the flickering light to demonstrate the very manner in which they would destroy the enemy. But this time, after the centuries during which it had been the Apache people against the world, it would now be Apache against Apache.

It was, of course, up to old Victorio, who—once the wailing began—took his own bitter counsel in the shadowy interior of his own lodge.

And, in the western part of the country, it was up to Naiche, whose son had been killed.

A few miles east of Tombstone, among some gently rolling hills, a ragged outcrop of reddish rock rose from the earth, an accidental wall that stretched nearly a mile north and south like a giant compass needle. Within a large fissure in the rock was an alcove where some ancient passerby had left a spiral scratched into the wall. There in the alcove, Naiche and his nephews placed the body of his son and sealed it with rocks.

Later, Naiche dismounted before the Bird Cage Theatre, hitched his horse to the railing, and noticed for the first time that behind the swinging doors, a large and rarely used interior door was shut. Grief mixed with dread, and Naiche hesitated on the wooden sidewalk, then pushed his way into the saloon. He stood blinking, his eyes adjusting from the intense sunlight to the gloom inside, and something flashed past his head and exploded. Shards and splinters of glass flew into the air behind him and a spray of liquid soaked the back of his head, his neck, his bare shoulders . . .

"Get out of here!"

The voice arose from some deep place, a guttural howl. Naiche took a step forward into the shadowy room.

"I said get *out*!"

Another bottle crashed against the wall behind him, whiskey and fragments of glass exploding harmlessly. The back of Naiche's neck and his shoulders were seized with cold as the whiskey from the first volley evaporated.

"Minnie," he said.

"You bastards." Her voice was quiet, icy. She stood in the middle of the room next to one of the round wooden tables. "You pigheaded barbarians, what *is* this? It's not human, I'll tell you that. Human beings don't do this kind of thing."

"Minnie, people have been killed. My son—"

"What do you mean, *people* have been killed? You pigheaded Apaches have killed each other. Like animals. *Animals!* Who cares if animals kill each other? You've shot my son, *my* son, and you've maimed three women. Disfigured them, *ruined* them, like they were dogs or toys or—"

Minnie stopped. She loomed enormous before Naiche. "Get out," she said. "Get out of here." Her shoulders heaved, and she sat down at the table and put her face in her hands. Naiche stood still as a rock.

"It's over," Minnie said. "It's over. I don't know why I ever thought we could—" Suddenly she was on her feet. She marched around the table and up to Naiche, her face glowering into his.

"What're you gonna do about this? I'll tell you what I'm gonna do. I've brought those poor women here, and they're gonna stay here where no one can gawk at them. They can stay as long as they want, which won't be very long, but where will they go? Where can they go with their faces carved up by you savages? So they can stay here. With me. This place is closed. It ain't a saloon anymore. It ain't a place where you people can come. *No* one can come here. No Apaches, none of you savages, no men, no men . . . not ever again through those doors." She turned her back to him.

"I will avenge this—" Naiche began.

"*Avenge* it?" Minnie spun around. "Is that all you can say? Is that all you can imagine? Vengeance? What, are you going to go cut pieces off them too, or kill 'em? Hang 'em upside down over a fire? Get out of here. Get out of here. Go get your *vengeance*. I hope you choke to death on your vengeance . . . Oh my God!"

Minnie was staring over Naiche's shoulder. He turned and saw a man and a woman in the doorway. An Apache, and a white woman with eyes as wide as saucers. Naiche heard Minnie Bignon behind him burst into tears.

~ ~

Twenty-three

The ravaged faces stared at him. Naiche's face was pinched, turned inward somehow, like a very old man. Minnie's round baby face had collapsed, her cheeks streaked with tears, dark bruiselike blotches below her eyes.

"Stop," Little Spring said in Apache. "Stop all this." He turned and saw that Muriel had stepped back against the door-jamb and held one hand over her mouth. Her fingers had streaked the dust on her cheek before balling up into a fist. Her black irises were small, like pinpricks against the whites, her face an unspoken question—a rebuke.

"No, wait," Little Spring said. He faced the other two. "What's happened here? Why are you saying these things?"

He saw Naiche's shoulders sink. He watched Minnie slump into a chair, put her head in her hand, and shake her head slowly back and forth. Little Spring had never heard her speak anything like the words he had overheard as he and Muriel approached the familiar entrance of the Bird Cage Theatre.

He had been right . . .

The farther the train rattled into Apacheria, the more excited Muriel grew, clutching Little Spring's arm and looking with dancing eyes at the landscape hurrying past the open window of the carriage. He teased her, asking how it was she was so wide-awake, and she replied that it was the dust and the sparks that flew all around and were sucked in the window and were covering her face and his, giving him, she said, a Mephistophelian countenance. A what? he asked. "You look like the devil," she said, laughing.

Muriel's duenna, Adelaide Buchanan, had explained early on, with a wink of her eye and an understanding grin on her freckled Scottish visage, that she had no intention of being a meddling busybody. For most of the train trip south and west she had amused herself reading penny-dreadful novels disguised in the dust jackets of the works of Charles Dickens.

As the train passed west of Silver City, Muriel was amazed at the dead white *playas*. She spotted some distant specks in one of them—birds wading in water? No, Little Spring explained, the water was a heat mirage. The birds were real.

She listened, eyes wide, as they rattled through Apache Pass north of the great ramparts of the Chiricahuas, and Little Spring told her about his father's camp high up in the crags, the place where he had been born and from which Juh had directed the Apache triumph.

"They're like a fantastic giant's castle," Muriel said of the Chiricahuas. "It's as if the world here was once full of a race of giants."

"It was," Little Spring said. "We had to rid the world of the giants when we came here. They were monsters who ate everything they found. It was the Apaches' first great victory."

Muriel smiled, a broad and welcoming smile, and he told her of the monsters and the twin Apache boys who had gone abroad to kill them long ago when the world was young.

But the farther they penetrated into the familiar landscape of his home country, the more uneasy Little Spring grew. Inside, behind the smile and the stories and in spite of Muriel's dazzling eyes, he felt an increasing sense of disquiet.

He had been gone a long time, he rationalized. It would be a big change to be back among his people again.

No.

He was bringing with him a white woman, a woman who he was determined was going to be his bride. None of his people knew about this, of course, and he could not be sure how they would react. To her. To the idea of his marrying a White Eyes. His father? His mother? Lozen? What would they think? What would they say?

Yes. That was it.

But no, there was more.

The clammy hand he had felt in the dining room of President Roosevelt's White House—it was with him now. Something was wrong.

He looked into the deep brown eyes of this amazing creature beside him. They were flecked with green. He scanned her face, now so familiar—the upcurve of eyebrows that gave her a look of permanent curiosity, the narrow nose with just the slightest button of a tip, a jaunty thing, and the delicate whorl of porcelain ear—he devoured these details with his eyes and felt jubilant, powerful. She was perfect. But still, underneath the elation, hidden but lurking just beyond his grasp, was an icy understanding that something was wrong here in the land they hurtled through . . .

He had been right.

At the station, they had left Adelaide sitting comfortably with one of her novels and their baggage while they went to arrange lodgings. Little Spring had been puzzled that the streets were empty during the short walk to the Bird Cage Theatre. But what was *this*—Minnie screaming about vengeance, cursing Apaches, and Naiche standing like a broken lance? And Minnie now weeping, an enormous weeping hulk?

He reached out and took Muriel's hand, cold in his, and led her to one of the tables. He held her hand as she sat, let it go, and turned to Naiche.

"What, old father?" he said in Apache. "You must tell me what. I have brought this woman with me. We came with happiness and I will introduce her. But here there is death. I'm right, aren't I?"

Naiche nodded, an almost imperceptible motion of his head. "Your father has gone to the Red Ground Country."

Little Spring groaned. For a moment he believed he had

been struck in the stomach. His father's face flashed in his mind and he willed it away, turning his head. His eyes were pinched. Tears welled up and he blinked them away.

"Patch, what is it?" Muriel put her hand out to touch him but withdrew it. He closed his eyes, turned his head to her.

"My father died. He was an old man." His eyes opened. "I wasn't here."

"You didn't know . . . You couldn't have . . ."

"When?" Little Spring asked.

"Six days ago," Naiche said. "He was on his way . . ."

"At midmorning," Little Spring said. "Yes?" That was when he and the others had been in the dining room at the White House and something had reached for him. He shuddered somewhere deep inside.

"Yes. He died on his horse," Naiche said. He mentioned an Apache place name.

Only an hour earlier, Little Spring thought, only an hour earlier, he had gone by that place. It was a slight depression in the San Simon Valley, within view of the railroad tracks. His father had not been far from home when he died. Little Spring sat slowly down in a chair at the table next to Muriel. Again he took her hand and stared at the floor between his feet. For several minutes the only sound in the room was Minnie snuffling.

Presently, Little Spring looked up at Naiche and glanced over at Minnie. He turned his head and pointed with his lips at the broken glass on the floor. "And that?" he said. "The talk of vengeance?" He relinquished Muriel's hand.

Slowly and in a voice that was little more than a whisper, Naiche began to speak, to recount the events of the past two days. While he spoke, Minnie looked back and forth between the two men. Her big baby face glowed with outrage.

The old Indian, Naiche, spoke in Apache, an extended series of liquid and guttural and sibilant syllables in an almost unbroken stream that went on and on, and Muriel Freeman had the odd sense that she might not really exist here in this room. Naiche stood motionless as he spoke, his eyes staring off into the distance, as if seeing whatever events he recounted. He was dressed, she noticed for the first time, in a blue denim shirt and baggy black trousers. A white strip of cloth was wrapped around his head, over graying black hair. His feet were encased in elaborately beaded moccasins. The big woman, Minnie, sat motionless as well, leaning on her forearms folded on the tabletop, her eyes the dark blue of newborn infants' eyes and brimming with moisture. The skullcap surmounted with pink silk roses that perched on her head somehow added to the sense that she was an enormous baby.

As the Apache words tumbled on, Muriel's sense of being disembodied grew. She longed to reach out and take Patch's hand, but dared not move. His face suddenly was unfamiliar to her, a mask of the face she knew, expressionless, motionless, unreadable. Only the black pupils seemed alive, though they too were motionless, as if unseeing.

The alien arrhythmic words ran on, like a stream, and the strangeness was nearly overwhelming. Anger, sadness, regret, these were presences sitting with them at the tables in grim visitation in this outlandish, crude saloon where the only sound was the fugue of the Apache's voice and the only light came from a gas lamp in the gloom in the rear and the shock of white sun lighting the doorway and glittering from the shards of glass strewn about on the floor in the sawdust.

I don't belong here, I don't belong here.

Vertigo grasped Muriel and her vision began to close down. Only details. The old man's mouth moving, thin lips opening and closing senselessly. Ugly lips. Not words, not language, only a distant noise. The big woman's eyes pulsed blue-black with resentment, dark folds below them. Muriel was oppressed by the notion, the sense of a violin string and a hand turning the knob, relentlessly tightening the string to an impossible tautness, and she had trouble catching her breath.

Am I going mad? Or is this fear, terror?

She dug the fingernails of one hand into her elbow and concentrated on the pain until her eyes cleared. Naiche, the old man, had fallen silent. Patch had not moved, his face still a mask. But something had happened to him. Perhaps, Muriel thought, it was the strangeness of all this, her senses gone awry, her mind gone perfervid. The others in the room were faded, not blurred but not substantial. But Patch . . . She searched for an answer.

Her father had brought home a strange device once, a pair of what looked like spectacles mounted on an apparatus of polished wood and brass, and a small pile of cardboard strips, each bearing an identical pair of photographs. Buildings. People. Dogs. Her father had inserted one of the strips, the dogs, a pair of black cocker spaniels, and handed the contraption to her. She peered through the spectacles and the spaniels seemed to have grown, to have been transformed, infused with what? Vividness? It was magic for a little girl. A stereopticon, it was called.

She looked at Patch. It was he, yes, but another Patch as well. A transformed Patch, but how? The details of his face, his black hair pulled back into a knot and a tail descending, the set of his shoulders, the veins raised on the back of his hands, forming the horizon line of mountains on the smooth coppery skin . . . the same, but he filled the room, vivid now and taut, still as a cloudless sky, and she knew he was about to move, to gather the world into himself for a moment and spring forth like a beast of prey, a lion . . .

Stop, stop. You are acting like an overwrought schoolgirl, imagination gone wild . . . Is this what they mean by the vapors?

Muriel found she could smile to herself about that, about the vapors, and the room took on normal dimensions and she wasn't at all surprised to find that Patch was now standing— but how had he done that without her seeing it?

"Tom is here?" he said. "Big Ears?"

Minnie nodded. Her eyes glanced upward.

"And the women, they will come here?"

Minnie nodded. "It'll be made over into a home. For as long as they want to be here. They can't stay . . ."

"No. They will need children."

Minnie looked up. "What?"

"Some of our children. To help them. Young children."

Little Spring looked over at Naiche, who nodded.

"And the vengeance?" Little Spring said.

"We wait," Naiche replied. "They'll come."

"What about Victorio's grandsons? The bodies?"

Naiche turned his head and pointed southward with his lips. "They were taken to the Mule Mountains."

"Who took them there?"

Naiche mentioned three Apache names.

Little Spring walked behind the chair Muriel was seated in and put his hands on the topmost rung.

"I've been rude," he said. "This woman is Muriel Freeman. Her family lives in Chicago. I brought her here—she chose to come here with me to see our country. To meet our people. It was my intention—" He stopped.

"I've told you about these people, Muriel. Naiche, the son of Cochise. A leader of Apache people. Minnie Bignon. The mayor of Tombstone, mother of my friend Big Ears. Tom. These two, they helped raise me, taught me."

"Muriel?" It was Big Minnie. She tried to smile. "That's a pretty name."

"Thank you," Muriel said.

"I'm sorry," Minnie went on, but stopped and waved a hand limply at the room.

"This isn't the world I wanted to show you, Muriel," Little Spring said. "This isn't the world my father saw for us Apaches. I am ashamed. I am ashamed before you for what my people have done now. Some of my people. But I can't ask you to stay here."

Muriel turned in her chair. "I don't know what's happened. You can't just—"

"I'll tell you, but first I'm telling you this isn't a place for you now."

"You want me to leave? To go home to Chicago?"

"No. More than anything in the world, I want you here, but it isn't right. Not now."

Muriel stood up from the chair and turned to face Little Spring. "Perhaps," she said in a voice that had the ring of icicles snapping off a roof, "perhaps you will first be good enough to tell me what is going on here. I am not moving an inch until I understand. And when I do understand, then we will discuss what I am going to do. I hope I'm not fracturing any ancient Apache custom by speaking this way, but no one, not even my father, simply tells me what I'm going to do."

She spun around and sat down with her arms tight across her chest and her jaw set. Across the room at her table, Big Minnie's mouth was agape. Slowly a hint of a smile crept over the corners of her mouth.

"Bravo," she said quietly, and her eyes flickered back and forth nervously.

Ten minutes later, after listening without a word while Minnie and Naiche alternately spoke, Muriel uncrossed her arms and folded her hands on the table. Her face was pale, chalky, cheeks faintly tinged with green.

"I'd like something to drink, please," she said. "Whiskey would be fine." She cleared her throat. "Minnie will surely need some help with those poor women." She turned her head toward Patch. "I'll be here."

"Where have you been?"

Tom Jeffords Cleveland Bignon lay in a large four-poster bed in one of the rooms on the second floor of the Bird Cage Theatre. A lacy pink coverlet was drawn up to his chin, and his head, with a large white bandage wrapped around it, lay among puffy white pillows. One bare leg, with bandages tight around his thick thigh, stuck out from under the covers.

"You look good in pink," Little Spring said. He was leaning against the doorjamb with his arms folded across his chest.

Tom Bignon looked up, smiled, frowned. "Your father . . . I'm awfully sorry. And then all this . . . A hellish homecoming."

Little Spring nodded.

"Everybody, it must have been every Apache in the world, was at your father's camp."

"Who shot you?"

"I don't know. One of the men with that madman Nakahyen. Maybe him. There was a lot of smoke, confusion. Say, what are you smiling at?"

"They say they found you lying on the floor all naked, wearing nothing but that Colt in your hand."

"Well . . ."

"You're a brave man, Big Ears."

Tom Bignon beamed.

"Breaking the house rules," Little Spring added.

"Yeah, that'll teach me, won't it?"

The two men looked at each other.

"Her name is Inez," Tom said. "Mother says she lit out, probably back home in Mexico by now. Say, did you ever hook up with that girl you were talking about, the one from . . . ?

Little Spring nodded. "Muriel. She's here. Downstairs with Minnie. You'll meet her. They're going to throw you out of here. No men allowed in here anymore. You can stay with me."

"Where?"

"I don't know yet."

"What's going to happen?"

"I don't know."

"Mother's scared there'll be a civil war . . ."

"East against west. Brother against brother. Like you people had. Maybe not."

"What are you gonna do?"

"See my mother. Then I don't know."

Tom shifted his leg and winced. "Lozen's over there. With Victorio."

"She's his sister. It was her great-nephews who were killed."

"Yes, I know, but—"

"When do they say you'll be walking?"

"A week, maybe two."

"Maybe less," Little Spring said.

"We're all really sad about your father," Tom said.

Little Spring turned to go.

Ishton's wickiup was built from fresh willow branches and stood not far from a copse of cottonwood trees lining one portion of a dry shallow wash that snaked through the low ground among several small hillocks about three miles east of Tombstone. Two hundred yards upstream was the camp of one of her cousins, several wickiups and a temporary corral in which six horses stood with their noses to the sun, now low in the west.

As Little Spring approached his mother's lodge, he noticed a young boy emerge from one of the distant wickiups and throw an armful of grass into the corral. The horses turned to look at the boy and they slowly turned and plodded over to the grass lying on the dusty ground. The boy disappeared into one of the lodges.

He heard movement, and Ishton ducked and stepped outside. Her face, her beautiful face, now was aged. Circles were dark under her eyes, her cheeks drawn in. Still beautiful, Little Spring thought. She was smaller. It was her hair. She had cut off a foot of it, maybe more. He stood before her, within arm's reach.

"Mother," he said ceremoniously.

"Yes."

"Ishton." It had been his father's name for her. It meant *the* woman. It meant beyond—exalted above—all other women.

"Once," she said. She glanced up at him.

"And now. Still."

"Just an old Apache woman. It's enough. You're home," she said, changing the subject.

"Yes, and—"

"They say you brought a woman with you. A white woman."

"Yes."

"You plan to marry her, make her an Apache woman?"

"I have no plans now, Mother. Not now."

Ishton looked out across the hills, glowing gold in the sun.

"One day," she said, "I would like to read and write." She looked back at him from underneath her thick black eyebrows. "When all this is over. Then you will show me what books of yours I should read." She smiled at the thought and turned to face the east.

"They put Naiche's son over there." She mentioned the name of the outcrop that lay eastward, out of sight. She turned south.

"Naiche had Victorio's grandsons taken out there," she said. "In the mountains."

Ishton stepped past her son and sat down heavily on the ground near the door to her lodge.

"Tomorrow you will take them to him."

She looked up at him.

"And tomorrow I will go meet your white woman."

Twenty-four

Victorio's grandsons lay in the back of the buckboard like two gigantic worms. They were wrapped in coarse blankets under a tentlike blanket erected over them to keep the sun from too rapidly doing its work. A brisk breeze blew from the north, so the nauseating stench of decay only occasionally invaded Little Spring's nostrils.

Apaches had every reason to fear the dead, and in spite of his sophisticated white man's education at Princeton University in the United States, these fears tugged at Little Spring with all their ancient insistence as the wagon proceeded through the desert scrub toward Victorio's camp in the foothills near Silver City. A man's spirit—especially that of a young man cut down violently—was inclined to lurk about near the body seeking revenge even for the merest slight incurred during life, never mind for the outright insult of being killed. Little Spring had plenty of other matters to think about on this long and dreary trek, but when the wind let up and the stench spread, the old fear intervened and sent his thoughts scattering.

The two horses in the traces plodded along with placid resignation—a good sign. Horses were especially adept at sensing the presence of malevolent spirits. With a flick of his wrists, Little Spring thwacked the reins on their backsides, and they quickened the pace somewhat. He had no interest in being abroad during the night with this cargo.

The sun, still high in the sky but behind him, warmed his shoulders reassuringly. He thought about his mother, Ishton.

By now she would have made her way into Tombstone, striding through the streets with that deliberate gait of Apache women, putting the toes down first with each step like a queen, and she would have met Muriel. They were about the same height, those two, both with hair the color of ravens—two kinds of beauty. How would they see each other? Beneath the white world's manners and the Apache's elaborate courtesies, would they seethe with hostility, some unfathomable form of jealousy? Or . . . would they see each other through his eyes? No, of course, they would see each other with their own eyes and their own opinions . . .

Off to his right, Little Spring noticed two thin wisps of smoke perhaps three miles away curling up from the foothills of the Peloncillos and vanishing into the blue tent of the sky. Victorio's people had moved eastward—at least some of them. They would be watching him now, had been watching him. The fires were an announcement to that effect. He tugged lightly at the right-hand rein and the team swung rightward, heads bobbing now in the direction of the smoke. Under him and behind, the buckboard creaked and the corpses wobbled back and forth. He smacked the horses' rumps, easing them into a trot. And then he saw the horsemen approaching.

Six of them emerged from behind a rise about a mile ahead of him and, in a tight knot, headed directly his way at a gentle, unhurried lope, kicking up the dust of the desert in feathery swirls. Behind them the Peloncillos lay like a sleeping guard dog. Soon he recognized them: boys, now men, whom he had hunted with in the summers, boys he had bested in footraces and wrestling matches and the other games that made Apaches into warriors.

He pulled up and waited as they drew near, spreading into a tight semicircle before they stopped twenty yards away. Each held a carbine pointed at the sky. One of them said Little Spring's name, and to him and then to the other five, Little Spring replied in kind.

"You come," the first one said, "in the manner of a Navajo. Or a woman. Why is that?"

"I have brought the husks of Victorio's grandsons," he said, "so they can be properly put to rest. Perhaps I should have slung each one over a horse like a sack of flour."

Several of the men before him involuntarily tightened their reins and their horses obediently backed away.

"Will you take them from me now and carry them to Victorio?" he asked. "Or shall I proceed?"

They gestured him to go forward, and took up a position to his side, the side from which the breeze came, he noted, and he brought the team to a fast walk. Wordlessly, the small procession moved up the rise toward the two thin strings of smoke disappearing in the air. Far off to the north a thunderhead had come into being over the ragged teeth of the mountains, and a transparent gray sheet of rain hung partway down to the earth.

Less than an hour later, with the buckboard left standing out of sight behind some large yellowish slabs that had tumbled down the sides of the mountain eons before, perhaps in the time of the monsters, Little Spring stood outside Victorio's wickiup while the old warrior told three of Little Spring's recent escort to take the corpses away and leave them hidden in the traditional manner. The old man had changed little since Little Spring had last seen him. Perhaps he was slightly stooped with age, but he remained an imposing figure. Perhaps the sheets of muscle over his chest and his arms had become more sinewy, stringier, but he appeared to have lost little in the way of strength. He still glowered at the world from under his thick brows, one black eye straying wildly to the side. The fissures that ran down from his nose past the corners of his mouth might have deepened slightly.

Victorio turned to him and they exchanged condolences for the dead. The old warrior talked quietly for several minutes, recounting some of the more notable achievements of Juh during his lifetime, referring to him only as "he who was among us." During Victorio's recitation, Little Spring glanced around the temporary encampment. As in all camps, women went about the chores of preparing food, cooking, scraping hides, repairing clothes, while small children darted and wobbled here and there. A few men considerably older than Victorio sat in the shade of the piñon trees sprinkled here and there, watching the world pass by with rheumy eyes. Otherwise, the camp was empty of men.

A little boy, perhaps four years old, approached with his large black eyes wide and stood a few feet away from the old warrior. Like others in camp his age, he was naked and dirty, and he carried in his chubby right hand the branch of a piñon tree, which he had evidently stripped of needles and twigs to make himself a war club.

Victorio looked down at him, amusement in his eyes.

"Is this the enemy, Grandfather?" the boy asked, holding his club in front of him.

Victorio laughed. "This is Little Spring, the son of the one who was our leader."

The boy stared up at Little Spring.

"Don't stare, boy," Victorio said. "My grandson, Long Arm. When he was born, one of his arms was longer than the other."

"When is the enemy coming, Grandfather?"

"Run along," Victorio said, and the boy turned and ran off, brandishing his club from side to side at imagined adversaries.

"Long Arm will grow up to fight Apaches?" Little Spring asked.

"I hope not," Victorio replied. "But Apaches killed his brothers. Even Long Arm knows that such a thing cannot stand."

"You have spoken long and honorably about my father," Little Spring said. "You knew him well. As a warrior. What would he have said about this killing?"

"Who can tell? He is not here."

"They tell me my father came to your camp before he died. To talk about some other killings. The miners. You are surely the last person to speak with him. What did he say then?"

"We spoke of the world, how it is changing. Out there." With his lips, Victorio pointed generally to the north. He explained that terrifying the strikers back to work hastened the day they would be gone forever. "But I am losing my interest in the world out there. I am interested now in being an old man with my memories of Apache glory when the world was simpler. I want to live out my life as a real Apache should."

Little Spring nodded thoughtfully. Was Victorio saying that he was stepping down from his role as leader? All this talk about being an old man . . . After a few moments during which both men were silent, Little Spring spoke.

"In the United States," he said, gesturing vaguely north, "the President has set aside some land where creatures like bears and elk and pumas can live without being hunted. They are called refuges. They can live there forever, without any of the White Eyes' roads or towns. No one can go into these refuges except to look at the animals."

Victorio glanced over at him. "The White Eyes do strange things," the old man said, scorn rising in his voice. "I've seen those things they call desks, with all the little square holes in them. They put everything into a different hole. It's their way. They build buildings they use only one time a week. That is where they put their god. They put all those Indians on little pieces of the land—those reservations. So they are going to put all their bears and elks and deer into a hole too, a refuge." He shrugged. "Their ways are not ours."

"And Apaches should stay here, in Apacheria, and live only the old ways, by the old laws."

"Yes."

"Like the white man's elk. In a refuge."

Victorio frowned. His mouth was clamped shut, his jaw thrust aggressively forward, but a slight flickering of the eyes suggested a man who may have been ambushed.

"I see no reason to talk of these things with you," Victorio finally said. "You've lived in their world. For four years you only visit Apacheria."

"My father told me that every Apache had standing before his leaders."

"I'm not your leader, Little Spring."

"Then who should I speak to in order to learn the purpose of all this?"

"These days, my son-in-law is concerned with such things. Here, in the country of Mangas Colorado, he now speaks the most persuasively."

"You have been fortunate," Little Spring said, "to have many daughters, all of them strong and beautiful. All have brought son-in-laws to your camp. Who of these should I speak with?"

"Nakahyen." The old man turned, stooped, and disappeared into the dark recess of his wickiup.

Muriel Freeman threw herself into the numerous chores involved in converting what had been a saloon and theater into a provisional refuge for the three disfigured women who huddled miserably in one of the upstairs rooms, faces bandaged and eyes staring, seeing nothing. For Muriel, it was only the physical routine of the chores, shoving furniture here and there, making beds, that kept the shock and horror of it all from overcoming her. Even so, she went through the motions with only half her mind. The other half was in turmoil.

Big Minnie had immediately seen a kindred soul in Adelaide Buchanan, and the two women worked through most of the night with the easy coordination of a team of horses in the traces, pausing only to administer as much maternal comfort as was possible to the three victims of vicious Apache righteousness. In the morning, a handful of men had appeared at the swinging doors, sent by Naiche to help, and Big Minnie shooed them away as peremptorily as she might have swatted some bothersome flies. Muriel had caught herself staring at them, their Mongol-like visages so much the echo of Little Spring's but so fearsomely, incomprehensibly, alien.

The gap between her and this world yawned, and as the men slipped away, Muriel realized that here—among women of her kind, however foreign to each other they all might be, and certainly were to her—was her only reassurance, her only bulwark against the vertiginous sense she felt again of not existing at all.

This has been an awful mistake. It's hopeless. It cannot . . . I cannot . . .

She was alone in the barroom with its round tables of crude dark wood, fixing a few strange desert flowers in cheap vases to put in the bedrooms of the poor women upstairs, when she sensed another presence in the room. She looked over her shoulder to where metallic white light filled the doorway and gleamed dully from the floorboards. The floor had been swept clean of sawdust during the night.

A figure stood silhouetted in the pallid aura, an Apache woman. Muriel watched as the woman stepped out of the rectangle of light toward her. She wore a dull-colored blanket like a shawl over an ankle-length skirt of yellowish hide. Her black hair was cut off roughly—as if chopped—above her shoulders. She looked in Muriel's direction but not directly at her from coal-black eyes that were, exactly, the eyes of Little Spring. A sister? A twin sister? Muriel realized that she was shuddering.

The woman stopped some ten feet away, positioning herself precisely between two tables, as if minimizing the taint of either. Her eyes swept down from Muriel's head to the floor and back, then off to the side. Was this Apache face hostile? Or just alien?

"I'm . . . my name is Muriel Freeman," she said. "I came with your—"

"With my son."

"I was so sorry to hear about your—"

"My son's father."

Muriel's heart sank. She had read in silly novels of hearts sinking and thought it was merely an expression. This woman's voice was as flat, as colorless, as unwelcoming as . . . as you'd imagine coming from a ghost. She was perhaps an inch taller than Muriel, but Muriel felt dwarfed, insubstantial, excluded.

Oh no, oh no.

Muriel blinked back tears that swelled in her eyes, impelled by the despairing knowledge that she could not hold up this world as it collapsed suffocatingly around her. Idly, nervously, she pushed some of her errant hair behind her ear with the back of her hand. She noticed that she was still holding a stem with a floret of lavender daisylike blossoms in her other hand. She turned and stuck it in the vase, and turned back to see that the woman—Patch's mother—was now a few steps closer. Patch had said her name was Ishton—*the* woman. Was it a name that she could say? What was the right thing to do here? Was *anything* right in an awful place like this, where they could cut off a woman's nose? Courtesy? Here?

The woman's head was now tilted ever so slightly to the side. Her black hair with its ragged ends had moved with her head—hair like iron. Was the tilt of her head a softening? Her eyes were unfathomable in their blackness.

"Come with me," the woman said. She turned and strode out of the saloon in a gait so regal she might well have borne a crown on her head, or a jug of water balanced there. Muriel followed her out onto the wooden sidewalk and blinked in the sunlight. She caught up and walked to the side and a pace behind the woman. She kept reminding herself that this was Patch's mother—whatever the import of that might be.

They proceeded in silence down the dusty streets past ramshackle wooden storefronts and saloons, turned down another street, passed several houses that appeared to be residences, continued on until suddenly the town of Tombstone gave way to open scrubland. Minutes later they were in the shade of some trees whose leaves rattled slightly in the wind. Everything in this country seemed so brittle.

Outside a rude, semiglobular hut made of branches, Patch's mother turned and sank gracefully to the ground, her legs crossed before her. She nodded to her left, and Muriel sat down as bidden.

"My son has chosen you," she began. Again her voice was flat, without expression except for an odd lilt that Muriel had come to associate with Patch but which she now assumed was common to Apaches speaking English. "It is his right to make such choices. And I am not surprised. He has spent a great deal of time among you people. We—I knew this might happen."

Muriel felt as though she were poised for flight. Far off to her left she saw a loose cluster of huts similar to this one. From somewhere in their midst a fire sent a thin serpentine line of smoke into the air. A few little children were playing some sort of game with what looked like sticks and a ball. She could hear their occasional shouts and cries, high-pitched familiar noises in an unrecognizable world. The hills around were covered with grass, dotted here and there with misshapen bushes of some kind, an unpromising landscape under a sky that was too big.

"No white blood runs in Apache veins," Ishton was saying. "None that we know of. There is Mexican blood, and the Mexicans are our oldest enemies. There is the blood of other tribes—Navajo, Yuman, Comanche, even Papago. We have fought with all of those people. Perhaps it is time there was some white blood."

The thought flitted through Muriel's mind that she was being looked upon as one might a prize female specimen in a cattle-breeding scheme, brought in at some expense to enrich one bovine feature or another. It was not a comfortable thought.

"Ah," the woman said. "You are frowning. We Apaches see things differently than you. There have been times when we have been so few, so many killed, that we survived only by having many babies. A few men can make many women pregnant. And any baby can be brought up Apache. But we also fall in love, just like you people. The days of many wives have been passing."

She made a sound, something like a snort, and Muriel looked up to see what might have been a smile leave her face.

"Many wives make a man feel proud, but they shorten his life." She snorted again and glanced slyly over at Muriel, and Muriel found that she was smiling.

"What has happened here since my son's father died is not right, not the Apache Way."

Muriel glanced up. "It's certainly not anything I can understand . . ."

"No. And this is not a time for you to come."

Muriel began to bristle inwardly.

"The anger here, the trouble, is over how Apaches are to be with white people. They—" Ishton gestured behind her to the east. "—those over there think the ways of white people will make us sick. Others think differently. So there is hatred here now, and they have started killing each other about it. My— My son's father, he held them apart all these years . . ."

She stared off at the cluster of huts. A dark bird arrowed over them, a crow, and vanished over the low hill beyond.

"My son is young. Too young to lead. But he will have to try now. He is the only . . . You being here, that does not help. Here a leader must stand above the dispute. He cannot with you here. You will have to leave. Maybe you'll come back later."

The woman's sentences followed each other like shots from a gun, and Muriel was left breathless. Yes, she would go, leave this awful foreign blood-reeked savage place where nothing made sense and the air was searingly dry, brittle. It would be such a relief. Just a mistake she had made. Anyone could make a mistake. This terrifying woman was right, there was nothing she could do here, this uncivilized place with its barbarous . . . It was not her place, couldn't be her place.

Early this morning she had watched Patch set off with two others in that old wooden buckboard, naked to the waist all three, wearing buckskin moccasins and white breechcloths around their waists, and she knew why they were going—to disinter bodies and take them off to their grandfather, that man they called Victorio—and it seemed utterly strange, utterly not her world. At first she hadn't even recognized Patch standing before her on the wooden sidewalk in those Indian clothes, saying he would return in a day or two, leaving her in this god-forsaken ramshackle town with these women.

Now, in her mind's eye, she saw him again, standing before her, almost a silhouette against the bright dusty street, a tiny leather pouch hanging around his neck on a leather thong, and like being hit by surf rolling, roiling, boiling up a beach, she yearned for him, physically ached from her groin to her temples to have him standing with her, touching her hair with his long brown fingers, his breath on her throat.

Muriel stood up slowly from the ground and turned to Patch's mother.

"Your son told me your name. Ishton. That it means *the* woman. Thank you for telling me all this. I honor everything you say. I have no interest in making matters here more difficult than they already are. For now, I'll go back and see if I can be of any further help to those women, and wait for your son to return. I'll tell him what you have said, and if he agrees, I will go, of course."

Not knowing what else to do, Muriel bowed her head slightly before the older woman, turned, and walked past the brittle trees toward Tombstone, wondering if it were she who was mad, or if it was just this place, or the whole world. Somewhere she could hear her father laughing approvingly.

"That's my girl!" He was laughing. "That's my girl. Pretty as a seashell, but rawhide and steel where it counts, by God."

But he had always approved of her, hadn't he?

Geronimo arrived in Tombstone a few hours after Little Spring set off to fetch the bodies of Victorio's grandsons. He sat grim-faced in one of the empty saloons drinking whiskey from a crystal glass, listening to Naiche and two others explain what had transpired since the wailing for Juh. He interrupted their recitation a few times to ask terse and pointed questions, and finally stood up, shaking his head.

"And Little Spring is now taking the bodies? By himself?"

Geronimo shook his head and made his way outdoors on bandy legs. Over white leggings and a breechcloth he wore a black jacket and a dusty black top hat. He threw the top hat on the ground in disgust, turned to glower into the gloomy saloon, and barked out a few short orders.

Several hours later he and Naiche arrived by buckboard at the foot of a hill beyond which Victorio's camp was located.

Painfully, he climbed down. To the west the sky was red with the dying sun, and the edges of black streaks of cloud glowed with metallic intensity. Followed reluctantly by Naiche, he walked almost crabwise through the scrubland to the top of the rise from which he could see the dozen or so wickiups of Victorio's extended family and a vast pile of twisted cedar logs standing like a tepee, waiting to be set on fire. A few men were standing near it. Geronimo made his way down the slope, through the wickiups, and to the fire. He looked neither left nor right as he walked but was completely aware of the stares of Victorio's people as he and Naiche passed among them. Reaching the site of the fire, he sat down with a grunt and crossed his arms over his chest. Naiche sat down several feet away.

"Light it," Geronimo said to one of the men, a young man he didn't recognize. "We will talk now."

He sat still as a rock, staring at the flames as they began to lick their way up into the wood, alive, voracious, implacable. He wished he had some Irish whiskey. His bones ached, every last one of them, and he knew he might well be facing the end of the world.

His world, at any rate. Well, let it come, he thought. It's as good a time as any . . .

He watched the men assemble—first Victorio, looking old and angry as usual. The man's eye had strayed even farther since Geronimo had last seen him, and he looked like a lunatic. The two old warriors nodded to each other. Geronimo noticed that Victorio did not look in Naiche's direction. Several younger men Geronimo didn't recognize approached and sat down, then the slender man called Nakahyen, the prophet. To Geronimo's old eyes, he looked snakelike—supple and muscular but as if there were no bone inside. Snakes were not appreciated much among Apaches. The man's face was set in an expression of . . . what? Contempt? Geronimo had seen faces like his, white faces in Washington, and he was quick to perceive any trace of condescension. It was detectable on this prophet's face now in the orange light.

The last to sit down was Little Spring, who took a position at the far end of the arc of men now lit by the fire. Geronimo caught his eye and pursed his lips narrowly. The fire crackled in the silence, and after a few moments Geronimo cleared his throat and spat on the ground in front of him.

"I am an old man now," he said. "A very old man. At night when I go to sleep, I wonder if I will see the sun again, or if I will have gone away to see what Ussen has in store for all of us at one time or another. I wonder if I will see some of the warriors I fought with for so many years. I wonder if my family whom the Mexicans slaughtered will be there to welcome me. I am happy to go. I've spent a long time here. I would *like* to go now. I am tired and old and every bone tells me it is time to lie down.

"But I cannot go yet. I cannot lie down. I cannot go now because my people are making me ashamed. I shudder with a pain and an anger greater than any I have ever felt at the thought of Apache warriors killing Apache warriors."

He paused, and in the silence Victorio said, "Geronimo, Geronimo, you cannot speak of such things. You killed Chato with your own hand."

"Chato was a traitor," Geronimo snapped. "He chose to lead the White Eyes against us. He was the enemy. No one here has killed more enemies than me, Victorio. Not even you. So you will not question me about such things.

"Victorio, you and I fought and killed and lost loved ones for most of the years of our lives. Why? To protect our land, to have our way of life. To have our place where our people, our children, could live in this world. I am proud of what you and I did. I have no regret that I killed so many. And you and I, we were honored among our people for killing so many enemies. In our day, a man's valor was counted in only such a way. And that's what we taught our sons and grandsons. That's what we taught our daughters."

Geronimo slowly and painfully got to his feet. He turned his back to the fire and faced the men in the half circle. He did this not so much to achieve a commanding pose but because his back was growing cold.

"We triumphed!" he said, his voice rising. "Alone among all the People who lived here, *we* triumphed. We won our own land, we live in our own land. The landmarks we hold sacred— they are all around us now. They are like what the white man calls standards. Flags. He plants his standards to define his land. Our standards were planted here by Ussen and our ancestors and we fought to preserve them and we *won!*"

His voice fell to a whisper barely audible over the fire, which now reached high into the night air. The men in the circle had to strain to hear him.

"The time of killing is over. It has long been over. You, Victorio, you and I, killing is what we have always known. It was all we knew. It is all that we have been able to teach our people. And so we see what happens when we have no enemies to kill. We kill each other. Are we to become two people? Two people seeking vengeance on each other?

"I'm proud of what we achieved, Victorio, you and I and many others who are now dead. But I'm ashamed that we had so little else to teach our children. And I'm angry that we haven't found a new way to be Apache.

"We are old now, Victorio. Maybe it's time for us to stand back from the fire, to leave these councils to others. Let others talk. Let others decide how Apaches will live in this world."

Geronimo walked away from the fire, his body swaying side to side over his crooked old legs. He walked beyond the spot where he had sat, and toward the darkness where the women of Victorio's camp sat listening. He stopped and cocked his head.

"For all the Apaches' fierceness," he said, "we wouldn't have won without the wisdom of the man who has left us so recently. It was he who told us how we could win against the White Eyes, and we all buried our knives in the ground in agreement. His blood now runs only in one body, his son. His son may be young, but his voice should be heard."

Geronimo sat down. "Come along, Victorio. And Naiche. You too. Let us sit back here and listen."

The men sitting in an arc around the fire looked silently at the ground before them. Naiche rose slowly to his feet. His mouth opened as if to speak, but snapped shut. The light of the fire danced in his eyes, and he looked directly over at Victorio.

"How brave are you, Victorio?" he said.

The warrior with the one eye askew stood up, looked to his left down the row of men, then to his right. His glance fastened briefly on the eyes of Nakahyen, then he looked away.

"I wish my people well," he said, and turned toward the dark. A twisted cedar log on the fire slumped and fell inward, and as the other logs rearranged themselves around it, a shower of sparks flew up into the night air.

BOOK THREE

∽ ∾

Destiny

After one year from the ratification of this article
the manufacture, sale, or transportation of intoxi-
cating liquors within, the importation thereof into,
or the exportation thereof from the United States
and all territory subject to the jurisdiction thereof
for beverage purposes is hereby prohibited.
> —Section 1, Article XVIII,
> Constitution of the United States

Twenty-five

1921

No one called him Little Spring anymore.

The name had fallen into disuse several years after he discredited Nakahyen the prophet who, once exposed before the People, was allowed to leave Apacheria rather than be killed, as some thought appropriate. Almost everyone believed that Nakahyen went to live among the Comanches in Oklahoma where he became a storekeeper. But there were stories also that he joined an itinerant Wild West show based in Kansas City in which he was nightly gunned down by "cowboys," and died a few years later of shame and alcohol poisoning. In any event, Nakahyen disappeared into the world beyond Apacheria and was not heard from again.

The people of Apacheria eventually came to call their new leader Juh, which means "He-who-sees-ahead." It was not so much a name as a term of honor—the core credential for office. For it had been Juh who had led the Apaches to their triumph over the armies of the United States and to the establishment of the sovereign Apache nation in 1885. In all the history of the Apaches, no man had done so great a thing—not Cochise, not Mangas Colorado. In the minds of the people, the name Juh had already come to embody wisdom and courage and craftiness—the very coefficients of leadership—and so they called their new leader by that appellation as he emerged in time as the one who could guide Apacheria to its destiny.

For the new Juh had vision. He had a vision that appealed to the young men who had been brought up hearing stories of Apache heroism and glory, of lightninglike Apache raids, of the evident superiority of the Apache Way over any other, be it Mexican, American, or any of the other tribal people who now lived like zoo animals on reservations. Even the most traditionally minded Apaches recognized that the world around them, at least in the United States, was changing rapidly, dramatically—and there was no way that the Apache nation could stand totally apart, immune. And so they had listened as he counseled patience, and they had joined him in creating his grand scheme . . .

Among the stories the Apaches liked to tell at night— sometimes with useful embellishment, the better to make a moral clear to the listeners—was one that told how the prophet Nakahyen stood up to speak after the three old warriors had retired from the immediate light of the fire that night long ago when many thought a civil war might erupt in Apacheria. He rose to his feet supple as a snake and addressed the Apaches with his eyes closed, his hands upraised. He told them of the dream that had come to him.

In his dream, the night had unfolded its wings like an enormous bat and blanked out the moon, bringing total darkness and cold to the world. This, he explained, meant that so long as some Apaches lived in the false lights of Tombstone, the moon and the stars would not be permitted to shine. It portended the end of the Apache Way altogether.

The men around the fire listened carefully, and one after the other, each spoke, probing the prophet's dream for different or additional meanings. Then, when all the others were finished, the one they called Little Spring in those days spoke. He said that Nakahyen's dream had no meaning. And that was because Nakahyen almost surely hadn't had such a dream. He had, instead, made up the dream and its meaning, just as he had made up so many other things. His name was not Nakahyen; it was a Comanche word having to do with lightning. He was not an Apache, but a Comanche.

He, Little Spring, knew this from the records the White Eyes kept in those days.

The records of the Indian agent in Oklahoma showed that the Apache woman whom Nakahyen claimed as his mother—the one who had gone off to live among the Comanches on the reservation in Oklahoma—had died giving birth. Her baby had been taken in by a Comanche woman, but it died of the coughing disease before six months passed. Meantime, the Comanche woman herself gave birth—to a son named for the lightning that flashed during the night he was born. This, Little Spring said, was a dangerous omen, as any Apache well knew even if the Comanches didn't. And as the Comanche boy grew, what was boyish mischief became intolerable cruelty, and when he was fourteen he was banished by his own people before the Indian agent could take action of his own. He had wandered here and there among the Indians in Oklahoma, including the Kiowas and the few Apaches who had wound up there. In the year 1900 he had vanished from Oklahoma. That was the same year he had arrived in Apacheria, claiming to be an Apache prophet.

This, then, was Nakahyen. Not an Apache, but a Comanche. Not a prophet, but a liar.

As Little Spring began speaking of these things, the one who called himself Nakahyen glowered into the fire with angry defiance, but as the story went on, his expression turned to alarm and then fear. When Little Spring was finished, the "prophet" stood, shouted something in his real tongue, and fled out of the reach of the council fire. But he was caught and dragged back into the light.

Through the rest of the night, the men debated the manner in which he should be killed. Most thought he should be hung by his feet head down over a fire in the old Apache manner, while others thought they should wait till morning's light and hold a footrace, the winner having the honor of dispatching the liar with a knife. But finally they listened again to a suggestion by Little Spring.

In the morning, while all the Apaches watched, including the women and children of Victorio's camp, the Comanche was stripped of everything he had that was Apache. The pouch around his neck was taken from him, and the piece of pink cloth and the bullet he said were from Mangas Colorado were thrown into the remains of the council fire. His clothes were stripped off and burned and, while he was held firmly on the ground, one of the Apache men lightly carved a picture on his chest—the head of a snake with its tongue flitting out. And while the women and children howled with amusement, the "prophet" was sent running, bleeding, and buck naked, through the camp and eastward.

Several young boys and girls, shouting with laughter at his humiliation, followed him on horseback for several hours all the way to the Rio Grande, into which he sank up to his neck and swam to the other side . . .

Another story the Apaches loved to tell—and embellish—around their campfires and in the log homes they had taken to building for themselves was about the invasion from Mexico.

On the morning of March 9, 1916, a Mexican some called a revolutionary and others called a hoodlum led a group of soldiers across the border into the United States. This was Pancho Villa, who had already begun to lose battles with other revolutionary forces in the internecine chaos that was Mexico. And like the megalomaniac he was, Villa decided that his best course was to get even with the United States, which had withdrawn its support from him in favor of another revolutionary, a man named Carranza.

So Villa and his men harassed Americans who lived or worked south of the border between Mexico and New Mexico, and then, in a fine madness, launched an invasion of the Colossus of the North, riding with guns blazing into the small and utterly insignificant border town of Columbus, New Mexico, which was only a few miles away from Apacheria. The Mexicans killed eighteen people, including one Apache family who had been trading there, burned the barracks at Camp Furlong, a forlorn little American military outpost nearby, and disappeared across the border.

President Woodrow Wilson would have preferred to turn the matter over to the Department of State and issue a severe warning to the Mexicans, but he was under great pressure to flex Uncle Sam's biceps in the face of such an outrage—the first invasion of American territory since the War of 1812—and it was, after all, an election year.

So two days after Villa's raid, a brigadier general at Fort Bliss in Texas, John J. Pershing, received orders from the Secretary of War to exact a devastating justice. He was to form an expeditionary force of some five thousand American troops—including cavalry, engineers, artillery, and eight aircraft, JN-2 Jennies from the First Aero Squadron of the Signal Corps' aviation section. They were to cross into Mexico to capture Pancho Villa. It was to be the first tactical use of aircraft by the United States.

These forces all began to gather west of Columbus, preparatory to their retaliatory raid, and the buildup was watched with something bordering on amusement by Apaches camped out in the hills to the west. The consensus among the Apaches was that Pershing and his Buffalo Soldiers and his flimsy flying machines would no more be a match for Villa and his men than a similar U.S. force had been against the Apaches thirty years before. For the Mexican revolutionary hoodlums knew the countryside in northern Chihuahua much as the Apaches had. In the Apache camps, bets were placed and young men dreamed.

Taking matters into his own hands, Little Spring—who was not yet considered the main leader of Apacheria—left immediately for Washington, D.C., and obtained an audience a week later with President Wilson, his onetime college president. There he explained that Pershing's force would surely not succeed quickly, if at all, and that a lengthy invasion of Mexico with troops from the hated United States thundering around Mexican communities would only bring further ill-will between the two countries. Anti-American sentiment among the

Mexican populace was strong and well known—however irrational, Little Spring said tactfully.

But a deeper hatred, he said, existed between Mexicans and the Apaches, and it probably never could be eliminated. The bad blood went back three centuries. Further, Villa's raid on Columbus had resulted in the death of an Apache family, and the raiders, fleeing back home, had raced through the eastern corner of Apacheria, burning down several rancheros along the way. The nation of Apacheria was, then, equally aggrieved by this unwarranted attack. And finally, Little Spring pointed out, the Apaches still knew the territory where Pancho Villa had gone into hiding, and, he reminded the President, they had always had more success there than U.S. troops, even the Buffalo Soldiers who were assigned to General Pershing.

Little Spring proposed a joint "military action" whereby Pershing's forces would position themselves along the border to intercept Villa if he returned northward, while the Apaches pursued him into the mountain fastnesses. And so it was done.

Three weeks after the invasion of Columbus, New Mexico, and approximately twenty acres of Apacheria, two hundred Apache warriors sang and danced around their great fires, and the next morning went on the warpath for the first time in three decades, led by Little Spring, who was then in his early thirties. It took only a week to track down Villa's men in the Sierra Madres—in all, some four hundred ragtag soldiers who were by now exhausted, running on reduced rations, with ammunition at a low ebb. They were in three separate camps deep in the mountains, and on a fine morning as the sun rose over the mountains to the east, the warriors struck with all the old ferocity—a ferocity latent in their lineage.

In all, Pancho Villa's force was reduced to a band of some twenty men who fled south with Villa into obscurity. About eighty men simply disappeared into the wilderness. More than three hundred revolutionary corpses were left to become skeletons in the canyons, and the Apaches returned to their land and celebrated their victory for more than a week of joyous dancing and feasting. Pancho Villa, instead of becoming lionized for being bold—and quixotic—enough to attack the great bully, the United States, which is what he had hoped for, was instead reviled among his countrymen thereafter as the stupid one who had aroused the smoldering fires of the Apache savages and paid the price.

The Mexican revolution ran its course, and the United States government publicly acknowledged the debt it owed its neighbor, Apacheria. Privately, a considerable number of officials in the United States government saw how useful the Apaches could be, and filed this insight away.

Thus did Little Spring become a legend among his people, eventually to become known as Juh.

Of course, the new Juh's wife, Muriel Freeman, the mother of his three sons and his daughter, had other names that she called him privately. Some of these were fond terms, while others were more mischievous, employed whenever she judged that He-who-sees had grown too grand "for his britches."

His old friend, Tom Jeffords Cleveland Bignon, usually called him by his Princeton name, Patch. Tom now called himself Thomas Bignon, Esquire, for he had gone on to study the law in St. Louis once the gunshot wound in his thigh healed that summer in 1906. Now, fifteen years later in 1921, his name was carved in large letters into a long mahogany sign over the door to his fine, book-lined, walnut-paneled offices in a one-story building across the street from the Bird Cage Theatre in Tombstone. And Patch—or Juh—who was the main recipient of Thomas Bignon's legal advice, still called him Big Ears, but only in private conversations.

The sovereign nation of Apacheria had its own laws, of course. These were few and simple: little more than the traditional canons of proper Apache behavior. It was the convoluted law of the Americans that Tom Bignon had studied in St. Louis, and it was on behalf of Apacheria's dealings with the United States that Tom Bignon dispensed legal advice.

Tom Bignon was blessed with several avenues by which he

could obtain the practical sort of advice he needed along with updates in the law. Three of his old classmates at Princeton had taken seriously President Wilson's motto for the college's graduates—"In the nation's service"—and held important offices in the departments of Justice and the Treasury. By keeping in comradely touch with these old friends, Tom derived a good deal of information about what steps the American government had in mind at any time, for example, with reference to the recent amendment to the Constitution, and to the Volstead Act that called for its enforcement.

Much to the apparent surprise of the temperance movement, the United States Congress, and the state legislatures that eagerly ratified the amendment, human nature remained obstinately unaffected. Prohibition produced an immediate open season for clandestine distillers and bootleggers. By 1921 untold thousands of citizens were engaged in the business. No government, state or federal, had thought to develop the capacity to do much of anything about it. In every city of any size at all, formerly small-time hoodlums had taken on the task of supplying restaurants, clubs, and the proliferating speakeasies with Demon Rum, John Barleycorn, and what came to be called bathtub gin.

Capitalism ran rampant. Already the hoodlums were engaged in the all-American task of competing for markets, and the result was turf wars between urban gangs that before had contented themselves with operating local brothels, running numbers, and other small-time rackets. Nowhere were the turf wars more openly fought than in Chicago. A commission on crime there announced that ten thousand crooks dwelled and worked in the Windy City, stealing up to $12 million a year—a low estimate, most people thought.

Tom Bignon's second major source of insight into this new world was none other than Abner Freeman, now in his sixties and retired from business except for his string of elegant "men's clubs." Like most people of means everywhere in the United States, the members of the crown jewel of these clubs,

Packard House, were not about to do without fine Scotch and brandies, regardless of what the United States government said. And Abner had presciently laid in a several-year supply of these luxuries before Prohibition went into effect, imported perfectly legally from the British Isles and the Continent. But his other clubs, with clienteles of lower status and not quite such refined tastes—and paying lower annual dues—had to be satisfied with whatever arose from the new order of things. This, of course, plunged Abner Freeman into the middle of Chicago's gangland turf wars.

Tom Bignon, a confirmed bachelor, made a point of making the three-day train journey to visit the old man and the Packard House at least three times a year. Abner, who still retained much of the buccaneer spirit that had made him rich in the first place, enjoyed Tom's company immensely, for Tom was both good-natured and wise for his years—and especially insightful at navigating the ambiguous realm where what was not quite illegal merged cloudily into the illegal. Indeed, Abner liked to refer to Tom as his "consigliere," a term he had picked up from one of the gangs that began in the latter weeks of 1920 to sniff around his string of clubs like a dog exploring a neighbor's yard.

In early spring of 1921, Abner wired Tom in Tombstone, saying that "the dog seems about to lift its leg." And that translated into: "Come, I may need you."

Tom had trained the Apache men who operated the telegraph office in Tombstone to consider any wire to him, any message however innocuous, as urgent. So the young telegraph operator arrived on the wooden sidewalk outside Tom Bignon's office at six-thirty in the morning and hammered on the door. Tom stuck his head out the window on the second floor where he maintained a small but well-equipped apartment, spotted the messenger through bleary eyes, and a moment later opened the door to the street wearing a silk bathrobe that was a source of considerable amusement among the Apaches in town. A man dressing like a woman.

Tom ignored the smirk on the messenger's face, took the yellow paper in hand, and read it, saying "Damn" to himself. He went back upstairs, marched through the small living room into the bedroom in the rear, and told the two young Mexican women who were lying drowsily in his bed that they had to run along.

"*Qué? Qué?*" they said, and flopped over on their stomachs. Tom swatted them playfully on their backsides, explaining that he was leaving for two weeks and had to pack his clothes.

"Out, out!" he said, and shooed them, complaining, out of the bedroom. In the living room they continued to complain as they dressed, and eventually took to giggling. A few minutes later Tom emerged from the bedroom clad in a gray suit with vest, a pair of three-hundred-dollar tooled boots, and carrying a soft black leather valise. He looked at his watch, noting that he had a half hour to catch the train east to Silver City, and only then noticed the writing on the mirror over the fireplace. One of the girls had written in lipstick and in Spanish, "We will be waiting," and this was accompanied by a sketchy but exceptionally lewd drawing.

Tom smiled.

What a life I have, he thought. Who could ask for anything more?

Two and a half hours later Tom Bignon stepped off the train in Silver City, a wholly different place than it had been when Victorio's young warriors terrified the miners into going back to work fifteen years earlier. The transformation had been old Naiche's idea, though of course he hadn't lived long enough to see it.

Naiche's idea was to start another Tombstone on the eastern side of Apacheria in order to attract people from, and visitors to, New Mexico, just as the old Tombstone attracted such people from Arizona. In 1917 Little Spring, as he was still known then, presented Naiche's idea to the council of eight who, in a loosely organized manner, oversaw Apacherian affairs at that time. But he presented Naiche's idea with an original twist.

Tombstone had stayed much the way it once was in the 1880s, to all intents and appearances a raw frontier town full of saloons and bawdy houses, wooden sidewalks and poker tables, swinging doors and singing whores. Its success was due to a widespread and deeply felt nostalgia for what people imagined were the days of the Wild West. As the western states of the United States got more and more civilized by temperance unions and Christian churches, mortgages and Main streets, Tombstone in Apacheria was about the only place where at least some of the accoutrements of the Old West flourished. People would pay good money for a few days in such a goodhearted, tawdry place.

But there was a wholly different class of people with money to burn—lots of money—and it was Muriel Freeman who reminded Little Spring that it was increasingly difficult for these people to find a welcoming place to gamble away thousands, to drink and eat capaciously if genteelly, and in general to enjoy elegant surroundings free of blue laws and blue noses. Tom Bignon, with his ear to foreign ground, confirmed that the blue laws were only going to get stiffer, meaning that the rich would have to travel farther to enjoy themselves. Why not to Apacheria instead of Europe? Why not to Silver City, which lay three hours south by train from Santa Fe, New Mexico?

And Santa Fe, finding itself a backwater town of six thousand ever since the railroad had passed it by, was now in the process of reinventing itself. There were architects up there inventing a whole new kind of building style called Neo-Pueblo, blocky buildings with round, handmade walls of adobe brick and stucco, all colored earthy brown, a mixture of Spanish and Pueblo tradition. Santa Fe was billing itself as a different kind of place, a City Different, with quaint Indians hanging around in blankets, and quaint Spanish-speaking people hanging around in serapes, all being charming to each other and to any visitor, all under the beautiful southwestern sky. The tourists were on their way.

And if to Santa Fe, why not a bit farther south, to a grand and elegant mecca of gambling and good liquor, refined entertainment, and all this among some real Indians, the Apaches?

The tribal coffers contained plenty of money to rebuild Silver City into such a mecca, and the income from the two combined would permit the tribe to close down all the mining in Apacheria. Copper in great abundance had been discovered near the old town—now gone—of Bisbee, and American mining companies were clamoring for the right to mine it. Why let the Americans take from Apache land that which they found so valuable and use it all up? Little Spring asked. Why not instead have Apaches mining the rich ore that Americans were all too happy to spend gambling and playing? That money could pay for all of the things so many Apaches now appreciated and wanted—modern medical care, automobiles, education. Why not leave the copper and the silver and the gold in the ground, as in a bank, for some other day in the future when it would be all the more valuable?

The council of leaders agreed unanimously with this grand vision of Little Spring's, and it was then that he was dubbed Juh. All eight men buried their knives up to the hilt in the ground, and the word went forth around Apacheria.

The new Juh had a model very much in mind for this new magnet for the American rich: Packard House, the central jewel in his father-in-law's tiara of men's clubs. He left all the details to his wife Muriel, who, of course, knew the names of all the different kinds of furniture, linens, chinaware, glassware, chandeliers, draperies, tapestries, and art that would have to adorn such a place.

Muriel Freeman threw herself into the project with a gusto that left heads spinning. She had her own vision of Silver City, and it was not restricted merely to building a copy of Packard House in the dry foothills. The old miner's shacks, the three saloons, the general store, stables, and outbuildings, were all torn down. She easily talked the Southern Pacific into replacing their old and ramshackle railroad station with a modern one built of stone with a fine pitched roof of blue-green slate. Apache funds paid for a railroad siding built as a resting place for visitors' private Pullman cars.

The haphazard, curved, and often muddy streets of dirt were replaced with graceful esplanades of gravel that made a rich sound as the wheels of a fleet of motorcars passed over it, a taxi service for those who preferred to ride rather than walk from the station to—and between—the three grand houses that were constructed more in the manner of the mansions of Newport, Rhode Island, than Chicago's Lake Shore Drive. In these four-story mansions with whimsical towers and playful mansard rooflines, and tall graceful windows to match the high ceilings inside, were room after elegant room for gaming, eating, and drinking. Each of the three buildings provided forty comfortable bedrooms and suites upstairs for the visitors, all with the most up-to-date plumbing fixtures and splendid views of the surrounding landscape.

On the northern end of this new town, a racetrack was laid out with viewing stands and betting services hooked by telegraph to all the major tracks in the United States and Mexico. Beyond the track were stables of horses and mules that would take the rich on well-catered excursions into the surrounding forested hills and even into the mountains beyond, to inspect the old ruins, to bathe in the natural hot springs, to hunt mountain lion and deer, even to visit a traditional Apache summer camp and eat mescal and venison around a vast campfire.

Soft-spoken Apache men served as croupiers and dealers in the gaming rooms, which were watched over by yet other Apaches with expressionless faces and black eyes that saw everything and bespoke a delicious latent danger. Near the three mansions, small cottages were homes for the women— all non-Indian—who, carefully selected by Muriel and under strict rules, were allowed to freelance their favors to that portion of the male clientele who came unattended by their wives or mistresses.

In Silver City, everything was managed with elegance, grace, and dignity. It was expensive, to be sure, which served to winnow out the kind of people who might be disruptive. In the two years since it opened, the wealthy had come in droves. Many would stop off in Santa Fe and enjoy the quaint pleasures it provided for a day or two—the astounding, chili-infested local cuisine, the wares of pueblo potters and Navajo silversmiths sold in the plaza—and then proceed south, relieved to spend a week or two amid the comforting and at the same time exotic and sinful splendor in Apacheria.

Disembarking from the train, Tom Bignon waved off one of the young Apache taxi drivers and decided to stroll over to the log house on the western edge of town that served Patch and his wife Muriel as a residence and an office when they were in Silver City.

It was a one-story structure built around a central open courtyard where Patch would make a cheerful fire for his guests to sit around and talk into the night. It had a flat roof, on which the couple often slept at night, particularly in the summer, under the revolving stars. In back were stables that housed two mares and a gelding, all the progeny of a large black horse that had belonged to Lozen, the Warrior Woman. She was now in her late sixties and lived in a camp in the Peloncillo Mountains to the south, overlooking a vast sea of grass in the Animas Valley and dreaming of the old days. Lozen was among a handful remaining of the generation that had led the Apaches to independence, and the only one who was still lucid.

Tom Bignon arrived at the log house with the glow of perspiration on his forehead. In the shadow of the ancient cottonwoods that shaded the office end of the house, he felt the perspiration vanish in a cooling instant, and went inside, blinking while his eyes adjusted. The office consisted chiefly of a single large room with three sofas ranged around a large fireplace built of stone. At the far end of the room were two enormous matching rolltop desks. One was Muriel's, at which she performed her tasks of overseeing the amenities of Silver City, the day-to-day management of the town's business being left to one of her husband's cousins. The other desk was Patch's. He had removed from it all the cubbyholes, and used it more as a bookcase than a desk.

Patch was sitting alone on a sofa facing the fireplace, moccasined feet crossed at the ankle and resting on a low table fashioned from a six-inch-thick slab cut from a single tree. He was wearing traditional white leggings, a light blue oxford shirt open at the throat, and his hair was pulled back into an ebony ponytail.

He looked up when Bignon entered the room. "Big Ears," he said.

"Patch."

"Sit down, if you don't think it'll wrinkle your suit."

Bignon dropped his valise on the floor and sat down. "Where's Muriel?" he asked.

"Settling an argument. Some of the girls sent away for those new kind of dresses. The ones that come down to just above the knee."

"They're called flappers," Tom said.

"The dresses?"

"The girls who wear them."

Patch nodded. "My cousin doesn't think they're proper clothing for the escorts."

"What does Muriel think?"

"She thinks they're fine."

"Good. I'll bring her some from Chicago."

"She won't wear them."

"But you just said—"

"She thinks they're fine for the escorts. Why are you going to Chicago?"

Tom reached into his jacket pocket and pulled out the telegram. "It's from Abner."

Patch read it and put his feet down on the floor, suddenly

transformed, like a mountain lion that has heard a hoof scrape a rock.

"Which dog is lifting its leg?" he asked sharply.

"My guess is it's that guy Torrio. John Torrio. The Italian."

"They're all Italian."

"No, there's an Irish gang up there too. This Torrio, he was born in Italy, Sicily, grew up in New York City on the Lower East Side. His uncle was a guy called Colosimo, Big Jim they called him. He ran a string of brothels in Chicago, wore a lot of diamonds."

Patch wrinkled up his nose. "I met him once. A vile man."

"Five or six years ago," Tom continued, "he asked his cousin—this Torrio chap—to come to Chicago and get into the business. He started out running one of those joints on Bedbug Row, then he graduated. Ran the House of All Nations for a while, then became Big Jim's right hand. Apparently he's a tough little guy. Looks like a weasel."

"You're talking about Colosimo in the past tense."

"He fell for an opera singer and left his wife last year. That doesn't go over with those Sicilians. They evidently think a man who'd dump his wife doesn't have any loyalty. Undependable. So last May, I think it was, Big Jim went to a restaurant he owned on Wabash Avenue and some hoods came in with Chicago pianos and mowed him down."

"Chicago pianos?"

"Tommy guns. You know, those—"

Patch nodded and a little smile played in his eyes. "Maybe you could bring me one of those, along with the dresses for Muriel."

"Sure. Now, Torrio took over Big Jim's business, and they say he's expanding into bootlegging, narcotics, a lot of other rackets. Building an empire. He's the one nosing around Abner. Abner's been buying hooch from the Irish guys, O'Banion's gang. So he could get himself caught in the middle."

"Abner should get out of the business," Patch said. "Retire."

"The old bandit is too proud to do that."

"I know, I know." Patch shook his head and sighed. "Find

out what you can about this man Torrio. And tell Abner to keep his back to the wall."

"I'll be back in a week," Tom said.

"Don't forget that, uh, Chicago piano."

Twenty-six

Rasheen definitely had the look. Thick dark eyebrows, almond-shaped eyes with pupils like coal, a prominent but narrow nose, and a narrow but full-lipped mouth painted a glossy deep crimson. This much of her was directly visible. The rest of her was also visible, but glancingly, fetchingly, beneath voluminous folds of nearly transparent chiffon, all designed to correspond to a common fantasy about what an Arabian odalisque should look like. Rasheen swayed prettily under the transparent veils as she massaged the knotty and nervous shoulders of Abner Freeman as he lay on a cushioned table in the room in Packard House that was called the Harem.

Rasheen was relatively new at Packard House, and a great favorite, even though most of the members were perfectly well aware that her real name was Jessica Wilbur and that she came from Des Moines, Iowa, not Baghdad. Even so, she affected an odd, all-purpose foreign accent, and dropped hints about a noble past in one emirate or another. She was an especial favorite among the older members, about whom she was particularly solicitous.

"You're so tense, Mr. Freeman," she said, kneading the trapezius muscles and the back of his neck. "So stiff."

"Oh!" Abner said. "Oh, by God, that's . . . oh."

"I'll get you all relaxed. Loose."

"Not all, I hope," Abner said, and heard Rasheen titter prettily as she pinched his ear. Her hands moved down to the small of his back, fingers searching successfully for each small point

304

that made up the mosaic of pain that bound his back like chain mail.

"I'm worried about Mr. Field," Rasheen said presently.

"Marshall Junior? Why?"

"The last time he was with me, he—well, he turned all red. I thought he was having apoplexy. Or a heart attack. He was gasping something terrible."

"Well, Rasheen, the man is seventy years old."

"But what if . . . ?"

"Oh, don't worry about that. If it happens, what better way for a man to . . . well, I see that it would be a bit trying for you, wouldn't it? I'll have to think about that." Abner Freeman heard a tap and looked up at the arched doorway fifteen feet away. Old Jenkins stood there, blushing. The man's been working at Packard House for fifteen years, Abner thought, and he stills seems surprised at what goes on here.

"What is it, Jenkins, for God's sake?"

Rasheen turned to face the old factotum and arched her back. Jenkins turned even redder. "Yes, Jenkins, we're busy." She smiled broadly at him and he dropped his eyes to the floor.

"Sir, there's someone here asking to see you," he said. "A Mr. Torrio and another gentleman."

"Mr. Torrio is no gentleman, Jenkins. He's a viper. Tell him I'm busy. I *am* busy, dammit. Tell him to come back in an hour. What time is it now?"

"Five o'clock. He seems quite insistent, sir."

"An hour, Jenkins."

"Yes, sir," the old factotum said, looking crestfallen and turning to leave.

"Only an hour?" Rasheen sighed. "In my country . . ."

Abner Freeman laughed, but inwardly he winced at the mental image of the self-assured face of the little man with opaque brown eyes whom they called the Brain.

Shortly after Apache independence, now almost three decades in the past, United States troops lowered the American flag over Fort Huachuca, handed it to Naiche, and, with little further fanfare, pulled out, a long stream of mounted cavalry, mule-drawn artillery, caissons crammed with gear, heading northwest to Tucson to be reassigned to duties elsewhere. For two decades the fort was left to itself, a ghostly place of empty barracks and a row of small officers' houses gathering dust and the messy webs of black widows. The wind blew sibilantly across the great parade grounds, which turned from well-mowed grass to weeds and finally gave in to the invasion of desert scrub plants—mesquite, prickly pear. The land was given over to kangaroo rats and the occasional coyote.

In 1917, however, just as his wife was developing her grand scheme for Silver City, the new Juh was laying plans of his own. Fort Huachuca was restored; the several barracks buildings where enlisted men had slept on narrow cots were now warehouses. The officers' quarters had been razed—all but the general's house that had stood in the middle of the row. This house now housed a telegraph and various other forms of equipment useful for keeping track of the coming and going of merchandise. Stables were rebuilt to house the several mule trains, and other stablelike buildings arose where solidly built Ford trucks were housed.

The merchandise arrived from across the border with old Mexico. It moved from the reconditioned fort, by mule train and often now by Ford truck, west through the bone-dry badlands between Apacheria and California, and eastward through the vast, sparsely uninhabited llanos of southern New Mexico into the equally uninhabited realms of trans-Pecos Texas.

Mexican smugglers who thought to carry their wares to other points along the border—El Paso, for example—rather than into Apacheria, soon disappeared from the world, but not without a trace. Their skeletons would turn up in remote canyons and on mountain trails, found by yet other smugglers or innocent vaqueros searching for their wandering cattle. Soon enough it was ubiquitously understood in the borderlands of the northern Mexico states of Chihuahua and Sonora that the Apaches owned the border. It was patrolled by what was called the Apacheria Police, who always courteously offered to guide any stray smugglers to Fort Huachuca. If the smugglers refused the offer, they were of course promptly dispatched into whatever afterlife they believed in and deserved.

And, of course, the baser elements of human nature being unalterable, there were always a few hapless Mexican smugglers who believed they could evade the Apache patrols and make a better deal elsewhere. Thus, from time to time, the police had the welcome opportunity to hone their skills and satisfy the ancient warrior spirit that dwelled undiluted in the Apache heart.

At approximately the same time that John Torrio and his colleague announced themselves at the door of Packard House in Chicago, the new Juh emerged from the shadow of one of the warehouses at Fort Huachuca, spun to his left, and shot the figure across the alleyway three times in the chest. Instantly, he spun to his right, threw himself into the dust, and, as he did so, fired three more bullets into the head and chest of another approaching figure. From the little crowd standing fifty yards away, whoops of approval rose over the echoes of the revolver fire. The two wooden figures, the late afternoon sun shining through their mortal wounds, swayed in the breeze.

Among the group of Apache policemen, who were variously dressed in combinations of Apache and western clothes, stood a white man with a self-satisfied paunch, massively wide hips, and a prodigious red moustache. He nodded his head approvingly. He was Charles T. Holly, lately retired from the New Orleans police force and recently hired by Juh to operate a more formal training school for the Apache police, to learn the arts of urban warfare.

Charlie Holly spat on the ground, tugged his broad-brimmed hat farther down over his eyes, and said, "Not bad, not bad. But if there'd been another man out there, you'd just be lyin' in the dirt with your thumb up your ass. If you don't stick to the goddamn walls, you're gonna be so much red meat."

Juh grinned, white teeth gleaming from his dusty face, and got to his feet.

"Now, you men," Charlie Holly went on. "Me and Juh set that up so y'all would see a bonehead mistake. Don't matter how good a shot you be. You expose y'self like that and it's all over. You Apaches, of all people, you should know that, for Christ's sake. Now let's go get something to eat. Tonight you men of A team're gonna see if you can take that building over there." He pointed across the parade ground to the house that had been the general's. "And B team is gonna come with me and see to it that you don't."

As the others walked off, Juh approached the big white man. "What do you think?"

"Wellsir, let me tell you, these boys of yours have all got the one most important qualification for this kind of work."

"What's that?"

Charlie Holly spat on the ground again. "They like it."

Old Jenkins ushered the two men into the wood-paneled library in the east wing of Packard House where Abner Freeman sat in a large leather easy chair next to a small fire that burned in the fireplace, despite the season. It gave off little heat into the room, the fireplace being a poorly designed one, both wide and deep.

Abner stood as the two men entered the room. He was carefully attired in a dark suit and expensive western boots that added an inch and a half to his long frame. Jenkins said, "Mr. Torrio, sir, and . . ." The old factotum looked nervously at the second, larger man who entered the room after Torrio.

"Glad to meet you, Mr. Freeman," Torrio said, handing his pearl-gray homburg to Jenkins and putting out his right hand toward Abner. He was short—perhaps five-seven—and nattily dressed, a trim-looking figure with an erect, self-confident posture and a smile that struck Abner as smug. Smug as a snake. By contrast, the other man was large—almost as tall as Abner, and broad across the chest. He had a large coarse-featured face—thick lips, heavy black eyebrows, dark eyes that looked resentful. A thin scar ran from his ear to his chin. He stood behind Torrio, glancing around the room.

"Torrio," Abner said, shaking the little man's hand. It was a damp hand with a firm grasp. "Sit down. Can Jenkins get you something to drink?"

"Scotch."

Jenkins nodded and turned questioningly to the bigger man, who merely nodded. The old factotum quickly left the room. Torrio sat down on a leather sofa beside the fireplace, and his companion sat at the other end. Abner took his seat in the armchair.

"We met a few years back, didn't we?" Torrio said. "At Big Jim's restaurant. Caruso was there, remember? Caruso loved the place."

Abner bridled inwardly. Torrio's mentioning Big Jim was not to establish a link between the two men but a reminder that Colosimo had been assassinated. And obviously at the command of Torrio, his trusted lieutenant.

"I know the purpose of this visit, *Mister* Torrio. I want to be perfectly clear at the outset. I have a long-standing relationship with Mr. O'Banion, a very satisfactory relationship."

"Two years," Torrio said. "That's not so long a time. A lot has changed in two years."

"And some things have not."

"Of course you know," Torrio said, "that the Genna brothers now have the, uh, sole distributorship to the South Side, and my people have the midtown area."

"I know that is how you people want it. I don't believe Mr. O'Banion agrees."

The large man on the sofa spoke, his voice surprisingly high in pitch, and phlegmy. "North of the river," he pronounced. "O'Banion."

"That's the way it'll be," Torrio said. He leaned back in the sofa and spread his hands in a welcoming gesture. "It's better this way. No more arguments, no more killing. That's stupid. Everybody suffers. I hate all the killing. Businessmen like yourself—you should appreciate some peace on the streets. A little certainty in an uncertain world."

Hypocrite, Abner thought. You appalling hypocrite.

Jenkins entered with two highballs of Scotch and handed them to the two men as swiftly as he could before vanishing from the room. Torrio sipped his drink.

"You don't get *this* stuff from O'Banion."

Abner said nothing. He crossed his legs and folded his arms across his chest.

"A secret, huh?" Torrio said with a smirk. "That's okay. I suppose the members here—" He waved his hand around the room. "—wouldn't drink the kind of stuff O'Banion deals."

"Mr. Torrio, I happen—"

"I'm just trying to avoid any unnecessary violence, Mr. Freeman—"

"—to have some business to attend to—"

"—it's bad for business—"

"—so if you'll excuse me—"

"—and it costs lots of money—"

"—I have to get on with—"

"—funerals and all."

Abner Freeman stood up. "Good night, *Mister* Torrio."

"I just wanted to come around to all our new midtown customers and tell 'em how it is now. No surprises, you know? Get up, Al. It's time to go. We've taken enough of this gentleman's time."

The two men rose.

"Oh," Torrio said. "How rude of me. I forgot to introduce you to Al here. He's from New York, like I was. He's learning the ropes. Abner Freeman, Al Capone."

The large man's eyes flickered around the room.

"Nice," he said in his high, phlegmy voice. "Maybe I'll join sometime." He smiled, an ugly smile that did not include his eyes. There were no laugh lines, no lines of any sort, around this Al Capone's eyes, as though he wore a mask.

The two men let themselves out through the door, and as it closed behind them with a solid click, Abner thought about how closely you have to pay attention if your house gets infested with rattlesnakes. It had happened to him once in

Texas, years earlier when he was a lot younger, a lot fuller of piss and vinegar, and a lot stupider.

"Vermin!" Abner shouted.

Charlie Holly sat comfortably in the dark in one of the upstairs rooms of the general's house at Fort Huachuca. He was smoking a twisted black cigar and, with one part of his mind, listening to the rain that had begun to patter on the tin roof overhead about five minutes earlier. It was getting louder, as was the wind. In the room with him, invisible now to the eye, was a large wooden table where the telegraph key and its associated wires and wooden boxes sat. Beyond the table, and also invisible, a window was open and the breeze fluttered through it noisily.

Ten members of the B team were deployed outside the house, four downstairs, and two lying flat against the peaked roof. Impregnable, Charlie thought, then thought how unwise it was to get cocky. He took a long pull on his cigar, and the tip glowed dully a few inches in front of his eyes.

Tightly rolled son of a bitch, Charlie thought, and jumped when he felt something go past his head, saw the glowing tip of his cigar disappear and felt it burning his paunch.

"Ow! Shee-it!" he yelped, swatting at the sparks burning holes in his belly. "God damn . . ."

A match popped into flame to his left and flickered behind a cupped hand. Peering at him from slitty eyes was the boss man, Juh. He had a big son of a bitch of a knife in his hand, blade maybe ten inches long, and his teeth were gleaming in the light, like a big cat about to eat its prey. Juh turned and lit an oil lamp beside the telegraph key. As the light began to penetrate the gloom, Charlie Holly saw that three other Apaches were standing against the walls, black eyes dancing in the dim light. They each stood, arms crossed, grinning at him like a goddamn horde of bloodthirsty Tartars. Jesus, Charlie thought, what scary goddamn people.

"What'll we do with him?" one of them asked.

Charlie chuckled. "Now, how in the hell did you boys—"

"Hang him by his feet," another Apache policeman offered.

"We can give him to the women," another said. "They cut him up into little bite-sized pieces. Old Apache tradition," he explained. "After two days you don't feel nothin'."

Charlie chuckled again. "I just can't imagine how you did this. How'd you get up here? You didn't come up the stairs, they're too creaky. And you didn't get up on the roof—"

"Why wait for the women?" asked the third. An enormous knife blade materialized in his hand, gleaming.

Charlie laughed. "Now, see, if this wasn't a game, I could get two of these men, blow 'em away, but the other two of you would get me. So you fellows won. Let's have a drink. Now I know you got plenty of hooch around here, that's one thing for damn sure." He stood up. "I just can't for the life of me figure—"

Juh leaned over to the window, cupped his hand, and gave forth a sound that reminded Charlie of night birds in the Louisiana bayous.

"You're gonna want to learn how a pigeon sounds if you're gonna use birdcalls," Charlie said, relieved to have found a fragment of urban wisdom to pass along to his pupils.

The black trucks pulled into the alley at two A.M. and noisily backed up to the loading dock like two black cows. Deliveries were typically made between midnight and four, more for appearance' sake than out of any fear of the police. Dion O'Banion bragged with some accuracy that he owned the police. But if some of the few remaining bluenoses saw bootleggers dropping off the stuff in broad daylight, they'd start beefing about the cops not doing their job, and it could get messy.

Of course, the police were "owned" by Johnny Torrio, as well, and in their precincts, by the Genna brothers too. Everybody was pretty happy owning and being owned. There was plenty to go around. The mayor himself played footsie with the three major gangs, just being careful not to invite all three leaders to the same occasions. The mayor had not achieved his position by being tactless.

The men in the truck who backed up to the loading dock behind Ellison House that night knew all this. They knew that Ellison House was one of the fancy "men's clubs" run by that old Freeman cowboy, a place where small-time executives in the railroads and stockyards went to get genteelly fucked, and not to discuss business, which is what they told their wives sitting at home with the brats listening to the radio. The men in the truck also knew that across the alley from Ellison House, the big pile of stone was a onetime mansion now broken up into apartments where old people, mostly, lived out the rest of their lives.

It was a routine delivery on familiar ground, but the men had been warned to be on the alert. Things were heating up between O'Banion and that little shit Torrio. Torrio was trying to carve up the whole city, and in the carving up, O'Banion's turf would be shrunken to north of the river. The guinea bastards who'd come to O'Banion's flower shop where he hung out to tell him all this had been flung out on their shiny sharkskin suit bottoms. O'Banion told them that if he saw them again, he'd hang their greasy corpses on hooks like sides of beef.

So the men in the trucks were on the alert, half of them standing guard with guns ready while the other half unloaded the trucks' contents onto the loading dock. It was quiet in the alley except for the grunting of men. It was quiet in the alley until the staccato racket began, the awful flames from thirty tommy guns erupting, a violent endless crescendo. The men from the trucks writhed like mad puppets, and screamed and fell one after the other onto the concrete, case after case of hooch exploding open, falling from the loading dock, splintered and sundered, glass shards and splatters flying; and the hooch, pungent and raw, flowed onto the concrete from hundreds of shattered bottles, merging there with the warm pools of blood in the silence that finally descended.

Twenty-seven

When Tom Bignon, a bit rumpled and heavy-headed from sleeping on the train, disembarked and made his way through the crowds to the train station's cavernous lobby, he was accosted by a boy with a sooty face and a cap, waving a newspaper and shouting *"Gangland massacre! Gangland massacre!"* which was almost exactly what the banner headline of the Chicago *Tribune* said, as well. It was an afternoon extra, a special edition put out with such breathless haste that no one had noticed that the word "massacre," which appeared in forty-point type, readable from fifty yards, had been spelled with only one S.

The paper, with its enormous typo, would soon become something of a collector's item, and one of the copy editors at the *Tribune* had already found himself looking for some other line of work.

Tom Bignon took the paper, gave the kid a nickel, and scanned the story that commanded the two right-hand columns of the front page. In a matter of seconds he had fresh ink on his fingers and he knew it was O'Banion's people who had been massacred. He suspected, along with the reporter, that it was Johnny "the Brain" Torrio's work. He also knew what the reporter did not know, that Ellison House, "a fashionable and exclusive men's club," was in fact a ritzy brothel owned and operated by Abner Freeman. Further, he knew that Ellison House, having so flagrantly been caught receiving alcoholic beverages in quantity, would have to be closed down. The feds would act, even if the city itself was reluctant to.

Of course, there was a loud and outraged call in the newspaper for someone to put a halt to these gangland wars, to stanch the flow of blood in the streets. Did the city of Chicago, the great and mighty hub of commerce and culture in the nation's midsection, have no civic pride whatsoever? Were its elected officials too craven and cowardly to take matters in hand?

Tom looked up from the paper, found the telegraph office at the far end of the lobby, and walked briskly to it. There he sent the same message to Tombstone, Silver City, and, on a hunch, to the old fort at the base of the Huachuca Mountains. That done, he marched out onto the street and flagged down one of the black Model A Ford taxis that waited near the station in a line as patient as cattle.

A half hour later he was ushered into the high-ceilinged library in Abner Freeman's house where the old man greeted him fondly and launched into a tirade that began, "That vile snake of a Sicilian, that goat-fucking lowlife bastard son of a guinea sow . . ." and went on for a minute or two until he ran out of wind and bestial metaphors and subsided into a low leather easy chair, his long legs sticking straight out to the floor.

"What are you going to do?" Tom asked.

The old man gestured with both hands in irritation. *"Do?"* he barked. "Do? What can I do? Sit here while the gimlet-eyed feds close down Ellison House, that's what I can do. And then they'll try and find out who owns it." He snorted in contempt. "Well, that'll stump the bumbleheaded . . . They'll confiscate everything, everything there. I was up all last night billeting the girls and the staff. Couldn't leave them there hanging in the wind. So the feds'll get a big house full of furniture and food and hooch. That's all they'll get. But goddamn it—"

"They could do the same thing again," Tom said.

"You mean Torrio, the little weasel. I've thought of that. Put me out of business, one place after another. Well, I've circled the wagons. No more deliveries of hooch from anyone. Not O'Banion, the mick blockhead. Imagine letting your people walk into something like that. Not from Torrio and his crew of rats, or any of these other guinea bastards. We'll get along on what we've got."

"How long can you do that?"

"Three months. Four at the outside."

"Maybe something should be done about it before then. Can I get a drink?"

"Oh my God, forgive me, Tom. How utterly rude of me." Abner leaped out of his chair, stepped to the fireplace in two long strides, and pressed a button hidden in the paneling.

"New system. Electric. Hated that goddamn bell the missus used to ring, like someone calling in the goddamn sheep. What do you mean, do something before then?"

"Patch has been thinking something like this might happen."

"Now, Tom, I know that Muriel and Patch think I should retire from all this, go somewhere by a lake and sit on my duff and molder away like an old piece of cheese. But—"

"I think Patch has something else in mind," Tom said. "You know how these Sicilians talk about family loyalty—"

"Family loyalty?" Abner interrupted. "That little excrescence, Torrio—he was the one who assassinated Colosimo. Didn't pull the trigger, but . . . Colosimo was his wife's uncle, for God's sake."

"Right," Tom said. "But in the Apache Way, a man's in-laws are the most important people in the world. It's always been that way, they tell me."

One of Chicago's residents in 1921 was an old Apache woman who married a white man from Tucson three years before independence. When he left the West, she went with him. Her husband had long since died, but the old woman still lived in a three-room house in the far northwest section of the city, occasionally tending her three grandchildren and puttering in a small backyard garden where she grew mostly roses, which is how she came by the name Rosie. Rosie had long since ceased speaking Apache, and that entire way of life had slipped so far off into memory now as to be more like a dream, and she seldom if ever spoke of it. As tenuously connected as she was, however, Rosie was the only Apache who lived in Chicago and all of surrounding Cook County.

In the ten days that followed the massacre at Ellison House, the Apache population of Chicago increased by two thousand percent.

Counting Juh, who arrived with his wife Muriel to pay her father an extended visit, bringing with them two trunks of clothes and other things, twenty Apaches came, the other nineteen slipping into the city in small groups on different days. Dressed in the manner of laborers, with caps and overalls, they were hardly to be distinguished from other more or less swarthy folk from various parts of the world who arrived daily in the city seeking their fortune. The nineteen Apaches, all members of that nation's police force, vanished into the nooks and crannies of the city as easily as they would have disappeared into the rugged landscape of Apacheria.

During the ten days after the massacre, the streets of Chicago were quiet. It was as if the massacre had stunned everyone into a silent consideration of the stakes involved. But of course both sides, the O'Banion people and Torrio's, were not so much stunned as taking their time to figure out their next moves.

They called Dion O'Banion "Deanie." He had the face of the choirboy he had once been before rising to the top in the rackets on the North Side and personally ordering the death of at least twenty-six men, and probably more. An oddly fastidious man, O'Banion was morally horrified by the peddling of flesh and wouldn't permit any brothels to operate in his territory on the North Side. He spent most of the days in his florist shop, the only place of legitimate business where he was ever found. He had a knack for floral arrangements.

It was a strong if relatively new tradition in Chicago that whenever a big shot died—either a gangster or a city official—the other big shots bought their floral tributes from O'Banion's flower shop. Some of the fancier ones went for $5,000.

The smell of fresh-cut flowers, as much as their beauty,

tended to clear Deanie O'Banion's mind of extraneous matters and let him concentrate. On a Thursday afternoon, Deanie emerged from the back room that he cooled with massive blocks of ice and where he kept a lot of flowers. He had left a discussion in the front of the store to pick out some gladiolas for the finishing touch on a floral arrangement the mayor's office had ordered. With five stalks bearing tightly furled peach-colored gladiola buds in his hand, he flopped down in a chair.

"That slob Capone," he said, pronouncing it Ca-pony. "Torrio's guy, his lieutenant. Torrio loves him like a brother. The scar-faced guinea, how could anyone love a kisser like he's got? Anyway, he loves him like a brother. So . . . need I say more? Thursdays he hangs out at Colosimo's."

It had been over a year since Colosimo's Restaurant on Wabash and Twenty-second Street in the red-light district had had a name change. It was now Salvatore's, but people still called it Colosimo's.

"Deanie," one of the two men protested, "he's gonna be surrounded with goons, what with—"

Deanie O'Banion was on his feet. A rare expression of anger darkened his cherubic face. He threw down the gladiola stems on the floor and stepped on them, crushing several of the buds.

"You want me to tell you how to do it?" he said, his voice icy with contempt.

"No, no, we'll—"

"Good. Now beat it. Tell me tomorrow it's done."

That night at eight o'clock, Al Capone was seated at a booth in the rear of the dining room at Salvatore's Restaurant. He was with another of Johnny Torrio's most beloved people, Frankie Yale (née Uale) from Brooklyn. Yale had been partners with Torrio in New York, and hired Capone after Torrio left for Chicago. It was like a nice family reunion, Frankie having come in from New York that afternoon on the train.

It was widely believed that Frankie Yale had made another trip to Chicago a couple of years back at the express invitation of Johnny Torrio to kill Big Jim Colosimo. An out-of-towner was better for such things, not being known or recognizable and therefore able to get close. Frankie Yale had happily obliged his old friend, taking Big Jim out in front of his own restaurant as he was about to follow his opera-singer sweetie into the backseat of his limousine.

Frankie was now head of the Unione Siciliana in New York City, nominally a society to promote Italian culture, and he came to Chicago every now and then with nothing on his mind but to exchange information, to keep in touch, to coordinate things if it was needed. So Frankie and Al, the old buddies, were sitting in the booth, forking veal piccata into their faces and talking about the recent massacre. A dark-haired girl in a red sequined dress sat to Capone's left, bored. She wasn't hungry. On the far side of the booth, a blond girl in a darker red sequined dress sat looking at Frankie Yale with an expression of awe on her face and, under the table, her hand delicately placed on his crotch.

"Hey," Frankie said when his plate was cleared and his wineglass drained. "Get up a minute, will ya? I gotta take a leak."

"Aww," the blond girl said, and swiveled her hips out of the booth.

Frankie squeezed out of the booth, patted her on her bottom, and whispered in her ear, "Don't forget that, angel face. I'll be right back." He made his way through the tables and looked meaningfully at the three men seated at a table near the door. They nodded back, and one of them rose and followed Frankie out of the dining room.

Five minutes passed, and the man returned to the dining room, looking pale, like the blood had been drained from his face. He strode through the tables, pushed his way past a waiter with a tray full of plates, and approaching the booth, said, "Al, Al, shit, you gotta come."

"What?" Capone said. "What? Get outta the way." Both girls swung out of the booth looking flustered, and Capone, glancing at the door, shoved his way out from the table.

"What? What?"

"I was standing outside while Frankie took a leak, you know, at the top of the stairs. He didn't come out so I went down. He's—"

Capone swiveled around. "Beat it," he said to the two girls. "Go home." He pushed the man ahead of him, and the other two, sitting by the door, stood up and followed them.

Capone took the stairs down three at a step and pushed open the door to the men's room. "What?" he said. "Where— Oh, shit."

Frankie Yale was sitting on the can, with his pants down around his ankles. He was leaning back against the wall, his head leaning to the side at too big an angle. The blood had spurted out onto the walls and the floor around his feet. It had turned his shirt red across its entire front, and it glistened from his bare knees. The sideways slash that had opened up his throat had also laid bare two of the greasy white vertebrae in his neck. Blood was still leaking out of him.

Capone and the three bodyguards left Frankie Yale sitting on the can, drenched in his own blood, and departed Salvatore's Restaurant by means of a back staircase that led into a basement full of rats and into an alley. Five minutes afterward, three men with tommy guns rushed into the restaurant and charged toward the booth at the back wall, pulling up short when they saw it was empty.

In a fit of pique, one of the men fired a burst of twenty rounds or so into the mirror on the wall behind the booth, and the hoods fled amid screams and the sounds of glass shattering.

"This is barbaric!" Johnny Torrio exclaimed. "What is this, we've gone back to the Dark Ages?"

In earlier days in New York, Johnny Torrio himself had taken a few enemies out with a knife, but more out of necessity than any preference. Guns, particularly the new submachine guns, were more efficient, less messy, more devastating, and more civilized. You didn't have to get even within smelling distance of your prey, and you didn't get his blood all over you.

Al Capone had never heard his boss raise his voice, but the little man had been ranting for five minutes now, in a rage at the killing of his beloved pal Frankie, and increasingly enraged too that the "goddamned micks" would resort to a knifing. And of an out-of-towner. Johnny Torrio had a vision—a vision of a nationwide cooperative venture he called a syndicate. Getting the turf straightened out in Chicago was just the first step. Carving up the big markets nationwide was the goal. He was talking to Frankie Yale about this—about putting New York City on the same footing, then Philadelphia, Kansas City, the whole thing. Agreed-upon boundaries, an end to warfare, national organization. Order. The orderly pursuit of business with only one enemy to worry about—the Law. And now . . . this hit . . . Frankie Yale of New York. Another unforeseen interruption of progress . . .

Al Capone was just a little miffed that Torrio had made no comment whatsoever about how narrowly he, Capone, had escaped his own death at the hands of the three hoods O'Banion sent in the front door of Salvatore's while the other—or others—had sneaked in the back and done their work in the men's room.

It coulda been me, Capone kept thinking. It coulda been me sitting on the can with my throat hangin' open.

"So what're we gonna do about it, Johnny?" he asked.

Deanie O'Banion's flower shop was located at 738 North State Street, right next to the Holy Name Cathedral where Deanie regularly went to mass and, occasionally, just to sit quietly by himself in a pew toward the rear of the nave. Deanie believed himself to be a "swell fella," the kind who did favors for people in his territory, handing out bills to the needy, taking care of things. He didn't see attendance at mass as hypocritical. He liked the Church, liked its rituals and music, and prayed there as devoutly as any man. Religion and business were, simply, two different things in Deanie's mind. God did favors for the people on earth, just like Deanie did favors for his wards, but God didn't do business and didn't care about business. Simple as that.

Deanie felt safe under the vaulted ceiling of the Holy Name Cathedral, so he would go there some evenings just to think, when even the ritual of floral arrangement wasn't enough to clear his mind. In the supernal quiet, among the familiar icons, he could relax. And, he knew, the guineas were respectful of the Church's ancient role as sanctuary.

On Friday night Deanie sat in his favorite pew, watching a few of the faithful lighting candles at an altar far off to his right, and pondering the death of Frankie Yale, which he had heard about that morning. He knew the night before by ten o'clock that his boys had missed Capone in the restaurant. It wasn't till the next morning that the killing of Frankie Yale hit the streets. And he knew that none of his people had done Yale. A knifing! Nobody did that anymore. But Deanie was shrewd enough to know that Johnny Torrio would assume that Yale had been taken out as an O'Banion hit, so he was taking precautions.

He had entered the cathedral from an alley in the rear, and stationed two of his men in the alley to cover him when he left. Sitting in the House of God, it came to Deanie with a sudden revelation what his next move should be. It was simple. He would simply get word to Torrio that it hadn't been his hit, he didn't know anything about it, didn't know Yale was in town, had nothing against him, and nobody, not anyone in his group, ever used a knife anyway.

He crossed himself, arose, and went out the back into the alley. It was pitch-black and he stood still, waiting for his eyes to adjust, breathing the smell of garbage and hearing the low scuffling of rats. Where were those guys?

He took two steps sideways, to his left, and ducked reflexively when something banged his head. He reached for the gun he kept in a holster under his armpit, and froze. Off to his right were the cathedral's garbage cans; to his left and above him a fire escape clung to the back of the building. He looked up and, in the gloom, saw a more opaque shape above him, a shape that resolved itself into the bottoms of four shoes.

He could now make out the bodies above the shoes, and he gagged and ducked back to the cathedral door. His two men were hanging from the fire escape, garroted in the shadow of the cathedral, hanging from the fire escape that was part of the church! Whoever had done it was probably still out there. His heart pounded in his chest, and he slipped back into the cathedral.

It wasn't right. It wasn't right. He noticed that he was still holding his gun in his right hand. That wasn't right either. Not here. He holstered it, crept back down the hall to the nave, and slipped back into his pew. They could be anywhere out there, everywhere. He had no choice. He resigned himself to sitting in the wooden pew, now so uncomfortable, for the rest of the night, safe in the House of God.

The following day, a Saturday, Deanie O'Banion stuck his head out the carved front doors of the Holy Name Cathedral and watched the street for several minutes before striding down the sidewalk, head high, to his flower shop. At approximately the same moment, Juh and Muriel Freeman, accompanied by Tom Bignon, boarded a train from Chicago to New York, where they would in turn take another train to Washington, D.C.

Twenty-eight

The man sitting across the desk from Juh was heavyset and evidently self-satisfied. He was America's leading lawyer, and had been for a year now, and already the ugly winds of corruption had begun to blow around him—accusations, innuendo. Harry Daugherty, Ohioan and kingmaker, could care less. Like a puppet master, he had engineered the political career of fellow Ohioan Warren G. Harding, now President, and his reward was his present office—Attorney General of the United States.

The only thing President Harding did without first consulting Daugherty was to play out his poker hands in the rooms upstairs in the White House where, on any night, the so-called Poker Cabinet met and played cards amid the smoke of cigars and the clink of ice on glassware. Official receptions at the White House were dry, but the new law of the land did not apply to the rooms upstairs. The administration spoke severely about the evil of drink, the need to enforce the laws, and few spoke more severely than Daugherty about such matters—but he and his cronies were hard-drinking men, and he for one had begun to develop the telltale signs of it, a reddening of the nose, the presence of tiny dark squiggles of veins showing on the cheeks, and from time to time a slight yellowing of the eyeballs.

Harry Daugherty showed all those signs plus an irritating cough this morning in his office, and he told his foreign visitor, this leader from Apacheria, that it had to do with the dampness of the Washington climate to which he still hadn't adjusted.

324

To Daugherty's right and about ten feet away sat another man, who had been introduced only as Mr. Hoover. What position he held was left unsaid. Juh was not surprised by this rudeness. It often occurred in situations where people, such as U.S. government officials, did not know him. To such people he was just another Indian, presumably a primitive with so slight an understanding of the white man's ways as to render certain common courtesies unnecessary. The surprise people experienced on hearing him speak in fluent, easternized English was to his advantage.

This Hoover was a young man, perhaps in his late twenties, thirty at the outside, and he wore what appeared to be a perpetual frown on his young features. His jaw seemed locked into a position slightly askew, making his grimly set mouth off center. Mr. Hoover sat with his legs crossed and his arms folded across his chest, looking contemptuous. Juh could not tell what Mr. Hoover was so contemptuous of, but he suspected that it was both him and Hoover's superior, the Attorney General.

Their meeting had been established at a request from the vice-president's office, but Mr. Coolidge was unable to attend it. As a matter of law enforcement, it concerned the Department of Justice most directly, and, it was widely known in Washington, the upright Coolidge detested Daugherty and his cronies.

After some awkward pleasantries, Harry Daugherty cleared his throat and said, "Now what can we do for you, Mister, ah, Jew?"

"Juh," Juh said pleasantly. "It's an Apache word, of course, and a lot of people have difficulty pronouncing it. I am here because we Apaches are deeply concerned about the outbreak of violence that's affecting both your country and mine." He leaned back and watched Daugherty take a second look at him. "We have made efforts to put a stop to illegal activity— smuggling, mostly—that takes place on our borders. As you know, we are very few—only fifteen thousand of us now, half of them children. Particularly on the eastern and western borders of Apacheria, we have a great deal of open space, remote land. Empty. Even so, we have been quite successful patrolling our borders to keep these . . . elements out."

He looked back and forth from one man to the other. Daugherty sniffed, and Hoover seemed to tighten his grip on his chest as he frowned more deeply.

"But," Juh went on, "I'm aware that our success causes additional difficulties for our neighbor, the United States. For these people simply go somewhere else."

"It's stupid," Hoover said. "Idiotic. You can't legislate morality. This moronic attempt called Prohibition is the worst Pandora's box anyone can imagine. It's only going to get worse, when all these scum start taking real advantage. Some of them aren't the usual stupid criminals."

The Attorney General looked afflicted. "Edgar, it's the law of the land. It's our job to enforce it."

Hoover snorted. "Yes. Nobody else seems to give a damn. At the local level, I mean. That's why the Bureau of Investigation needs reorganizing, it needs—"

The Attorney General interrupted. "Mr. Jew, this is a matter we discuss often here, as you can imagine. Mr. Hoover here is our assistant director for operations in the Bureau of Investigation, and no one detests crime and criminals more than he. A regular firebrand." Daugherty smiled with his lips, and Juh thought it not a pretty sight. It was, he thought, surely the Attorney General that this Hoover didn't approve of—among many other things, of course.

"I have come," Juh said, "to suggest a cooperative effort to put an end to this terrible business. We have learned—from interrogating the smugglers whom we apprehend—that this appears to be highly organized. Even in the hinterlands where we are."

Hoover sneered. "What's the matter, Mr. Huff, are the gangs beginning to bother your operation there in Silver City?"

"I'm sure that our gaming casinos appear to you here in the

United States as what your lawyers call an attractive nuisance."
Juh smiled ingratiatingly. "But perhaps their very attractive-
ness can be put to use. To our mutual advantage. These people
want to control all such activity in America. I can't imagine
they'll overlook so lucrative a center as Apacheria, where, of
course, our laws differ from yours in some ways . . ." He
shrugged. "You have a great many constitutional constraints
that you must, well, heed. Impediments in some ways, I
suspect—I mean to dealing with the organized activities of
these people.

"Everywhere," Juh continued, "even in my country, there is
always a certain amount of chronic law-breaking. It's part of
the human condition, something that governments can contain
but never eradicate altogether. But what we are seeing now—
all of us—goes beyond that level. It could get completely out
of hand.

"In the last century," he went on, "the U.S. troops arranged
with Mexico to permit what they called 'hot pursuit.' Of us
Apaches, of course. Your army was given permission to follow
us into Mexico if the opportunity arose." Juh smiled. "I would
offer something similar here . . ."

Harry Daugherty coughed and coughed again, spluttering
behind his desk.

"Goddamn humidity," he said, gasping. Hoover unfolded
his arms and sat forward in his chair.

Daugherty stopped coughing, wiped his mouth with a white
silken handkerchief, and pulled a watch on a chain from his
vest pocket.

"Edgar, I have another appointment. Perhaps you and Mr.
Jew could discuss this further. Of course, this administration is
in favor of cooperative ventures of this sort. Benefit us all.
Gentlemen?"

Juh and Hoover stood and took their leave, spending the rest
of the morning discussing law enforcement. At lunch, a three-
course spread at the Golden Door, one of Mr. Hoover's favorite
places, they were joined by Tom Bignon, whom Juh introduced

as the Apache nation's equivalent of Attorney General. The discussions continued on into early evening.

Deanie O'Banion lost the war. On May 4, 1921, at three-thirty in the afternoon, three swarthy men who were new to Deanie entered his flower shop. One of the men introduced himself as a Mr. Stavropolous and explained that he was in the process of opening up a Greek restaurant about ten blocks to the south on State Street and wished to know if the O'Banion people might be interested in becoming his supplier. He had an odd accent, which Deanie assumed was the way recently arrived Greeks spoke English. They spoke of prices and other matters for a few minutes; and Mr. Stavropolous looked happier and happier, finally sticking out his right hand and saying, with a broad smile, "Then it's a deal."

O'Banion offered his own hand, which the man pumped enthusiastically, reluctant, it seemed, to let go. And when the other two Greeks pulled out their weapons and pointed them at O'Banion, his right hand was still in the man's iron grip. He made a move to reach the gun holstered under his left armpit, so the first of seven bullets fired that day in Deanie's flower shop went through his left hand, shattering the fine bones, before entering his chest. The other six bullets slammed into his chest and head in rapid succession, and before the echo of the shots had subsided, the three Greeks were on the sidewalk, piling into a long black hearse that pulled away from the curb and headed south.

The following day, Johnny Torrio and Al Capone were invited "downtown" by the police, along with the Genna brothers and several of their torpedo men, but they were all released after some desultory questioning. Meanwhile, O'Banion's body lay in state at the Szarbi Funeral Home, ensconced in a bronze casket that cost ten thousand dollars, with solid gold candlesticks burning and silver angels presiding over each end. Thousands of people filed past the bier over a period of three days, including Chicago Mayor Bill Dever, the Gennas, Al

Capone, and Johnny Torrio, who had sent a three-thousand-dollar floral tribute, which was among the others that filled the room with a blaze of color and a nearly palpable cloud of perfume.

Between the casket and the flower-bedecked wall, several of O'Banion's lieutenants stood patiently and devoutly, tears in their eyes. These included Hymie Weiss, the onetime soup man who had dropped an unpronounceable Polish name for Weiss and who, rising quickly in O'Banion's organization and finally to number two, had given up cracking safes two years earlier, for administrative duties. Weiss was only twenty-six years old at the time, and O'Banion had been like an older brother to him.

Among the mourners who filed past were most if not all of O'Banion's customers, and these included Abner Freeman, tall and straight as a ramrod, his silver-haired head rising above those in the line nearby. Outside the funeral home, he encountered Johnny Torrio, who was standing on the sidewalk with three other men. Torrio looked up, smiled his weasel smile, and said, "Mr. Freeman. The micks are done, finished. They'll all go back in the woodwork where they came from. Maybe we should talk again."

Abner eyed the man with the dispassion of a scientist looking at an unusual zoological specimen.

"Perhaps we should," he said presently. "Yes, perhaps we should. Call me. Once all this—" Abner gestured toward the funeral home. "—is behind us." He turned and strode away.

The next day it rained lightly, a fine drizzle from a gray sky accompanied by a sudden cold snap. It seemed that the world itself was weeping as Deanie O'Banion's remains, encased in his bronze casket, were lowered to their eternal rest on a pretty hill in Mount Carmel Cemetery, only forty-odd feet from a mausoleum where a former archbishop moldered in the ground. A priest who had grown up with Deanie in the slum called Little Hell presided in an unofficial capacity over the lowering of the casket and said three Hail Marys and the Lord's Prayer.

The story went out that it had been Angelo Genna's two most accomplished torpedoes plus an out-of-towner who had hit O'Banion in his flower shop, but another story went around as well that it had been some hoods Johnny Torrio brought in. Each side—Torrio and the Gennas—assumed it was the other side that had accomplished the deed, and they never spoke about it, except to agree between themselves on how to carve up the North Side once they jointly ran the remaining O'Banion people out. Chicago was in the hands of the Sicilians.

Johnny Torrio had to admire the old man. He had balls, that was for sure. Here he was, basically a small-time operator of a small string of brothels—elegant ones, but a brothel is a brothel—standing in his library with the wood paneling and the fireplace, explaining *his* decision to go with Torrio as a supplier and saying that he expected better terms than what he'd paid O'Banion. Torrio and his product were "untried." What balls. Untried? There wasn't any other product to try.

Torrio listened as the man outlined the terms he would accept, and kept a pleasant smile on his face. At the same time, he was curious about the other two men who were in the room with Freeman. One was a chubby white man with a limp, introduced as Tom Bignon, and the other was an Indian named something like Hooh. The old man's son-in-law. Torrio had never seen an Indian, that he knew of, only pictures in the pulps, and this guy Hooh didn't look much like the drawings or the photographs. For one thing, he was wearing a suit. He did have a feather tied to his hair, which hung down behind his neck, and he had those high cheekbones. Eyes on him that looked like some kind of slit-eyed python. But this was definitely no run-down savage. The guy spoke English as good as him—maybe even better, Torrio admitted to himself—though with a curious lilt.

It wasn't clear to Torrio why the Indian and the other guy were here. He noticed that Capone was staring at the Indian like he was something in a zoo. Al was a sharp guy, but he was a bit light on manners. Torrio reflected that it took more than a two-hundred-dollar suit to make a gentleman.

"Okay, okay," Torrio said when the old man appeared to be finished listing the ways he wanted to do business. "Sound okay to you, Al?"

Capone took his eyes off the Indian and nodded. "Yeah."

"Good," Abner Freeman said. "Now, my son-in-law has something he would like to discuss with you. I'm sure you've heard about Silver City, the Apaches' gambling resort. Juh is, I'm sure you also know, the leader of the Apache nation, and Tom here is his . . . well, I suppose you people would call him a consigliere."

Tom Bignon nodded at Torrio, a twinkle of amusement in his eyes. The Apache was looking at him without the slightest trace of expression, ebony eyes shining but utterly opaque.

"Yeah," Torrio said. "I've heard about your place down there. Very successful, I'm told. I'd like to hear more." It had not occurred to Johnny Torrio to turn his eyes to the West, a region that seemed too alien and remote to a man whose life had been spent exclusively in the canyons of two cities that were built, essentially, on the European model.

"First of all," Juh said, "I would like to tell you how much I admire the Sicilian—" He hesitated. "—manner of doing things. It reminds me of our own way, the Apache Way."

Torrio smiled broadly, ingratiatingly. "That's right. You people whipped the U.S. Army, set up your own shop. Nation. I like that. All these other Indians . . ." He shrugged.

"Like you Sicilians," Juh proceeded, "loyalty to the family is paramount. And we think of our entire tribe, all our people, as family. Any Apache is always right if he is opposed by an outsider. We have never tried to change our enemies, only to control them. To know where they are, what they think, and who they trust. We avenge wrongs to our own, but we know that vengeance is food that is best served cold. We have a saying: 'False in one, false in all.' We do not suffer liars. Perhaps, Mr. Torrio, this sounds familiar to you."

"It does."

"We are a small nation, Mr. Torrio. Surrounded by a very large one, the United States. Its interests are not always the same as ours. We need to be powerful beyond our numbers. Like you. And we have learned that you cannot be powerful without money."

"That goes without saying," Torrio said.

"What the Apache people are proposing, Mr. Torrio, is that two groups with such similar outlooks on . . . life, on the United States government . . . two such similar groups might benefit from cooperating. Perhaps there is a possibility that two and two could add up to more than four."

Torrio nodded, thinking that this was going to be easy.

"The Apache people would like to get to know you better. And discuss ways we might work together to our mutual benefit. So what I am proposing is that you, and Mr. Capone here, and your lieutenants, pay us a visit in Silver City. Once you have matters here in hand. We would like to show you our business there, our country, and several other affairs of which the United States government is . . . well, not aware of."

Juh's dark face creased into a smile, white teeth glowing. It was, Torrio thought, the smile of a predator, but an innocent predator.

"Sounds swell," Torrio said. "What about the Gennas?"

"As you wish," Juh said. "But we assume that you are what we call the chief."

Twenty-nine

"I worked in Chicago until recently," Rasheen said in her peculiar accent. Only her neck and head rose above the froth of white bubbles in the oval-shaped bathtub that was sunken into the floor. Behind her head, a large window stretched from the floor to the ceiling; beyond, forested hills rose into distant blue mountains. Rasheen's shiny black hair was piled casually on her head, and Al Capone couldn't imagine what kept it up there.

"Yes," she went on, "I liked it in Chicago. The Packard House was very elegant, and I worked in the most elegant part, the Harem. But I came down here just two weeks ago. For my health."

"Your health?" Al Capone asked. He was sitting in shirt-sleeves, trousers, and bare feet on a stool a few feet from the edge of the sunken tub. "Someone after you?"

Rasheen laughed, a merry sound. "Oh, no. Not like that, Alberto. Not like that at all. It's the dry climate here. It's good for my . . ." A soapy hand with long fingers came up through the froth and she touched her long thin nose. "The sinuses," she explained.

Al Capone was a family man, which didn't mean that he avoided the dolls, not at all. A casual piece here, another there, it went with the job, same as eating good food in restaurants, but this Rasheen had really knocked him out. She was like some kind of exotic flower, like something from the Garden of Eden, musky, an irresistible perfume drawing him like a bee into her voluptuous petals . . .

333

All day she had guided him around this Apache joint, showing him the gaming rooms, the drawing rooms, the racetrack, the stables, telling him it was the altitude when he started huffing and puffing, and then back here, in his suite, on that huge bed . . . The thought of it!

"Alberto," she said. He liked it that she got his name wrong. He hated his name, Alphonse. "There's something I must tell you. The truth."

Capone's eyelids dropped slightly over his eyes, the only sign of caution. People who said they were going to tell the truth usually weren't going to. She worked for these guys, these Indians, and maybe she was a plant, going to try to wheedle something interesting out of him. But he knew you never told any woman, even your wife, anything about business. Never. So what was this *truth*? He smiled.

"Tell me," he said.

"I'm not Arabian."

"No?"

"No, it's an act. For the Harem at Packard House."

Capone appreciated a good act. "So what are you?" he asked.

"Bulgarian," Rasheen said with a big smile. "My father was a count in Bulgaria, my mother a maid in his castle. He never recognized me as his daughter, so I emigrated to the United States."

That's bullshit too, Capone thought. She's probably a Jew from New York, but so what?

"Come in here, Alberto. The water is hot and I want to give you a massage." No change in the accent, he noted. Arab, Bulgarian, Capone didn't care if it was Eskimo. She lifted a sleek leg out of the froth and he watched the suds slide from it.

Capone stood up and unbuttoned his shirt. "Look, beautiful, you get your sinuses all squared away, I'll set you up back in Chicago. A nice apartment. Looking over the lake. Your own place. You think you'd like that?"

"Alberto, you do know how to take care of a girl." Rasheen crooked her finger at him, beckoning him into the froth.

The next morning, Juh led a caravan of automobiles that took the Sicilians, seven in all, bouncing across the arid valleys of Apacheria to old Fort Huachuca to inspect the warehouses and to hear the nature of the Apache smuggling operation. Out of tact, Charlie Holly, the onetime New Orleans cop, had been dispatched to spend the day in Tombstone, which he was happy to do.

The visit went smoothly enough, both Torrio and Capone carefully looking at each and every detail, nodding approvingly, asking expert questions. The other five men from Chicago, all uncomfortable in their city clothes out in the dusty landscape under the southwestern sun, trailed along behind, saying nothing but glancing with implacable suspicion at the Apache "police." None of them had ever seen an Indian before, and these men were dressed in various mixtures of attire—moccasins, boots, regular trousers, white leggings, western-style shirts, leather vests over bare chests. They all wore their hair pulled back with single long braids hanging well below their shoulder blades and watched the Sicilians from narrowed eyes that looked Mongolian.

The five gangsters all had the same unspoken thought: it's one thing to work with the micks and the hunkies and the Jews and the other immigrants—even the chinks—but these Apaches! Look at the eyes on 'em . . . like headhunters from Borneo or wild animals or something. Why was the Brain so intent on getting together with these savages out here in the middle of nowhere? They probably fuck goats and eat people. The boss, this guy Hoo, sounded like any businessman, and the lawyer, the tubby guy, he looked like any lawyer, but these others . . .

Johnny Torrio, on the other hand, seemed pleased, even delighted, with this exotic company. He told Juh that he'd read up on the Apaches over the summer and he admired the way they'd always taken care of their enemies.

"It was you guys against the world. Same as us. Anyone got in your way, got unreasonable . . ." Torrio drew his finger across his neck and smiled. "I guess the people around here, in Arizona and New Mexico, I guess they still hate your guts, huh?"

"A lot of them are still scared of us," Juh said. "So they hate us, yes."

"That's it. Fear. Keep 'em pissing in their drawers and they're yours. I was talking to some of your guests last night, a classy crowd you got there. Let me tell you something, your rep for being bloodthirsty savages—people like that. It adds spice. Like a little background buzz. Like they're not sitting around in some drawing room in Europe with a bunch of fairies. Here there's always the possibility, somebody gets out of line and . . ." He shrugged. "Did you know that?"

"I hadn't thought of it just that way," Juh said. "But I guess you're right."

"Yeah. It's a good operation you got here. Like a big cruise ship in the desert—you got everything here. Most people come for a week, two weeks, right? Get away from everything, the law, their jobs, their wives, all that. I'd like to put one of these together. Maybe across the border in Canada. But those Canadians? Stuffed shirts, let me tell you . . ."

Johnny Torrio found that, oddly enough, he felt almost comfortable with these strange people. He could tell that his soldiers thought the Apaches were like something out of a bad dream or a zoo or both, but he felt increasingly at ease with them. He was enjoying passing along some old Sicilian wisdom to these grateful, if unwitting, recruits to the grand scheme he had in mind.

What the White Eyes had long ago dubbed Little Walnut Creek trickled prettily through evergreen woodland and down into the lower ground near Silver City. About a half mile from the northernmost of the Apaches' three casino hotels, its eastern bank was open ground sparsely ringed by low desert scrub plants—sagebrush, snakeweed—the desert reaching its upper altitudinal limits at this place. On the opposite bank, ancient cottonwoods rose against the sky, their branches all askew, in the anarchic habit of cottonwoods.

In the open ground near the creek, a long table had been set up some twenty feet away from a tepee-shaped pile of gnarled cedar logs. Folding chairs of wood and canvas were arranged around the table. A light, refreshing breeze blew down from the mountains.

About an hour before sunset, the Sicilians arrived in the clearing, accompanied by Juh, Tom Bignon, and two Apaches who had been introduced but whose names the Sicilians could neither pronounce nor remember. They discovered there, in the clearing, that the tables were covered with platters of food—antipasto, several steaming serving bowls of pasta of various kinds, venison steaks, bottles of red wine, and a dish the Sicilians did not recognize.

Juh explained that this was mescal, made from cooking the fleshy parts of the century plant in a pit oven. Many times in their long history, he said, when the Apaches were forced to live on the run from their enemies, mescal and some dried bacon jerky had been enough to keep them alive and capable of sixty-mile treks day after day.

"You might want to try some of it," he said, smiling. "But we won't be offended if it isn't to your taste. Now please . . ." He spread his arms to embrace the tables. "Please eat." Juh sat down himself, then stood again. "I've asked the women to leave us in peace while we eat and do business. They'll join us later, around this fire of celebration." He gestured with his head toward the tepee-shaped pile of twisted cedar logs that awaited the torch.

The diners fell to, eating eagerly and well after the long day bouncing across the alien landscape. Slowly the sun descended to the horizon and slipped down behind it, leaving a deepening reddish glow in the western sky that turned a bright vermilion. The sun's direct light was replaced by flames that licked hungrily upward among the cedar logs, lighting the clearing as if it were day.

As they ate, Juh recounted the story of an earlier feast that had taken place near this spot almost a century before. It was when a group of pioneering American miners invited the Apaches to come to their camp and eat, and when the Apaches were all gathered around the tables, some of the miners, secreted behind bushes and a woodpile, opened up with rifle fire and killed most of the Apaches, including women and children. In those days, Juh explained, the Mexican government paid fifty dollars for an Apache scalp.

"That was the beginning of our trouble with the Americans," Juh said. "For more than a half century, we tried to make peace, but always had to return to the warpath. The United States government sent treacherous men here. In the end, we resolved our differences. We drove them away. But we regard the United States government with suspicion still—much as you do." He smiled happily, and the firelight glinted from his white teeth.

During this account, the Sicilians were seen to glance nervously around the clearing and low grass and scrub around it, and Juh concluded by saying, "As you can see, we are alone here in the light of the fire. Mr. Capone, would you like to look around on the other side of the fire? To reassure yourselves?"

Capone grinned and forked a swirl of pasta into his mouth. "Nah," he said.

Juh leaned back in his chair at the head of the table. Next to him, Johnny Torrio wiped his mouth decorously with a white linen napkin. "Mr. Torrio and I—" Juh began.

"Johnny, please. Call me Johnny."

Juh bowed his head slightly toward the little man. "Johnny and I have been talking this afternoon about how well the Apaches' interests and your own fit together. We have talked about expanding these interests—forming a syndicate that can . . . influence all of the business from Chicago west. Before we go any further into the details, I would like to propose a toast."

Juh held up his glass, and the others followed suit.

"To loyalty and friendship," he said. "The loyalty and friendship that can exist only among those who consider themselves a family."

Somewhat startled by the man's naïveté, the Sicilians raised their glasses in salute, brought them to their lips, and, with Juh, tipped the glasses skyward. Before they had replaced the glasses on the table, two dozen Apaches stood as still as stone at the edge of the clearing, not twenty feet away, in an arc. Each had a rifle pointed at the men around the table.

The Sicilians didn't speak, didn't utter a sound of surprise. One of them, turning to look over his shoulder to see what the men opposite him were staring at, reached under his jacket, and three shots sounded as one. The man's head exploded, and he crashed onto the table, dishes scattering. Across from him, blood, brains, and pasta sauces sprayed onto the shirt and into the face of Al Capone, who sat without moving, his face gone ashen.

In the echo of the rifle fire, Juh, Tom Bignon, and the other two Apaches stood and backed away from the table, while the riflemen stepped closer. They wrenched the Sicilians to their feet and ran rough hands thoroughly over their bodies, removing weapons and tossing them into a pile between the table and the fire.

"Now your clothes," Juh said.

"What? What?"

"Take off your clothes. The women will be here soon." He paused. "Oh, not your escorts. Apache women. You've heard, of course, what Apache women liked to do when the warriors brought captives back to camp. No? Well, they'll choose one of you, maybe two . . . It's a terribly long and drawn-out way to die. The ones they choose will wish they had been hung over a fire like the rest."

Johnny Torrio stared at Juh with a hatred that glowed. "You savages. You goddamn savages."

Juh nodded. "Some customs die hard. Now, the clothes. You won't be needing them where you're going."

The Sicilians began to peel off their clothes. One of them, a man who looked barely twenty but had eyes that seemed older, glared at the two Apaches who held their rifles on him.

"Fuck this!" he shouted, and ran at them. He found himself spinning in the air and landed on his back in the dust, a rifle barrel pressing into each temple.

"Take him," Juh said, and gestured toward the creek with his head.

The two Apaches, joined by a third, dragged the Italian toward the creek. He twisted and writhed until the butt of a rifle struck his forehead and he sagged into semiconsciousness. The Apaches dragged him through the creek and under a large branch of one of the cottonwood trees. Producing rope, they lashed his wrists behind his back and tied his ankles together. Deftly tossing the long end of the rope over the cottonwood branch, they hauled him up off the ground, feet up, head three feet off the ground.

"Let me explain, *Johnny*," Juh said, turning to face the little man now standing in only a pair of white undershorts. "You're pissing in your drawers, Johnny," he said. "Take them off."

Torrio did as he was told.

"It would take maybe two days for a man to die hanging like that," Juh continued. "We Apaches aren't without pity. The fire we build under his head brings death much sooner. Think of it as a kindness."

The hanging man had regained consciousness and began to writhe, screaming unintelligibly. Below him, the three Apaches piled up small branches, forming a miniature tepee. Torrio, Capone, and the three others, standing naked in the light of the celebratory fire, felt their arms wrenched behind them, wrists bound painfully with coarse rope. Their compatriot across the stream continued screaming, a desperate howling sound, and the Italians watched with horror as a light was struck in the gathering gloom across the creek.

"You may want to sit down to watch this," Juh said. "Whoever the women choose won't get to sit again in this life."

"What do you want?" Torrio asked, his voice rising. "What the fuck do you *want*?"

Juh raised his hand, and the flame on the other side of the creek winked out. The dangling man was blubbering. The naked men were all shivering violently despite the heat of the fire at their backs.

"I want you to go home to Chicago and go about your business. At least some of you. I want you to remember your dinner here. Especially how one minute we were alone and the next there were twenty Apaches standing in your presence. Out there—" Juh pointed out into the low scrub around the clearing. "—there's no place for a man to hide. Where did they come from? They came out of nowhere. Like ghosts. And they will be somewhere near you wherever you go for the rest of your lives."

He paused.

"From time to time one of them will appear and give you instructions. If you fail to follow these instructions . . ." Juh grinned in the firelight. "You remember your man Yale? You heard about O'Banion's two bodyguards at the cathedral?" He mentioned three other deaths that had taken place that summer.

"We will tell you exactly what you can do, and what you can't. Do you find this acceptable? You have a few minutes to decide before the women come. Let me assure you, they all hope you refuse."

Johnny Torrio's face looked as if he had aged thirty years in five minutes. He nodded. "Yeah. Yeah," he said. "Okay." His voice was a barely audible croak.

"How many of these men here," Juh asked, "do you want alive? It's a question of who you want to know that you are working for the Apaches."

Torrio's eyes narrowed and he looked thoughtfully at his compatriots, one after the other. Across the creek, the hanging man was moaning softly.

The following afternoon, Juh and Tom Bignon sat on one of the sofas in front of the huge stone fireplace in Juh's office quarters. Across from them, a man with a perpetually fierce expression on his face, his jaw set slightly to the side as if he had been in an accident, listened with complete attention as Juh explained the previous night's events and what import they held for law enforcement in Chicago and eventually, perhaps, most cities of the United States. Johnny Torrio and the men who had come with him—minus the one who had been shot at the table—were on a train steaming north.

"All right, Mr. Huff," the man said. "The hoods'll be kept to the small stuff. The chronic stuff that goes on no matter what anybody does about it. Small potatoes."

"And," Juh said, "anytime one of these people gets too ambitious, you'll hear about it. Surely that will happen too. You'll get your arrests, Mr. Hoover."

"I have one question," J. Edgar Hoover said.

Juh smiled.

"It's hard to believe you're not going to take your cut."

"We make all the money we need right here," Juh said, gesturing around him.

"Then what's in it for you. For the Apaches?"

Juh leaned back in the sofa. "Mr. Hoover, the Apaches are warriors. It is what we do best. Why waste talent?"

DEL REY® ONLINE!

The Del Rey Internet Newsletter...

A monthly electronic publication, posted on the Internet, GEnie, CompuServe, BIX, various BBSs, and the Panix gopher (gopher.panix.com). It features hype-free descriptions of books that are new in the stores, a list of our upcoming books, special announcements, a signing/reading/convention-attendance schedule for Del Rey authors, "In Depth" essays in which professionals in the field (authors, artists, designers, salespeople, etc.) talk about their jobs in science fiction, a question-and-answer section, behind-the-scenes looks at sf publishing, and more!

Internet information source!

A lot of Del Rey material is available to the Internet on our Web site and on a gopher server: all back issues and the current issue of the Del Rey Internet Newsletter, sample chapters of upcoming or current books (readable or downloadable for free), submission requirements, mail-order information, and much more. We will be adding more items of all sorts (mostly new DRINs and sample chapters) regularly. The Web site is http://www.randomhouse.com/delrey/ and the address of the gopher is gopher.panix.com

Why? We at Del Rey realize that the networks are the medium of the future. That's where you'll find us promoting our books, socializing with others in the sf field, and—most important—making contact and sharing information with sf readers.

Online editorial presence: Many of the Del Rey editors are online, on the Internet, GEnie, CompuServe, America Online, and Delphi. There is a Del Rey topic on GEnie and a Del Rey folder on America Online.

Our official e-mail address for Del Rey Books is delrey@randomhouse.com (though it sometimes takes us a while to answer).

✎ FREE DRINKS ✎

Take the Del Rey® survey and get a free newsletter! Answer the questions below and we will send you complimentary copies of the DRINK (Del Rey® Ink) newsletter free for one year. Here's where you will find out all about upcoming books, read articles by top authors, artists, and editors, and get the inside scoop on your favorite books.

Age _____   Sex ❑ M ❑ F

Highest education level: ❑ high school ❑ college ❑ graduate degree

Annual income: ❑ $0-30,000 ❑ $30,001-60,000 ❑ over $60,000

Number of books you read per month: ❑ 0-2 ❑ 3-5 ❑ 6 or more

Preference: ❑ fantasy ❑ science fiction ❑ horror ❑ other fiction ❑ nonfiction

I buy books in hardcover: ❑ frequently ❑ sometimes ❑ rarely

I buy books at: ❑ superstores ❑ mall bookstores ❑ independent bookstores
❑ mail order

I read books by new authors: ❑ frequently ❑ sometimes ❑ rarely

I read comic books: ❑ frequently ❑ sometimes ❑ rarely

I watch the Sci-Fi cable TV channel: ❑ frequently ❑ sometimes ❑ rarely

I am interested in collector editions (signed by the author or illustrated):
❑ yes ❑ no ❑ maybe

I read Star Wars novels: ❑ frequently ❑ sometimes ❑ rarely

I read Star Trek novels: ❑ frequently ❑ sometimes ❑ rarely

I read the following newspapers and magazines:

❑ *Analog*	❑ *Locus*	❑ *Popular Science*
❑ *Asimov*	❑ *Wired*	❑ *USA Today*
❑ *SF Universe*	❑ *Realms of Fantasy*	❑ *The New York Times*

Check the box if you do not want your name and address shared with qualified vendors ❑

Name _____
Address _____
City/State/Zip _____
E-mail _____

page

Be sure to look for this
alternate-history novel of
Nazi invasion in the American
Southwest by Jake Page!

OPERATION
SHATTERHAND
by Jake Page

**The Indians lost America once.
They are not about to
lose it again . . .**

OPERATION
SHATTERHAND
by Jake Page

Published by Del Rey® Books.
Available in your local bookstore.